MOST VALUABLE PLAYER

A. M. WOODY

VIKING

VIKING
An imprint of Penguin Random House LLC
1745 Broadway, New York, NY 10019
penguinrandomhouse.com

Copyright © 2025 by Amanda Woody

Viking & colophon are registered trademarks of Penguin Random House LLC.

Edited by Dana Leydig
Design by Sophie Erb
Text set in Adobe Caslon Pro

Library of Congress Cataloging-in-Publication Data is available.

First published in the United States of America by Viking, 2025

Manufactured in the United States of America
BVG

ISBN 9780593695425
1st Printing

The authorized representative in the EU for product safety and compliance is
Penguin Random House Ireland, Morrison Chambers, 32 Nassau Street,
Dublin D02 YH68, Ireland, https://eu-contact.penguin.ie.

BOOKS BY A. M. WOODY

Exes & Foes

Most Valuable Player

They Hate Each Other

To the people who feel trapped in a cycle of pain.

To those who lie awake at night wondering how anyone could bother to love them.

To those who feel undeserving of other people's time and efforts.

To those whose walls are made of steel.

You don't need to earn a kind, gentle love.

You're already worthy of it because you exist.

* CONTENT NOTICE *

Please note that the list below contains plot and character spoilers. For those who may not require content notices, consider skipping to chapter 1 to maintain narrative ambiguity.

- Discussion and depictions of trauma and mental health.
- Mentions of bullying and queerphobia (off-page, invasive flashback).
- Discussion and depictions of grooming and abuse from a character's past, beginning when the victim was thirteen and the abuser seventeen. Emotional abuse is seen on-page via manipulative verbal conversations. Physical and sexual abuse are stated to have happened but are not depicted on-page.
  - Scenes detailing these events do not go into descriptive depth or put readers "in the moment" of the past abuse.
  - The abuser is a recurring character, and the story features tense moments between them and the victim.
  - The abuser restrains the victim once (grabbing their arms) and throws another character onto the ground.

CHAPTER ONE
CAM •

Mason Gray, your face is mine.

I mean that fondly, of course. Now that I've had a few weeks to get to know Elwood High's new varsity football team water boy, I've decided to offer him a taste of what it means to date a strapping young lad.

It should be the easiest "yes" in years. I'm single. He's single, probably. I'm spectacularly attractive. He's symmetrical from the neck up. I'm a big fan of all the genders. And he wears beanies and rainbow gloves, so I'll eat my own ass if he's not a little fruity.

Most importantly, I know Mason Gray has eyes for me. Whenever I glance over from the field, he's watching me from the sidelines in his water boy jersey, tapping his clipboard. Clearly trying to be as cute and dainty as possible to fit that soft boy aesthetic that drives women feral.

"Well, Cameron," he said politely when I called him out for his hungry gaze just last week, his smile never reaching his eyes, "I'm probably watching you because you're the quarterback, so you're usually holding the ball."

His pitifully obvious desire for me is bursting at the seams, so I'll spare him time to get to know me. Because I'm a good person.

"He's going to say no," Darius—our biggest linebacker and team captain—tells me as we jog a warm-up lap around the track wrapping the football field. The Southfield Hawks aren't here yet, so I have plenty of time to acquire Mason as my boyfriend and make out with him passionately behind the bleachers. It's usually the first thing my partners ask of me, anyway, so I'm fully prepared to get it out of the way if it means I can proceed to stare at him unblinkingly without being labeled a creep.

"Why would he reject me?" I ask with a cheeky smile. "I think he'd be honored. It's the first time in years I'm asking someone out, rather than the other way around."

Darius wipes beads of sweat from his warm brown forehead, or maybe he's massaging away the headache he likes to pretend I give him on a weekly basis. "Sorry, why exactly do you need to pursue the guy who has a track record of rejecting everyone who wants to date him?"

"His face."

"What about it?"

"It's high-quality," I say with a scoff, because shouldn't that be obvious? "And it looks soft. And he has nice skin."

He really does. Mason is more pleasant to look at than anyone I've ever met. He's a smooth plain of pale ivory, and his lashes are long and as deeply obsidian in color as the feather-soft hair constantly rumpled atop his head. His eyes are big and round and perfectly spaced apart and a sweet honey brown. My carnal desire to stare at him means I must be attracted to him.

Which means his face is mine.

"Don't do this, Cam," Darius pleads, slapping a beefy hand on my shoulder. "We need your ego for the game."

As if anything could wound my rock-solid ego.

Five minutes later, I approach Mason. He's writing on his clipboard, pretending like he can't see my hulking figure in his peripherals, his cheeks appropriately flushed considering my proximity. "Hey, water boy," I say.

Mason spares me a glance. "Yes, quarterback?"

His eyes are astonishingly cold in comparison to the warm color of his irises. "You and me," I say, jabbing a confident thumb into my chest. "I'll be the sun to your moon if you'll be the tides to my beach."

Fucking nailed it.

Mason scrutinizes me with measured intensity. "Are you having a stroke?" he asks.

Uh . . . hmm. Can't say that's ever been a response to my poetry. "I'm asking you out," I explain, in case he's not well-versed in romantic dialogue like I am.

"Why?" Mason asks.

Yet another response that catches me off guard. I'm starting to feel like a deer in headlights. But okay, fine, he's making me work for it. I can respect the game. "Because you have bewitched me, body and soul," I say with a gleaming grin.

Mason gives me a contemplative nod. "You like that movie?"

"What."

"*Pride and Prejudice*," he says, his arctic eyes unblinking.

Damn it. Of course I'd pursue the one person alive who's into that romancey shit. "Just because it's not my line doesn't mean I can't mean it," I point out.

"Okay. What about me, exactly, has bewitched you, body and soul?" Mason's maintaining his eerily pleasant, robotic expression.

It's possible I'm starting to squirm. Some of the benchwarmers gearing up nearby are snickering as they listen. The fluorescent stadium lights come alive, and though they illuminate the entire grassy field and gunmetal-gray bleachers, I feel like they've activated specifically to pin me under a spotlight. "Your face," I squawk.

Mason blinks at me.

"I fuck with it," I clarify. "Please go out with me."

I'm not used to tacking on a "please" for anything, but fine, I'll throw him a bone.

Mason Gray's narrow shoulders deflate, like he's just released a sigh, and then he returns his harrowing gaze to his clipboard. His face hasn't flinched once, despite how high his flames of flustered passion must be writhing. He opens his mouth, and I massage my vanilla-flavored lips together, preparing.

"That's an awful idea, but thank you."

. . . Oh.

Okay, it's okay, he's just playing coy. Which means I need to lock into full-force seduction mode. "How can I sweeten the offer?" I ask, leaning over him with a knowing smirk, my eyebrows waggling. He's at the perfect height that I could rest my chin atop his head. "What do you desire from me, water boy?"

"Distance," Mason says flatly. "Stop breathing on me and jog another lap."

I think I choke on my next inhale. The heightened laughter of the huddled juniors is like acid in my ears. Coach Barnett, who's been yelling at people nearby but also eavesdropping, kneads his fuzzy eyebrows. Clearly they don't understand we're locked in a game of cat and mouse, which Mason is dragging out to make the end result more satisfying.

"Is this environment not romantic enough?" I ask with charmed laughter. "I know a perfect restaurant down the street. Low candlelight, soft music, waiters with accents. Shall I give you a ride after the game?"

I notice a muscle work in Mason's jawline, and he closes his eyes, folding his clipboard into his chest. "Cameron Morelli," he says, as soft as he looks, "I would sooner star as the lone twink in a porno featuring the entire football team before ever accepting an invitation to dinner with you. Does that clarify the situation?"

. . . I don't. Understand. "You don't want to date me?" I ask, just to be certain.

"I do not," he confirms.

"Are you, like, sure?"

The words are pathetic, and they're also mine. To which Mason Gray continues smiling his polite smile, the kind that doesn't show his teeth or crinkle his face, and says, "Yes, but thank you for the opportunity."

What . . . do I do.

I decide to run another lap to sweat this off, my brain scrambling to extinguish the short circuit fire roaring into its fleshy folds. Why? Why? Why—

"Told you," Darius says beside me, sweat shining on his temples, matching my pace as I sprint around the track's inner ring to flee my demons. "He's out of your league, anyway."

I wheeze in protest. The sentence has never been uttered, yet there it is, another verbal backhand to my opposite cheek. Who's the one with the eyes often described as "sea blue" and "cerulean" and "sapphire" depending on the lighting? Who's the one with the golden-brown hair streaked with glittery highlights? Who's the one with the perfectly cut midsection that could be mistaken as a bed of skin-colored rock?

Oh ho. So Mason thinks he's out of my league?

"No," Darius says. "I'm telling you that as a fact."

Well, he's going to regret it.

"Sometimes I think you don't know when you're talking out loud, Morelli."

I finish my lap, skin shimmering beneath the humble luster of sweat, and beeline for Mason, who's peeling back the film over a case of water bottles. "Hey, water boy," I say sharply.

His chest swells with a fatigued inhale, and he cranes his neck back. His black hair is swept over his brow like it's been molded by a gentle, flattering breeze. "Yes?" he asks with infuriating calmness, as if he didn't just knee me in the sack moments ago.

"You . . ." The words tangle in my throat.

"Me?"

"*You.*" I hack through the blockage and spit. "Am I not sexy enough?"

He blinks a few times. "Um."

"Sexy," I say impatiently.

"Yes, I heard that part."

"Is that why you turned me down?"

"No," he says.

"So I *am* sexy?" I demand.

Before Mason can confirm, Anup Kumar, wide receiver, glides into the conversation like a lubricated dildo. He folds one massive arm around Mason's skinny shoulders and gives him an affectionate squeeze, his shaggy black curls restrained by a bandanna. "Is this guy bothering you, babe?" he asks sternly.

"I'm very bothered!" I snap. "Ask Mason why he hates me!"

"You're out of your damn mind if you think I was talking to you, Cam."

"Are you bullying our precious assistant, Morelli?" Jody Jackson, punter and pastiest blond man alive, sidles up to Mason and fondly pats his beanie. "Leave Mason alone. Can't blame him for not wanting to date your ugly ass."

"*Ugly?*" I shriek.

Mason shakes his head in earnest, though his perfect level face isn't giving anything away. "Cameron is attractive, sure, but—"

"You're dating a sexy college girl?" Anup asks.

Mason's snowy-white cheeks start to redden, and he lifts his hand self-consciously over his mouth, like he's concealing inaudible laughter. "I'm single."

A direct punch to my throat. So being single is better than being with me. Got it.

"That's not it," Mason says in exasperation, and maybe Darius is right about the whole *talking out loud* thing. "It's nothing to do with your looks."

"So it's his fuck-ass piece-of-shit personality," Anup figures.

"The personality doesn't help," Mason says, kicking me directly in my esophagus.

"Or you're straight," Jody suggests.

"I'm not," Mason says, cleaving my chest open.

"So it *is* the fuck-ass piece-of-shit personality." Anup gives Mason a hearty smooch atop his beanie, oblivious to the critical hits I'm suffering. "It's okay, baby. I expect he only wants you for your brain cells, anyway."

Unfortunately, Mason doesn't get the chance to defend my intelligence. Coach Barnett notices the congregating mass and blows his whistle, shattering the sound barrier. "Morelli! Kumar! Jackson! On the field!" he yells, and so we sprint away to complete our high knee jogging, side lunges, and assorted tortures. All the while, I can only contemplate my place in the universe.

Why did Mason Gray reject me?

There's this uncomfortable nagging in my chest. Cam Morelli is supposed to be . . . well, perfect. He's well-liked by everyone, a shining star among a dome of murky darkness. I've put years of work into this face, this body, this personality, to solidify my position as one of the most respected seniors in school. Everyone knows my name because I've hand-carved a positive reputation for myself.

Why doesn't it work on Mason?

My skin feels prickly. I can't remember the last time I asked somebody out—usually, people are propositioning me every month, and I go along with it for a few weeks until we break up. I don't care about the connotation that comes with it. It's better that I'm too romantically active than otherwise, and it's better that the negativity is based around my number of partners rather than the queer thing. I tested the waters and "came out" last year by dating one of the JV lacrosse guys, and thankfully people seemed more gossipy about the fact that he was the fifth person I had dated in three months than the fact that he was a guy.

Every popular person in school has at least one negative feature attached to them, whether true or false. It's better that I can control what that feature is—in this case, being hard to tie down.

I was shit out of luck in middle school. It's better this way.

Is that connotation the only reason Mason isn't interested in me, or is it something else?

Eventually, people begin to flood the stands—students dressed in Elwood High merch, faculty members, and parents. Not mine, though. Today is the first game they're missing because they're busy swapping saliva over a dinner table for "date night." The sun melts into the horizon, bathing the sky in a crisp October orange despite the lingering September date, and the other team arrives to warm up beneath the looming scoreboard. I'm still heated.

That's an awful idea, but thank you.

I readjust my shoulder pads, secure my face mask, tie my cleats tighter, and try to get serious. I can't start slacking because I'm in a bad mood. Especially because Coach Barnett has been in contact with a scout from the University of Alpine who's been observing Darius since freshman year and just caught wind of me when I joined the team last year as a junior. I have to keep on top of my game if I stand any chance of earning myself a full ride, or the last two years of obsessive training and bulking will have been for nothing.

As the hum of roaring high schoolers washes over the field, annoyance plucks at my veins. Seriously, it's not like I have a crush on Mason. I don't get those. Butterflies? Not in this chiseled abdomen. If anyone is pining nearby, it's probably for me. I'm one of the tallest and most well-built seniors in school, thanks to my dad's one good gene and the aforementioned obsessive training and bulking. My skin is a natural, flattering golden brown, which gives me the mysterious and sexy air of an ethnically ambiguous man.

"You are *tan*, white boy," Anup tells me whenever I bring it up.

But basically, with my long eyelashes and dagger-sharp jawline, I'm irresistible. What happened here?

It's the fourth quarter when everything goes wrong.

I huddle up behind Nate, our center, eyes wandering the sea of white helmets clashing with the brutish red of the opposing team. Everyone is braced, waiting for the call. My gaze flicks to the sidelines, where Coach Barnett is massaging his peppered goatee. Mason stands beside him, expression neutral as ever.

Nate snaps the ball, and I close the leather between my gloves while the crowd wails with excitement. Anup is trying to escape the guy on his flank—Ravi's down the field, faster than the player targeting him. We're about to score. With twenty seconds left, we'll tie the game, and all Jody has to do is score the extra point for the win—

Suddenly, a heavy weight collides with my side, drilling me into the ground with enough force that the air nearly leaves my lungs. I blink blearily, looking into triumphant eyes behind a garish-red helmet. "*Stay down, bitch!*" he yells.

He's done it. He's cracked me. I don't know where it comes from, but suddenly, I'm not on the field anymore. The turf is a coarse bedroom carpet. The people looming over me aren't football players—they're other students. Eighth graders. Laughing, speaking behind hands, looking down on me with amused, disgusted eyes.

Do you think he's . . . ?

Like mother, like son . . .

I'm not that kid anymore. I've taken appropriate steps to ensure I won't ever find myself in that position again. But knowing this matters little. The pure, unbridled rage that spills out of me would be extremely ugly if I wasn't . . . well, me.

Suddenly, I'm on my feet, and I'm tearing my helmet off, and so is he, and my fist lands on his face before he can even curl his hand. He staggers beneath my knuckles and hits the grass, blood spurting from his nose.

The chaos that follows is flattering, actually. As his team surges toward me with an explosive battle cry, my team rushes to keep them off me.

Just like that, the game is over.

CHAPTER TWO
CAM

"I'm the victim."

I'm seated on the bench before the vacant field, arms knotted over my chest, the evening sun causing my skin to glitter a flattering golden sheen, probably. At this point we've had our after-game meeting and the bleachers have been cleared of onlookers, leaving me to look at nothing but gaping emptiness under blazing fluorescent lighting. A warm breeze combs across the green turf and white spray paint, cooling the beaded sweat along my hairline, and the heat radiating from my cleats is intense enough to fry the rubbery track under my feet.

Barnett rubs his gleaming bald head, his light-brown face drawn with weariness. "You punched another player, Morelli," he mutters.

"He called me a bitch," I point out. It's the closest to an explanation he'll get—I'm not going to tell him I had some weird PTSD war flashback. "Look, Coach. I'm a big guy, so I have a lot of testosterone. When someone disrespects me, it's natural that my response is to punch him. Haven't you watched hockey? They're duking it out all the time."

"You're an eighteen-year-old high schooler, not a salaried hockey player," Barnett says despairingly. "Also—and I'm asking this politely—please stop bringing up your testosterone when I speak with you."

"I'm just defending myself." I lean my elbows against the helmet nestled in my lap. Since the stands are cleared, there's no audience to defend my appropriate reaction to being insulted. "I didn't hit him that hard. He was barely bleeding."

"The quantity of blood is irrelevant, Morelli." Barnett looms over me with all of his five feet and seven inches, his expression contorted with severity. "This is the final straw."

I blink up at him. "Final? Were there others?"

There's a snicker behind me, and I whirl my head around. Mason Gray is standing on the track, hugging his clipboard, the breeze ruffling his perfectly styled black hair. Has he gotten prettier over the last two hours?

"Laughing about something, water boy?" I demand.

Mason gives me another pleasant, toothless smile. "I wouldn't dare, quarterback."

I whirl back to the coach and jam my thumb in Mason's direction. "Shouldn't he be sweeping the end zone or something?"

Coach Barnett tips his head back like he's casting a silent prayer to the Heavens Above, then walks to the bench and fumbles through a bulky tote bag. He pulls out a manila folder and tosses it into my lap. "I was planning on pulling you aside after the game anyway," he says darkly. "Even before you decked another kid in the face."

I flick open the folder and find my transcript staring up at me.

Health Science—C

English 12—D

Precalculus—F

World History—C-

Independent Reading—D

Gym—A

"Notice anything?" Coach Barnett asks.

"Crushing it in gym," I say, grinning in triumph. "Hell yeah."

Coach pinches the bridge of his nose. "Morelli," he says, slow and deliberate, "you don't meet the minimum-required GPA to play on the team anymore."

He may as well have just spit directly into my mouth. "What the *hell*?" I snarl, shooting to my feet and causing my helmet to roll onto the field. "The year just started!"

"Yet you're already failing courses. And now you've punched a person."

"Again, he called me a bitch," I point out, huffing. "I had to prove I wasn't a bitch."

Coach Barnett swallows another deep breath, like my mere presence is suffocating. "I can't ignore this, Morelli. The school's rules apply to everyone, even our leading quarterback. There needs to be a change, or this is your last game."

The weight of his words comes crashing onto my shoulders, causing my knees to wobble. Everything inside me screeches to a stop—my heartbeat, my blood flow, my breath. "W-Wait," I croak, raising my hands defensively. "I don't understand. That scout is going to be here in a few weeks. If I don't play, my chances of being recruited . . ."

And getting a full ride . . .

I realize my fingers are trembling and my voice is hitching around my words. The confident, indomitable Cam Morelli isn't supposed to snivel.

So I lower my palms and level my face.

"That's why you need to get your act together," Coach Barnett says, stroking his gray goatee in solemn thoughtfulness. "You're a late bloomer in the recruiting process, so this is your only chance to grab his attention now that you've met his height and weight requirements.

You've worked hard over the last couple years to get to this point, Morelli. *Very* hard. It would be a shame if the reason you didn't get an offer is because of your transcript."

I resist the urge to flop onto the turf and start writhing in frustration. He's not wrong. I've been working overtime, particularly this past year, to bulk my body and perfect my skills through training and conditioning. If only I'd thrown myself full force into this sport freshman year, maybe I'd already be verbally committed to Alpine University. Or maybe another few scouts would've taken note of me, and I'd be exploring my options.

But I didn't. Because it hadn't been my plan, up until sophomore year.

"I'm ordering you to get a tutor," Coach Barnett continues, oblivious to my mental anguish. "And a therapist. God, *please* get a therapist."

"A tutor?" I croak, ignoring the other sentences.

"Yes. A person who helps with schoolwork and—"

"I know what a tutor is."

"Well, I can never be sure with you." His bushy eyebrows tent with sternness. "Preferably a straight A honors student with a willingness to tolerate bullshit."

To my utter horror, his attention turns to Mason Gray. I snap my head around so quickly that my neck cracks. Mason offers a timid wave and says, "Coach Barnett asked me about it before warm-ups. I'm happy to help."

So he knew.

This slimy bastard *knew*.

My entire world is succumbing to the flames of Hell, wrought by the Devil Herself. Was his rejection of my advances another way for him to escalate my upcoming misery he was clearly aware of? Does he really hate me that much? "Stop," I say, shaking my head. "Please, fuck all of that, I'm begging you, anyone but him."

Mason's lip crinkles down. "Why?"

"You said you'd rather be skinned alive than date me!"

"I did not."

I groan, swinging back to Coach Barnett. Football is the one thing I have after I forcibly carved my name into the varsity team last year despite never having played in anything but recreational leagues. I'd known until now that I would probably excel in the sport if I devoted my life to it—I have raw talent, and that's a fact nobody on the team can deny. My current situation is the only proof that I'm not the same little brat I used to be. My parents sacrificed *everything* to get me here. My status on the football team is evidence that it was worth it, evidence that I can do something to benefit them for once.

I'm getting a goddamn full ride to play football in college. It's my fault that we had to come out here, so I'm going to do everything I can to ensure I don't plunge my parents into more debt, regardless of whatever turbulent inner feelings I have about college.

I can't tell them I've failed. I won't allow it.

I'll do whatever the hell I need to if it means getting back on the field.

Mason steps between me and Coach Barnett, wearing that mild smile. "Don't worry, Cameron," he says, using my full name like the little jerk he is. "Together, we can boost your pathetic grades and get you off the bench."

I nearly choke. "Pathe—?"

"I hope you're excited to get started with your lessons," he interrupts, his dark eyes glittering with innocence and hatred. The fluorescent stadium lighting settling over the town gives his pale skin this infuriating, ethereal glow, like he's descended from holiness to speak with me. The detached gaze and cagey body language don't add much to the "polite" atmosphere he's aiming for. "At this rate, you likely won't graduate senior year, let alone touch another football."

I look at Coach Barnett in horror, waiting for him to address this outrageous accusation. He merely shrugs.

"You want to get back on the field, and I want to . . . help the team," Mason continues in that soft voice, tapping his clipboard against my shoulder in an act of war. I go to smack it, face gnarled with a scowl, but miss it by inches. I swear his indifferent smile widens. "So let's be respectful, okay? There's something commoners call *hard work*, and with it, you can accomplish anything."

I hunch over, because he's dealing me blow after blow, railing his words into my chest with the force of curled fists. Coach Barnett doesn't seem to care about the verbal mugging happening directly in front of him.

"Anyway." Mason draws his clipboard into his chest. "Even if I have my reasons for helping, this offer is still one-sided. So, it would be nice if you could be my ride over the next few weeks. I found your number in the roster, so I'll send you my address. Good night, Cameron."

With that, he reaches for a backpack beneath the bench, slings it over his shoulder, and proceeds toward the locker room behind the end zone, leaving me bleeding out, my jaw hanging open, my eyes nearly bugged from my head.

Today is the worst day of my life.

Almost.

I'm not sure how I'm going to tell my parents about my *issues*. I'm almost glad they took a day off from child-rearing, because it would've been worse if they had to watch me whack another guy in the face from the bleachers. My dad probably would've vaulted onto the field just to wrangle me into a choke hold until I sputtered out an apology.

I hurl my backpack into my passenger seat and plop into the driver's spot. Everyone is gone—I'm usually the only one who doesn't carpool. People have invited me, but . . . I don't know. It's better this way. I love the camaraderie, and I love the feeling of my teammates depending on me, but the thought of spending a lot of time with these people outside the sport makes me itch and squirm. Maintaining the mask of Cam Morelli is harder the longer I cling to it. If I went to all the team dinners and carpooled every day on top of attending all the parties going on every week, my exhaustion would shatter the damn thing.

To maintain the image, I can't get too close. They might start to see the fractures I've been gluing together over the past four years.

I peel out of the parking lot and head into the darkened, early-autumn world. I can already hear my mother's concerned questions rattling around in my head.

What's different this year?

School's never been your forte, but you've never failed classes. Why now?

I won't be able to answer, because I don't know how. My transcripts aren't remarkable—certainly not as perfect as pretty boy Mason Gray's—but it's rare I'm ever below a C in any class. I guess I've been distracted. College is an ever-looming threat on a horizon that inches closer every day. Which means more loans, more debt. Even though my parents took plenty of that on by moving us away from our old town. An issue they made sure to hide from me, until I heard them muttering at the kitchen table at midnight two years after moving here.

And suddenly, things started making sense. The reason they shared a car rather than having their own like previously. The reason Dad suddenly ventured into "handyman" territory despite being horrible at it, rather than calling people to fix issues around the house. The reason the thermostat was uncomfortably low in the winters. The reason the tension always rose around Christmas or birthdays, when they had to shop for presents.

That was when I decided I was going to do everything in my power to keep us from sinking lower. My brain is big, sure, but it's not hardwired for academics, so I knew I wouldn't earn myself a scholarship based on intelligence.

Football, though?

I can do that.

I wish I'd known about the money situation earlier. I hadn't found out about it until the end of sophomore year, which only gave me the summer to practice and build my body for junior year. I made the varsity team easy, but took a back seat to the senior quarterback, and couldn't put my skills on display as frequently as I wanted. Even though Darius's scout took note of me toward the end of the season, impressed by my capabilities when the senior quarterback twisted his ankle and needed to sit out, he still told Barnett that I wasn't big enough to be fully considered. He promised he would return the following year to take one more look.

I would've been big enough if I'd taken football seriously in my younger years. Why hadn't I cared? Especially considering I knew how *good* I could be?

Whatever. The recruitment thing isn't even my only issue with the future. Financial concerns aside, will *Cam Morelli* thrive in college like he does in high school? Or am I going to have to rebuild myself from the ground up once again?

I groan at the empty interior of my car and watch the passing landscape to cool off. Elwood is a decently-sized town smothered with forestry and pricked with local businesses, restaurants, and a strip mall. Trees tower over every road, turns are sharp and angled, and ditches frame the streets, blanketed with dead leaves and branches as we sink into fall. I like this place. It's more scenic than the dull, dingy suburbs we came from.

There was a state park down there, too. I used to take meandering walks through the trails behind the school so I could find rocks to paint and add to my collection. The trees were a place to escape to where I didn't have to worry about fists and laughter.

Until they found out and started hunting me for sport.

I don't have to worry about that anymore. I'm big enough that people won't test me like they used to. If I wanted, I could probably find some woodland trails to go scavenging in. But . . .

Cam Morelli isn't that kind of person.

After a few ninety-degree turns along unpaved roads, I make it to my little house, separated from the neighbors by a curtain of pine and maple trees. As October creeps closer, splashes of red and orange are becoming more visible on the leaves. This house is way smaller than our place downstate, but with its wide glass windows and ten-minute walk to Lake Evergreen, it's more freeing and open than the prison we left behind.

It takes me a long while to collect myself enough to head inside. When I push through the door, I come to a horrific sight.

Mom is giggling like a fifth-grade girl with a secret, her peanut-brown waves pinned back. The scent of freshly baked brownies wafts through the air—probably an apology gift for having emotionally neglected me. "Nico, *please*," she says at the kitchen sink, plunging her gloves into soapy water. "If I break any more dishes, we're going to need a new set."

Dad's trying to sidle up behind her, ignoring her attempts to shrug his gigantic bear frame off. "Well," he says smoothly, the criminal, "we can just take funds out of Cam's minisafe."

"Ah, poor Cammy. Writing the code on the bottom in Sharpie . . .

How's he going to survive?" Mom grins and twists her head, allowing him to peck her lips.

I gag so loudly that I nearly make myself throw up. Which, based on today's events, would be perfectly appropriate, if not expected.

Both of them whirl toward me. "Cammy!" Mom says happily, beelining for me so she can plant a squishy kiss on my forehead. She's dressed in her favorite pink dress, which means she must've really been looking forward to abandoning me, her most precious person, for their traitorous date. "How was the game, bun?"

"Well," I say, shifting my weight. Disappointing Mom is the worst thing in the world, next to being rejected by some water boy with a magnetic face. "Something happened."

She arches her thin eyebrows, and I think I'd rather drown myself in the dishwater nearby than have to admit my wrongdoings. "Meaning?"

I glance at Dad, who's looking all dapper and shit with his sleeves rolled up and his tie tossed over his shoulder. "I can't listen?" he asks defensively.

I wrinkle my nose.

"All because I dared to steal your mother for a night." He scrubs a muscular hand through his dark hair, sighing. "Come on, Cam. I've got a client who can *only* come in tomorrow night to finish his full body, and your mom and I haven't gone out in months. Cut me some slack, yeah?"

I continue glaring at the villainous man. Mom thumps my head as if I'm to blame for this whole situation, then snaps, "Both of you, living room."

I fold my arms, searching her face. The area around her eyes, where she's painted concealer over dark circles from her late shifts in the OR. She's been a nurse there for a few years, and agreed to take on exhausting weekly twelve-hour shifts so she could have Fridays off for my games. Yet another burden she has to shoulder because of me.

Dad lumbers over like the big, clunky man he is. I inherited his height, but his stout physique, scruff, and overabundance of tattoos swathing him from the neck down don't help the fact that we look nothing alike. (I begged him to give me a sweet lioness tattoo when I turned eighteen, but he said he was booked solid at the studio. I checked his schedule. Haven't trusted him since.)

But okay, while they chose the worst day to bond over medium-rare steak or whatever married people do, at least I walked in on them being happy. The air of our old house was tight, the silence unbearably loud. While my dad moved soundlessly, every step my mom took quaked the floorboards.

Bottom line, fine. Maybe I'll let the date slide.

Mom pulls us into the living room, then sits me on the left cushion of the love seat and props herself on the right while Dad takes the recliner chair. "What happened?" she asks tentatively.

"Well . . ." The word comes choked. I feel like there's a giant, swollen testicle in my throat. I blink through the burn in my eyes, which happens on the rare occasion that two eyelashes fall into them simultaneously. "I got benched because of my grades. And for hitting another player. So now I have to be tutored by this guy who rejected me. Otherwise, I'm not sure I'll be on the field by the time that scout from Alpine University comes to look at me."

It's the barest bones of what I can offer. My parents take this in, silent, and I brace for a scolding session that's going to leave me groveling at their feet and begging for forgiveness. Hearing that I might not even be able to do the bare minimum for them by getting a full ride . . . I'm sure this doesn't feel good to hear. As expected, Mom looks at me in slight horror.

"You? My sweet baby?" she whispers. "Got *rejected*?"

. . . Oh.

Dad's mouth, halfway open and about to spill words, snaps shut. He clears his throat. "Aubrey, I don't think that's . . ."

"Why?" she demands. "You're so handsome! And you have a great personality."

My previous annoyance comes reeling back into my chest. "That's what I'm saying!"

Mom taps her chin, wearing a soft frown. "Maybe he has a partner?" she suggests.

"He's *single*, Mom."

She palms her mouth, face straining with dismay. "My God."

"Aubrey," Dad cuts in, scratching at his coarse beard, "maybe we should focus—"

"Clearly this boy doesn't deserve you if he can't see your amazing qualities." Mom smooths a hand through my hair with a sunbeam smile that warms my chest. I'm sure she's thinking about the *scout* situation but doesn't want to show the worry on her face. "And you threw a punch at someone because . . . ?"

The acknowledgment of my *altercation* causes me to flop back with a scowl. I'm not sure I can find the words to explain the real situation, so I go with the bare bones again. "This guy sacked me and called me a bitch."

Mom's brows shift together. Dad's massaging his face like he's trying to rub our conversation out of his skin. "Hitting people isn't like you, Cammy," she murmurs. "Is there something you're not saying?"

Of course she sees right through my attempt at nonchalance. Images come roaring to the forefront of my brain. Seeing people crowded around me on the turf. Flashing between the field and the party from eighth grade. The laughter and whispers as I sat frozen, trembling.

"I'm failing my courses," I decide to say. "But I've got an A in gym!"

"Obviously," Mom says with a wave of her hand. "You have my natural-born athletic talents."

I can't help a grin. In high school, Mom earned a full ride to college for volleyball, so this is high praise. After she got pregnant, though, she and Dad dropped out to take care of me.

"But your other classes?" she asks, her voice firming. "You need a minimum number of credits to graduate."

The words slip out of my mouth before I can even contemplate them. "Then I'll get a job in Elwood instead of worrying about college."

The silence tells me everything I already knew about their opinion on that idea. Dad folds his beefy arms. Mom kneads a knuckle into her temple, which makes my chest twinge. I hate when she looks tired like that, especially when I'm the reason for it. "You need a degree," she says sharply. "We're not discussing this again."

My teeth latch together with frustration. Whenever the topic arises, it forces me to remember that we were well-off in our old town, until the bullshit (*my* bullshit) forced us to pack up. Dad had been months away from opening his own studio.

Today's finances stress them out, even if they won't admit it to my face—they mutter about it plenty at the kitchen table when they think I'm asleep. That's why, if I *have* to go, I need this scout to find me as impressive as he finds Darius. If I have no choice, the least I can do is spare my parents the added financial distress. Everything is riding on securing a spot in the NCAA. Earning a full ride and Name Image Likeness deals, sacrificing my entire college career to the sport of football so I don't sink them into a worse situation . . .

An apprehensive shiver scratches down my spine.

Anyway.

Mom fixes me with a severe look. "Get back on the field. Let this boy tutor you, even if he did dare to reject you. Right, Nico?"

She shoots a look at Dad, who says, "Yes, ma'am."

Still no mention of the scout. They probably don't want me to feel even more pressured by bringing it up.

Mom pinches my cheek, and I squawk, wriggling away from her. "Fine," I say irritably. "I'll go along with the tutoring, but only for you." Besides, most of these Division I schools require a high GPA, so even if I did play the best game of my life, it won't be worth much if I can't prove I'm academically competent. And I usually am. It's just . . .

I don't know. I don't know why I can't focus this year.

Sighing, I stand and shuffle down the hallway to the bedrooms— one on the left, one on the right, and a bathroom between that we all share. The walls are uncomfortably barren compared to our old house. Years ago, our place was decorated erratically with framed pictures, award certificates, and Pride paraphernalia. The counters would be overcluttered with vibrantly painted rocks, and the halls smelled over- poweringly floral. I used to stop at a local flower shop on my way home from school and pick up bouquets for Mom once a week.

Though that was eventually ruined, too, when I got found out, and they would rip the heads off the flowers, then force me to walk home with the stems.

Maybe I should consider stopping at a flower store and picking up the hobby again, now that I can. But is that something Cam Morelli would do? Buy flowers for his mommy like some kind of elementary schooler? Does he also play board games with his parents and hand- paint rocks and take cutesy little walks through the woods?

It's better to avoid doing anything out of character, I guess.

I push into my room and walk right past my six-foot-tall poster of Beau Rainey, a recent college football player who was one of the first openly bisexual Division I athletes in male sports. I've had his face plastered on my wall long enough that the edges are curled inward and the tape is peeling the paint. He decided against pursuing the NFL, but that hasn't stopped me from worshipping him since I discovered his existence.

I can't look him in his cavernous black eyes right now, so I flop onto my bed and drag my phone out of my pocket. I have a message from an unknown number.

> Hey! This is Mason. Meet me at my place tomorrow. There's a cute coffee shop we can study at. Let's say 10 a.m.? Here's my address.

Fucking gross. I swipe the message away, growling. Down the hall, I hear Mom burst into laughter, probably because of some joke her clown husband just told. Which maybe sounds nice, even if that traitorous man is the one making her do that. With them being so busy lately, it seems their moments of genuine joy are becoming fewer and fewer.

Whatever. If the college conversation is off the table, I'll need to get over this rat's ass of a situation and focus. Fine, I type back.

My phone buzzes again before I can pocket it. Looking forward to seeing you! :)

I groan a cuss, slamming my face down into my pillow.

CHAPTER THREE
MASON

"I appreciate what you do here, Gray."

I blink out of my daze, eyes lifting from the shoulder pads I've been disinfecting, palm crinkled under the dampness of the cloth. "Huh?"

Mr. Barnett, who's been counting helmets on the nearby rack, turns to me with his tablet tucked under his arm. Now that the other players (Cameron Morelli) are gone, his strict coaching expression has softened to its tired-dad state. "You've been a huge help," he says, swinging his keys around his finger. His "time to go" signal. "Keeping those hooligans in check."

I smirk. "Never heard someone use that word before."

"It's an adequate description of these players."

I hike my backpack over my shoulder and follow him out the locker room door. It's a crisp late-September day, a welcome contrast to the hair-frizzing mugginess that's been assaulting the town. My fingers tingle at the thought of October on the horizon—cozy sweaters, pumpkin spice lattes, scary movies, bonfires.

"So, this situation with Morelli," he says as I climb into the passenger seat of his maroon minivan. "How are you feeling?"

I shrug, which encompasses my feelings about the situation. "It's fine."

I'm not sure it is, but it's another excuse to be out of my house and it's a distraction from my unruly thoughts, so I'll take what I can get at this point. Even if it means having to spend my time around a sleazy jock who apparently prefers to punch his way through his problems.

Mr. Barnett gives me a skeptical look.

"I'm not *excited* about it," I admit as he pulls out of the parking lot. "But the team needs Cameron, even if he's . . . like that."

Mr. Barnett nods solemnly, clearly wishing this weren't the case. "I know he's a lot, but once you get to know him, I think you'll find something more complex hiding beneath the surface."

Complexity in a single-brain-celled organism like Cameron Morelli? An enticing thought, though I'm keeping my hopes low. "Mm," I acknowledge, leaning against the window and watching headlights roar to life on passing cars as evening rolls over Elwood.

Mr. Barnett chuckles at my cynicism. "He's ditzy and arrogant, but try to be polite."

"Obviously," I grumble. Being polite, neutral, and boring is my entire personality. It's why I knew Cameron only wanted to date me because he liked my face. Nobody but one person has ever been attracted to me beyond my appearance, has ever gotten to know me through more than just small talk before asking me out.

I've been told I have one of those universally nice, androgynous faces. Long lashes and big doe eyes and thin brows and smooth skin that apparently doesn't harbor the right conditions for body hair to adequately grow. A straight nose, slender lips, and an angular face that probably looks sharper than usual because I lost so much weight last year.

People are more likely to call me pretty than handsome. But I've never been addressed as anything other than "sir" and "mister." I'm just feminine enough that I've heard my name passed around at parties by straight guys when they inevitably got asked who they would fuck if they had to choose a guy in the school. Yet I'm masculine enough that some girls seem comedically astonished (even offended) when I tell them I'm mostly attracted to men, except on a blue moon. As if every queer guy in the world needs to have some kind of physical or verbal indicator that exposes their fruitiness, and if they don't, it's *misleading*.

It sounds like a silly problem to have. I'm not sure it *is* a problem, considering everything else I've been dealing with.

But it's precisely because of what I'm dealing with that it's becoming more disconcerting. The way people look at me. Having to wonder who's genuine and who's not makes it all the harder to move on.

We had problems. Plenty. Authenticity wasn't one of them.

Basically, I'm not surprised Cameron Morelli asked me out, despite most of his former interests being girls. At least I didn't have to drag the truth out of him. He willingly admitted he asked me out for my face, unlike others who dance around their reasoning when I ask point-blank.

You're just really interesting.

It's easy to talk to you.

You seem like a warm, fun person.

Lies. I'm not interesting. I can't hold a conversation. And I'm certainly not warm and fun. It's why I haven't made any friends in the seventeen years I've been living in this town.

But that's not something I need to spiral about right now.

We snake through the town's varying hubs of activity—the strip mall, a cluster of business buildings, the local gallery (my favorite place), Annie's Brews (my second favorite place). We drive along Lake Evergreen, where people lounge around in sweats along the sandy, twig-laden beach, before branching off into a subdivision.

Tension prickles under my skin. My garage lights are on, shedding warm gold over the beige house. Instinctively, my eyes fan the area—the sidewalks, street, porch, roof. Nothing seems out of the ordinary. "Thanks for the ride," I say, scooping up my backpack. "I'll start the study sessions with Cameron right away."

"Take care of yourself, Gray," he says, offering a friendly wave.

I jog up to the porch and push inside. The interior of my house is no brighter than the exterior, save for the chandelier over the kitchen table on its dimmest setting. My father is on the edge of a chair, mindlessly scrolling on his laptop, the light overhead casting lengthy shadows across his worn, tired face. His skin seems more sallow than usual, and the bags under his dark brown eyes sag further.

He unglues his attention from his screen to look up. "Mason," he says, relief flashing across his face. He probably thought I was Mom. "Been missing you around here."

His words scrape my chest just deep enough to unearth some guilt I've been burying. I don't intentionally avoid my father, but it's a side effect of staying out of this house as frequently as possible. "Yeah," I mumble. "Been busy with games and practices. And the gallery. It's easier to study at the coffee shop, too, so . . ." I glance at the digital clock above the stove. "Where's Mom?"

"Out."

"What was she upset about this time?"

He doesn't answer for a long moment, like he's carefully considering his words. He doesn't have to, since it's just the two of us, but he's used to it. Weighing every syllable is something I'm familiar with, so I won't chide him for it. "I didn't buy organic yogurt when I went grocery shopping earlier," he says.

She's blown up over more menial things. The other day, I was running late for a shift at the gallery and tossed a spoon from a pudding cup into the sink on my way out. When I got home, I had to spend the next two hours hand-washing every single dish in the kitchen while she breathed heatedly over my shoulder.

I amble into the kitchen, hands working through the darkness as I pry a glass from an overhead cabinet and fill it with water, then nudge it toward him. Wordlessly, he scoops it up and drains it. "You never hydrate," I say quietly.

A smile lifts his lips, but it's the fake kind I learned from him. The one that functions as an aesthetic. "Good thing I have such an attentive kid. I might shrivel up otherwise."

I want to press him about . . . something. Everything. Why is he sitting in the dark, browsing article headlines? Has he looked over those brochures I sent him? He never responded to my last few texts about them.

I know better than to press, because he'll probably shut down. So I leave him and head down the hall. I don't have anywhere to be, so I take a shower to scrub the pungent macho energy of the football field off my body, then disappear into my bedroom.

The pastel paintings on the walls relax my shoulders. They're smaller ones gifted by the gallery, painted by local artists with my favorite colors. Soft lilac purples, peachy pinks, baby blues. Vibrant horizons and frosty mountains and radiant skies. I trail past the dusty guitar in the corner of my room, as well as the dried-out paint set and canvas I abandoned not long ago. The bookshelf filled with novels, which have makeshift bookmarks trapped in the middle. A pricey camera I received as a gift, which I used to take pictures of things I found lovely. Until I was informed that my definition of *lovely* could use some work.

It's not wintry cold, but I fish out my fuzzy flannel pajamas anyway, check to make sure the window is locked, and crawl into my bed. I guess I'll do homework so I can help Cameron focus on his. As I prop open my notebook, though, the sight of my screen lighting with a message locks my muscles tight.

I won't look. I don't need to look.

I should probably eat something.

I climb off the bed and start down the hall toward the kitchen but slide to a stop when I realize Mom is home. She's sitting across the table from my father, arms knotted over her cardigan, her blue eyes frigid enough to send ice crawling up the walls. They're having a tight, irritable conversation, her fingers trembling with anger.

At least they aren't yelling. Yet. Quietly, I go back to my bedroom to avoid getting close enough that Mom will notice me and demand I take her side about something. I retrieve an emergency peanut butter snack bar from my desk drawer, then sink into my bedsheets. As my glazed eyes rove the textbook section we're supposed to read before Monday, I nibble my snack.

But I can't ignore it. I know who the text is from, because there's nobody else who would want to talk to me on a Friday night. If I don't look now, I might do it during a time when I'm less stable. So I should get it out of the way.

I pick the phone up.

> Hope you're well. I understand if you don't want to talk. But I'm always here for you :)

A lump expands against the walls of my throat. My fingers fumble along the screen, typing and retyping messages, the words blurring more with each attempt.

> Don't text me.

> Please don't text me, but thank you.

> I'm fine. Good night.

> I'm okay, how about you?

> I miss you. We can talk for a bit if you want to call?

> Are you in the area? I don't want to be home.

I pause above the send arrow. When I blink, the crooks of my eyes are moist, and my vision blurs. My heart stops beating and instead begins to throb. Ache. I delete my message, then his, and wrestle under my sheets. Somewhere in my shallow breaths and dazed thoughts, I find myself pulling up a number I've never used, because Cameron should know that we're studying tomorrow.

I'm not looking forward to it. Tutoring a notorious flirt of a blockhead who measures his worth in muscle. He generally dates more popular people clinging to his peripherals, so I'm not sure how I ended up in his hunting grounds. Especially considering our interactions have been limited to me twisting open his water bottle and handing him towels.

Your face. I fuck with it.

How does that guy attract so many people with such a pompous personality? He's attractive, sure, and maybe I've caught myself watching him from afar whenever I drag myself to parties. But not because I'm lusting after him. It's more like I'm envious. What does it take to accumulate that much confidence?

I gulp in a breath, annoyance tingling in my skin. At least mentally whining about Cameron Morelli is masking my previous lamentations about . . . him.

Until one more text lights my screen, right as I'm about to send

Cameron a message. Even though I never responded, it's like he knows I'm looking at my phone. It's the kind of message that freezes the blood in my veins.

See you soon <3

CHAPTER FOUR
CAM

I wake to multiple rude-as-hell messages from people who are no longer my friends.

> Big D(arius): You brought this on yourself. Sorry man 😬

> Anup: This is your karma for harassing my son

> Jody: Maybe don't punch people shitass

This, atop the fact that I'm reading them before nine o'clock on a Saturday morning, an hour before I'm supposed to become Mason Gray's personal escort, means this is setting up the permanent death of my happiness.

I writhe out of my sheets and fumble through my dresser for my sexiest casual clothes. If I have to be around him, I'll ensure he regrets his rejection of my perfectly innocent advances. I opt for a black V-neck sweater that showcases my high-definition collarbone and roll back my sleeves. Bitches love rolled-back sleeves.

As I stumble into the kitchen, the smell of greasy meat wafts through my nose. Dad's at the stovetop in a T-shirt that exposes the tattoos winding up his wrists, stirring eggs, a flowery apron slung around his neck. "You're up early," he notes.

"Study date with the water boy." I peek over his shoulder. Sausage patties and bacon pop and sizzle in the pans beside him. I'm still a growing young chap in need of sustenance, so I can't reject protein so readily available for the taking. I reach out to snag some bacon, and Dad whacks me with his spatula. "Ow!" I hiss, reeling back.

"Are you shitting me, Cam?" he demands, his nostrils flaring above his thick beard. "You're going to take food out of a burning pan with your bare hands?" He drives me away from the stovetop with his elbow, grumbling, because I'm apparently the hardest kid in these United States to deal with. "Really, how will you survive on your own? Who's going to stop you from stuffing your hands into boiling oil? Or sweeping broken glass together with your bare foot? Or tripping over your shoes in the hallway and concussing yourself on the wall?"

"I've only done those things once!" I choke out, throwing my arms into the air with exasperation. "Sorry I'm not some genius Einstein–Benjamin Franklin–Isaac Newton–Leonardo DiCaprio–type ass!"

Dad massages his bushy brows. "Go sit. I'll bring you breakfast."

I tromp over to our rounded wooden table, plopping down. Moments later, I'm drooling over a fresh plate of crispy bacon, cheddar scrambled eggs, sausage patties, and buttered toast.

Dad slumps into the seat beside me. "So?" he asks, combing down the scruff around his lips. "Am I forgiven?"

The smell of food has driven me into a drunken stupor, forcing me to reorient myself. Was I mad at him for something? Probably. "Sure. Hopefully it'll get me through whatever suffering Mason is about to inflict." I chug my glass of milk—a torture I endure every morning. If the claim that milk builds strong boners is true, mine are slowly becoming indestructible.

"You're going to start trying, right?" he asks, watching me tear into a strand of bacon. I expect he might bring up the scouting opportunity, but of course he doesn't. My parents probably don't want their desperation to show. "If you fail, you're repeating senior year. You're not getting a job instead of going to college."

I shudder at the thought, especially considering I already have one extra year of schooling under my belt from when I was held back in sixth grade. I'm not ready to go through *another* fresh start, and then have to do it all again the moment I graduate. "I'll try," I say, chomping into a sausage patty. "But if the water boy gets *sassy*—"

"You'll relish it, because it means he's tolerating your bullshit." Dad scoops my plate up and brings it to the sink like he hasn't just roundhouse-kicked me in the neck.

"What *bullshit*?" I demand.

"Your personality." He shrugs and adds, "The fake parts. And your abysmal behavior."

I've been gagged. Where is this coming from? I want to throw something pointy at him, but he gives me a sudden, cutting glare that brings my boiling blood down to freezing temperature.

"You hit someone, Cameron James," he says darkly. "I thought we raised you better. How many times do I have to tell you to drop the macho act you've been playing? You pretending to be someone you're not is hurting others."

Hearing his voice drop to such a low, irritable tone causes my intestines to twist into painful knots. I'm sure he's been hanging on to this since last night—waiting for me to cool down before confronting me. And the thing is . . .

He's not exactly wrong.

"Sorry," I mumble. Cam Morelli doesn't speak softly, but I guess I can be Cameron for the moment. It's just Dad.

"Use your fists again and you'll have to do a hell of a lot more than say *sorry*." He's glaring at me with unyielding intensity. "I don't know what's got you twisted up lately—"

"That party."

Dad's brows quirk. The words slipped out before I could chew on them.

"It . . . When he hit me, I remembered that party," I whisper. Even mentioning it causes my limbs to seize and my chest to pound. The air thins rapidly in my lungs, but if I don't persevere and choke it out, Dad is just going to push until I crack open anyway. "From eighth grade. I realized I didn't have to take it. Like back then."

I'm not going to let him question me further. Besides, if I linger, he'll find new ways to insult me, so I lunge upright, hitch my backpack, and head to the door.

"Thanks for breakfast," I call to him. "I'll be back—"

"Do you still think about it? That night in eighth grade."

I falter, his voice cutting through my attempt at indifference. "Huh?"

"What happened." Dad's expression is neutral, his voice level and cool. "How often do you think about it?"

Clearly he's not willing to let it go. But I'm not going to indulge him when I'm already about to endure the shittiest Saturday in all of history. "Not often" is all I say, before pushing through the front door. The gold morning sun is weaving through the trees, though the warmth doesn't reach my face.

I drop into my car and toss my backpack aside, then plug Mason's address into my phone.

The route is scenic at least, not that driving along the lake makes my situation more acceptable. The waves seem extra frothy and gray today—a sure sign of impending doom. I zigzag through run-down roads caged in by looming trees, then creep through a midsize subdivision. The sight of similarly colored houses makes me wrinkle my nose. Places like this, with their perfectly curated lawns and identical slanted rooftops, remind me of the town we narrowly escaped.

I pull into the driveway of a beige house with a porch wrapped around the front, furnished with a swinging bench. There's someone sitting on it. A pale middle-aged man in a faded T-shirt, black scruff climbing his cheeks. A cigarette dangles from his lips, causing wispy smoke to trail into the air. Frantically, I pull Mason's number up and call him.

"Good morning, Cameron."

Even the sound of his sweet, mellow voice makes me want to projectile vomit. "Water boy," I snap. "I'm here, but there's a creepy man on your porch."

There's a beat of silence. Then, "That's my dad."

"Tell your dad that blinking is healthy," I order.

"You're early. Like twenty minutes early."

I don't feel like mentioning that I was desperate to escape my father. "And?" I ask coldly. "What, should I have shown up tardy like some hoolig—"

I choke on the rest of my words, my heart skipping. What am I doing, sounding like a responsible, eager, bright-eyed pupil ready for studying? Cam Morelli should've shown up a half hour late. And he sure as hell wouldn't use the word *hooligan*.

Thankfully, Mason doesn't question it. "I'll see you at our scheduled meeting time," he says, and I can hear him smiling through the words. "Goodbye."

I choke on my dismay. "You're going to make me *wait* for twenty whole *minutes*?"

No response. He hung up on me, the bastard.

Thankfully, though, he doesn't take that long. Just as I'm considering booking it home (that porch man is giving me shivers), Mason appears at his front door. He's wrapped in a turtleneck, scarf, and beanie that blends with his midnight-black hair. All this combined with his skinny jeans makes it look like he's trying to haul late autumn into town with sheer willpower. Is he trying to look as cute as possible to twist the knife into my wound of rejection?

Without a glance at his father, he jogs to my car, then tosses his bag into the back, nearly zipper-slapping me along the way. "Hello," he says, a calm, vacant smile toying at his lips. His eyes are burned pink—from fatigue, maybe? "I'm flattered you were so excited to see me this morning that you came early."

I hiss like a cat. Flattered? Excited? For *him*? "Just tell me where to go, water boy," I snap.

"Annie's Brews."

I furrow my brows. "Annie's who?"

His smile flips into a scolding frown. "Cameron Morelli, you uncultured swine."

"Pardon the fuck?"

"Any coffee-drinking high schooler is lost without Annie," he says, wagging his slender finger in my face. I resist gnashing my teeth at it. "I don't know how you've survived this long."

"Never had coffee," I grumble. Mr. Gray eyes me through the windshield in this "I could charge your car at any moment" way, so I start backing out of the driveway. Until I catch Mason's expression in my peripherals, twisted with dismay, his brown eyes shot with horror.

"You've never had *coffee?*" he demands.

I sigh, pulling onto the street and heading toward the subdivision exit. "Which way?"

"Left—but, okay, tea? Hot chocolate?"

"Not interested."

Mason slumps down into his seat until the belt is notched under his chin. "You're hopeless," he says in quiet defeat.

Like I asked for his irrelevant opinion. I draw calming breaths, trying to remind myself of why I'm doing this. It's for my football career. So I don't have to be a benchwarmer by the time the scout shows up to examine Darius and me.

Mason gives a lofty sigh. "We're just studying, Cameron," he says wearily. "It's not like I'm making you get your genitals waxed. You don't have to be so clenched up."

"I'm being forced to study with a snobby asshole who hates me, just so I can play football. It's *worse* than getting my balls waxed," I mutter.

"I don't hate you. I just find you rude and inappropriate."

It's like he wants me to eject him from the car. "If you can't see my natural charm and charisma, that's your problem." I jut my chin higher, and despite my father's warning voice in my ear, I say, "You should feel lucky. I could've offered myself to anyone else."

Mason presses a palm over his mouth, like he's concealing a smile. "But you deigned to choose a lowly peasant," he says solemnly. "Why, pray tell, did you descend from your royal pedestal of perfection to offer yourself to a modest commoner such as me?"

I turn my music up to the max because I'm not dealing with this shit right now.

I continue along the road hugging Lake Evergreen, watching sunlight bounce off the rippling water, before pulling into a building complex across the street from the sandy shores. Mason guides me along the cracked sidewalk to a shop with fogged windows and a faded sign reading ANNIE'S BREWS. The interior walls are paneled with wood, and golden lamps decorate the perimeter. Bookshelves are scattered along the hardwood, tucked beside leather couches, love seats, and rounded tables. The aroma is sweet and nutty. A handful of people are lounging around—some on laptops, two in business suits, and a couple of sophomores I recognize.

"Mason!" A young woman with wildly curly hair stands behind the barista counter, dressed in an I LOVE YOU A LATTE! apron. She waves, a gigantic smile plastered on her face. "What are we having today?"

"Hey, Annie." Mason treads closer, massaging his hands like we came in from a blizzard. "Cinnamon-twist latte, please. Extra sweet?"

Her grin wavers, and her eyes search him intently. "That kind of day, huh?"

"Yes." Mason's voice comes uncharacteristically dull and flat.

"I see." Annie offers me an expectant smile before I can stick my nose in whatever they're talking about. "How about you, hon?"

I wave my hand halfheartedly. "I'm okay. Never had coffee, so . . ."

Annie gives me this look like I've just killed a golden retriever directly in front of her.

"I know, right?" Mason demands. "I have no idea how he stays awake at school."

"Sheer willpower and natural strength," I explain. Obviously.

Mason snags my elbow and tugs me to the counter so I can see all the fancy contraptions behind Annie. His hands are as silky smooth as they look, which doesn't make me feel any better about him. "What do you like, Cameron? Sweet? Spicy? Nutty?"

I sniff stubbornly. "None of the abo—"

"Make that two, Annie," Mason says, ignoring me like my words mean absolutely nothing. "He can try my favorite drink."

I want to protest this attempt to coerce me into drinking caffeine, but Annie turns away from us to do whatever baristas do. Mason plucks out his wallet and stuffs a ten-dollar bill into the ceramic tip jar, then scurries away from the counter. Sighing, I follow after him, adjusting my backpack straps.

"So," I say, watching Mason plop onto a love seat in the corner of the shop and shed his shoes. He's wearing socks with smiley face marshmallows because he has that adorable soft-boy image to protect. "What did she mean? When she asked if it was 'that kind of day.'"

Mason sinks deeper into the cushion. "She usually knows when I'm having a bad morning."

"You have enough of those that she has a special drink for you?" I ask, skeptical.

"It's just extra whipped cream."

I huff, flopping down beside him and peeking out the sprawling window nearby. The brick business building next door is in the way of a great view, but the edge of the lake still peeks around the corner. "You don't *have* to tutor me if you hate me that much," I mutter. "Like, damn. Even the barista lady sees it."

Mason massages his temples with exasperation. "How many times do I have to say I don't hate you?" he asks coolly.

"Why else would you be having such a shitty morning?" I demand.

He gives a brief, sassy eye roll. "I know this may be beyond your comprehension, my liege, but there are problems that exist outside of *you* in this world."

I'm about to pack my ass up and haul it home so I can tell my parents I'm officially closing the book on my education. There's no way putting up with Mason Gray is worth the money I'll be making as a Division I college football quarterback.

Except it *is*, because money.

Damn it.

Annie appears suddenly at the back of the love seat to hand us our cinnamon-twist lattes. "You boys enjoy," she says, and as she turns to leave, a ten-dollar bill drops onto the cushion.

"Wait!" Mason grabs it, eyes glinting with frustration. "Annie, take my money."

"Not from my favorite customer." She tosses a wink over her shoulder, then jogs off before Mason can launch the bill back at her. I pop the lid off my coffee and stare suspiciously at the whipped cream. Does this guy walk around town getting shit for free because he's that irresistible?

"You're dramatic." Mason draws his cup to his lips, then melts into the couch, his eyes fluttering. "I come here pretty frequently. It's nice to get away."

I should learn how to think with my mouth shut.

Before I can ask what subject we're starting with, Mason flaps his sweater sleeve and says, "Try it!"

I want to remind him I didn't ask for this, but he's so eager that I feel compelled to bring it to my lips. I take a gulp, and sugary heat explodes through my mouth, frying my taste buds before laying waste to my throat like liquid fire. "Fuck," I gag.

"Sorry." Mason tosses a sleeve over his mouth and laughs. "Should've said to sip."

"No shit?"

"Well, if your mouth ever regains feeling, try it again. I'll take it if you don't like it."

Ah. It's all making sense now. "You ordered this for me knowing I would hate it, just so you could have a second drink," I say accusingly, glaring him down across the couch cushions. "This was part of your plan, you manipulative little bitch."

Mason spreads his hand further over his mouth, but his eyes are crinkling, which means he must be smiling wide. "How was I supposed to know you wouldn't like sweet drinks?" he asks innocently. "I thought they'd be your favorite. Since your personality is so soft and syrupy."

It's like he wants to be launched through the glass windows of the establishment. I don't have any intelligent response to offer. My brain-power has been all but drained over the last several minutes, simply from trying to keep up with him. It's all I can do to tear open my backpack and start rifling angrily through my books.

Mason snickers, apparently documenting this exchange as a win, and pulls out his precalc textbook. I guess that's what we're starting with.

And thus commences the most agonizing few hours of my life.

Okay, so maybe it's not that bad.

Precalc sucks, but the thing about math—at least, high school math—is that it's mostly straightforward. There's no hidden themes or subtle meanings to search for, like in English. So, with Mason walking me through these questions slowly, taking it step-by-step until we both have the answer, we get it done relatively quickly.

Next comes health science. He took the class as a junior, so he has knowledge in it. Next, world history. Basically, he reiterates everything I failed to pay attention to in class, but in simpler words and shorter sentences.

English is torturous. I swear we spend two hours going through summary notes of *The Great Gatsby* because I can't remember anything about it, even though I just watched the Leonardo da Vinci version a few days ago.

"The teachers are asking these questions, so you should be prepared to answer them," Mason says when I ask why I should give a shit. "Whining won't make a difference."

Now I'm a whiner. Even though I gave him my coffee out of the sheer kindness of my heart, he's still insulting me.

"You hated it, and it was free," he points out.

Whatever.

As time passes, more students come to occupy the seats until the place is bustling. I recognize some people from lower grades, but nobody I can confidently call my friend and request to save me from this madness. Still, there's something undeniably cozy about it all. The soft lighting, the warmth of the café, the sound of the coffee death machine whirring, the muted chatter. There are worse places Mason could've chosen.

The last class is independent reading, which is where we read books through the fifty-minute session and then take ten minutes at the end to write about what we just consumed. "What book have you been reading this semester?" Mason asks, eyeing my backpack.

"Uh. None?"

He offers a weak, frustrated smile. "What do you do during class?"

I give him a thumbs-up. "Sleep."

"Mm. I thought you were too busy running on willpower and natural strength to fall asleep in school," Mason says, thrumming his fingers along the brim of his empty coffee cup. There's this smug calmness about him that makes the muscles tighten in my neck.

"I could stay awake if I wanted to, coffee boy," I snap. "But I don't have anything interesting to read, and I took it as a blow off, so—"

"Yet you're failing." Mason is nearly unblinking, his level expression unflinching. "'Read book' is the bare minimum you have to do to pass the 'read book' class. Are you purposefully trying to fail senior year, Cameron Morelli, or are you just genuinely that incompetent?"

Oh my *God*? I open my mouth to protest his audacity, but my voice doesn't come to me for several seconds. "Fuck you," I squeak out.

"Hmm." He pokes my thigh with the toes of his marshmallow socks, then fumbles through his backpack and fishes out a slender novel with an illustrated cover, which he tosses into my lap. I scrunch my face at the image, which depicts two people pointing accusatorily at each other. "Read it. Enough that you can do a daily report at the end of class and turn it in. Start it now and I'll let you know when a half hour is up."

I'm ready to crack my skull open on the mahogany bookshelves. "Can't I read it at home?" I ask pleadingly.

"No, because you won't." Mason furrows his thin brows at me and says, "That's why you need a tutor, right? Someone to hold you accountable?"

"You can't keep me here," I snip.

"No, but I can snitch to Barnett."

My lips peel back into a scowl. I've been inwardly deliberating the question for a while, so I might as well pose it. "Why do you care?" I demand.

He tilts his head sideways, though his expression doesn't flinch. "About what?"

"*Me.*" I gesture violently to myself. "My tutoring. My football career. What's in it for you?"

Mason gives me a lingering look that's probably meant to look empty. But I notice his gaze flick away, like I've reminded him about something. His jaw flexes—a fracture in his composed expression. "Didn't I mention there's a world that exists outside of you?" he asks coldly. "Why do you think it's your business to know?"

He actually looks miffed that I asked. I'm not sure why the realization makes my heart stutter. Now that I'm thinking about it, though, I've never seen Mason express *actual* emotions. He's always perfectly poised, unruffled. Seeing this tiny break in character is strangely exhilarating.

"You're spending hours of your day tutoring me and trying to get me back on the field," I say, poking deeper into this unexpected chink.

Can I make this guy angry? What would a pissed Mason Gray look like? "You can't pretend I'm *not* involved. There has to be a reason you said yes to this. I'm wondering what that is."

Mason's brow twitches. "Keep wondering," he says, his voice tight, and before I can try to goad him any further, he strides off toward a neon sign hanging over the bathrooms.

Hmm.

I'm interested, admittedly, but Cam Morelli would probably let it go and move along. So when Mason returns from the bathroom, that's what I do. I pick up that romance book, because the sooner I get started the sooner I'll be able to leave.

"You've done well for your first session," he says. "Thank you for making this experience mostly painless by listening to me."

I almost say *you're welcome*, but there's this playful glint in his eyes that reminds me of when my dad slides jabs at me beneath his compliments. "You say you don't hate me, but you take every opportunity to insult me," I snap, scrunching my nose.

"Sorry." Mason's smile spreads, and just when I think I might get to see his teeth for once, he covers his lower face with his sleeve again. "You make it too easy."

"You think I'm dense."

"Not true," he says with an offended gasp. "It's more like, if I was to shout directly into your ear, I think my voice would probably echo quite a lot."

"What the hell is *that* supposed to mean?" I ask squeakily, on the brink of shooting to my feet and squaring up. He's insulting me—I can *see* it in the amused crinkle of his giant brown eyes.

"Don't worry your pretty head about it." Mason waves me off with his free palm. "Aren't you supposed to be reading? An engaging romance awaits."

I scoff, snapping the rom-com book open in my lap. "Why do I need to read twenty chapters about a heterosexual couple hate fucking just to pass my class?" I grumble, to which Mason makes a quiet chirping noise. Did he just *laugh*?

"If it's any consolation, I've read eighty percent of the book, and they haven't had sex."

Well . . . that doesn't sound too bad. "I thought most romances were just porn," I admit. It's why seeing this book cover made me feel instant dread.

Mason must notice the relief on my face, because he lifts an eyebrow and says, "I thought you would've wanted a smutty book to read. Considering your . . . uh." He clears his throat and says, "Knack for relationships?"

His words instantly sour my mood. And my throat. I have no interest in discussing that subject, and I'm at my limit for tolerating his sass, so I irritably ask, "If I send you a paragraph about the first thirty pages before Monday, can we leave?"

Mason's pleasant expression wilts. "Fine."

Hell yeah. I've made it through my first tutoring session having accomplished plenty, so my impending football career is still within reach.

. . . Yay.

Right. *Yay.* I'm excited about that.

"Let's go, then," I say, hiking my bag onto my shoulder.

"Go ahead." Mason snuggles deeper into the love seat, rooting himself. "I'll walk home."

I tent my eyebrows. "I thought you wanted me to be your ride?"

"I spend most of my days here or at the gallery. But thanks for driving me."

I'm not interested in what he's saying, nope, not even a little, because he's still the brat who cruelly rejected me. So I won't wonder about why he looks so tired and whether or not he was crying last night, or why this is the only place I've ever seen his shoulders relax, or what the deal is with the smoking man with the sunken eyes on his porch. "You stay here all day?" I ask, for lack of anything better to say.

He shrugs, then fumbles through his book bag for something to do. "We can study again in a couple days when you start collecting homework. Try to stay focused in class. It'll make sessions easier if I can jog your memory rather than teaching you from scratch."

"Meh." I fish my keys out, then falter. "You going to that bonfire at Ravi's?" I'm not sure why I ask—I don't want to see him twice in one day.

At the mention of the bonfire, though, Mason curls in on himself. "Uh. Well. Maybe? I don't . . ." His knees fold into his chest, and his eyes glaze, like he's deeply deliberating his answer. "I guess . . . yeah. I should probably get out . . ."

His voice fizzles away.

"If you go, stay away from me," I say, huffing. "You've been rude enough today. Probably because of how much you hate me."

That earns me another eye roll. "You may not believe this," he says dryly, his face the flattest and most bored it's been this week, "but my opinion of you is overwhelmingly neutral. This *bad blood* or whatever that you've created between us? It doesn't exist."

"You're right," I say sharply.

"Oh?"

"I don't believe you."

"Oh."

"I can feel your animosity. It fills the air around us," I snap, gesturing at the coffee shop.

Mason nods thoughtfully. "That's a big word, Cameron Morelli. I'm impressed."

"Fuck y—"

"Aren't you leaving?" Mason flutters his annoyingly long lashes. "Or are you stalling because you want to spend more time with me?"

I have to swallow a gag. "See you tonight, then," I say, backtracking to the door, because his playful little statement doesn't deserve acknowledgment. "From a reasonable distance."

"I didn't agree to—"

I'm out the door before he can finish his sentence.

CHAPTER FIVE
MASON

"Hey, honey."

There's a hand on my shoulder. The sensation sends a panicked jolt through my body, and I hurl upright with a gasp, slapping the wrist away. "Don't!" I snap.

"It's just me, Mason."

Annie's familiar voice slows my heartbeat. I'm nestled into the love seat in Annie's Brews, a couch pillow tucked under my beanie. The world beyond the café windows is pitch-black, and the chairs have been upended onto rounded tables. "Did I hold you up?" I ask, grimacing.

"Never." Annie tugs me to my feet and hands me my backpack as we head to the door. She closes it behind us and twists her key into the lock. Though darkness has cloaked the town, the overhead moon provides just enough light to cast silvery twinkles along Lake Evergreen. Despite the serenity of a calm night in Elwood, my apprehension begins to mount. My eyes flit around, searching the uneven cracks and foliage plaguing the parking lot, scanning the shadows behind looming streetlights.

"Have a good night," I say quietly, and I start to walk toward the main road, but she catches the crook of my arm.

"What are you doing?" she asks, raising a stern brow. "You don't have a ride?"

I swallow with apprehension. I don't normally stick around until closing time—I foolishly fell asleep, though, so now I get to deal with *questions*. "It's fine," I try to say, but she's already anticipating my response and shaking her head.

"Absolutely not. You're not walking home alone when it's this dark."

Well. I can't exactly run away, because she'd just confront me the next time I show up at her shop. So I reluctantly follow her to her beat-up vehicle, climbing into the passenger seat.

As I start mindlessly pointing her down the correct streets, I can't help but reflect. Honestly, I expected I was walking into the most frustrating day of my life. That's usually how Cameron Morelli leaves me feeling—he's that overconfident, conceited "I don't take orders from anyone" type of jock. He whined about everything, sure, but when it came time to get serious, he had, against my expectations, gotten serious.

We're starting to approach a crossroad where if I tell her to turn right, we'll end up at my house. If I tell her to turn left . . .

It'll take us in the direction of Ravi's bonfire.

I rub my palms against my tired eyes. Most of me wants to go home. Parties aren't my forte—my egregious small-talking skills leave me with acquaintances instead of friends, because nobody finds me interesting to be around. But I've spent years of my life avoiding social circles and shying away from friendships because I felt . . . or I was *promised* . . . that I wouldn't need them. And maybe I don't. But I can't help feeling lonely.

I made an oath that I would try to get myself out there. That I would go places I'm invited, talk to people who approach me.

So I say, "Take a left."

The bonfire is already roaring in Ravi's backyard, and there's upward of four dozen people hovering around it, clinking plastic cups, enjoying nostalgic pop music. Dim golden string lights zigzag over our heads, illuminating the trees lining Ravi's yard. A white foldout table decorated with alcohol and a cooler hugs the wall beside the glass door.

I stand beside the fire, the heat of the crackling flames washing my face, and sip my drink, watching embers spiral away from the billowing smoke. A few people are talking in pairs or small groups, but I don't know most of them by name. I should probably consider finding someone I've had pleasant conversations with.

Just then, there's an onslaught of noises—the glass door slamming open, deep voices booming into the night, laughter shaking the ground. The varsity footballers are here. Thundering out of the house are Anup, Darius, Jody, Nate.

And, of course, Cameron Morelli.

He's wearing a gleaming smile, and my traitorous heart does a higher-than-normal bounce. With his plaid shirt, peeled-back sleeves, and black pants rolled to his ankles, he'd fit in well in a college crowd. The highlighted streaks in his brown hair catch in the firelight, causing them to sparkle gold. The hearth's glow is flattering against his warm skin.

A lanky arm slides around my neck, and a voice says, "The team darling!"

The unexpected feeling nearly sends me lurching into the fire. It's Anup, wearing a signature sly smile that indicates he knows a little more than you. I return it, though seeing him makes my stomach twitch. Where he goes, the rest of the team follows, and I'm not sure how thoroughly I want to be perceived tonight.

"How's my baby?" he asks, squeezing me against him. "I heard you had to hang out with our most unbearable player today."

I know he's being polite, seeking me out to talk to me. He probably saw me lingering by the fire, pathetically alone, and feels like he owes me something since I refill his water during games. I won't hold him long here.

"I'm fine," I say with a neutral smile.

"Back off," comes another voice. Darius, the middle linebacker and team captain, is now taking up his usual excessive amount of space in the semicircle around the fire. He raises a thick, weary brow at Anup. "Nobody wants to be that close to you."

"Aww! Tell him that's not true, Gray."

I can't say I'm comfortable, yet part of me doesn't mind the friendly physical contact with another person. Before I can respond, Anup unhooks his arm from around me, then peeks into my cup.

"Got booze?"

"No," I say.

"You driving?"

"No."

"Then let's get some vodka into that cup!" He tries prying it from my fingers, but I hold tight, inching away, my throat suddenly tasting like bile.

"It's fine," I say faintly. "I don't drink anymore, so . . ."

"Bobbing for apples!" another voice cries, and suddenly, Cameron is jogging circles around us, pumping his fists with excitement. "Ravi's filling the blow-up pool! I'm going to kick your asses, *ha-ha-ha-ha*!"

He runs off with a delighted hoot. I don't think he noticed me, which is fine. I'm nothing but a temporary tutor and the guy who rejected him—a title I'm happy to keep.

"Oh my God, I have to push him in, oh my *God*—" Anup laughs maniacally and takes off after Cameron. He was probably glad to have an excuse to leave. Darius isn't as lucky, and now he's stuck adjacent to me, swirling a drink, grimacing at the footballers wreaking havoc.

A sudden howl yanks my attention sideways. It's only been ten seconds, and Cameron is flailing in the pool of apples, roaring curses while Anup and Jody shriek with laughter. The sight of him writhing in a shallow kiddie pool is ridiculous enough to make me laugh, forcing me to throw a hand over my mouth.

He's kind of funny. Sometimes.

"Seems like they have it out for Cameron today," I say to Darius, thankful to have a conversation starter. I have to take initiative. All the social skills I should've learned as I grew up were robbed from me, and now that it's senior year, this is my last chance to practice them.

Though, did I have to think this hard earlier, when I was with Cameron? I can't remember ever straining or searching for conversations. Maybe I'm just not as worried about his opinion or something.

"Better this than confronting him about the game he lost for us," Darius says, sighing while Cameron hikes himself onto the grass, sopping wet.

"I'm surprised you're not angrier."

"Eh. Cam screwed up, but he's our best player. His skills are off the charts—he came out of nowhere at the end of the last season. He can throw a bullet halfway down the field into a receiver's hands *as* he's being tackled. He's amazing, so we get over his issues." Darius shrugs his broad shoulders. "And we have no reason to hate him."

I smirk. "Seems like you could find something if you squinted."

Darius laughs, and then it's quiet again. Damn it. What topic should I bring up next? He's probably fumbling for a reason to step away. "You . . . You can . . . go," I say feebly.

His eyes, which were glazed on the fire, sharpen so they can look at me. "What?"

"You don't have to stay here. Um. With me," I clarify. I can already feel heat seeping into my face, and I hope the flames aren't bright enough to illuminate it. "I know you'd probably rather hang out with the guys."

Darius laughs in a low rumble that shakes the ground under my feet. "You're kidding, right?" he asks skeptically. "I have to spend every waking moment with those dipshits. I'd much rather be here right now."

Oh. Right. "I guess it's quieter," I agree. Since I can't maintain a conversation to save my fucking life, and all.

"It is. Besides, I'd prefer to hang out with you."

That gives me pause, and I knit my brows. He's back to watching the flames snap and twirl, nursing his cup against his lip. Why would he say that? To make me feel better? "I don't have much to say," I admit. "Sorry. If you feel obligated to stand with me . . ."

"What are you talking about?"

Darius looks both baffled and vaguely annoyed, and I think I've screwed something up. Panic closes my throat, but thankfully, my phone rings—the perfect escape. Thoughtlessly, I swipe the screen and bring it to my ear as I jog away. "Hello?" I say, the haze of anxiety clearing.

"Mason?"

My heart plummets into my stomach. The air leaves my lungs in one shaky exhale. "Don't call me," I sputter out, and I disconnect, but it doesn't matter. His word, low and smooth, still reverberates in my ears. It's been so long since I've heard him say my name.

My pulse rams against my throat and water glasses my eyes. My phone hums.

> Sorry if I caught you off guard. If you aren't ready to call, I'm happy to text. :)

Ah. This isn't good. My thoughts are an incoherent mess. My stomach twists and flutters and aches. My fingers are moving.

> I'm sorry, I don't think we should text.

I told myself I would never apologize to him again. Yet here I am, my first two words to him in months.

I'm sorry.

> I understand. Let me know if you need anything. I'm always here for you.

He's never said something like this before. Does that mean he's maybe . . . ?

I massage the wetness from my eyes, shoving my phone in my pocket. I don't want to be here. I can't do this right now. So I power walk to the glass door, then round the corner into Ravi's kitchen, nearly slipping on a trail of water leading into the house.

When I look up, it's because I'm slamming face-first into a naked Cameron Morelli.

CHAPTER SIX
MASON

Okay, he's not *naked* naked. He's wearing stretchy Hanes, which are soaked and clinging to him in all of the . . . uh. Places. That you might expect.

It's the only thing I comprehend before I realize I'm falling.

I ram so hard into him that I rebound backward, and my heel slips in the water left behind by his dripping body. He tries to catch me but doesn't have the proper footing, and my weight drags him down. I don't know how he does it in the split seconds we have before we collide with the ground, but somehow, his hand finds the back of my head, and he manages to twist us a full one hundred and eighty degrees.

He hits the tile floor on his back, and I land flat on top of him.

It takes me a few perilous seconds to understand what's going on. How did I slip backward and end up on top of him? But, no, why does that matter when I'm *pressed fully against Cameron Morelli's half-naked sopping-wet body?* I choke out a pitiful noise and instinctively throw my hands out to push myself away. Both of them land on his smooth, toned chest below his razor-sharp collarbone. His tan skin is warm despite the coolness of the kiddie pool.

"I'm sorry" is all I can croak, fire roaring into my face, and I throw my (now-damp) body sideways off his without touching him.

Cameron seems disoriented. He's blinking at the ceiling, like he, too, isn't quite sure what happened. "Are you okay?" he asks in a suddenly stern voice. He swings upright and scrutinizes me with severity. "You didn't hit your head, right?"

"No," I say, wrenching my eyes away. Looking at him while he's in a state like this isn't doing my face any favors. Worse, this isn't how I expected him to respond—with concern rather than a cheeky quip. I'm glad the party is fully in the backyard, because I don't think I would've survived the embarrassment of being seen by our classmates in this position. "Why did you do that?"

"Do what?"

"Turn us midfall. You could've hurt yourself."

"I was more worried about hurting you," Cameron admits, clambering to his feet. He offers me one of his sprawling quarterback hands. "I'm twice your size. It's better you fall on me."

"Don't underestimate the damage I can do," I say, a weak attempt at a joke as I place my hand in his. It wraps fully around mine, then hoists me up with ease. He smirks at this claim, and I'm not sure why, but the sight revs up the heat blistering in my face again. It's just different from the snide, insufferable reaction I expected. "What are you doing, exactly?"

"Looking for towels." Cameron sighs deeply. "No luck in the living room."

Cameron Morelli was looking for towels in the living room. That's more on par with what I expect from him. "Try the hallway closet," I suggest, starting forward. Naturally, I slip in the water puddle again, because my worn tennis shoes haven't had traction in over a year. Cameron catches my wrists, more prepared than earlier, apparently, though it does nothing to stop my face from colliding with his damp bare collar for the second time today.

"Come on," he says, clicking his tongue. "You're on the football team. How can you be this uncoordinated?"

"All I do is hand out water," I rasp, peeling backward and squirming out of his firm grip.

"That's a lie. You also fold towels. And you're . . ." He pauses, a scowl etching into his face as he looks me up and down. "Well, you're Mason Gray, and that helps plenty."

My brows arch into my forehead. "I'm not sure what you mean," I admit.

"You're, like. I don't know. The rock."

"For what?"

"Our team."

I scrunch my face with skepticism. But he's not snickering or grinning, so I guess he's serious. "How exactly am I a rock?" I ask, smirking. "My hydration skills are that impeccable?"

Cameron rolls his eyes violently. "I mean, yeah, you're pretty on top of that, but I'm talking about your personality."

I don't know what he's getting at. When I merely stare at him, he groans in exasperation and flings his hands in the air.

"I don't know, man," he snaps. "You have a really calming presence. The vibe on the team is completely different from last year. Whenever games would get too intense or start to spiral, it's like everyone forgot how to play. We have a running bit now where when we're getting stressed, we just look at you for thirty seconds."

The heat ravaging my face from earlier is still in full force as I try to wrap my head around these words. "Why?" I choke out in bewilderment.

Cameron looks ready to bash his face into the drywall. "I told you, you make people feel calm," he snips. "You constantly look bored at games. You're never impacted by anything going on. I guess it reminds us that we're just playing a game." He pauses, then tacks on, "It helps that you have a symmetrical face. Everyone likes looking at you."

I should've expected he'd slide in a flirtatious remark, but he's not waggling his eyebrows. In fact, his words were abnormally clinical, like he was making an unbiased observation.

"Symmetrical?" I ask, passing around him to follow the nearby hallway. I swing open the closet doors. The towels are still here from when we had our team-building beach day this summer, so I grab a couple, then turn and drape one over his dripping shoulders. "That's not a word most people use to describe me."

Cameron starts scraping himself down. I don't realize I'm watching him dry off too studiously until he snaps, "Stop staring, unless you're going to shower me with one-dollar bills."

I squeak out an apology and look away.

"What words do people use to describe you, then?" he asks.

"Cute. Pretty." I lower my eyes, a familiar, imaginary voice brushing the curve of my ear, strained with anger, and mumble, "Tempting."

Cameron doesn't respond. After a long moment, he says, "You can look."

I turn my eyes back to him. His underwear is on the floor and there's a towel knotted at his hip. I've seen him shirtless when he runs laps, but up close . . . Well, now I understand the appeal of Cameron Morelli. (Not for myself, of course. It's a good look, but I'd never be intimate with a person who'd lord it over me forever.)

"Do people really say you're *tempting* to them?" Cameron asks, scooping his underwear off the floor and heading down the hall. I guess I'm supposed to follow, so I do, until we reach the laundry room. The dryer is already spinning, and he pauses it so he can throw his boxers in with the rest of his clothes.

Only then do I realize how conceited that word sounds. "I don't mean it like I'm really sexy or something," I choke out defensively. "Um. I've just been told that I have a certain kind of body that . . ."

My voice fizzles away. Cameron's observing me with a calm expression I've never seen him wear before. I can't stand it anymore, so I demand, "Are you sure you didn't hit your head when we fell? You're acting strange. Not as annoying as usual."

I think I snapped something inside of him. His mystified expression dissolves into one of dread, intense enough to contort his entire face. I blink, and when I open my eyes, someone else is standing in front of me. His broad shoulders are back and he's giving me a glittery smile and his eyes are brimming with an overabundance of confidence.

"Am I acting different, or are you just distracted by how good I look?" he asks cheekily.

I stare at him.

He stares back.

"What?" I ask.

"I need to go yell at that motherfucker outside." Cameron starts striding to the sliding glass door I came in from.

I watch him blankly. It's like he flipped a switch, and suddenly, everything about him changed without a moment's delay. I only come to when I see him sliding the door, and a rush of cool wind flutters through the house. "It's too cold for you to be out there naked," I tell him.

"Well?" Cameron throws his arms up—a sight I'm becoming familiar with. "My clothes are in the dryer because Anup decided to be a whole entire dick. I don't have options, so I guess I'm just putting my tits out today free of charge."

I avoid snickering at the recollection of him flailing around in the water.

He ventures out into the dimly lit backyard. I'm not sure why I even came inside, so I follow him to rejoin the party. The bonfire is still a roaring mass of wood and flame, spitting embers into the air and shedding warmth over the clusters of teens fluttering around it like moths. Some football players are tossing a ball around underhanded so it won't get tangled in the string lights.

Jody catches sight of Cameron's predicament and hoots, causing the rest of them to turn and start whistling. "Suck a thousand cocks, Anup Kumar!" Cameron growls, sticking his middle finger up. Anup is too busy hunched with laughter to respond.

I inch away from Cameron, eyeing his back. The shadows slicing through the backyard cause his muscles to appear more defined, jutting from his skin in little ridges and hills. He's abnormally big for a high schooler, even a senior, which I guess goes to show just how desperate he is to impress that scout from Alpine University. Through the grapevine, I heard he was told last year that he'd need to bulk up and gain weight if he wanted to be seriously considered. I wonder what kind of regimen he had to follow to get his body to look like that over the past year. Strong and sturdy, not fragile and flimsy.

Cameron groans at the sound of everyone's hilarity. My stomach chooses, at that particularly random moment, to groan alongside him. Loudly.

He immediately spins toward me to stare.

I fan a palm over my stomach, embarrassed. "Sorry," I mumble. "I've been running on coffee and a blueberry muffin today."

Cameron's brows are furrowed and his eyes—turquoise under the nearby light—are shot with concern. Suddenly, he turns to the yard and shouts, "Who's sober?"

He's glaring at the varsity football players, all of whom snicker again at the sight of his towel. Darius glances around, then heaves a fatigued sigh. "Guess that's me," he says somberly.

"Emergency Taco Bell run," Cameron snaps, and he takes my shoulder, shaking me around. "Aren't you guys always creaming your pants over this guy? How do none of you know that the only thing your precious water boy has eaten today is a muffin?"

No. No, no, no. My face is flooded with scorching heat again, made worse by the fact that everyone immediately gasps in horror and sprints toward me.

"My baby!" Anup says, gripping my face and squeezing. He's far, far gone. "Don't worry, Big D will get you some precious sustenance."

"Why haven't you eaten?" Jody demands, shoving Cameron aside to get a closer look at me. "What are we supposed to do if you get sick or something? Bad enough this asshole next to me had to get benched. The team literally won't survive without you there to keep everyone cool."

There it is again. Another proclamation that I do more for this team than hydrate them. I don't understand why they're being so nice—I guess they just know I'm a lonely person trying to get myself out there, and they're being supportive.

I'm so lightheaded I can feel numbing tingles in my fingers. Normally, being surrounded by several muscular guys who only have eyes for you is a bi boy's dream, but it's suffocating. So I do what I always do and turn my lips up into a small smile, keeping quiet. They'll stop eventually. They'll get bored of me and my lack of response. I just need to stay collected—

Someone yanks my sweater, hoisting me out of the center of attention. Suddenly, Cameron is inches from my face, allowing me to zero in on him. "What do you want?" he demands, rattling me around again. "Darius is going to get you something so you don't pass away."

He's still speaking in an exaggerated manner, his movements agitated and dramatic, but his voice is strangely low. Steadying.

"It's fine." I shrug out of Cameron's grip. "I'll eat when I get home."

"Look, Mason. Taco Bell is right around the corner." Darius swings his keys around his thick index finger. "You do plenty to help Barnett and the team. And you're suffering through tutoring Cam. It's the least we can do."

"Suffering?" Cameron chokes out.

"I love you, man, but you're a pain in the ass."

Everyone nods in agreement. Cameron whirls away with a dramatic sniffle.

"So," Darius says, looking pointedly at me, "text me your order and I'll be back."

He walks off, followed closely by Anup and Nate, who are asking how many things he'll buy them while he's there. A deep, baritone "Zero" resounds through the yard.

"Come on." Cameron's voice is back to how it usually is—obnoxiously loud and lilting like a frat boy's in college. He nudges me toward the bonfire before I can properly react to anything that just happened. "You need heat. You'll stand a better chance against the Grim Ripper if you're not both malnourished *and* hypothermic."

Despite the frustrated pounding in my temples, a smile cracks my face. How can he say words like "hypothermic" in the same sentence as "Grim Ripper"? "Reaper," I correct gently.

Cameron glares at me, the flames accenting his tan face nicely. Then, "I need to text Big D your order. What do you want, water boy?"

"I guess . . . a black bean soft taco."

"He's going to punch my sack if he finds out I sent him away to order one dollar's worth of food," Cameron snaps. "Come on—work with me."

I swallow nervously. I don't have much money—allowance doesn't exist in my house (I simply do the chores I'm asked to by my mother, who says my reward is the roof over my head). The only pocket change I have is when the artists tip me for volunteering to watch the gallery. But I can probably afford a little more, so I say, "Two black bean soft tacos?"

"And?"

"Uh . . . a veggie burrito supreme?"

"*Now* we're getting somewhere." When he finishes texting, we return to watching the flames. Ravi must've added more firewood, because it's soaring higher, shedding golden light farther across the backyard. Cameron keeps one wary eye on me, and I wonder how he'd react if I pretended to faint. The thought of him squawking and running circles around my unconscious body is so amusing, I have to shield my mouth to prevent laughing.

"Why do you do that?" He points at my palm. "Your teeth rotting or something?"

I lower my hand, the smile fading away. "Just a habit."

That smile of yours . . .

"How did you get here?" Cameron asks.

"Annie drove me."

"How are you getting home, then?"

I shrug. "Walking, I guess."

Cameron gives me an incredulous look, like I said something absurd.

"What?" I ask defensively.

"You can't just walk around in the middle of the night by yourself. And when you're starved half to death. What are you thinking?" he demands. I'm about to ask why he's concerned, but then he flips course and playfully says, "If you reconsider your rejection, maybe I'd even be willing to drive you home."

"I thought you couldn't drive," I say accusingly, raising a brow. "Isn't that why you sent Darius to Taco Bell? Because he's the only sober one?"

"I'm sober, too. But someone needed to stay with you to make sure you don't pass out," he says, scoffing.

"And you decided to take up the mantle. I'm honored."

"Don't be. It's my duty as a strong, competent man."

I smirk, scooping my knees tighter into my chest. "Sure," I whisper.

Darius arrives minutes later with Anup and Nate, and it's only when I smell food that my hunger reels to the surface. My stomach roils with nausea, and Darius has to meet my trek toward him halfway to hand me my bag. "How much do I owe?" I ask feebly.

"This one's on me." Darius claps my shoulder, and I nearly buckle under his strength. "Oops. Sorry. Go eat—you don't look good."

I can't muster a protest, so I stagger back to the fire, flopping into the grass. The other guys swarm Darius to claim the extra miscellaneous food. After mowing down tortillas, beans, and cheese, my stomach stops aching, and my nausea trickles away. Cameron returns from the mob, sniffling and empty-handed as he sinks into the grass. His team must still be irritated with him about yesterday's game.

"Better?" he asks, analyzing my face.

"Yeah. You didn't have to set that up. Thanks."

He purses his lips.

"I'm not being sarcastic," I say, laughing.

His eyes widen a fraction, like I said something strange. He turns to the fire, and his cheeks glow a tinge of pink.

"What?" I ask nervously.

"It's nothing." He leans on his palms in the grass, gazing into the flames. "You should stop covering your smile."

My body goes rigid. I hadn't even realized . . . Ugh. *Shit.* I need to be more careful. "Want the rest of my food?" I sputter out, swallowing my embarrassment. "I'm full, so—"

"Hell yes." Cameron snags the bag and rips out a soft taco, though his face scrunches when he bites into it. "I forgot this was black bean. What, you don't trust their meat?"

"I'm vegetarian."

He gasps hard enough to nearly choke himself. "No shit?"

I have to catch myself before I can laugh again. "You're not going to tell me how inconvenient that must be?" I ask skeptically. "Or demand what happened to make me like this?"

Cameron answers with a shake of his head. "Why should I? It's not my business."

I should've expected that response from the "if it's not about me, I don't care" guy.

My phone vibrates in my pocket. When I remember its existence, I also remember why I went dashing out of the yard earlier. The ever-present pit in my stomach triples in size, weighing down my back and chest and shoulders.

What am I doing here, really?

The rest of the night passes in a blur. I don't remember Cameron driving me home, but he must, because suddenly I'm flopping into bed, dressed in cozy pajamas. I swipe away the messages, documenting my lack of response to the final one as a win. Though his texts do seem a little kinder than they used to be.

I stuff my face into my pillow, trying to steer my attention elsewhere. Where else could it go but to Cameron Morelli? Faintly, I can remember his grip on my shoulders. The way he strutted around with that towel clinging to his waist, fully confident in his stature. What must it be like? To look like that? Feel like that? To have the certainty that you can protect yourself?

I raise my skinny arm and peer at it through the dark. My lower lip trembles.

I want to be like that.

CHAPTER SEVEN
CAM

A blueberry muffin and coffee? *Seriously?* How can such a smart guy be so clueless and neglectful? Someone needs to keep snacks on hand for that little shit before he evaporates.

I'm not being sarcastic.

An invasive image of Mason tossing his head back in laughter brings my perfectly valid negative thoughts to a screeching halt. The way his fine black hair fluttered with his head. The way his eyes crunched up at the edges. Those two seconds are going to haunt me for the rest of my life. The moment my pathetic monkey brain forgot about the hostility I hold for Mason Gray, because apparently he has a glittery smile that can burn through retinas. It's a safety hazard. No wonder he's always covering it.

I don't think my heart has ever stopped before. I've been in plenty of relationships over the past few years, but getting *butterflies* is a concept that's always existed outside of my understanding. So what's different about this runt?

He's abnormally silent on the way to his house, his eyes flitting around, present but glazed, like only half his conscience is awake. As he heads inside, my mind reels back to the moment he slammed into me inside Ravi's house. When he landed on top of me, looking frazzled, his face flushed with embarrassment. Seeing him ruffled was sort of captivating.

But the awareness of our positions caught up to me, and suddenly, his cool, slender hands on my chest were someone else's.

Come on, Cameron . . . You want to prove the rumors wrong, right . . . ?

If he had been anyone else, I probably would've shoved him off instinctively. But Mason Gray has this strange effect on the people around him. Rather than getting lost in my remembrance of middle school, Mason's touch anchored me to the present. It doesn't make sense—he was clearly as disheveled as me when we fell—but the atmosphere around him is always calm and peaceful even when he isn't.

I wasn't lying when I said the team has a running joke of looking at Mason when they're feeling particularly agitated, because seeing his unwavering composure and apathy settles their nerves. I guess that's why I didn't have a meltdown when he landed on me. Unlike the moment I got sacked yesterday on the field. I was so distracted that I didn't even notice I'd slipped out of character until Mason pointed it out.

Are you sure you didn't hit your head when we fell? You're acting strange. Not as annoying as usual.

He's perceptive. I need to be careful.

By the time I get home, all of my charisma has been depleted. Mom and Dad are asleep, evidenced by the silent house that screeches under my muscle mass as I maneuver to my bedroom. I bet Mason would float noiselessly down the hall like a ghoul.

I practically stumble through my door. The remaining strength in my limbs melts away, and I follow after it, knees colliding with the carpet. Ugh. *Parties.* To this day, they're still difficult to manage. Faintly, my father's voice from this morning cracks through the crevices of my skull.

Do you still think about it? That night in eighth grade . . .

I groan, slapping my face into the carpet. But being on the floor—envisioning people standing over me, whispering, grinning—isn't making my situation better, so I drag myself upright.

I realize my closet door is open. Maybe Mom came through earlier looking for something (she uses part of my closet for some of her spillover clothes that don't fit into her own) and forgot to close it.

Staring me dead in the eye is an assortment of old painted rocks meticulously organized in neat little rows. One of them is striped with rainbow colors. Another looks like it's soaked in blood. The rock beside it has a mustache.

I can't believe how much time I used to waste on menial shit like that. I wanted to throw them out once after some guys found my "buy a lemonade, get a free rock" stand and decided to pelt me with them in fourth grade. But Mom got teary-eyed, and the thought of her crying nauseates me, so I kept them around. I even went back to painting more after a while, though I made sure it would be where nobody could see.

I don't remember organizing them like this. She probably did.

I slam the door and turn to the wall so I can lock eyes with Beau Rainey's absorbing black ones. Football. Right. He's my idol. A Division I champion who made countless NIL deals. The kind of guy I'll become if I can better apply myself to my studies. If I can just focus.

I drag myself to bed and unlock my phone to find a message waiting.

> Thanks again. Feeling better. Well, as good as one can be after eating Taco Bell lol.

The flutter in my chest makes me want to projectile vomit. So I saw the guy smile one time. That doesn't mean I need to act like an eighteenth-century virgin who faints every time they get mildly flustered. I still don't understand *why* I keep feeling flustered.

Maybe it's because he's forbidden fruit.

. . . Yeah.

It's obvious how much Mason would rather light himself ablaze than be around me. He rejected my advances with shameless cruelty, so he's *off-limits*. If Hades and Perstephanie taught me anything, it's that when you can't have what you want, that makes you . . . like, you want it *more*.

So Mason is the forbidden fruit whose juicy interior will remain untasted. Which means it's only natural I'll fall harder for dorky shit like "a smile luminous enough to provoke the envy of the night sky" or whatever. I can't let it get to me.

I send him a passive-aggressive thumbs-up emoji and then toss my phone away, trying to think about anything but crinkled brown eyes and glittery white teeth.

CHAPTER EIGHT
MASON

Cameron is picking our next study location, which probably means we're going to be reading textbooks over the glossy waxed floors of a gym called Masculine Man. But he refuses to confirm anything as we take the twisty roads through Elwood.

It's Tuesday afternoon. Mr. Barnett ordered us to forgo practice today, because Cameron's grades are of the utmost importance—getting him back out there apparently takes priority over me helping keep the boys quenched or cleaning and storing equipment.

The last couple of days have been uneventful. Thankfully, I haven't received any texts since Saturday, which means my mental health is on the climb. Anytime I see that jumble of numbers flash across my screen, it drags my "moving on" progress back. It should be simple to block him, but I need to know what he's saying. These sporadic texts allow me to keep an eye on him in my periphery. I don't *want* to, but if he shows up, I prefer the heads-up text to no warning at all.

Cameron pulls into a decrepit parking lot outside of what looks like the jankiest, sketchiest bar in the region. The windows are fogged and gray, and there's a cracked wooden sign reading HOLE IN THE WALL. The beige paint is stained from water damage and the cement between the bricks is coated in grime.

Cameron gives me this pleased, self-satisfied smirk. He's in a scoop-neck T-shirt and pale jeans, both items a size too small to fit his bulky figure. He's always wearing things that hug him to show off how trimmed and godly he thinks he is.

Though, just because I'm scowling doesn't mean it isn't working.

"Welcome to the best burger joint in town," he says, kicking open his driver's door.

"Is this environment conducive for . . . studying?" *For anything?*

"No, but it has food. Not coffee shop pastries—*real-ass* greasy American slop for growing young men." He grabs his backpack and tromps toward the entrance. It's a beaten-down place on the edge of town, and all the businesses nearby are in a similar state of disrepair.

But it's too late for me to suggest elsewhere or remind him that I'm a vegetarian, so I follow after. I wasn't planning on buying food anyway, so whether or not it's a burger joint doesn't make a difference. Aside from the fact that the smell of sizzling meat and oil will probably send my stomach into a sobbing frenzy.

We walk inside, and it's not as scary as I figured. It's got that old-fashioned black-and-white-checkered floor, shiny and pristine, alongside bubbled crimson booths and a neon jukebox.

Cameron grabs my wrist and heaves me toward the counter, where a college-aged girl sits on a rounded stool in a vintage red-and-gold waitress uniform, scrolling her phone. Just as I'm about to remind him about the meat thing, he points at the menu and says, "We get these burgers once a month but never the vegan ones. So I forced my parents to come here yesterday so we could try them. They're fucking incredible."

I follow his gaze to the menu and blanch when I see they *do* have vegetarian options. "If you came yesterday, why come back today?" I ask, furrowing my brows.

Cameron wrinkles his nose, like my question offends him. "I told you, I had to try the vegan burgers to make sure they were good."

"But why?" I'm having difficulty comprehending the implication.

"How can I study if I'm worried about whether you're going to starve to death?" he demands, striking me with an accusatory glare.

He says it in his usual Cameron Morelli way, like I'm to blame for his woes, but . . . I don't know. Against my better judgment, the ice crackling along my connection to him thaws, just a little. "I appreciate your commitment to studying distraction-free," I say seriously.

Cameron squints at me, trying to determine whether I'm being sarcastic. While his precious brain catches up, I decide to place my order for a mushroom Swiss veggie burger, because I'll feel guilty if I don't get something after he came here yesterday just to taste test for my sake. He forfeits his suspicions, leaping up to the counter to order the triple-patty Monster Special.

We find a rounded booth in the corner. I pull my beanie lower over my forehead, watching his arms at work as they hoist textbooks out of his backpack. "If you can eat burgers frequently and look like that, you must have a decent workout routine," I hear myself say before I can deliberate over whether I want to put up with his ego.

"I mean, you're at the practices," Cameron says, smirking. "You don't pay attention when Barnett sends us around the track doing high knee jogging?"

"I do, it's just . . . that's cardio, right? And stretches? So you probably lift weights." I clear the waver from my throat and squeak out, "Any tips for beginners?"

Cameron's eyebrows soar up to his hairline. "You want to start working out?"

"Want" is a strong, wholly inaccurate word. *I want to look like you*, I nearly say, but I chomp on the words. I go with "Just looking to get bigger."

Cameron sips the soft drink he purchased with smug nonchalance. "What, and ruin your cutesy soft-boy aesthetic?"

Leave it to Cameron Morelli to ruin a nice moment with his personality. Though, I'm not sure why I brought the subject up. It's not like I'm getting a gym membership, and I don't have workout equipment to put his tips to use. "Forget it," I mutter.

Cameron is quiet for a long moment, and when I peek at his expression, he looks contemplative. He scratches his neck and exhales slow, then says, "I can show you my workout routine if you want to come over after this."

I look between his eyes, my own bewilderment reflected in that greenish-blue hue. There has to be a catch. Like *I'll let you come over if you promise to give me one teeny-tiny little blow job.* Before I can prod him for his price, the girl at the counter calls our names, and we climb out of our seats to retrieve our food.

When I see the mountainous burger waiting for me, I nearly trip over myself. "I'm supposed to eat this?" I ask as we reclaim the booth.

Cameron is already unhinging his jaw to fit the triple-patty monstrosity in his mouth. He pauses, mouth agape, to glance over. "Sit on it," he suggests.

I roll my eyes, then press a napkin against the burger and lean down, squishing it. Grease and cheese pools to the bottom of the basket, staining the waxed paper and curly fries. I manage to scoop the sandwich's weight into my hands and sink my teeth into it. Flavorful juices and seasoning burst through my mouth, delighting my taste buds. I make a noise of stunned approval as I chew, and Cameron smiles with satisfaction.

"See? Knew you'd like it. Wouldn't have brought you here otherwise."

He speaks so casually, one could almost miss that he's being nice. That he actually took time to come here and make sure I wouldn't be eating a burnt slab of mushroom on a bun if he brought me. "I hate breaking my jaw to get my lips around it, but the flavor is great," I admit.

Cameron, the teenage boy that he is, nearly explodes with laughter. Maybe I should be irritated at another display of immaturity, but his mirth is sort of intoxicating. The edges of my mouth rise, lips parting to unveil my teeth.

That smile of yours . . .

Instinctively, I release my burger so I can shield my mouth. Cameron notices the sudden movement, and his bluish eyes glint with interest. "I don't get why you do that," he says. "Why cover them? The real ones."

"What?" I pluck a curly fry from the basket and plop it onto my tongue. It's been a while since I've had greasy, fatty food—I usually opt for snacking on leftovers in the fridge or old pastries at Annie's— so a full meal like this is refreshing.

"You smile behind your lips," he explains. "Those are the fake ones. And when you have a real smile that shows your teeth, you cover it." He grabs a napkin from the dispenser and smears it over his face, spreading the grease to his cheeks.

"Interesting," I say through my mouthful of Swiss. Are my "fake" smiles that obvious? "Maybe I don't have a lot of confidence. You wouldn't get it, being the most arro—ah, confident person in town."

He doesn't catch the jab, sadly. It's cute when he notices I'm making fun of him. "What's there not to be confident about?" he asks, framing his face with his hands.

Changing the subject around Cameron Morelli is easy. "Have you always been this way?" I ask, nonchalant. "I don't know how you're so self-assured."

Cameron's eyes flicker with apprehension, like I've caught him in a lie, and his fingers press deeper into his burger, squeezing juice out of his patties. "Of course," he snaps.

"Nobody knows who you were before ninth grade," I point out. Though, I can't imagine Cameron being anything other than *this*.

"I was perfectly fine and mentally stable," he says sharply. He shoots me a menacing glare, daring me to contradict him, before promptly changing the subject himself. "Are you coming over to see my workout equipment or not?"

Oh. I'm surprised he's following up on that—I guess his offer was genuine. "There's no reason to," I mumble. "I don't have equipment, so even if you came up with a regimen, I couldn't practice it."

"You could. You'd just have to come over after every study session," he says, shrugging.

I tilt my head in bafflement. Cameron Morelli keeps startling me today. "I thought you preferred to spend as little time around me as possible," I say with a knowing smile. "Who are you and what have you done with the real Ca—"

"I *am* Cam Morelli," he snarls, so harsh and heated and sudden that instinctively, I reel away from him, my eyes widening. I'm not sure where his unexpected intensity came from.

"Sorry," I hear myself say. "I'm sorry. I didn't mean to."

You didn't mean to what? a voice mutters in my ears. *You know you've done something wrong, but do you know what? What are you apologizing for, Mason?*

Cameron must notice my change in expression because he relaxes as suddenly as he tightened, his brawny shoulders loosening, his contorted face leveling. "Sorry," he grumbles. "I didn't mean to snap."

I watch his hands, unresponsive. They're clawing into the knees of his jeans.

"Anyway, yeah," he says, holding his chin high as he reclaims his grip on his burger. "Of course I want to spend as little time with you as possible. Why would I want to be around someone who'd rather get lobotomized than go out with me?"

My eyes nearly roll into the back of my head. Apparently, Cameron believes the only reason someone could reject him is because they have a deep, unfounded loathing for him. "What would it take for you to stop claiming I hate you?" I ask wearily.

"Prove you don't." He smirks like he's got me cornered.

I knead the bridge of my nose. What's something I could do to appease Cameron Morelli? I don't want to get closer to him right now when he's probably still riled up, but I also don't have other ideas. So I say, "Come here."

"Why?" Cameron demands, though he lowers his face so it's a foot from mine. At this distance, I can more clearly see the smattering of colors in his irises, the long lashes, the hairs in disarray on his golden-brown brows. "So you can look into my eyes as you tell me how much you'd rather get your hand slammed in a car door than—"

I lean forward and kiss his greasy cheek.

His sentence disintegrates. He blinks, eyes widening with perplexity.

"I," I say calmly, grabbing his chin, my stern gaze locking with his. "Do. Not. Hate. You."

Cameron's stare flicks between my pupils. A split second later, he's reeling back and smacking his head against the booth. "The hell?" he chokes out.

I return to my burger and bite a chunk to avoid bursting into laughter.

Cameron doesn't whine about me hating him for the rest of the study session.

CHAPTER NINE
CAM

Mom and Dad are at work, thank Christ, because I can't fathom how they'd react to me bringing home a Disney prince like Mason. I get the "can't resist a cute face" flaw from *both* of those losers, and Mason has one of the most aesthetically pleasing faces I've ever seen. Every time I look at that twerp, despite the emotional trauma he's given me, I'm *still* hopelessly mesmerized.

The studying itself is fine. I guess. I'm pretty distracted, and Mason notices, constantly asking me what I'm thinking about and redirecting me to the subject I'm working on. Now that I know how effective a tutor Mason is, and how grounding his presence is, I'm certain my grades are going to steadily improve. I'm getting closer to being on the field, showing off my skills to the scout who's been following Darius.

It should be elating. So why does my skin itch, and why is my stomach sinking?

It's a pretty uninteresting session, until Mason receives a call that causes the table to vibrate. For a while, he lets it ring face down, staring at it blankly before flipping it over and revealing the name "Dad." He exhales, then slips out of the booth to take it. As he's walking away, the bones in his back tightening, the sound of yelling echoes through his receiver.

"I'm busy," he mutters. "Why is she shouting? Tell her I— What's that noise?" He pauses, still as stone. "Put her on the phone." Another beat. "Mom? Hey. Uh. No, what you're feeling is valid, I'm sure, but— I'm out. It's important, so . . . stop talking for a moment."

Mason wanders farther from the table, but the establishment is small and there's someone in the bathroom, so he can't retreat out of earshot.

"Put it down and stop yelling. Honestly, it's embarrassing . . ." His shoulders slump and his voice quiets. Then, angrily, "Go for a walk or something. Just get away from Dad. I'm busy."

He slams his phone into his pocket, then storms to the booth and slides in, snatching his pen. He starts jotting notes down with heightened vigor.

"I'll come over after this," he says, his voice strained. "To work out."

"Okey dokey," I say, smooth, casual, and natural. I'm not going to ask about it, even if I'm curious. I don't want him prying into my life, so I won't pry into his.

Cam Morelli doesn't worry about other people's problems.

I shouldn't have offered him access to my workout resources. What was I thinking? Being around him makes it difficult to remember the kind of person I'm supposed to be, and I have no idea why.

I can't exactly retract the offer because I'm not a complete asshole, so we end up at my place. I draw him toward my bedroom and fumble for workout clothes that won't slip off his figure, then toss them over. He's been staring unblinkingly at my poster of Beau Rainey and seems surprised when the clothes land in his arms. "Oh, we're actually doing this," he says, looking at the outfit with dismay.

"How can I give you a plan if we don't know what works for you?" I ask skeptically, shedding my pants and shirt to pull the looser clothes over me. Mason's face burns pink, and he charges to the bathroom to change. I'm not sure why he's flustered, since he's seen everyone's bodies in the locker room.

When he returns, he's wearing my shabby old workout clothes. The shirt hangs low enough to expose his collarbone, and he's had to tie the shorts as tight around his narrow waist as they allow. "So, exercise," I say as we descend into the basement, and I awkwardly do a twirl with my arms extended because Mason Gray is in my *house*, wearing my *clothes*.

Mason looks between everything, intrigued. The elliptical, treadmill, weights, chest press machine, exercise bike, yoga mats, and so on. "You have a whole gym," he says with amusement.

"I wanted to get bigger after I moved, so I put years of allowance money toward equipment. My parents chipped in, and I've built my own little exercise haven over the past few years." I turn the TV on, filling the basement with casual lo-fi. "What are you hoping to get out of working out? Fitness? Stress reduction? Bulking up? Improving—"

"Bulking up," Mason says, desperately enough that my brow pops. "I want . . . If I had a body like yours, maybe I wouldn't be so . . ."

He doesn't complete his thought, and I decide not to press. "It's important to warm your body before exercising," I say, guiding him to a yoga mat opposite me. "We'll start with basic stretches. Sound good?"

Mason nods, though he's fumbling with his fingers and his eyes dart around the basement like he's mapping out escape routes.

"Squats." I clasp my hands and lower myself, then rise and gesture for him to try. He mimics my position, pointing his toes forward and holding his hands out flat, face down. His palms are shaky. Instinctively, I wonder if it's because he hasn't eaten before remembering that we just stuffed our faces a couple of hours ago. Why is he so anxious?

Mason doesn't descend nearly as far as he should for a proper squat. "Ow," he remarks.

"Spread your legs wider and try again."

Mason's lip flinches into a smirk. He spreads his knees apart, and though he sinks lower, his face strains again when he comes back up. "What's next?" he prods.

He wants to move on after one and a half squats? I decide to swallow my laughter. "Message received," I say, and I thread my fingers, then rise to my tiptoes and reach for the ceiling. "Stretch like this. As high as you can go."

I catch that he spies the hint of skin showing beneath my shirt. He mirrors me as requested, the T-shirt sleeves bunching at his shoulders, exposing his pale upper arms. Despite how tightly they're tied, the shorts he borrowed have already slid down his waist and are resting on the flare of his hips.

"Touch your toes," I instruct, bending over and grazing my tennis shoes. He attempts to do the same, though his hands barely dangle past his knees. "Lower."

Mason gives an irritated sigh that further amuses me. Like, he asked to do this, didn't he? We've only been at it for forty seconds and he's already whining. "Can't," he snaps.

"Move your legs farther apart and try again," I instruct.

Mason gives me a skeptical glare. "I'm starting to think the only reason you let me come over was so you could ask me to spread my legs for you."

At that point I'm sipping on one of the water bottles I brought downstairs, and I hack violently on it. As I try to sputter out a response to defend myself, Mason widens his stance as ordered and forces his fingers lower so they're nearly touching the ground. I think I catch the faintest glimpse of another smirk.

Is he teasing me?

"Lower," I snip, and I reach over, pressing my hands flat to his back and pushing down. He squeaks with pain and immediately swipes my hands away.

"Are you trying to kill me?" he demands, slinging himself upright to stare daggers.

I huff at him with displeasure. "The more flexible you are," I say, rolling my hand dramatically, "the wider you'll be able to spread your legs for me. Since apparently that's why you think I invited you here."

"Is it not?" he asks with a weak, uncertain smile. Something about the defeated way he says it bothers me. Is he seriously anticipating that I'm going to invite him to bed after our workout? Is that why he's been so apprehensive?

"Why would you think that?" I grumble. "I hardly know you."

Mason stares at me long and hard for several seconds, his expression unreadable. "Did you not just ask me out last week because you're attracted to me?" he asks coolly.

"I said I like your face because it's symmetrical," I squeak out. "That doesn't mean I want to fuck you."

Mason cocks his head with curiosity. "You don't?"

"Why would I?" I demand, taking an uneasy step back. The intensity in his stare is unnerving, like he's trying to dissect me. "Like I said, I barely know you."

"I thought you were trying to sleep your way across the entire graduating class."

"Well, that's a lie."

"Then why," he says softly, "are you doing this for me?"

I stare at him blankly. He returns it with heightened concentration that makes me want to crumble away.

"You tested a burger place's vegan options to make sure they would taste good for me," he says slowly. Maybe he feels guilty about cornering me, because he stretches for the ground again. "You specifically chose a studying place with food so you wouldn't worry about if I was hungry. Now you're offering to make me a personal workout routine. If it's not because you want me to *spread my legs* for you, then why?"

Mason rises, then decides to reach for the ceiling, now deliberately avoiding my eyes.

"If it's not for anything in return," he says, quieter, "then that means Cameron Morelli must be different than who I thought he was."

By the time he finishes, I feel like all of my intestines have been brutally squeezed between tight fists. My breath is coming in short, panicked spurts. What is he talking about? The things I'm doing . . . Aren't they things normal people would do? Cam Morelli is well-liked, meticulously crafted to resemble the most popular people in my previous school. Confident, boisterous, fun-loving, flirty. He looks out for himself, but that doesn't mean he's a dick to everyone around him. He has friends because he's a decent, loyal guy.

Isn't it normal for Cam Morelli to help someone with their workout routine? To bring them to a burger place to indulge in some greasy slop?

How is this out of character?

I guess Mason never really *knew* Cam Morelli outside of brief interactions, and maybe assumed the worst of him because of the "gets around" rumor I've allowed to be tied to him. I don't need to have an episode over the fact that he's poking daggers into my stone walls. They're still perfectly solid and sturdy.

I decide the only thing I can do right now is move the subject. I just need to get through this session and pretend like I don't care as much as I do. "Lunges," I say, hoping I sound casual. I frame my hips and put one foot toward him, squatting down. "Try one."

He gives me another dubious look, clearly seeing through my distraction attempt. Nonetheless, he does as commanded. But as he sinks down, he wobbles and topples over with a groan of misery. I snag him beneath his elbows, keeping him upright.

"You're trying to humiliate me," Mason says tightly, the hollows of his cheeks rosy as he wriggles out of my grip.

"They're basic stretches," I point out, grinning.

"Hmph."

"You're pouting."

"Hmph."

"Acting cute won't get you out of warm-ups."

Mason's face deepens further in color, and he gives me a solid push, forcing me back to my yoga mat. "What's next?" he asks sharply. "Stretching isn't going to make me bigger. I'd rather jump right into the weight lifting and stuff."

I remember sounding like that a few years ago. Back when I thought curling an hour a day would make me an indestructible force of nature. "If you don't stretch before working out, you could injure yourself. You'll be more sore, achy, and you'll tire out faster." I reach out, jabbing his forehead with my index finger. "If you want to get stronger, do it the right way. I wouldn't have been able to meet the weight requirement for that scout from Alpine University if all I'd focused on was lifting over the past year. Besides, stretches *do* help you build strength. Squats are a staple of bulking."

Mason scrutinizes me like he thinks I'm tricking him. Then he tries another lunge, and though he wobbles again, he manages to keep upright. "Annoying jock," he murmurs. "Why can't you be this competent with your schoolwork?"

I make a choked scoffing noise. "Rude?"

"It's an innocent question," Mason says, fluttering those long black lashes.

"Bullshit," I snap. "You're just mad that I'm making sense."

"Hmph."

"Your pouting isn't as cute the second time around."

"Hmph."

Okay, maybe it is. I'm sure as hell not going to tell him.

We move through an assortment of stretches and warm-ups. He loathes them, but none so much as the sit-ups. I pin his feet with my weight, my arms hugging his propped knees as he struggles to lift his head off the yoga mat. "Come on," I encourage. "I'll let you up after five."

He groans, arching his head back with annoyance. His skin is already gleaming with traces of sweat. It's not a bad look on him.

Another trip and stumble, courtesy of my heart. I don't know where it comes from or why it strikes now, but I brush the unfamiliar sensation away. First stomach flutters, and now my heart is literally skipping? How? Why? I can't remember this ever happening.

Worse, I still can't figure out what's different.

"Two crunches," I say, slapping his kneecaps. "Just get your shoulders off the ground."

With a pained grimace, Mason hurls himself upward so fast he nearly bashes my forehead. "Fuck your crunches," he snaps, his fiery eyes inches away.

"One more, then," I say, smiling sweetly. Pointedly deciding not to count those lashes.

He flops onto the mat with a choked sob.

Eventually, we move on to cardio. He maintains a light jog on the treadmill for two minutes before petering out. He lasts half that time on the bike. He holds a wall squat for twenty seconds before ducking out. And the chest press machine . . . It's not looking *great*.

"How about some curls?" I suggest, setting two ten-pound weights in his palms. The longer we test his limits and strengths, the more he appears to deflate. While he moaned and groaned through stretches, there was still an aura of determination around him. Now it's withering away.

I instruct him how to properly curl, and he does it himself, silent, before I notice his wrists shaking with strain. "That's enough," I say, reaching for them, but he evades me.

"They're only ten pounds," Mason snaps, the rims of his eyes reddening. "If I can't handle these, I'm a lost fucking cause, right?"

The ferocity in his words startles me backward. Am I missing something? Where is his sudden desperation coming from? "I said you'd have to build yourself up slowly, right?" I ask, leveling my voice. In the back of my head, I know that Cam Morelli should shrug this off and act like he hasn't noticed Mason's apprehension. But . . . I don't know. I can feel the anxiety radiating off him, and it reminds me of my old self, back when I first came to this school and only had the summer to reinvent myself. "It'll come easier with time—"

"Maybe I don't have time to grow slowly," he whispers.

I scrunch my face at such an ominous claim. "What?"

He must've let something slip, because panic flickers across his expression, and he drops the weights so suddenly that I jump. "Thanks for letting me try your equipment. I should get home."

Mason tries fleeing up the stairs, but I'm not going to let him escape so easily after what he just said. I catch the crook of his arm, swinging him toward me. "I feel like you're expecting something out of this that isn't going to happen," I say sternly, the words coming in a jumbled rush. I don't want to upset him, but he needs to hear it. "It might be months before you start noticing a difference. But you can't skip the stage of warming your body."

Mason's glaring at the floor now, like he might melt into it if I release his arm. "How long did it take you?" he mumbles.

"I've been working on my body for four years. When I started, I was pretty twiggy." I scratch my neck with a sigh, wishing I could read his mind so I could understand his intentions. "I started bulking up because I felt people would take me more seriously. And maybe I wouldn't get pushed around anymore."

Mason stiffens, peeking up at me. "You've been bullied?" he whispers.

Ah . . . fuck. Fuckedy fuck. I didn't realize he might ask *questions*. Why the hell did I say that? I'm normally so good about watching whatever past-related words come out of my mouth, so how did I screw myself so thoroughly? My brain didn't even warn me to hesitate before I yapped.

"I was a well-balanced and emotionally sound individual," I say sharply.

He stares at me, unconvinced.

Shit. Okay, I can make this situation fine. Maybe it doesn't matter if he knows hints from my past—just telling him about a few incidents shouldn't mean that my ruse is up. Besides, it's pretty clear he's onto me, so if I give him something to latch on to—an excuse for this behavior he finds bizarre—it's possible he'll stop prying.

"There were some issues. We lived in an aggressively *traditional* small town in the middle of nowhere," I say, trying to keep my voice light and indifferent. "My mom was an out-and-proud bisexual woman. Had the bumper stickers and shirts and fridge magnets and everything. I was an easier target than her, so . . ."

Even mentioning the barest details of the conflict makes me feel like the walls of my chest are closing in. Mason examines me studiously, like he's attempting to read past my purposefully vacant expression.

"Anyway!" I hack through the awkward silence and say, "I tried building muscle during the summer I moved, then in ninth grade. It took a while, but I bulked up, edited my life, and now I'm a fucking pleasure to be around."

Mason's thin lips furl upward. "An absolute pleasure," he agrees, though he drawls the words enough that I know he's being sarcastic.

"When I tried jumping into bulking, I made myself miserable. My body hurt all the time. I did more research and found out that the excessive training I was doing was more likely to stunt my growth than help it, so I had to slow down and start from square one. Trust the process or you'll damage your body."

Mason fidgets, despising this truth I'm forcing him to acknowledge. "Okay," he says softly.

I'm buried so deep in my own confusion that I hear myself blurt something genuinely uncalled for. "Is it your parents?"

Mason tips his head again. With his face lightly flushed and the scant amount of sweat shimmering on his forehead, he's even nicer to look at than usual. It's distracting. "What about my parents?" he asks suspiciously.

"I . . . uh . . ." Damn it, how do I back myself out of this corner? It's been nestled in the crook of my brain since that phone call at the restaurant, but I'd decided *not* to stick my greasy (though perfectly sculpted) nose into his business. "You've been cagey about why you wanted to bulk up, and I wondered if it had to do with your living situation," I decide to say.

Mason's muscles seem to snap tight and strain in his limbs. For a moment, I think he's getting angry. Despite this tense situation, my heart still thuds faster because I can't help but want to see it. He's shown that he can be annoyed and prickly and exasperated and amused but only in faint, dull bursts. It's like he's wrapped his emotions in a thick cloak, barely allowing them to poke through when they start rising.

I want to see them. His emotions.

Just as I'm thinking he might spit infuriated words at me, it's like someone pops his building pressure with a needle, and suddenly he's going lax, his posture slumping with exhaustion. "My parents have a rough relationship," he mumbles. "My mom loves yelling and throwing things, but it's never been physical. So. Nothing to do with them."

Then what? I want to ask, but I feel I've pried deep enough, and an attempt to dig further will strike a concealed nerve. Even if I'm curious to know what might happen, even *desperate* to know, it's probably better that I don't make him more uneasy than he already is. Despite his knack for bantering, his body language hasn't loosened much since we arrived. Something about this situation unnerves him.

"Has someone at school been giving you trouble?" I try.

"Of course not," he says stiffly.

I don't know him well enough to determine whether he's lying. To lighten the mood, I reach out and ruffle his damp black hair. "I'll come up with a training plan," I say, smirking when he swats my hands away with a scoff. "We'll come here after studying for light exercises. Once your body gets accustomed, we'll step it up a notch. And so on, until you're where you want to be. But."

I shoot my index finger into the air.

Mason winces.

It's subtle. Brief. Nobody else would probably notice.

I do.

I see myself in his eyes.

I'm eight years old. Ten. Twelve. Fourteen.

I freeze, finger hovering.

He's watching it.

I used to do that with their knuckles.

Stare. Wait. Anticipate.

I lower my palm. Slowly.

He returns his eyes to my face.

Okay. I see.

It's an inkling. Nothing more.

"You need to make sure you're eating right," I continue, like I haven't noticed anything. His gaze is sharp again, and I wonder if he even realizes what he did. "Full meals. Protein, vegetables, fruits, grains. It means not skipping meals or running on sugar and coffee."

Mason looks crestfallen, like he was hoping I'd forget about his atrocious lack of nutrients. "Just because you caught me on a day when the muffin was my only source of food doesn't mean I'm always—"

"What did you eat today before we went out for burgers?" I demand.

Mason opens his mouth to protest but can't find the words. Eventually, he says, "Coffee and a peanut butter protein bar."

"Mm. Hmm. Mm-hmm."

"I'll try eating healthier, okay?" Mason says with an aggravated huff. "I just don't have many opportunities where I can make a meal in peace because my house . . . is like that."

I hate the implication, and worse, I don't know what to do about it. "Can you make food when your parents are in bed?" I plead.

Mason dons this strange smile I've never seen before. It seems genuine but with an underlying tinge of lingering skepticism. "You must love the art of being active if you're that worried about my health."

He's poking and prodding again. Just like I've been poking and prodding him. I feel like we're locked in a ballroom masquerade dance, both of us attempting to lead, both trying to sneak glances under each other's sequined mask to see what really lies underneath. He's frustratingly observant. Maybe he feels similarly about me.

But Cam Morelli isn't supposed to be a perceptive person. So why am I doing this? Why am I so fixated on sliding his mask up when I should just let myself be entranced by its design?

I prop my knuckles irritably on my hips. "Do you think I'm some one-dimensional fuck without empathy?" I ask with as much haughty disdain as I can muster. "You're helping me study, so I can help put muscle on your bones."

Right. It can be as simple as that.

Mason's lips waver, and suddenly, he's tossing his head back in laughter. For the second time, I catch a glimpse of his bright, magnetic smile. How it pushes into every fragment of his face, brightening his features and causing the air to sparkle. How does a smile have the power to slow time? It doesn't, but every moment seems to drag, as if my brain is intentionally stalling its own perception to cling to this radiant image.

Then he throws his hand over his mouth, shattering the illusion.

"What's funny?" I growl, my face reddening. "I'm never inviting you over again."

"No, no, you *have* to now," he says brightly, and I swear his golden-brown eyes are legitimately glittering. They're more captivating than the mask. "Cameron Morelli, you fool. You've given me the perfect blackmailing material."

"The what?" I squawk.

"I've caught you caring about someone other than yourself. Just what is the team going to think when I tell them you're capable of being a sweetheart? I think it would cause mass chaos—"

"Don't."

Mason blinks at the sudden seething anger in my voice.

"I'm not," I snarl when he doesn't respond, fingers curling up into my palms. My heart is back in my throat, and alarm bells are clanging against the inside of my head, overwhelming my senses with desperate fury and dread. "Don't go spreading false shit about me. Whatever you think I am, you're wrong. I'm not . . ."

I'm not a sweetheart. I'm not gentle. I'm not a kind, softhearted boy. I didn't paint rocks for fun. I *didn't* buy my mom flowers on my way home from school every week. I *didn't* hum while taking meandering walks through the park. I *didn't* constantly get chided on the local recreational football team for picking dandelions and daydreaming instead of putting all of my focus and raw talents into practicing. I *didn't* stay at home all weekend playing board games with my parents because I had no friends.

Cameron Morelli doesn't exist.

He's not allowed to.

"Sorry," Mason says.

I focus on him, panic zipping through me in nauseating waves. He's watching them again. My hands. I need to relax, and fast, because I'm frightening him. But the thought of my costume being forcibly peeled away, exposing me for what I am to everyone I've convinced to like me . . .

I can't let that happen.

"Sorry," Mason says, softer, like he's afraid of startling me with his already meager volume. "I was kidding. I didn't mean to . . . I wasn't trying to . . ."

His eyes meet mine, and I can tell it takes all of his courage. I don't know what he sees there, but it's enough that his body—which had begun to stiffen and brace—suddenly relaxes. I can't say for sure, but part of me thinks he's recognized that my anger is stemming from panic. Not from something worse.

He takes a hesitant half step forward and reaches out, placing his hand against my collar. The tips of his fingers press into the hollow of my throat, as cool as they were when he fell on me a few nights ago. "Just breathe, Cameron. It's not your fault. Okay?"

"What the hell are you talking about?" I snap, before inwardly cursing. Why am I acting like such an ass, especially after the way he keeps reacting to my anger? Getting this riled up is ridiculous.

But something's different this time. His body language has changed.

He's not closing up, not pulling away or watching my fists. His hand is still flat on my chest, partially atop my shirt and partially digging into my skin. Something about his touch is strangely centering.

I feel like I'm on the football field during a game. Watching the defensive line, pacing, tapping my feet, a spiraling ball of nerves.

And then looking over at him. Mason Gray. Watching the game with vague, detached interest interspersed with glances up and down the bench to make sure nobody needs more water. Steady on his feet. Unmoving except to meander back and forth with no rush. Calm.

My heart rate is slowing.

"It's worse than what you said, right?" Mason whispers, peering up at me with furrowed brows. "The way you phrased it earlier . . . You said you were picked on because of your mom's reputation. But it's more than that, isn't it?"

I want to tear my eyes away from his, but they're too magnetic. I can't even blink. His hand is like a five-hundred-pound weight, keeping me pinned to the flat carpeting of the basement. His ability to see through everything I told him should terrify me, but his touch is like a soothing serum. It's comforting.

"How would you know?" I grumble.

"Because I . . ." Mason swallows, his fingertips curling up gently against my skin. "I also . . ."

His mouth hangs open for a lingering moment. Then he pulls his lips between his teeth, chewing the words away. He remains that way for several seconds before he speaks again. I don't know what to do but stand rigid, listening.

"I'm not going to tell anyone what you said," he murmurs. "I'm sorry people treated you so poorly because they had bad opinions about your mom. Because of whatever other reasons you won't say." He pauses, his jaw shifting like he's deliberating his next words. Then,

"I just think you should know that it's not your fault. The way people hurt you. That's all."

He tugs his hand away.

I'm free now, so I start walking to the staircase ascending out of the basement. "Come on," I say flatly. "Let's get you home."

If Mason is annoyed, frustrated, relieved, or anything else by my complete and utter lack of response, it doesn't show. His face is back to its base state. Unbothered. Neutral.

He follows me to my car, and we don't exchange any further words that day.

CHAPTER TEN
CAM

I'm about to roll under the silver bench and sink through the turf to the earth's core if I have to do this much longer.

It's the first game of the season where I'm benched, ripping my hair from my head as my team fumbles down the field, barely held together by the second-string quarterback. Roger isn't bad, but it's obvious my teammates don't trust him with the ball like they trust me.

I feel naked, sitting there in my jersey without my padding and helmet, resisting the urge to yell instructions as Roger looks around for another receiver. Coach Barnett is already taking a risk by letting me sit on the sidelines rather than banishing me from the field—I shouldn't draw attention, especially if people from the school board are here with their power of "suspension." God forbid the incoming scout sees that permanent blemish on my record when he next comes to observe Darius and me.

"Anup is open," I hiss, clutching my head. "Come on."

Suddenly, something soft obscures my vision. I tear the damp towel off with a growl to find Mason Gray beside me with a clipboard. "Cool off," he suggests with a smirk. He's dressed in that oversized jersey atop a snug, long-sleeved black shirt, another beanie nestled over his head.

"I'm perfectly cool," I snap.

He gently taps the top of my head with his clipboard, then moves along. I might've blushed and smacked it away if I hadn't noticed Roger getting sacked in the corner of my eye.

Not even Mason's presence is enough to bring me to a simmer. "Coach," I plead, inching toward Barnett, who's stroking the stray hairs of his silvery goatee. "It's been a week—I've been turning in homework. Paying attention in class. Can't you sub me in?"

He swallows a deep breath. "We have rules for a reason, Morelli. Once we see proof in your transcript, and once the punching incident fades from people's minds, we'll get you out there. For now, you're stuck."

Grumbling, I return to the bench so I can cuss to my heart's desire. But the moment I realize there's nothing I can do to get myself out on the field, something bizarre happens.

My interest evaporates.

Suddenly, I'm not watching the game anymore. It's an unexpected, disorienting shift that I'm not sure what to make of. Maybe this is normal for Cam Morelli, to not be interested in something I'm not involved in.

It's not, though, because football is supposed to be half of my personality. My talents and my confidence help me maintain my social standing. I need to stay agitated, riled up, pissed off, because *extreme passion* is required of every Division I player in football. It shouldn't matter that the only reason I played football earlier in life was because my counselor recommended it as a means of distraction from my circumstances. It's so much more than a casual escape now. It has to be, for my parents' sake.

Yet here I am, staring at Mason Gray as he marks data on his clipboard and towels people's faces while maintaining that mild look.

We haven't spoken about the workout session. It's been clinging to my thoughts like a parasite, its teeth needling into my brain. The way his frustration mounted until his eyes turned red with tears. The way he laughed unabashedly before realizing he wasn't covering it. The way his skin felt so cool and calming, like it was sapping the agitated heat straight out of my chest.

The way he told me, unprompted, that the things I endured weren't my fault. Like somehow, he knew that I still blame myself for . . .

Everything.

Maybe he senses that I'm thinking about him, or maybe he notices that I've been watching him unblinkingly, because he wanders over and sits on the bench beside me, thrumming his fingertips against his clipboard. There's a foot of space between our thighs. He twists the soles of his worn sneakers into the rubbery turf beneath us.

"You quieted down," he notes.

"So?" I ask irritably. "I thought you would've been happy to hear me shut up."

Mason gives me one of his sweet, phony smiles. "Your silence is indeed a blessing for those of us who live on the sidelines. Thank you for your sacrifice."

I seize the clipboard out of his hands and throw it onto the ground.

Mason's lips wobble, like he's about to laugh, but he quickly chomps on them. A few seconds later, he says, "I'm sorry, Cameron Morelli, did you just throw a temper tantrum?"

"No," I snap.

"Man-child."

"Fuck off."

"Adult toddler."

I seize the beanie off his head and throw that onto the ground as well.

Mason has to lift both hands to cover his mouth. "Teenage fetus," he breathes.

"Shut the hell up!" I shout, embarrassed heat flaring in my cheeks.

Mason's laughing fully now, half his face invisible behind his palms. The sound is crisp and sweet, and unfamiliar enough that some of the guys sitting down the sidelines are peering over with raised brows. "Or what?" he asks, apparently not noticing their curiosity. "I have nothing else on me that you can throw."

"I'll just throw you," I growl. "The trash behind the bleachers should do."

"How am I supposed to fulfill my important duties as water boy from the garbage?" he asks, clicking his tongue. "I thought I was a rock, Cameron. Won't things spiral without my presence?"

He's being so sassy that I can barely keep up. I stoop over and grab his beanie off the turf, then shove it over his head, pulling the edge over his eyes and nose. "Perfect," I snip. "Do me a favor and stay like that for the rest of the game."

"But then you can't see me," he protests, hands still fanned over his lips.

"That's the point, water boy."

"I thought you liked my face, quarterback."

"I did. Until I found out it belongs to a snide little bastard."

Mason snickers, then rolls the ends of his beanie up over his brows, exposing the warm honey-brown color of his irises. I'm glad it's murky and gray out today, because I don't think I could handle seeing the little gold flecks sparkling in the sunlight.

"Then," he says softly, "what's going on? Why did you get quiet?"

It's annoying that he even noticed. Everyone else on the team has been too frustrated and invested to pay attention to me. Or maybe they're purposefully ignoring me since my absence is half the reason we're flubbing this game. Darius is doing a good job with the defensive line, keeping the other team from running away with the game, but none of it is worth anything if we can't score.

"Mad about the game," I say.

"But that's not true," he replies. "You were mad the entire first half. Kicking and groaning and whining. Now you're different."

I scowl. We've been talking for a week—why does he get to see through me as if we've been best friends for life? "I'm still mad, just quiet about it," I try, to which he rolls his eyes.

"Actually, it looked more like you stopped caring."

"The only way you'd know that is if you've been paying attention."

To my surprise, Mason's snowy cheeks actually turn pink. I won't pretend the sight doesn't give me some satisfaction. "I happened to notice your grating voice was no longer ringing in my ears," he says coolly.

"Why do you care about my enthusiasm levels for this pathetic game?" I grumble.

Mason seems to consider this, like he's not even sure himself. He massages his thin lips, and I try not to stare. Try not to think about the way he smiles. The way his laughter irritates my heart in a way nobody else's ever has. I've been pondering it, trying to understand what it is about him that makes me feel uncomfortably fluttery.

Could it really just be his face?

"I guess," he says eventually, his voice quiet, "I'm just trying to figure you out."

I frown, tucking one knee up into my chest. "I'm extremely flat and shallow," I tell him. "I have no depth at all. So you don't need to worry."

"I might've believed that last week." Mason taps his clipboard against his chin, observing me from the corner of his eye. "I'm not so sure anymore. Are you acting this way because you're not playing, so you don't care? Or is it because of something else?"

"Am I not allowed to get bored of my team's shitty ballhandling?" I cry out, to which some of the guys nearby scoff and flick me menacing looks. I'm nervous now. Because what he's saying is starting to ring deeply within me.

Why did I stop caring? Why did I stop paying attention?

"Anyway, you rejected me, so why do you care?" I demand, scowling deeply.

"Just because I don't want to date you doesn't mean I can't be curious," he points out.

"You just like to antagonate me."

"Antagonize."

"What-the-fuck-ever."

Mason pulls his lower lip between his teeth again, which is a sight I'm becoming annoyingly familiar with whenever he's resisting laughter.

I fight the urge to pick him up and find the nearest trash can. "You're not coming to that beach party tonight, right?" I ask, shifting the subject. "If I have to see you one more time this week, I'll drown myself in the lake."

"Don't worry. I'm staying late to help Barnett clean up, so he'll drive me home."

"So . . ." I swallow, hating the dip in my stomach. "You're for sure not coming?"

"Nah. I'm pretty tired." His mouth quirks into a playful little smile, and he tacks on, "Unless you beg me to come on your knees."

I know he's not actually flirting with me, considering he hates— or at least *dislikes*—me. But I'd be lying if I said my face didn't feel ten degrees warmer after that. "Cam Morelli begs for no one," I say sharply, and he laughs into his hand.

"Then this lowly peasant won't hinder Your Majesty with his presence." Mason wanders off without another word, leaving me itchy with aggravation and feeling like I've just been insulted.

I hate the fact that I feel strangely disappointed.

CHAPTER ELEVEN
MASON

"Thanks again for the ride," I say to Mr. Barnett as he pulls into my driveway.

He pats my beanie fondly. "Have a good night. Don't do anything too wild."

"I'll keep the debauchery to a minimum," I tell him, returning his smile as I climb out of the car. I could've gone to the beach party—I usually look for any excuse to get out of my house—but today, I'm clocked out and exhausted. I've gotten five texts, each increasingly more frantic.

> I miss you. Please, can I just see your face?

> Just once. I'll stop bothering you, but I know that's not what you want.

> How much more space do you need?

> I promise I'll do better this time around, please respond.

I'll do better. I'll be better. For you. Just give me a chance.

My head has been plagued with thoughts of him all day, to the point where I could barely choke down the turkey sandwich I fixed myself for lunch last night. Which I only did because I knew Cameron would text me about what I'd eaten.

The remembrance makes me smirk as I wander up the porch steps. Seeing him in his element while we were working out was endearing. It's clear he knew what he was talking about and was maybe even eager to impart some wisdom about exercise on me. He was never pushy or irritated when I couldn't fulfill his requests for lunges or squats or the minutes I could run.

Finding out that he was in the same boat a few years ago is comforting. I assumed Cameron Morelli was born with a strong figure and handsome face, and that's why he's egotistical. Even though we've only had two study sessions, I feel like there's a lot more beneath the surface when it comes to this big goofy jock.

The reason he moved here . . . Was it really just because of what he mentioned about his mom? How badly was he harassed that he felt he needed to change aspects about himself? And how far from the truth is this current version of Cameron?

Against my better judgment, I'm intrigued. Even more so when I looked over from my position on the sidelines and found him watching the clouds rather than the game. For a moment, he seemed uninvested. Almost *content* to not be on the field. Did he even realize it? And does it have something to do with why he's been failing his courses?

I push through the door, sighing. I shouldn't let this quarterback occupy my thoughts so frequently. Yet I can't help but remember the trace of disappointment in his face when I told him I wasn't going to the party. Could it be possible that after a measly week, maybe Cameron Morelli . . . ?

"—genuinely a pleasure to see you again, Mr. and Mrs. Gray. It's good to know you've been well over the last few months."

The familiar voice ricochets off my eardrums, freezing me in my tracks.

No.

The blood pounding through my veins crystallizes.

No.

"Oh, Mason!" Mom says, her face cracking with a wide smile. Her abundance of dark curls is in disarray, pouring around her heart-shaped face, and her usually pasty cheeks are flushed. "Finally you're home. Look who was sweet enough to drop by!"

Did he park down the street? Or was I too distracted to notice his car was out front? I'd been good about eyeing my surroundings—why have I been letting my guard slip?

"Mason," Dad says in greeting. His own hair is swept backward, a common sign indicating that he's been nervously swiping his hand through it. "I just texted you. Ah. We were talking about how busy you've been. With the football team, the gallery . . ."

The well-built person looming between them turns on his heel and grins at me. His pale blue eyes meet mine for the first time in months. They're exactly as I remember them—arctic, sparkling, like a snowy tundra in the north.

"Mason!" he says brightly.

An explosive chill scratches down my spine. His hickory-brown hair is a flattering, curled mess, and he's sporting coarse stubble around his jaw that makes him look older than twenty-two. He's wearing a white button-down, a pastel-blue tie, and slacks, as if he stopped by on his way to a dinner party. He's always dressed like a gentleman, adhering to his wealthy family's strict standards and demand that he maintain a proper image.

It's always been this way. He's never not been strong, capable, and confident. He was on student council for all four years. He was one of the most popular and well-received students in the improv club. I know because I used to walk to the high school after classes ended so I could watch him. He was the most valuable player on the varsity tennis team beginning freshman year, when he wiped the floor with the seniors during tryouts.

I lurked in his shadow for years, always watching him surpass every expectation his parents bestowed on him with ease and a beaming smile. I've never known a life without him. Our moms are—*were*—close friends, and they'd hoped to have their first children in the same year. But his mother settled down first and got pregnant, leaving her best friend to scramble for a husband so she could have her own child within a reasonable amount of time.

Four and a half years later, she had me.

There are pictures of us together. Sitting under a Christmas tree, him holding me swaddled in his arms. Him carrying me on his shoulders around a playground after school. Bundled up while building a snowman in the backyard. Sitting in his lap during crammed car rides, his arms wrapped around me. My parents left me in his care frequently, hoping his success and self-determination would rub off on me. And one day, when he showed me how to properly swing a tennis racket, and I purposefully kept messing up so he would have to touch me again to correct me, I realized it was more than admiration.

Though our moms grew apart (despite my own mother's desperate attempts to stay connected), it never hindered our relationship. As his family's wealth increased, and they pulled away, my grip on him tightened. And his on me.

Since my dad took over the business, they've been trying to squeeze into new crowds, he told me once when he was fifteen or so, his arm slung around me on the couch. I could barely hear him over my own agitated heartbeat. *I don't care if they think your family is poor or messy. That won't stop me from seeing you.*

He made me feel special. The way he smiled at me. The way his hugs lingered. My parents invited him over frequently and asked him to take me along whenever he ran errands or went to study. When he was sixteen and I was twelve (eleven?), he'd take my wrist and guide me around the superstore down the street if he needed food. I enjoyed those trips, though they stopped happening when his family hired a personal servant.

Then we got older, and I was fourteen (thirteen?), and this and that happened, and suddenly whatever, now we're here. Every panic response in my body tells me to run, but I can't move. I can't do anything.

I'm pathetic.

"What do you look like that for?" Mom asks, her cheery persona dissolving into a stern glare. "Apparently he hasn't been able to get ahold of you lately. You should know better than to be so impolite."

"Oh gosh, no, it's fine. Sounds like Mason has been busy. I'd hate to think I was bothering him," he says, offering her a wink.

She squeaks out a laugh and waves her bony hands in dismissal. "No, he really shouldn't treat you like that! You're family."

I keep hoping that if I stay as still as possible, I'll turn invisible. His eyes stay locked on me, twinkling with familiar kindness and warmth despite their frigid color. "I can't believe how long it's been," he says, still grinning despite my lack of response. "Can we talk in your room?"

He takes a half step toward me, and I mirror him, moving backward. My voice is lost somewhere in the cavity of my chest.

"Mason Gray, come here," Mom snaps, seizing the crook of my elbow and dragging me into the kitchen, where everyone's stationed. I want to dig my feet into the ground and pull, but I don't have the strength.

I probably never will.

Dad stares at the floor, like he doesn't want to see us interacting. He won't say anything, because he doesn't want to argue with Mom. Mom, who's looking between us with anticipatory eyes. "You're being ridiculous," she says after a heavy silence, and she points down the bedroom hallway. "He asked to speak to you in private. Go on."

If I disobey further, she'll fly into a rage. The last time I upset her, she made me scrub the grout out of the tile floor in the bathroom with a toothpick. I'd take that over spending a moment alone with him, but the end result will be the same.

He gets what he wants. Always.

So my feet move of their own accord, dragging me down the hallway. His shadow pours over mine, longer and wider, as he follows.

The creaking bedroom door is sharp and knifelike against my eardrums as it swings shut. He's probably taking in my room. Other than additional pastel paintings gifted to me by the local art gallery, it's the same. The half-read books, the dusty guitar, the canvas I haven't thrown away, the capped camera I haven't used in a year.

"Seems like you're getting out there." His words are gentle, not tinged with frustration like they used to be. He props himself on the edge of my mattress, another smile lighting his face. "That's amazing. You've always struggled with socializing."

I feel like my head is stuffed with cotton balls that are absorbing all sounds and thoughts before my brain can process them. He's complimenting me.

"Sorry for surprising you. I didn't know how to reach you, since you're ignoring my texts—"

"I blocked your number," I blurt. I hide my trembling fists behind my back, and when he notices, his smile widens incrementally.

"Come on, Mason. If you're going to say that, you should at least turn off your read receipts."

My face pales.

"It doesn't matter. I know you've needed space. But it's been six months, and I miss you." His eyes soften, and he extends his arm, gesturing for me to approach. I'd rather die than let him touch me again. My muscles respond to the command anyway, guiding me forward, slipping my palm into his. My hands are cold. His are worse.

He grazes his lips against my knuckles, like he's savoring this moment. I hate how my body responds, stirring fluttery warmth in my abdomen.

"I don't miss you," I whisper.

The words sap away my fortitude, and suddenly, tears scorch the edges of my eyes. When he peers up at me, his gaze pained and uncertain, it shatters what little confidence remains. My fingers shiver harder, his touch igniting memories I've concealed—the feeling of him wrapped around me while I tried to sleep, the way he kissed my forehead so gently when he left for college, sitting in the darkness of his car because I didn't want to come home, curling up with him in his dorm and not having to worry about roommates, since his parents paid for a single room. His voice, full of soft reverence.

I watch vacantly as his mouth shifts to the back of my hand, to the crook of my wrist, to the veins of my forearm. "My birthday was a few weeks ago," he murmurs, cool lips working to my elbow. "You didn't text me."

Sorry. I swallow the word. I don't need to apologize.

"We've been friends for years." He continues in that soft, soothing voice, like he's trying to lull me to sleep. "We've shared so many moments. Don't they mean anything to you?"

I once promised myself I would never cry in front of him again. Yet beads of water leak down my cheeks, coagulating at my jaw, burning my tired eyes. "I *hate* you," I choke out, unable to muster the courage to stop him when he reaches up, framing my face in his palm. "You treated me terribly . . ."

"I know." He draws me forward, forcing me to step between his propped knees, and tugs my head to his shoulder. "I've had time to reflect. The things I said and did . . . I don't know how you could forgive me. Yet I'm asking for it anyway."

The familiarity of this situation is sinking into my bones, dulling my anger. The sharp edges of my resilience are being shaved to useless nubs. The longer his hands caress my skin, the more watered-down I feel, like all my frustrations, arguments, and characteristics are bleeding away.

"I'm better than that worthless man I was," he breathes. "And I'll stay better. For you. My sweet, gentle Mason."

My tears melt into the silky material of his shirt. I think I've lost weight again. Have I always felt this small and pathetic in his arms?

"We're good for each other. That hasn't changed, right?" He pulls back so he can reclaim his grasp on my face. Instinctively, I lean into his palms, enjoying the way his cool thumbs soothe the reddened skin beneath my eyes. "When I graduate, I'm taking a more permanent position at my father's company. I can provide you a good life like your parents want. Your mom hoped she'd find a way to bond our families, and this can be it." He smiles again, warm and inviting. "Maybe she'll ease up on your dad. And they won't have to worry about providing for you anymore. That's one less stressor in this house, right?"

I stare dazedly at him, clinging to his handsome, angular features. I'm sure people are falling all over him at college. Has he been warding them off because he still sees a future with me? He apologized. So maybe he's telling the truth? Could we go back to the beginning, when he did anything and everything to make me happy, showering me with gifts and affection, enabling my requests no matter how childish they were?

Probably not. But I'd be lying if I said I haven't envisioned this moment, those two words on his lips. *I'm sorry.* And I'd be damning myself if I pretended I don't fall asleep wishing I could roll over and find his chest waiting for me. I miss the kind words. The reassurances. The company.

I miss being loved.

My hands rise shakily through the air, fingers curling around his wrists. I miss this sensation, too. Of being held. Sought-after. Special.

"I graduate in December," he says, eyes glinting when he recognizes an opportunity to get through to me. "I'm closing on a house. It's big and quiet. Plenty of places you can entertain yourself with whatever hobby you're into. You can come live with me and finish senior year." He leans closer, face strained with desperation. "I'll take care of you. I know you're in your parents' custody until you turn eighteen, but I don't think they'd mind."

I'll take care of you. That's nice. The thought. I can barely take care of myself.

"I'll give you time to think about it," he says softly, stroking my hair. "In the meantime, I brought you something. Want to see?"

I don't answer, but that doesn't stop him. He reaches into his back pocket and slips out a velvety bag, then pops it open so I can see it glint in the bedroom lighting. It's a watery-blue gemstone on a silver chain.

"Your birthstone," he says brightly. "Aquamarine. Remember when you took astrology seriously? I thought you'd like this. Can I put it on you?"

I don't answer, but that doesn't stop him. He fastens the clasp around the back of my neck, and it falls against my collar like a fifty-pound weight, nearly buckling my knees.

"I won't force you to answer right away. But I don't want to give up on you. On *us*."

He kisses my hands like they're precious to him, like he treasures me. He stands and draws me into an unbearably gentle hug, then trails to the door with a quiet "I love you" that plumes through the bedroom air like a noxious gas.

Then I hear him talking to Mom. She sounds pleased. That's rare.

The beach is a twenty-minute walk.

I leave through the window. Only after his car drives away.

I want to make mistakes tonight.

CHAPTER TWELVE
CAM

"What about you, Morelli?"

The sound of my last name snaps me to attention. I'm sitting cross-legged on the grainy sand, watching the firepit dance and wriggle as a cool breeze sweeps the beach, tossing embers into the midnight-black air. I didn't realize that I'd spaced out until now.

"What?" I squeak.

Jody's watching, the flames illuminating his mischievous expression. "We're talking about relationships. Are you still ass sore that our precious water boy rejected you?"

The group of ten or so people cluttered around the fire laughs, because mob mentality or something. "He wasn't for me anyway," I say airily. "He's too . . ."

"Good for you?" Anup guesses, to which my boy Darius flicks his temple with annoyance. Anup scoffs, massaging his skin. "What? I'm right. Why would someone as sweet as Mason Gray date this lump of brainless muscle?"

"My brain is fully functional and very large!" I snap.

"Yeah—how's that going, by the way? The studying." Darius shifts his cross-legged position toward me, apprehension glinting in his eyes. The flames in the stone hearth emphasize how nervous he is. Today's game was messy.

"It's fine. His help is . . . like, helping," I explain.

"Very large," Anup whispers to Jody, and I hurl my empty pop can at his head, which he catches with his wide receiver reflexes.

"You've only got a couple weeks before that scout shows up," Darius continues, popping a stern brow. "I've already committed to Alpine University, but you have to win him over. And you can't do that from the bench. It doesn't matter that you're playing your ass off during practices and training every day if he's not there to see it."

Naturally, the mere mention of college, of being recruited, gives me a full-body chill. The word "scholarship" is a grating echo in my ears. Keeping my parents afloat is wholly riding on my college football career. If they don't have to worry about paying for my college, maybe Dad could open his own studio like he's always wanted. Maybe Mom won't have to work overtime in the OR and get up at four o'clock on Saturdays when she's on call anymore.

"Better stay focused, Morelli," Nate says, crossing his thick arms with a smirk. "Don't let Mason's pretty face distract you."

"I told you, I'm over it! We're obviously incompatible," I say with a violent huff.

"Mm. Then who gets to break up with you next?" Jody asks.

"Pardon?"

"You know." He gestures at me like I should, in fact, know. "You get into relationships and then people break up with you for being a player. I'm wondering who your next target is."

The implication causes irritated heat to flourish in my face. "The fuck are you saying?" I demand. "That I'm not *loyal*?"

"If the glass slipper fits," Anup says with a roguish grin.

I want to chuck something into the fire, preferably one of them. "I don't cheat!" I growl, lurching to my feet. Is that what my ex-partners have been saying? What *bullshit*.

"Then, why else are people breaking up with you?" Nate wonders. The crowd cluttering the fire stares at me, awaiting a valid answer. But would they even believe me if I said the truth? My track record doesn't speak in my favor.

All I can sputter out is a hearty "fuck you" before storming off toward the next ablaze firepit, where a few of my other teammates and random acquaintances are huddled, pumping music on a Bluetooth speaker. The sun is set and the stars and moon are in full bloom, shedding a cool white radiance atop the warm orange glow washing the beach.

People break up with you for being a player.

Jody's amused voice makes me squirm with annoyance. I knot my arms against my chest, wondering which of my exes planted that rumor. Did they all come together to collude against me by spreading misinformation? I don't care if people know I jump from shallow relationship to shallow relationship—I've made a point of tying that one negative trait to me so people don't come up with other worse shit. I *do* care if people think I'm a cheater.

I'm only like a month into senior year, so how is it already falling apart? Is my image going to start unraveling? I've spent so much time and energy building myself up, controlling the narrative around me, adjusting my personality and body and presentation so I wouldn't get trampled under people's shoes and cutting glares.

What am I supposed to do if it's not enough anymore? Even if I scrape my way through the rest of high school, what happens when I go to college? Am I going to have to start from scratch? And continue to keep people at an arm's length so they won't notice something's off? There's a reason I don't have any solid friendships. People I'd hang out with one-on-one outside of football practices and parties. Everyone is an acquaintance, which is what I planned from the moment I got here. It's my own damn fault, so what am I even bitching about?

I hate this. I hate everything. I hate *me*. I hate—

Just breathe, Cameron.

Suddenly, I feel the weight of Mason's palm against my chest. Resting lightly on my shirt. Cold fingertips nestled into my collar.

I heave a giant stabilizing breath, my eyes fluttering shut. I don't know why Mason appears so suddenly in my thoughts. But I decide not to question it, because the remembrance is easing the flustered heat coursing through my blood.

A sudden noise draws my attention. Down the strip of beach, several people are cheering and clapping, forming a circle around something near the next firepit. My first thought is *Fight*, so I sprint over and needle through the throng to see what's going on.

Only to find Mason Gray doing a keg stand.

My jaw drops so quickly that it nearly dislocates from my face. He's gripping the edges of the keg, sucking down beer while two of my second-string teammates hold his legs in the air. Moments later, he taps out, and they ease him back to standing again.

"Holy shit!" someone cries out—it's Ravi, who's swaying on his feet. "Gray is unhinged tonight."

Mason laughs into his hand. He's not wearing a beanie, so his black hair is a frumpy mess. He's still in an oversized jersey over a long-sleeved black shirt, faded sneakers, and slim-fitting cargo pants. Something glitters around his neck. I watch with sheer bewilderment as he's drawn into a group of five and allows one to push a beer bottle into his palm. All the while, he has one hand folded over his face, giggling uncontrollably, lowering it only so he can drink.

Something's off. I don't like the apprehensive feeling stirring in my stomach. Then I hear his next words, loud and clear, and bile rises into my throat.

"Hey, does anyone want to kiss me? I really want to be kissed."

His voice is so slurred it's hard to pick the words apart, and while most people around him laugh nervously, clearly aware of his drunken state, one guy grins and steps toward Mason. "I'll do it!" he says, sticking his hand up.

White-hot rage boils under my skin, causing me to break into a furious tremble. Who the hell does this guy think he is, taking Mason's request seriously as if he's not plastered out of his mind?

Mason doesn't even look like he's paying attention anymore. He's staring dazedly at the stars, fumbling with a pale gemstone dangling at his collar.

That slimy prick is reaching out to grab Mason's face.

"Are you *kidding me?*" I snarl, storming forward and seizing his shoulder, then wrenching him backward with such force that his heel slides out from under him. He collapses onto the ground with a loud "oof."

"Hey!" Mason's garbled voice reaches me, and I swivel on him, my fists balled and my jaw strained with anger. He instantly staggers back and raises his arms, bracing them, as if preparing to shove me away. "What's your problem, Cameron?"

The people who were in his group are awkwardly backing off to give us space. Even the guy I ripped backward is crawling out of sight, thankfully. I forcibly unclench my hands and relax my face, though irritation is still pulsing through me in overwhelming waves. "What's *your* problem?" I demand. "I thought you weren't coming tonight. Did you walk here alone?"

"So what? I can do what I want," he growls, stumbling closer to jam an accusatory finger in my chest. I guess now that I'm not as visibly mad, he's feeling braver about getting in my face. "I don't need your permission to do anything."

He flashes his middle fingers, then twirls around to walk away. The quick movement throws him off-balance, though, and he stumbles, his knees buckling. It all happens with enough lethargy that I have time to jump out and catch his elbows, coaxing him back to his unsteady feet. "What's going on?" I ask sternly. I've never seen him drink at a party before. If he's ever at one, he's usually hugging the shadows, watching people chat from a distance until one of the footballers notices him and drags him into a circle. "You seem off."

Mason gives me a blank, dead smile, lips pressed firmly together. "Hey, Cameron. What the fuck do you think you know about me?"

He's trying to provoke me, but it's not going to work. "Are you okay?" I ask.

Mason's breath hitches, like my response startled him. Suddenly, his lower lip trembles, and water sparkles in his eyes, threatening to escape down his cheeks. "I could consent," he rasps.

I stare at him. "Huh?"

"I'm guessing you yanked that guy away because you think I can't consent to being kissed." His shoulders break into a tremor. "It's my fault for drinking, so it's my fault if someone kisses me. I literally asked for it. You don't have to *save me*."

He's still thinking about that? "I don't care," I snap. "If someone kisses you while you're like this, they're taking advantage of you."

"Oh, well, excuse the fuck out of me. I didn't realize I was talking to the god of fucking consent." He sucks down a few gulps of his beer, which causes my teeth to latch together.

"Have you had any water?" I ask sharply. "Did you eat dinner?"

"Sure," he says with enough hesitation that I know he's lying.

"You'll get sick."

"Then I better find someone to kiss before that happens," he says, eyes roving over the beach. Everything he says is throwing me for a loop. I don't know Mason well, but this . . . this isn't *him*.

I massage my temple, sighing, and say, "I'll do it."

Mason blinks lethargically, words seeming to seep into his head. "Really?" he asks, snorting. "Even though I rejected you?"

"At least you know me."

Mason laughs into his cupped palm. The sight is saddening. I can almost feel the loneliness, the desperation, radiating from him. After several long seconds, during which his laughter sputters away and he merely stands there behind his hand, silent, he lowers it. His eyes are dull and lifeless, and he's wearing a deadpan smile.

"Then kiss me," he says.

"After you eat."

He scrunches his nose. "Huh?"

"You might throw up because you're drinking on an empty stomach," I say, placing my hand on his hair and digging my fingers gently into his scalp. He peeks up at my wrist in confusion but doesn't pull away. "Let's go to Burger King and get you an Impossible Whopper."

A glimmer of life returns to his eyes. "You know about their vegetarian options?"

"I've been looking up restaurants for when we need food runs," I say, shrugging. Shouldn't that be obvious, considering I told him I'd help with his diet and regimen?

Mason looks at me like I just spoke in a dead tongue. A breeze sweeps the beach, disturbing the glassy lake and crackling flames of the firepits. "That's nice," he says quietly.

"Yeah. I'm kindhearted as hell." I dig my fingers deeper into his head and twist, turning him to the weedy hill climbing up to the main road. "Let's go."

So we go.

Mason sways in my passenger seat as we head down the road. We come upon the fast-food chain just as the trees start thickening along the street perimeter, and when the glowing sign emerges from behind a cluster of pine trees, Mason gasps. "We're going to Burger King?" he asks hopefully.

How many times must I tell him we're visiting patty royalty before it sticks? "Try not to act drunk," I plead. "If the cops show up because some sixteen-year-old is toasted at the local BK—"

"Seventeen," Mason interrupts, scoffing. "Why does everyone think I'm so young? I'm very mature. The rest of me just hasn't caught up yet."

I don't have the mental fortitude to try to unpack why he's saying that, so I don't respond.

When we stroll inside, Mason shields his face against the fluorescent lighting. I seat him at a table, where he promptly rests his face in his arms. Then I pop over to the counter and order him a veggie burger and fries, as well as a cheese Whopper for myself. Because I'm a growing boy and deserve it.

As I wait for the food, I eye Mason. One might think he's asleep, but there's a tremor in his outline, like he's crying. When the baggie arrives, I return to his side and twist my knuckle between his shoulders. "Come on," I say. "Back to the beach."

Mason curls his arms tighter around his face.

"I said I'd kiss you if you ate, remember?"

The moment he lifts his head, eyes pink and puffy and rimmed with exhaustion, I jam the straw of the water cup between his lips. He chokes in protest, then begins to drink, obediently rising to his feet when I clasp his elbow and tug.

As night falls deeper over Elwood, so does an early-autumn chill, and as we leave the parking lot, I see raised bumps flecking his wrists. He didn't bring a jacket or come prepared for the cold, which seems unlike him.

I shouldn't care. If something happened to make him cut loose, how is it my business? But he feels different from the person I've been forced to be around. Is this the guy who's been hiding behind that sweet, feigned smile and dry voice? Someone a little angrier, more combative, more frustrated, more tired and impatient and . . .

Genuine?

I'm so deep in my thoughts that I don't realize we're at the beach again until a cold rush of water swills around my ankles. I'm standing at the brink of the midnight-black lake, which scintillates beneath the stars and moon as the water returns to its undisturbed state. Mason scarfs down his veggie burger, looking out emotionlessly across the yawning expanse. Every movement causes the pale blue gemstone around his neck to glitter. I don't remember him wearing that at the game. Maybe it was tucked beneath his jersey?

When he's done, I take his wrapper and hand him his fries. He goes to town on them like he's discovering potatoes for the first time. "Didn't you order food?" he mutters. "You could eat it instead of staring at me."

Oh. "Who's staring?" I squawk, plunging my hand into the bag to grab my own meat.

Mason smirks and continues shoveling fries into his mouth.

Eventually, I stuff the baggie in a trash can half-buried in the sand, then return to Mason's side. Music still thrums along the beach from Bluetooth speakers, and the firepits are still crowded with high schoolers who were at the game, their chatter and laughter echoing along the lake. "What are you hoping to get out of tonight?" I ask.

I avoid staring as he licks the salt off his fingers. "I told you," he says flatly. "To get drunk and kiss someone."

"Then, what are you hoping to forget? Or who? Your parents?" I don't understand that situation, since he hasn't clarified the circumstances, but I think I can paint a semi-accurate picture.

Mason sucks down the rest of his water, then jingles the remaining ice. "Hey," he says. "It was just my face, right?"

"Huh?"

"The reason you asked me out. It was because of my face." Mason's attention shifts to his ankles, which are plunged in the cold, murky water. His shoes, socks, and phone are bundled on the sand behind us.

"Yeah," I admit, because I literally told him so last week.

"And now . . . knowing what you know about me . . . would you still ask me out?" he mumbles.

I'm not sure where this is coming from. "Should I ignore the fact that you want to run me over with a tank while I consider my answer?" I ask skeptically.

Mason's mouth twitches upward. I've amused him about something again. "You're really not as confident as you pretend, are you, Cameron?" he whispers.

Embarrassment surges through me, which is becoming entirely too common around him. "The hell?" I demand. "I'm the most egotistical piece of shit this side of Elwood. You can't take that away from me because you're cranky."

Mason throws a hand over his mouth and laughs. The sound is warming and cute, standing in sharp contrast to the dulled parts of himself he's had on display. "You didn't answer me. Would you ask me out, now that you know me better?"

I consider it, putting aside my biases, from the fact that he rejected me by verbally sucker punching my manhood to the fact that I'm his least favorite person. I do love his face a concerning amount. The way his features are so soft and well-balanced, the visually pleasing contrast of his black hair against his ivory skin. Then there's that annoying-ass smile.

That aside, would I ask him out based on his personality?

I don't even have time to deliberate. The final, lingering spark of life remaining in Mason's eyes flickers out, leaving his gaze hollow and cold. "I know," he whispers. "I'm boring. I can't carry a conversation. The only reason people stand to be around me is because they like my aesthetic. So don't say it. I know."

His candor stuns me. Mason kicks his foot, causing water to arc through the air and glitter like diamonds beneath the moonlight before they melt into the lake.

I don't think my answer matters. If it's no, I'm confirming his assumptions. If it's yes, he won't believe me. I can feel the weight of this twisting, tangled ball of self-deprecation weighing him down, spreading its sharp tendrils into every fragment of his character. Shaving away all the intricacies of who he is.

I know how it works. Been there, done that. Yet I have a sinking feeling his demons are more gnarled and deeply embedded than mine. Mine sunk their claws into me in late elementary school, and only loosened their clutches when we moved somewhere I could scrub myself clean. Even still, I can feel the shadows of the puncture wounds they left behind.

But Mason . . . This aching atmosphere around him . . .

He's been living with this pain far longer.

I'm starting to understand Mason Gray. He's not just the cute, elusive water boy everyone wants to linger around because of his mysterious atmosphere and pretty appearance. He's a painstakingly crafted shell of a person who's been battered and worn down to his most basic functions, thoughts, and feelings. There's only one crack in his armor. His smile.

That's why he's always hiding it.

I'm not sure what to say. I guess he doesn't care, because suddenly, he's grabbing my shirt, dragging me in to kiss me. "Stop," I say darkly, and I snag his wrists, but he curls his grip tighter around the fabric. His proximity mixed with my reluctance sends a signal of panic reel-

ing through my skull. Mason's hands are someone else's. I'm not on
the beach, I'm in a bedroom. There's a persuasive, cool voice in my ear.

*You want to prove the rumors wrong, right . . . ? Or do you take after
your mom after all?*

Everyone thinks you're disgusting.

How can your dad stand it? His wife and son both being dirty, rotten—

"Fuck *off* of me!" I growl, and my hands fly out, pushing. Too late
do I realize that I'm not in eighth grade. I'm much bigger than the boy
I used to be; I'm at a beach party, and the person I've just shoved is a
drunk, emotionally stunted Mason Gray.

Of course he falls. He can't even stand without swaying. I feel like
I've just rammed a fragile glass flower off its pedestal.

Mason shatters when he hits the water. He lands flat on his back,
and the lake splashes up around him, soaking through his clothes and
wetting my pants. While I stare in horrified dismay, he looks around
with jaded, dead eyes, like he's not sure how he got down there. This
section of the beach quiets, the conversations dissolving as people
turn to see the damning image of me standing there, arms extended,
and Mason sitting in the shallow edge of the lake.

"I'm sorry," I sputter out. "I didn't mean . . ."

Nausea roils through me as Mason struggles to stand but only
gets one leg under him before he collapses onto his knees, further
drenching himself. He stares vacantly at his hands anchored in the
sopping sand.

"I'm sorry," I say again, and I kneel in the water, allowing it to
consume my jeans up to my thighs as I offer my hands. "I shouldn't
have—"

"My fault," Mason whispers. "It always is. So you shouldn't apologize."

His lips pale the longer he sits in the water, his clothes clinging pitifully to his frame. Slowly, I wrap my fingers around his wrists and lift, unrooting him from the beach. I rise equally as slowly, waiting for him to properly plant his feet.

"Let's go," I say, tugging him toward the bundle of belongings behind him. He scoops them up, shaken like a wet puppy. I've probably ruined his night enough, but I don't feel like I should leave him alone. "I'm taking you home."

He doesn't argue. He looks like he's on autopilot, expressionless as he shivers from remnants of lake water.

That's how I end up driving Mason Gray home.

It's a long journey with nothing to break the silence but the soft hum of my engine. I put his seat warmer on, but Mason hugs his arms the entire time, shaking in his damp clothes.

I have so many things I want to ask. Or say. But we're not close enough for any of them to leave my mouth. Still, it takes all my strength not to blurt something, because I know what it's like to feel so fucking alone you might as well disappear.

Maybe I don't need to ask anything. Maybe I just need to tell him that if he disappeared . . .

I would notice.

As we pull into his driveway, his body language changes. He closes in on himself and his eyes flit around the subdivision, picking apart every shadow like he's anticipating we might be jumped. Instinctively, I prepare myself to clock a bitch, but the street is quiet and vacant.

"Well . . . here we are," I say awkwardly as I guide him to his door. "Will you be okay?"

Mason's eyes fuzz with incomprehension.

I wait a moment, then try again. "Water boy?"

The word gets his attention, and he peeks up at me. "Quarterback," he says.

"Get inside and change into something warm."

His focus slips down his front, where his shirt and pants cling to his purplish skin. "Okay."

I start trailing backward, waiting for him to enter his house, but he doesn't. Just grips the edges of his wet jersey like he's lost all sense of direction and meaning.

"Water boy," I say firmly.

His head quirks. "Quarterback," he responds.

"Give me your house key."

He does, though it takes him several seconds of fumbling through his pockets. I use it to unlock his door, then pull him into his house. Just as I'm stepping over the doorframe and back onto the porch, I feel a light touch against my wrist.

"Don't leave," he whispers.

I swivel toward him in astonishment. He's staring at my feet, though his fingers are curling in around my wrist, his featherlight grip strengthening.

"I'll call him if I'm alone," he breathes. "Don't leave me."

Him? "What do you need?" I ask, closing the front door. He makes a barely audible exhale, and his shivering hand drops from mine.

"Just . . . stay."

Maybe that gets a smile out of me. I hope he doesn't notice. Cam Morelli shouldn't smile like this for anyone. Softly. Kindly. That's not who he is. I say:

"Then I'll stay."

CHAPTER THIRTEEN
MASON

I don't know how I'm still awake. I also don't know why Cameron is humoring me so late.

I drink two full glasses of water, take a brief shower to scrub the lake water off me, change into flannel pajamas, and brush my teeth. I don't throw up, which is damn lucky, though there's always tomorrow morning, when I'll be inevitably hungover. All the while, my hands itch to find my phone. Whenever it vibrates, it doubles in weight, causing my posture to sag.

I'm better than that worthless man I was. And I'll stay better. For you.

Those words have been swirling between my ears all night. I don't believe them. But I *want* to. I want to so *badly*.

"Are you sure?" Cameron asks.

I blink, orienting myself, and realize I'm lying under my covers while Cameron stands beside me, dressed in boxers. Why did he *strip*? "Am I sure about . . . what?" I squeak, my low body temperature correcting itself comedically quickly.

"That we can share your bed." He looks strangely earnest. I'm used to Cameron wearing a cocky grin and winking more than he blinks. His greenish-blue eyes glimmer like water under the golden aura of my bedside lamp, and his highlighted hair is appropriately stirred from beach wind.

I'm so busy staring that I forget he asked a question until he raises an unruly eyebrow and says, "I know I'm attractive, but I'm standing in my undies and getting cold and perky, so can I squeeze in or not?"

"Why are you in your underwear?" I choke out.

"Your clothes didn't fit me and my pants are wet. Remember?"

Well, it's not like I haven't seen him in a more compromising state (that being when he was in practically translucent underwear after being shoved in Ravi's inflatable pool), so I say, "Okay."

Cameron crawls over me to slip into the opposite side of the bed, his corded football muscles shifting here there and everywhere. He splays out on his back beneath the comforter, the heat of his body a mere foot from mine. I only have a full-size mattress, which could fit two lanky people without issue, but it's different having a bulky guy with a broad wingspan beside me.

I watch the ceiling swim, keeping my eyes anchored on a little divot to keep from getting dizzy. Then my phone buzzes, and I reach out, too tempted not to look.

"You like photography?" Cameron asks.

My hand pauses midair. I tilt my head sideways in confusion.

"You have a fancy camera," he points out. "And a guitar. And a paint set. Did you make these pictures on your walls? How can you say you're boring when you can do shit like that?"

He sounds so sincere that I burst into giggles. I squirm onto my side so I can peer at him through the dark. "Those pictures were given to me by artists since I watch the gallery for them sometimes. I'm not talented enough to make my own pictures."

"What's the canvas and paint supplies for?" he asks.

"They're dried out. Haven't used them in a while."

"Why?"

I'm not sure why he's pushing so hard. Does he feel that awkward lying in silence? "I'm not very good," I say with a shrug. "I don't have an eye for it. Same goes for the camera. None of my pictures are worth taking. The guitar is . . ." I clear my throat, wishing my lungs would open so I wouldn't feel like I'm gasping for air. "I thought it would be fun, but I'm useless with it."

"That picture you started painting looks good, though." Cameron furrows his brows. "The silhouette of a tree against the sunset. Why stop halfway through?"

The compliment burns my cheekbones. I almost want to turn and assess it—is it better than I remember? "The branches were too thick and the colors didn't blend," I say mechanically. "Someone pointed out that the lines were uneven because my hands are too shaky. Because of all the coffee. Which also applies to photography and guitar."

That should be explanation enough, but he stares like I've only further bewildered him. "I'm not an artsy guy, but I didn't notice uneven lines," he says. "Besides, isn't the point of hobbies to have fun?"

"It's not fun when you realize how bad you are," I mumble.

"Well, if you want to get good at something, you should put your entire ass into practicing or you'll be disappointed," he snaps. "It's like working out. You won't be ripped after the first set of curls—why are you laughing? I'm being so serious."

I'm laughing hard enough that my stomach is cramping. I clutch my abdomen with one palm and shield my face with the other. "I know you're serious, and that's the tragedy of it all," I choke out.

"You're drunk. Go to sleep."

"Yes. And no."

He wrenches his pillow from beneath his head and thwacks me. "All I'm saying is that your painting looks great and you should finish it, but also if you don't like the picture but still enjoy painting then you should practice until it looks the way you want."

The words tumble out of his mouth in a disorienting rush that makes me feel like my head is spinning. Somehow, I manage to decipher them, and my heart warms. "You really think it looks okay?" I whisper.

"Yeah. Call me whatever, but I'm not a liar." He clears his throat. "I used to spend half my free time painting rocks when I was a kid, and I can promise you none of them look nearly as good as the picture you started. You have talent."

He tries to say this indifferently, but there's a level of strain behind his words that makes me feel like he either had to choke them out, or he unsuccessfully tried to hold them back. "Painting rocks?" I ask with a tiny smile.

He shrugs. Apparently not willing to elaborate.

"What did you paint on them?" I press anyway, because I want to know more about such a strangely cute fact.

"Forget you heard that."

"Impossible. It's permanently tattooed to my brain now. 'Big beef-brained jock Cameron Morelli likes to paint rocks.'"

"Used to!" he croaks defensively.

I think, if he was my boyfriend, I would probably try to kiss the mortification off his face. "Please tell me you painted eyes and a mustache on one of them," I plead.

He opens his mouth to yell at me. Then snaps it shut.

"Oh my God, you *did*," I breathe, and I can't stop myself from laughing again, tossing my hands up over my face. "Do you still have it? Please, can I buy it from you? I promise I'll put it on my nightstand so I can cherish it every day."

"I'd rather swallow it."

"Cameron Morelli, you cruel, selfish tyrant."

Cameron grimaces at me. "You're more annoying when you're drunk," he snaps.

"What? No, no, you're just being funnier than usual," I tell him, smiling wider behind my hands. "Sometimes it's fun to poke you like a water balloon and watch you dance."

I'm probably being insufferable, confirmed when he literally starts squirming with aggravation beside me, like he's resisting the urge to push me off the bed. "I genuinely can't believe I have to lie here and accept your verbal violence," he mutters.

"Find a way to shut me up," I suggest.

Cameron gives me such a suspicious look that I dissolve into laughter again. This only worsens when he flatly says, "Give me your wet sock. I want to see how far back into your mouth I can shove it."

I gasp, trying to sound offended, but follow this up with another uncontainable grin. "Cameron Morelli, how vulgar of you."

"Can you stop saying my full name? It's creeping me the fuck out," he snaps, and it revs up my fit of laughter once again. As I struggle to breathe, I can't help but notice that he's shifted onto his side toward me, his head braced in his propped palm, and he's staring at the hands concealing my mouth. Like he's trying to see through them.

"Oh, Cameron Morelli," I say wistfully, to which he spits a cuss at me. "I think you're not the big, goofy jock you say you are."

He huffs in protest. "What would you call me, then, if not a sexy jock with a great ass?"

"I've never called you that," I remind him. "Not once."

"You've probably thought it, though."

Which is beside the point. "You surprise me," I admit, snuggling deeper into the bed, the tremors of uncontrollable laughter finally fading away. Though, I still can't seem to get warm after my kiss with the lake. "You open your mouth and I think you're going to talk about how many people you've dicked, but then you say something thoughtful. Or I think you'll make our study location at some arena, but you take me somewhere with vegetarian options you've already tested."

Cameron scoffs like I insulted him. "It's normal behavior."

"Going out of your way for someone else is thoughtful. Taking me to Burger King is thoughtful. Spending the night with me is thoughtful." My voice fractures over the last sentence, and I realize my eyes are stinging. Oh no. I'm not going to cry again, am I?

Cameron's expression softens like warming chocolate. "Hey, water boy."

"Mm?"

"Who hurt you?"

I stare at him. He stares back, perfectly nonchalant.

"Why would you ask something like that?" I mutter, twisting onto my back to return my gaze to the ceiling. Does he think we're suddenly best friends because we've spent a few hours together? Does he not realize how invasive he sounds?

"You've been wild tonight," he says, unfazed by my annoyance. He's still propped up on his elbow, facing me, waiting for me to look at him. It won't happen. "I don't think you're acting like yourself."

I squirm so my back is to him, glaring at the darkened canvases nailed to the wall. "And you'd know all about that, wouldn't you?" I ask coldly.

He doesn't answer for a while. I've probably irritated him with that comment. But I still feel him eyeing me, like he's hoping I'll blurt a tragic backstory to him in my drunkenness. "Look, don't say anything you're uncomfortable with," he says, reading my mind, "but it seems like you could use a talk. I'm here, so I thought I'd offer myself up."

There he goes again, this big annoying quarterback, saying coherent sentences that aren't about how amazing he is. I'm trying to stay bothered, but he's being patient, and that's not something I'm used to.

What would I even tell him? I doubt he wants to sit through alcohol-induced rambling about a person he's never met. Yet I still feel I owe him an explanation, since I ruined his Friday night by becoming a sloppy mess at the party. He took care of me. And he also shared a part of himself with me the other day during our workout session. So maybe if I just tell him a little tiny bit of the whole truth . . .

"Oh," Cameron says. "Your chain broke."

My elevated heart rate comes to a grating stop. I flip over.

"Here." He plucks something off the bed, dangling it so I can see the damage. "The clasp must've caught on your pillow."

I try focusing on the necklace, but my vision blurs in and out, and my airway is sealed.

"Put it on your table so the pendant doesn't get lost," he continues, coaxing it closer.

I can't move. I feel like my joints have been screwed into the bed, fastening me in place. It's broken. I broke it. On the first night. How did I do something so fucking ridiculous? I moan and whine about how he doesn't treat me well, and when he actually gives me a thoughtful gift, I break it? I'm pathetic, worthless *trash*. It's just like me to fuck everything up the moment things start to go right.

"I have to fix it," I breathe, grabbing the necklace. Maybe I can find a DIY video and pull out a hot glue gun. Maybe I can ship another chain here. Though, it's probably real silver—I can't afford to replace it. Would he notice if I got a fake chain? At least I didn't lose the aquamarine—

"What's wrong?" Cameron demands.

I don't realize until I swivel toward him from my upright position that I'm shaking violently, tears combing down my face and melting into my flannel top. "I have to fix it," I sob, though my fingers can barely hold fast to the jewelry. "I have to fix it before he notices or I won't know what to do or say especially when it's my fault and it's *always* my fault, so—"

My voice is choked away when Cameron suddenly slings his arms around me, one hand tugging my head to his shoulder. "Breathe, Mason," he pleads. "Holy shit, *breathe*. I've got you, okay? You're fine."

I hear myself hyperventilating. This paired with the warmth of Cameron's body brings me drifting back to my senses. I'm clutching him, stubbed fingers digging into the smooth skin of his spine, the aquamarine biting into my palm. I don't remember how I got myself in this position, but I'm sitting in his lap, legs wrapped unbearably tight around his waist.

"Hey," Cameron says, and he pokes my forehead, grinding his index finger into it. I manage to zero in on his startled-yet-earnest cerulean eyes, barely comprehending that his face is only inches away. "We'll fix it tomorrow before we study, okay? It's late and you're tired and drunk. So just . . ."

His finger drifts down, scraping the tip of my nose, the center of my lips, the curve of my chin, the hollow of my throat, before resting lightly against my chest.

". . . breathe."

I give a pitifully shaky exhale. As my breath swirls away, so too does whatever strength I've been clinging to. I slump against him, legs slackening. I had him in a death hold. "Sorry," I whisper, my tears staining his bare shoulder. "I'm a mess . . . Why are you even here . . . ?"

"You asked me to stay." Cameron's palm grazes the small of my back, his pinkie finding a trace of skin not concealed by my flannel. His warm finger tickling my ice-cold waist nearly sends a shudder through me. "Besides, if it keeps you from contacting whoever's making you feel this way, that's all the more reason to stay."

My lower lip trembles. Why is he being so understanding? Shouldn't

Cameron still be partying on the beach, shoving football players around and flexing at anyone who looks his way? Why is he sitting here, holding me in his lap like I mean something?

"I like this side of you," I whisper. "Cameron Morelli."

I can feel his veins tighten under his skin. He doesn't respond.

"Would you . . . ?" I swallow with unease, curling tighter around him, shoving my face back in his neck so I won't feel embarrassed for asking. "Would you kiss me now? I'm just . . . I could use a distraction, I guess."

"You're still drunk," he mutters.

"I know. I just. I guess I." I can't complete a sentence to save my life. I shouldn't be asking him for something like that. Isn't it horribly selfish, considering I rejected him so callously last week? Am I not basically taunting him by requesting that? But my head is full of bad thoughts right now, and I want them to slip away. I don't want to think about him tonight. The other him. Or the broken necklace. Or how he'll react if he finds out.

Cameron's index finger, which has been lingering torturously near the skin of my waist, suddenly rises under my shirt, scraping a slow, careful line up the indent of my spine. Pleasant tingles scurry across the nape of my neck.

"What shape?" he mumbles.

I blink blearily, melting further into his chest. "Huh?"

"I'm drawing a shape."

He's tracing patterns on my back. He's mostly using the pad of his finger, but every so often, I can feel the curve of his nail tickling my skin. After a few moments, I whisper, "Square."

"Right." He starts to stroke another shape into my back. The feeling is featherlight, but with enough pressure to send goose bumps prickling across my upper arms.

"Triangle," I guess.

"Mm-hmm." He keeps going, leaning his head sideways against mine, which is still cozy in the scoop between his neck and shoulder. Unwillingly, I can feel consciousness sliding away from me, quiet darkness seeping into my busy thoughts.

I feel him trace one more shape into my skin before I fall completely under. I'm too far gone to say it.

It's a heart.

JOURNAL OF MASON GRAY

IF YOU AREN'T MASON GRAY PUT THIS DOWN AND WALK AWAY, BUB!!!!

Journal #1—May 4

I'm not good at journals but I want to remember this moment forever so I went out and got one just for this! The love of my life asked me out today. YES MY BIGGEST CRUSH EVER LIKE HELLO??

He was acting weird all day, kissing my fingers at the mall, hugging me longer than normal. we got back to his car and he said he can't stop feeling butterflies around me (AHHHHHH!!!!) and that he wishes more people my age could be this mature. That's probably why I'm not good at making friends in school. I'm too mature for them I think.

Then he asked if he could kiss me (AHHHHH???) and pecked my cheek. I thought I was going to explode, my heart was pounding so much!

But he says I should grow up more before we tell anyone. That's fine. He'll be eighteen soon so people will probably think our relationship is weird. But if they just get to know me, they'd see I'm not like other kids and it would make more sense.

More soon!!!!!! In case it wasn't obvious: AHHHHHHHHHH!!!!!

CHAPTER FOURTEEN
CAM

Mason was drunk when he said it, so I won't let his words carry too much weight.

My back is getting sore from sitting upright on the middle of the bed, supporting us both. He's leaned fully against me, arms linked around my neck, his knees curled in around my hips. His breathing is slow, gentle, and warm against the crook of my neck. I know he's asleep, but I can't stop my fingers from wandering across the smooth plain of his back, trying to press warmth into every fragment of his frigid skin.

I've never seen Mason cry before. Or show any emotion that intense. I wish sadness wasn't the first one I got to see at full force.

Slowly, I lower myself until I'm sprawled on my back, Mason lying completely on top of me. His head rises and falls gently with my every breath, the strands of his obsidian-black hair fluttering with my exhales.

I probably shouldn't, but I can't help it. I smooth my hand slowly through his locks. They're as soft as I've imagined. Thick. Shiny. The perfect length and texture to twirl one's fingers through. My stubbed nails graze his scalp, and I can feel little bumps rise along the back of his neck, where my pinkie is lingering.

I hate that I like this feeling. His reaction to my touch. When I brush my fingers down his nape, he makes a quiet, pleasant noise against my shoulder, which warms my face.

I should stop treating him like he's my boyfriend and not just a tutor who shot me down.

Then I notice his hand curled up into a light fist against my chest, soft knuckles pressed to my skin. Again, I know better than to fiddle around with him like he's some kind of doll, but my curiosity outweighs my reasoning. I smooth my hand over his, unfurling his fingers until they're spread out. I press our palms together.

His is smaller.

There's a warm tingling that stirs in my stomach, which puzzles me. I knew this. Mason is several inches shorter than me and nowhere near as padded with weight and muscle. It's no surprise that my hands are bigger. But seeing them side by side is giving me this unrecognizable rush of emotion that feels almost carnal. Suddenly, I want to hide him. I want to wrap myself around him and make sure nobody looks at him the wrong way again.

The sensation is cringe-inducing. Really? One week, and that's all it takes for me to suddenly care about some snarky water boy who verbally kicked my ass when I tried to ask him out? The hell is wrong with me?

I draw his sheets and comforter around us, remaining on my back, allowing him to lie sprawled over me because he looks cozy and I know he's had a long night.

I like this side of you, Cameron Morelli.

I give him the kiss he was waiting for, pressing it lightly to the top of his head before I fall asleep as well, my arm around his waist and my hand in his hair.

When I open my eyes, there's a gaping emptiness beside me, the sheets rumpled and the pillow cold. A halo of light leaks in around Mason's bedroom shades, telling me it's probably well into the morning.

I crawl out of his bed and stuff my shirt from yesterday over my head, then hike my frigid, damp pants over my waist and creak the bedroom door open. Down the hall, I see Mason at the kitchen table, head bowed over a plate of buttered toast.

There's someone with him. The man I spotted smoking a cigarette on his porch, with hooded eyes and sallow skin, his dark hair hanging like a curtain over his forehead. He's reading a real, actual newspaper, like he's from the 1800s.

The air is stiff. I can feel it from all the way over here. Maybe I should interrupt it, but Mason suddenly mumbles, "You said you wouldn't let him in."

The man's jaded gaze flicks up to Mason. Then down to his paper. "You know how your mother gets," he says monotonously. "I can't do much when she's made up her mind. And she's not wrong. That boy can provide for you."

"You hate him."

"But he can get you out of this house," Mr. Gray says flatly. "He'll provide for you. He'll stay by your side. He'll make sure you're always fed and warm and comfortable. He'll give you anything you need. Right?"

I wonder who they're talking about. Is this the same person who gifted Mason that necklace? Who he threatened to contact if I didn't stay? Regardless, I shouldn't be eavesdropping, so I shimmy into the kitchen.

Mason's head pops up when he hears me, and I swear his eyes actually brighten.

"Toast," I say, nodding to his plate. "Good work."

He smirks at my attempt to compliment his sustenance. "Dad, this is Cameron," he says, gesturing at me. "He's the guy I'm tutoring."

Mr. Gray peers over his glasses to examine me. Before I can

extend a hand in greeting, he grunts an acknowledgment and returns to reading. He looks like he's half-conscious.

Mason rolls his eyes—maybe this is typical behavior—then points at his fridge. "Take what you want for breakfast. I made extra coffee in case you're tempted."

"You'll never make me a coffee drinker," I warn, wandering farther into the kitchen to take stock of his items. His fridge is painfully empty compared to the leftovers and unnecessary impulse purchases that stuff mine.

"Your first time was rough because you torched your mouth," he explains. "Maybe you should change flavors from sweet to nutty."

"The taste of nuts is the last thing I want in my mouth in the morning."

Mason laughs so suddenly that he nearly forgets to cover his face. His father seems momentarily distracted by this, looking over at Mason with bewilderment, like he's never heard his son laugh before. The man peeks over at me, I guess to get a better look.

I opt for a freezer-burned bagel and watery cream cheese. No wonder Mason rarely makes food for himself.

He's wearing the aquamarine necklace. I notice a pair of snipe nose pliers on the kitchen table and the broken clasp beside it. He must've taken one from another necklace or something. I wonder how early he left my arms this morning to fix it. There's a tremor in his hands, and his skin is pasty, the circles under his eyes more violet than usual. Lingering signs of a hangover, probably.

"Where are we studying today?" Mason asks as I stand in the corner of the kitchen, mowing down my bagel, out of reach from their strange energy.

"What about your gallery?" I ask. "Do they have anywhere we could sit?"

Mason's eyes widen, and suddenly, he's radiating so much sunshine that it singes my corneas. "You want to go?" he asks enthusiastically, looking ready to vibrate out of his seat. "Really? Actually?"

I can't help but smirk at such genuine delight. "Why not?" I say, shrugging. After last night, I'm not sure that recommending some ridiculous sporty place more befitting of Cam Morelli's personality is going to fool him.

Down the hall, a bedroom door opens. Mason's expression immediately deflates, then twists with irritation. "Let's go," he says, shooting to his feet.

"You haven't finished your toast—"

"I'll eat it on the way." He strides to the door in such rapid earnestness, it's clear he doesn't want to see his mother. Which is so wild to me as a certified mommy lover. He hikes his backpack up and gestures at me, his plate of toast in hand. "Let's go."

I don't think now's the time to question him. So I merely head after him and say, "Nice to meet you, Mr. Gray."

His father eyes me again. His lips part like he's about to say something.

Mason pulls me from the house before he gets a chance.

"I've never seen our son so eager to study," Dad says when I rush down the hall to scoop my backpack up. My parents are being aggressively average by watching separate shows on their respective laptops with their headphones on.

"How was the party, bun?" Mom asks. I pause on my way out to stoop over and let her kiss my cheek. I repeat this with Dad, because I guess I shouldn't show favoritism. "Has that water boy fallen for your charms and sensational personality yet?"

I can't help but grin at her insistence on calling Mason "that water boy" as her personal way of holding a grudge. "I'm sure he regrets rejecting me," I say with a dismissive flutter of my hand. "I'm a standout guy."

"Mm," Dad says, fitting his headphones over his ears. "Better start moving if you don't want to warm the bench with your ass again for the next game."

And he wonders why I prefer to hang out with his wife. "Have fun with whatever this is," I say, gesturing to their figures on the love seat, and then I'm rejoining Mason in my car.

"Were your parents upset that you didn't come home last night?" he asks, tucked up in a familiar ball formation. I try not to think about the way his hair felt under my palm, or how cool his skin was under my fingers. How his hand looked pressed to mine. The way I wanted to wrap them both fully in my own.

"Extremely." I give a solemn, wistful sigh. "They were waiting at the door so they could disown me. So you're indebted to me for the rest of your life."

Mason nods, expression surprisingly neutral. "And what does Your Majesty require of this humble, filthy peasant?"

The fact that he's letting me come up with something without needing proof makes me feel like a dick. "I'll just pardon you," I tell him. "Because I'm nice."

Suddenly, he leans over the middle compartment and presses his lips to my cheekbone. "That should suffice, yes?" he asks. "My liege?"

Oh. I think I'm royally fucked when it comes to Mason Gray. I'm not even mad that he's clearly mocking me, because his tiny grin makes my heart flutter. Why am I suddenly so whipped for this annoying-ass water boy?

Then we pull up to the gallery, and I get it. Mason is the sunshine incarnate. It's like every shadowy corner and crevice looming within his body disintegrates, overtaken by an explosive ray of light that further wrecks my poor, healing corneas. He's not even smiling, but the world encompassing us suddenly feels like a bright, warm place.

Because Mason is happy. Genuinely.

The building is weathered down but plaited with windows that provide a scenic view of the lake from a section filled with rounded tables and cushioned chairs. Exhibits scatter the shop, providing a winding pathway to the register that allows one to see every station, from photography to abstract to watercolor and so on.

Mason looks like a kid in a candy shop as he yanks me around by the wrist, showing me his favorite works and artists, his dark eyes ablaze. "It's beautiful, isn't it?" he says at one point, his expression painfully bright.

He's different here. Unrestrained. "Yeah," I say, though I've already forgotten the question and what painting he's referring to. Everyone inside recognizes Mason, greeting him with familiar smiles, and he's so eager to see them that he forgets to cover his own.

I have the feeling this is the closest Mason has ever been to being himself. He loves art. Paintings. Photography. He knows the difference between acrylic, oil, watercolor. As we roam—or as I'm dragged—Mason's fingers twitch like he's resisting the urge to find a paintbrush. If I'm being honest . . .

Maybe it makes me itch to find one, too. And a couple rocks out back.

Then I remember that canvas collecting dust in his bedroom. And I wonder who battered his self-confidence so low, to the point where he gave up on something that brought him joy. I must be pretty distracted because I don't even realize I'm "studying" until Mason says, "Cameron? Did you forget you can flip the page again?"

I blink at my history book and find that fucker Winston Churchill glaring up at me. Mason's sitting in the chair adjacent to me, facing the sprawling windows overlooking Lake Evergreen. He's leaning his face into his palm, observing me with amusement, the warm golden glow of the sun reflected in his eyes.

"The more you pay attention, the sooner you can get back to doing bench presses or seducing our classmates or whatever else Cameron Morelli likes to get up to," he says.

"I have many hobbies," I snap. "I'm more than a meathead with a sizable schlong."

"Name a hobby that isn't working out, football, or flirting."

Shit. I can't tell him about all the hobbies I *used* to have, because that's sacrificing another chunk of my image to him. He's already punched through some of the bricks in my wall, and as a result, he's received several peeks into who I am. He's gotten closer to the truth than anyone else just by spending a handful of hours around me. A few years ago, if I'd responded to this question with the truth—*finding flowers for my mom, playing board games with my parents, painting rocks*—I would've gotten beaten up.

If I had known Mason back then, I don't think he would've minded.

My silence must amuse Mason because he laughs into the back of his palm, then says, "Just teasing," and returns to his work. I do the same, relieved I didn't have to come up with something, but three seconds later, he's reaching over and tapping the skin between my knuckles. His expression has darkened.

"I'm sorry, by the way," he mumbles. "For last night. Trying to force you to kiss me. Making you stay for me." He curls his knees into his chest, gaze wandering to the lake. There aren't any boats out, so the water is a cool, reflective plain shimmering under the sun.

"You should pick up painting again," I blurt.

Mason tips his head, hair tickling his shoulder. "Why do you care?"

"Because you should do things that make you happy, even if you're bad at them." Maybe I should keep my trap shut, but I want to drive the point home. "It's obvious you like artwork. And isn't 'good' subjective? So something you think looks terrible probably looks amazing to someone else." I clear my throat awkwardly and say, "I'd hang your half-painted picture on my wall."

Mason's brows are high enough to blend into his hairline. Suddenly, he smiles. Eyes crinkling, face warming, cheeks flushing. And I think I'd hang this image up on my wall too, or maybe my ceiling, so when I opened my eyes in the morning, I'd be greeted with sunlight even on the cloudiest days. "Thanks, Cameron," he says.

But then his hand rises to finger the chain around his neck. The one decorated with aquamarine to make it look like jewelry. The shadows lengthen along his face, dimming his features until he's a husk of himself. The vibrancy flickers out of his eyes until they become two yawning expanses of dull loneliness.

"Have you been paying attention to what you're reading?" His voice is back to what I'm used to. "You have a quiz on Tuesday. Are you prepared? You're three chapters behind. Remember, your football career is on the line."

The thought doesn't make it easier to pay attention. The reminder that my entire future is riding on a game a couple of weeks from now is anxiety-inducing enough that I can barely zero in on the pages. And now, I'm just thinking about him.

I want to tear that shackle off his neck, wherever it came from.

Journal #2—August 23

okay maybe not so soon haha. I'm bad at journals. My boyfriend's (AHHHHHH) parents had a birthday party for him in their huge house. There were so many people he had to talk to, I was starting to feel lonely. But then he pulled me into his bedroom and pushed me against

the wall (LIKE WHAT EXCUSE ME HELLO HI) and kissed
me! He even used tongue. It was slimy but maybe it
gets sexy when you don't have braces. He let me touch
his back under his shirt and I was basically melting out
of my face the whole week.

    Is it weird to fall in love with your babysitter??

Journal #3—March 28

I keep forgetting to write in this annoying thing. We
told my parents about our relationship after my
fourteenth birthday (HAPPY BELATED BDAY ME). Mom
seems happy, which is nice because she's always such a
huge fucking grump.

    Dad looked weird about it and kept asking questions
like how long we've been dating and if we've kissed. We
lied about some of it (THE SCANDAL), but it's for the
best. Dad doesn't get that we're the same age at heart.

    We went to the aquarium for Valentine's Day because
I love sharks. He let me go on and on and held my hand
the whole time. Though, he doesn't get why I like them
so much since we're not near the ocean. I told him I want
to be a marine biologist, but he says I should find
something in Elwood. Apparently marine biologists work
sixteen to twenty hours a day (THE AUDACITY) and always
get sent to the hospital because of violent sea life. Guess
that's the kind of stuff they don't tell you in the online
research. Fucking thanks for the heads-up, Google.

    He brought me back to his house because his parents
were gone and he kissed me so long I could barely breathe.
I told him I love him. Maybe he'll say it back soon!

CHAPTER FIFTEEN
MASON

Elwood High barely wins their next game. It's only because Darius has the linebackers on fire, keeping the other team from running the ball. In the first half of the game, Cameron paces the sidelines, dressed in his loose jersey, the rain slicking his highlighted hair against his forehead, his clenched pearly whites displaying his frustration.

Periodically, I walk over and tap my clipboard against his head. He looks ready to rip it from my palms like he did during the previous game. But then he makes eye contact with me, and the sight of my calm amusement takes him down a few notches.

The second half is a little different.

It's strange. It's almost as if Cameron has designated himself a certain amount of time to loudly bitch and moan, and when he feels he's been dramatic enough, he stops paying attention. Several times I catch him leaned back on the bench, dazedly watching the clouds swirl by overhead. Or staring into the stands on the opposite side of the field, like he's trying to see if he recognizes anyone. Once, I even catch him twirling and pulling up strands of fake grass beneath his feet, like a toddler who's forgotten where he is.

It would be easy to chalk up his behavior to him being an egotistical quarterback who only cares about his team when he's on the field. But the more he talks about football, the more I'm starting to feel like he doesn't really . . .

Care?

I don't think he dislikes football. In fact, he seems to have fun on the field, and it's clear he loves camaraderie. But I don't think he holds as much passion for the sport as he pretends to.

I wonder if he's noticed himself.

His grades *are* improving. Steadily. Mr. Barnett has been keeping an eye on his transcript. I'm happy for him, because it's clear he'd much rather be in the thick of the action. And . . . I don't know. It's only been a couple of weeks, but I think, maybe, I don't mind studying with him. In fact, it's possible I'll even miss it. When it's over.

I still can't wrap my head around the fact that he spent the night in bed with me because I got drunk and begged him to stay. I don't think it's because he's started to care about me or anything. It's probably more like he's a better person than I thought. It's the same reason the football guys all pretend like I'm a staple of the team. They're nice.

But then, why did I wake in the middle of the night to feel him stroking my hair, even though he knew I was asleep?

In the days since, the weather has begun to reflect that coziness I've been waiting for. After the game we barely squeak by, I remember I'm supposed to be "getting out there" this semester, so I tag along with the footballers to the haunted corn maze slash cider mill. The sky sags with frigid gray rain clouds, yet pops of color wash the town as the tree leaves shift from green to crimson, pumpkin orange, and canary yellow. I sit atop a grated picnic table beside the looming corn maze, watching the first-string players toss a football around.

As I wrap my plaid flannel jacket tighter, my gaze wanders to Cameron. He's in a riveting battle against bumblebees that have taken an interest in his hot cider.

"*Fuck!*" he roars, sprinting in circles. "Oh my God they're going to sting me, oh *God*—"

"Put the cup down, Morelli," Darius pleads. "They want your drink."

"Protect this with your life!" Cameron cries out, and suddenly, he's thrusting the cup of hot cider into my gloved hands. He flings himself into the muddy grass and rolls around like he's on fire. This is followed by three bees who hover around the rim of his glass eagerly. Sighing, I place it at the end of the grated table, and the bees follow it, leaving us behind to drown themselves.

Cameron's head pops up, and he glares at me. "I told you to protect it!"

"Get another cup."

"You going to pay, water boy?" He scrapes his way to his feet, dirtying his pants, expression twisted with bitterness. I think he's going to try to insult me, but Anup comes sprinting over and slides up onto the picnic table, bumping my thigh with his.

"Sweet baby Mason!" he cries out, throwing his lanky arm around my shoulders and squeezing—a sensation I'm familiar with at this point. I can't help but notice the way Cameron's face flashes with annoyance, to which Anup grins wider and slides even closer to me, so he's inches away. "Will you go into the haunted maze with us?"

He gestures to the obscenely tall corn, which people have been disappearing into and then emerging from, frazzled and shaken or laughing hysterically.

"I'm not going in there!" Cameron croaks. "I have a phobia of tall corn."

"I'll buy you a cinnamon donut."

"Okay."

I snort at Cameron's predictability. Anup basically drags me off the table to join Jody and Ravi, who are waiting by the sprawling maze. I'm not sure why he's bringing me—probably because I've been by myself, and he wants me to feel included.

"Oh, thank God." Ravi sprawls a hand over his chest and sighs with relief. "Mason said yes. I won't die now."

"I didn't say anything," I admit, though Anup nudges me toward the group anyway.

Moments later, we're disappearing into the looming corn, and the boys are steering us around corners with no sense of direction or deliberation. Jody gets jump scared by a stationary scarecrow. The sound of a revving chain saw causes everyone but me to scream, and I find all of them clutching me at different points for . . . emotional support, I guess. As much as I love fall and Halloween, I've never been particularly affected by anything horror related.

A few minutes in, though, they decide they don't need me after all, because Anup turns to me and says, "You and Cam should go that way."

He points to a branch in the pathway we're approaching.

"What?" Cameron squawks, his eyes flitting around with terror. He's shivering like a wet dog, and I've lost count of the number of times he's snatched the edge of my jacket. "Why? The bigger the group, the less likely we die, right?"

"Yes," Anup says, "but consider this."

They all sprint away, laughing at the top of their lungs.

"You *fucks!*" Cameron shouts, and he starts to take off after them— until he remembers that I'm standing there. Reluctant to abandon me, he skids to a stop, sighs, and returns to my side with a scowl. "I hate them."

"Do you?" I ask with a skeptical smile.

He gives me a cutting glare, then starts down the other pathway. This lasts three seconds before he remembers where he is, and he hunches in on himself, eyes darting across the dim trail with anticipation. "It's scary now that there's only two of us," he chokes out.

I widen my eyes, offended. "You don't trust me to protect you?"

"I don't even trust myself," he snaps. "And I have abs."

We turn a corner, and a person dressed as a spider lurches out, causing me to wince and Cameron to shriek at the top of his lungs, voice cannonballing through the evening. Despite his howling scream and terror, he lunges in front of me and sprawls his arms out. Protecting me.

"Dude, relax, it's a costume," the spider says, shoving his hands over his ears. "I'm not going to kill you."

"*Water boy, run; I'll hold him off!*" Cameron roars, but I'm too busy hunching over with laughter. The spider sighs and wanders off to find someone more suitable to scare.

"Y-you . . ." I can't finish my sentence—at that point, I'm curled up on the ground, laughing so hard I can barely breathe.

"What are you doing?" Cameron demands, his cheeks red with humiliation or fear, I'm not sure which. He wraps a hand around my elbow and hoists me into the air like I weigh the amount of a toddler. His casual strength is attractive enough that it snaps me out of my laughter.

"Incredible," I choke out, smearing tears from my eyes. "I've never heard anyone scream like that before—"

"Stop," Cameron grumbles. He reaches out suddenly, and it's startling enough that I reel backward, heart plunging into my stomach. His palm hesitates twelve inches from me and slowly retreats. "Your hand. Stop hiding your smile."

"Oh." I clear my throat, feeling sufficiently awkward as I start walking off. "Well, let's find the exit."

The goose bumps are poking prominently out of my skin, and I realize that I'm cold despite the flannel jacket. I guess Cameron has this natural warmth that wards it all away, until you step too far out of his sphere.

Quickened footsteps approach behind me, and then two flaps of a jacket suddenly ensnare me, pulling me to a stop on the muddy pathway. I look down in puzzlement to find that Cameron has trapped me within the confines of his varsity jacket.

"Why?" he asks.

I can feel his firm, warm midsection pressed against my back—the rise and fall of his broad chest, the steady beat of his heart, which is maybe bigger than I thought it was. I try stepping out of his grip, but he tightens his hold around me, keeping the flaps of his jacket snug around my front. "Why what?" I ask with a sigh.

I feel a weight press into my beanie—he's resting his chin against my head. "You can't leave until you tell me why you cover your smile."

He means it, but I don't feel in danger. Maybe I'm even cozy. But if he realizes, he'll get smug, and we can't have that while I'm this vulnerable. "My smile is misleading," I say, staring vacantly at the wall of corn carving a path before us. "I cover it so people don't get the wrong idea."

I figure he's about to burst into laughter, but his voice comes in a dark mutter, and his frosty words scrape my ear. "I don't understand."

"You don't have to." It's none of his business. But when I try prying out of his grip again, he spins me at the waist, so I'm chest to chest with him, his warm breath unfurling against my forehead. I try looking past his shoulder, but he bumps my chin up with his index knuckle, directing my gaze to his stern one.

"Explain."

"Why should I?" I ask irritably. Our proximity is so distracting I can barely piece together a coherent thought. If he wants to banter with me, I'll be useless. His lips, sleek and pink, are enticingly close.

All it would take to kiss this annoying jock would be to rise to my tiptoes.

"You're my prisoner until you tell me," he says casually.

I scoff, steering my eyes away from his once again. "I don't even get a trial?"

His arm tightens around my waist, and heat flourishes up my neck and into my ears. I snap my hands against his chest, trying to keep a few inches of distance between us. Even if his body heat is comfortable.

"Why do you think people get the wrong idea when you smile?" he asks.

I groan, my head slumping back with exasperation. Why does he care so much? "My smile is too suggestive," I mutter. "Too flirty. It's not that complicated."

Cameron's eyes are so wide they look ready to pop out of his head. "Where would you get that idea? Your mom?"

"Of course not," I growl, and I shove him, squirming in his grip. Finally, his arms drop, freeing me. "Let it go. Now let's find the exit."

Cameron's brows are pinched and his face is wrinkled with displeasure. "Whoever said that about your smile is wrong," he says. "You've got a really nice, warm smile. It lights up your whole miserable face. So stop hiding it."

He says this so casually, like he doesn't know how heavy his words are. How deeply they dig. Snippets of conversations from long ago tickle my ears, always lingering in times of self-doubt.

Honestly, Mason, can I even trust you?

How can you lead someone on like that right in front of me?

Maybe you're too young to realize what that look says to someone.

There's a football-sized lump swelling in my throat. "Noted," I whisper. "Let's go."

Cameron remains stubbornly rooted for another few seconds. But he concedes, following after me, then inching in front of me, like he's willing to take the brunt of whatever's going to lunge out despite clearly being more scared than me.

"I don't know how this stuff doesn't get to you," he chokes out, still reeling half a minute after someone revs another chain saw nearby.

"It's not that scary," I mumble. The tall corn, people jumping out, cliché sounds of horror movies played on echoing speakers throughout the maze. None of it is comparable.

The moment Cameron suddenly reached for me flickers through my mind. Followed by the barest trace of a memory I've been shaving away. I've forgotten most of it, or what led up to it, because nothing matters but the fact that my own mistake is what caused it. The first time it happened. And all the times after that.

I'm good at unintentionally riling him up. Eventually, I learned what the "triggers" were for this rare side of him, and that I held the key to unlocking them all. My smile was the biggest one.

So if I hide it where nobody but him can see, I can throw that key away.

My smile belongs to him. And that's okay. He can have it if it means he'll stay happy.

Why wouldn't I want my fiancé to stay happy?

Journal #4—July 14

We got into a fight. We were paying our bill and I was talking to the server. When we got to the car, he asked me if I go around flirting with everyone like that. I'm like??? EXCUSE ME. He said it was obvious I liked her because of how I was smiling. I told him I was just being polite, but he said this isn't the first time it's happened? WHAT.

I don't understand so I don't know how to make it better. He won't respond to my texts. Guess I need to figure something out. He doesn't ask for much, so I'll try to make him happy. I don't want to be ungrateful or immature since he's done so much for me.

We spent yesterday at his place. Mom loves going over there and talking about what she'd change if she had money. She comes from a poor family so it's her dream to make it big.

Dad still gets this weird look on his face when he sees us together. He muttered something about the age of consent the other day. But that doesn't even matter if your boyfriend won't let you touch him anywhere that matters, right? Like, come on. I have BEGGED this man to fuck me and he won't. He's a gentleman.

I hope my parents can see how happy I am. He's always bringing me gifts and spending time with me. Saving me from their bullshit.

He likes when I say I love him. He says he's waiting for the right moment to say it back.

Journal #5—April 28

Fuck me. We got drunk when my parents were out. I remember most of the night but apparently he told me he loved me. Did I black out? He says it was when we were in bed but I swear I remember every moment until he fell asleep. He was kissing my neck for a long time. Is that when he said it?

He's upset. He's been waiting for the right moment to pop the L-word and when he does, his boyfriend ignores him and then FORGETS?? I'm a dick. I'll make it up to him somehow.

15 is close enough to 16, right?

EDIT!:

He didn't let me touch him but I still made it up to him.

CHAPTER SIXTEEN
CAM

"Try not to be annoying," I plead, eyes wandering between my parents as they clean up and prepare dinner.

"You'll find that I'm quite average, son," Dad says at the stovetop, flipping the vegetarian lemon chicken slabs sizzling in his massive pan.

"You look like the son of a Mafia boss."

"But I have the cuddly personality of a koala." He pops open the oven to peek at the cheesy scalloped potatoes. "Ask your mother. She was disappointed to discover I'm not the mysterious, dangerous bad boy I appeared to be."

Mom gives a wistful sigh from the living room, where she's fluffing couch pillows. "He ended up being perfectly levelheaded," she says solemnly. "Not a single toxic quality for me to fix."

If they're bantering like this before dinner, they're about to be insufferable. "Just don't show him baby pictures or start making out to make me uncomfortable," I snap.

"We'd never, Cammy." In the corner of my eye, I notice her tuck a giant binder under the couch. Predictable.

"What's got you so nervous, anyway?" Dad smirks as he hands me a collection of plates to set the table. "Could it be because this is the first time in years that you've invited someone over to dinner? Friend or *otherwise*?"

"Mason is coming to eat a balanced meal and then I'm showing him his workout regimen," I say shortly. "It's to pay him back for tutoring me. Not because I want to see him."

Then I remember that smile, and I realize I'm a dirty fucking liar. Christ, why am I so obsessed with that little asshole's teeth?

Except it's not just that, is it? I'm anticipating *all* of him. It's the dry wit, the calming atmosphere, the cutting jabs meant to insult me but mostly fluster me. It's his swooshing hair meant for tousling and cute hands meant for holding. It's those tiny moments where he feels comfortable enough to crack the ice fragments sealing him from head to toe, allowing me glimpses of someone much warmer, much happier.

I readjust the kitchen chairs for the fifth time. "You're sure that's fake meat?" I ask Dad.

"Ask me one more time, boy, and I'll tattoo my face on your ass cheek while you're sleeping," he growls, his annoyed eyes piercing through my face.

I scoff, turning to Mom and gesturing at him. "Not a single toxic quality, huh?"

She looks ready to console me for the verbal threat uttered by her husband, but then the doorbell rings, and she beelines for it. Who else could it be but the water boy, who's dressed in a knitted pumpkin-orange turtleneck and matching beanie, looking as cute and cuddly as always?

"Ah," Mom says. "This must be my son's failed conquest."

Oh. My fucking God.

Mason's pallid face colors, and his dark eyes flit over her shoulder to see me, slack-jawed and ready to careen out of the nearby window. "I . . . Hello," Mason says, extending a tense hand. "Nice to meet you, Mrs. Morelli."

Mom fans a palm over her heart, finding this endearing, apparently. "What a sweet, polite boy. Much sweeter and politer than mine. I'm sure that's why you rejected him, hmm?"

So my parents are planning on making me the *miserable* type of miserable tonight. Got it. "Hi, we don't need to discuss that either now or at any point in the future for as long as we both shall live, so let's move along," I wheeze out, nudging my mother aside and snagging Mason's hand. I tug him over the front step leading into the house. I can't help but notice the way his fingers press light imprints into my skin.

"Thanks for inviting me to dinner," he says, eyes widening when my father rounds the corner—this looming wrestler of a man wearing a floral apron.

Dad reaches his beefy hand out in greeting. "It's an honor, Mason. I'm Nico," he says pleasantly. "Nice to put a face to the man, myth, and legend who can put my son in his place."

"I wouldn't say that," Mason says, laughing uneasily. "Cameron does what he wants. But nice to meet you, too."

This feels suspiciously like a "meet the parents" date scenario, which makes me uncomfortably hot around the collar, so I clear my throat and grumble, "It's a quick meal before a workout. Can we skip the meet and greet?"

Dad's lashes flutter with an intense eye roll. "Like I'm a peasant," he mutters, trailing into the kitchen to retrieve the food.

"We're trying this plant-based chicken he found at the store yesterday," I tell Mason, seating him at the kitchen table. "Hope that's okay?"

Mason offers a little closed-lipped smile, toying with the gemstone on his necklace. "Thanks for being so thoughtful," he says lightly.

"You brought workout clothes, right?"

"No. I thought it would be a fun extra challenge to try exercising in jeans," he says, staring unblinkingly at me. I stare back, deciphering whether he's being a sarcastic little shit or not. He must notice my brain muscles straining, because he smirks and opens a plastic bag dangling from his arm, revealing a T-shirt and shorts.

Sarcastic little shit, then.

The meal goes as wretchedly as I expect. My parents ask Mason an assortment of embarrassing questions, from *Has Cammy been treating you well?* to *Are you sure you didn't reject him because you're dating someone?* to *Other than saving our son from his own incompetence, what do you do in your free time?* Mason takes everything in stride and doesn't seem to mind being grilled. I wonder when someone last asked him about himself.

"Cameron is behaving well," he says, smiling in that fake sweet way, like he's about to expose me for something dreadful. "I'm not dating anyone. And I like drinking coffee and working at the gallery."

"He also likes painting, guitar, and photography," I chip in.

Mom's blue-green eyes glitter. "Maybe we'll have you bring your guitar next time and play a song. None of us are musically inclined. Or artistically."

"I'm literally a tattoo artist," Dad says grumpily.

They're being annoying, but Mason laughs genuinely enough to cover it with his sweater sleeve. I guess it's not that easy to break a habit you've been doing for years. Evidenced by my mom, who occasionally glances around with apprehension, like she's afraid she left Pride paraphernalia out despite not having put anything on display since we moved.

When dinner is over and the dishes cleaned, Mason changes into his workout clothes and follows me into the basement. He glances up at the ceiling boards and smiles at the sound of my parents walking around and talking. "They're nice," he says softly.

"Meh," I grumble, folding open the paper I jotted his routine on.

"You feel like a family. It's sweet."

He sounds wistful. He's standing at a yoga mat, nudging the curled corner down with his foot. Something glints in my eye as he shifts around.

"You should take that off," I say.

Mason's hand reaches up, snagging hold of his necklace. "Take what off?"

It's strange, the way only his subconscious knows what I'm referring to. "The necklace," I clarify. "So it doesn't get caught on something and break again."

Mason's grip tightens around it. Reluctantly, he unclips the back with trembling fingers. "Is there somewhere safe I can put it?" he mumbles.

I retrieve a jewelry bowl from upstairs and set it on the counter behind the equipment. Mason drapes the necklace inside like it's a fragile newborn baby. "Ready?" I ask, positioning him on the yoga mat in front of mine. Mason's eyes haven't left the bowl. It's like he thinks the gemstone will leap out of the holder and plunge into the nearest vent. "Eyes here, water boy."

The nickname pulls his attention to me.

"Remember, bulking isn't a race. It requires patience."

"Okay," he whispers. "I trust you."

My heart squeals, which is probably a medical emergency, but I proceed like nothing is wrong.

We start with our stretches. He muscles through his discomfort as music echoes through the basement, his forehead gleaming from strain. He does better at sit-ups, his face coming closer to mine as I sit atop his feet, counting, trying not to wonder what he'd say if I leaned forward and bumped our lips together.

I don't know *why*. Why is he *different?* Is this . . .

Is this what attraction is supposed to feel like?

I've always liked looking at him. That's why I asked him out—if he said yes, staring at him unblinkingly wouldn't be (as) creepy. But after spending time with him, it's becoming more than the desire to look. I want to touch. To *feel*. I want to tug on his hair and smooth his palms out and trace the indent of his spine. I've never had that desire with my previous partners, and Mason isn't even my boyfriend.

It's half the reason people break up with me. The disinterest in physical intimacy. The other half being that I never let them get close enough to see the jostled bricks in my walls. It should've been the same with Mason, but somehow, he saw through the holes from as far back as he could've possibly been standing. All it took was a couple of hours of one-on-one interaction.

He's been chipping at them gently. He knows I have two sides, an exaggerated one and an authentic one, and a strange central line where the two blend together. He knows I'm a momma's boy and that I used to paint rocks and that I was bullied at my old school. And . . . I don't know. I think I've started to cut through his own fortified, looming steel walls. Centimeter by centimeter. Though, I'm still painfully in the dark.

All I have to go on is that damned necklace.

He's starting to get irritated with the stretching. I can tell because when we're doing a partner stretch, our legs spread into a V and our sneakers pressed flat against each other's, he pulls forcefully on my hands as if to punish me. But I'm used to exercises like this, so I merely follow his tug and stretch over my open legs, smiling knowingly.

"Trying to hurt me?" I ask skeptically.

"Hmm?" His gaze is detached and cold. "Cameron Morelli, why would I want to see you in pain? Could it be because you added a stretch to my regimen that literally forces me to spread my legs for you?"

I hack on my own saliva. "It wasn't intentional!" I choke out.

"Oh." He leans back, pulling my arms again, stretching me so far forward that I'm starting to feel the ache in my thighs.

"Wait, I'm serious, I didn't mean—*ack, water boy, mercy, please!*"

Mason heaves a sigh, straightening up and freeing me from the excessive stretch. But his eyes are glinting with amusement, and I realize he's not actually annoyed—he's just pretending to be so he can torture me.

Little. Shit.

"I have a new stretch," I say darkly, and his expression shifts at my tonal change. "This one works your abdomen."

"Crunches again?" he asks, sounding miserable.

"Worse." I fold my legs in so our feet are no longer pressed together, then yank on his hands, sliding him across the ground and into my lap. He barely has time to rasp out a confused noise before I'm jamming his fingers into his waist and rib cage, causing him to suddenly shriek and wriggle against my iron grip.

"*Wait!*" he cries out, laughter raking his body as I poke at every sensitive spot on his midsection. He's trying to wrench his arms free, but they're pinned firm between our chests, thanks to the arm I have wrapped unyieldingly tight around his back. *"Don't you dare, let go, I'll never forgive you, I'll tell your mom—"*

The rest of his words dissolve into uncontrollable laughter. The sight of his smile in full force, so close to me, his lashes sparkling with tears, his cheeks peachy pink, his forehead shimmering with warmth, is too much.

It's too much.

The hand I'm using to torment his waist slides up his abdomen, his chest, until it's latching around the back of his neck. His honey-brown eyes, glazed with delirium, sharpen the moment his forehead falls to mine. His hands, which have been pounding against my chest, fall still and unfurl. The tips of his fingers graze the skin above my collarbone. Cool. Centering.

We sit frozen for several seconds, an echo of the night I drove him home from the beach party, his legs curled around my waist, his weight positioned atop my thighs, his face invitingly close. His thin lips are pressed firmly together now, but the edges are curled upward, like he's still fending off his previous laughter. His breaths are tight, quick, and the sound makes my chest thump harder. Neither of us care that our foreheads are sticky and will probably peel apart like glue when he draws back.

The point is that he's not drawing back.

But he rejected me. Right? He only took the tutoring thing up to help the team and probably to have an excuse to get out of his house. If not for that, he would be avoiding me at every corner, because he's made it clear my personality isn't his type. So why . . . ?

Why is he watching my lips like that?

I probably shouldn't. I ghost them against the outer corner of his mouth anyway, my face moving in against my instincts. His head twitches, like he wants to meet them, like he wants to correct my course. He decides to keep still, though, and allows my lips to brush up against his skin, a mere inch away from fully kissing him. His lashes flutter shut—he's still not pulling back. His fingers, though, are tensing against my chest, like he's bracing for the moment he might want to shove.

My gut feeling is telling me to stay away from his mouth. So I drag my lips lower, catching his soft, pale chin instead, my hand still pressed flush to the back of his slender neck. The faintest fragrance of something woodsy and warm tickles my nose. Did he dab cologne on himself before he came? Just for dinner and working out?

I press a slow, careful kiss under the jut of his jaw. My left arm remains hooked around his waist—it fits perfectly against me. My right thumb works the divot behind his ear, and he might be sensitive there, because I can feel his heart pulsing faster, deeper.

"Just my face?"

He gasps the words out like he's been clinging to them.

I pause, my lips hovering at the arch of his neck. "What?" I whisper.

He shivers as my breath unfurls against his skin. "It's because of my face," he says, and suddenly, he's pushing, his fingers digging into my chest. "It's not because you like . . . It's not because I'm actually . . ."

I want so desperately to hold on to him, to make him clarify his thoughts, but I can't keep him hostage like this. So I pull my arms away, and he immediately scrambles out of my lap, stumbling to his feet.

"I should go," he says, gazing toward the staircase leading out of the basement.

The last several seconds have happened so fast I can barely keep up with them. I've messed something up, though, so I sputter out, "Sorry."

"Huh? No, it's fine. Uh." Mason's eyes flick around with unease before returning to the stairs. The sudden, weak tremor in his arms furthers my guilt. I want to apologize again for assuming his body language meant he was on board with what happened. I should've confirmed with him verbally before . . . yeah.

He's already lunging up the stairs to escape me.

I drive him home in silence. I'm not sure what to say. I screwed up. Badly.

When I return home and start wiping down the exercise equipment, the jewelry bowl shimmers in the corner of my eye.

He left his aquamarine necklace.

Journal #6—October 31

Happy Halloween. I was invited to a party today but meh, it's just a bunch of kids acting like dicks, and he doesn't like when I go out on my own. I'll probably stay home.

We got in another fight. I told him I went to a bonfire where there was alcohol and he said I shouldn't go to places like that, especially since I still can't remember him saying he loved me. It just shows I can't handle my liquor.

Besides, he thinks some kids would take advantage of me. He's always saying people love to stare at me nowadays, and it makes him feel protective. I appreciate him looking out for me. Though, I wish he'd stop throwing out my clothes. I caught him tossing some of my favorite leggings the other day because apparently they make me look more "tempting." I'm not sure what he means. My ass is flatter than paper.

He's struggling this semester at college. I think he's lonely.

I started learning how to play the guitar. Mom has an old one in the basement from when she tried playing in some garage indie band. I tried playing him a song when he came home last weekend but was so nervous I messed up several times. He made a good point that it's pretty late for me to learn a new instrument anyway. Maybe I'll get bored and go back one day.

It was kind of fun.

Journal #7—April 2

Oh. My. God. I. AM. ENGAGED.

The ring is so beautiful. I can't stop staring. He took me to the park for the most romantic picnic for my sixteenth birthday a couple weeks ago (it was cold as shit). Then we went back to his house and almost didn't make it to his bedroom, he was so excited. I did a ton of research and think I did okay? He kind of dodged the question.

I love him so much it's gross. Mom is excited. I've never seen her light up like that. Dad was weird about it but he'll get over it once I'm eighteen. It's not like we're jumping down the aisle tomorrow. First he has to graduate, then he'll buy a house.

Sometimes I spend weekends up at college with him. I can't wait until the day I get to wake up beside him and don't have to leave.

Nobody understands me like he does. He thinks it may be because I don't have an easy personality to work off. He said there's nothing wrong with that, though, since we balance each other out. As long as he's with me, I'm okay around others.

He doesn't mind my personality. Even if I'm unlikable or boring, he's there for me. Sometimes I wonder if I deserve someone like him. I'm so happy he chose me. He could have anyone he wants, but I'm the one he put the ring on? Wild.

We'll keep it a secret until I'm out of high school.

CHAPTER SEVENTEEN
MASON

Because you should do things that make you happy, even if you think you're bad at them.

I smirk at the watercolor picture I've been doodling, Cameron's earnest words humming in my ears. I think it looks okay. Or I'm too distracted thinking about him to notice the flaws. The kindness hidden in his words. The way his eyes sparkle like pools of tropical water tinged a pleasant green. The way the muscles flex in his shoulders, the way his hand sprawled against the back of my neck last night, so big but so gentle and careful.

I couldn't handle it. The way he was holding me was too sweet.

For a moment, I was convinced that he cared about me.

I realize I'm smiling widely and my hand is rising to cover it. I know I shouldn't. The gallery opened an hour ago, and it's a Sunday morning, so I'm alone. The painters like to leave their calm, unbusy mornings and evenings to me.

I love it here. The vast windows overlook the lake, and autumn-gray light floods the building, making the need for overhead fluorescents unnecessary. Plus, I get to study my favorite paintings and imagine where I'd make room for them in my house. Or in my college dorm room, if I go. Though, I'm not sure what I'd pursue—I'm a good student, but my aspirations . . . When I try to come up with something, my brain gets hazy and sluggish.

What do I want to do with my life? I've never thought about it because a future has always been promised to me. I never knew what it would look like, only that it involved us being together. Married. Moved in. And I'd be free to do what I wanted.

Within reason.

I massage my ring finger, loosening it before reclaiming the paintbrush. The picture isn't innovative. I haven't painted in months, so I'm just doing an exercise to rekindle the warmth in my frigid hands, depicting a sun sinking into ocean waves. Part of me hopes Cameron will see it. Maybe I'll bring it to our next study session.

Maybe he'll show me his old rock collection.

The door jingles. Immediately, I lurch off my seat behind the register and plaster a friendly smile on my face. "Good morn—"

It's him.

His ice-blue irises carve through my body and inject frost into my veins. My limbs lock at my sides as his glacial presence washes over me, plundering me of warmth.

"Mason!" His grin stretches the skin around his sharp, stubbled jawline. "Your mom said you'd be here."

He's wearing a wool trench coat atop a collared sweater and slacks, as though he's prepared for a formal event. The only thing he ever leaves in disarray are his fine, soft dark-brown curls I could never stop running my hands through.

"This place is so cute. Definitely your vibe," he says with a gentle laugh. "But are you here alone? That doesn't seem safe." His gaze wanders the establishment, hands nestled in his jacket pockets, eyes tinged with disapproval. "You're only seventeen. And small. Shouldn't someone help you watch the shop?"

I don't realize how tightly my hands are clenched until a dull ache pulses up my wrist. I'm holding my paintbrush so fiercely it's causing my knuckles to throb.

He's wandering closer, one step at a time, pretending the artwork is intriguing. My eyes flit to the swinging glass door—it's the only exit, and he's in the middle of my route to it. The left side of the cashier counter is cemented into the wall, so I have to loop around the right unless I vault over it.

He props himself on the edge of the counter farther from me, expression pleasantly chipper. "That's cute," he says, nodding to my picture.

I look down at it. The sun is too misshapen. I oversaturated the color of the waves.

"You're not going to talk?" His dark, kempt brows meet at the center of his forehead. "I thought you were going to start responding to my texts, but you still won't even do that. Why are you acting like we're strangers?"

His desolate tone spears through the cracked, frail defenses encircling my heart. Guilt leaks from my chest, pouring into the rest of my body.

"Have you at least thought about what I said?" he pleads. "Won't you consider my apology? I don't want everything to be thrown away because I made poor decisions during a bad time in my life. You used to be excited when you saw me."

His marble-white hand inches over the counter toward mine, still clenched painfully tight around the paintbrush.

"You told me you wished you could wear your ring in public," he whispers. "You told me your mom finally seemed happy about something. I know I've made mistakes, but I also know I meant something to you. And maybe I still do."

The more he talks, the further I fall into a daze, slackening my grip on my mental fortifications. His voice is so low and compelling. I used to joke that he could spend his life narrating books—that his voice could draw any reader to any genre. He's good at luring.

"The ring looked good on you," he says softly. "It made me feel incredible. Knowing you wanted to spend your life with me . . ."

"Or knowing you had me on a more permanent leash?" I mutter.

I don't know where the words come from or why they sound like that, varnished with an anger I'm incapable of feeling. They leave a scorching hot feeling in my lungs, like they were coated in bile.

"That's how you feel?" His voice quiets. Unlike my mom, whose voice rises with her anger, his does the opposite. I'd always considered it one of his green flags. "That I proposed to *trap* you? Don't be immature. You broke our engagement off without batting an eye."

The word "immature" clangs around in my head, sparking irritated heat. "You thought you could do whatever you wanted the moment you had me tied down," I snap. After all the things he said and did, simply because he thought he could get away with them since we were secretly engaged, since my mom supported us . . .

"Don't do this, Mason." Aggravation flashes across his irises. They're always so cold in contrast to the warm, inviting atmosphere he brings to everyone else around him. "You always assume the worst of me. I loved you in every way that I could. I drove all the way home from college just to get you out of your parents' house at night. I brought you gifts, took you on extravagant dates, listened to you rant. How can you think that way about me?"

He lists everything rapid-fire, like he's been waiting for the moment to remind me of the things he used to do for me. More poisonous guilt clouds through my body, because he's right. Why am I even arguing with him? He's always right. "Sorry," I whisper.

"We wouldn't have this many problems if you would just listen to me and think things through before acting on your emotions."

". . . Sorry."

"I know I haven't been the best version of myself around you, but you never gave me the space or time to grow. You cut me off when things got difficult."

". . . Sorry."

He massages his forehead with weariness, then swings his legs over the counter and joins me, scooping me into a gentle hug, slotting me into his arms. "I didn't come here to scold you," he whispers, his lengthy fingers dragging through my hair. He smells of warm, spiced cinnamon. He knows it's one of my favorite scents. His palm unfolds against the back of my neck, holding my head to his shoulder, much more frigid than the one that was there yesterday. "I'm not upset, I promise. So stop shaking, okay?"

". . . Sorry."

"I adore you. And part of you knows that you'll never stop loving me. I'm not giving up on you, Mason."

. . .

"Hear me out. Please. Is there anyone who will love you the way I do? I promised to protect you, support you. I know your soul like the back of my hand. Genuinely, is there someone else who could be there for you? Who could fall for you?"

. . .

"Girls want bigger men who can protect them, so being bisexual doesn't do you any favors. And guys—muscly guys, who are your type—always look for prey like you. You're small and defenseless. Your face is seductive. They'll try to mistreat you. But I won't let anyone hurt you."

. . .

"Even if there *was* someone out there with good intentions, would they be capable of falling for you? You told me I bring out your good qualities. Do you think other people can see them without me? Do you think they'll be patient enough to wait for you to leave your shell, like I was?"

. . .

"You're not wearing my necklace."

His sentence is a scythe that slashes through my lethargic stupor and sinks my heart, which has been treading water since he stepped through the door. Instinctively, my fingers fumble along my neckline, seeking the jewelry.

It's gone.

My stomach twists into nauseating knots. I try to keep the panic from showing, but he notes the shift in my expression, because his jawline tenses. "You lost it?" he asks.

"No." I'm barely audible. "I didn't . . ."

"Is it not a good enough apology gift? I had it custom-made for you." His hand slides slowly down my face to nestle against the curve of my neck. He doesn't sound angry, but he rarely does when he's upset. He's good at masking it, until he's not.

"It's at a friend's house," I say, though the air is so thin in my lungs I can barely push the words out. "I was working out with someone and—"

"Why do you look like that?" he asks, his thumb notching beneath my jawline. One of his brows is arched, almost accusingly. "I told you I've changed, so you don't need to act so dramatic, okay? I'm curious, that's all." His thumb works deeper, like he's trying to push the answer out of my throat. "Who were you working out with? You hate exercise."

"Just a friend." I'm still whispering. "He made me a regimen."

"Oh? Who's this friend? You must be close if he's making a specialized plan for you," he says, his thumb now trailing my jawbone. I hate the urge to lean into his touch. He's being gentle right now, and if I show him I appreciate it, maybe he'll stay like this.

"Some guy I'm tutoring from the football team," I mumble.

"A football player." He speaks with perfect neutrality, but a tense atmosphere is building around his shoulders. "I take it he's a bigger guy? Popular? Knows how to work out?"

"I guess." I don't know why that matters, but he tends to fixate on meaningless details.

Sure enough, my confirmation further displeases him, and his hand drops to dangle at his side. "I haven't even met him and I know he's taking advantage of you," he says with a frustrated shake of his head. "Honestly, Mason . . . why won't you let me protect you?"

"What do you mean?" I ask, voice sharpening. Just a bit. "Cameron isn't taking advantage of me. He's paying a favor back."

"Let me guess—his plan involves touching you?"

I want to protest, but the words are wedged in my throat. Last night comes flooding back in a surge of feelings. His lips on my jaw, his arm around my waist, his fingers on my nape.

"Mm." He takes my silence as confirmation and steps back, disappointed. I almost follow him, wanting to plead my case. But why should I? He's not my fiancé anymore, not even my boyfriend. So why do I feel guilty, like he caught me cheating?

The door chimes.

Suddenly, I remember where I am. The foggy bubble wrapped around us pops, and the world swims back into focus, allowing the daylight to flood back into my eyes. I take a shuddery breath of relief—one that he notices—and look over his shoulder.

It's Cameron.

CHAPTER EIGHTEEN
CAM

It's my third stop of the day, so precious water boy better be grateful that I'm so kind and considerate. But if he's not here, I'm torching the whole gallery and then myself. I'm tired of shipping my ass across Elwood just to return his necklace to him, especially considering I'm missing out on an unofficial practice Darius is currently running in his backyard. He hosts those occasionally to make sure our muscles stay warm—though, it's rare that more than five or six people actually show up. His dedication to the sport scares even me sometimes. I try not to think about the tingle of relief in the back of my neck at the fact that I have an excuse not to be there.

Is the length of this necklace-related journey my fault for not contacting Mason before setting out on my quest to see him, as my parents indicated when I texted them my frustrations?

No. It's his fault for being unpredictable and elusive.

First I visit his house and meet his mother. She's a short lady with apple-red cheeks and a surplus of hair that coils to her neckline. She answers the door with eager eyes, but when she sees me, the excitement dissolves from her features.

"Who are you?" she asks.

She doesn't look anything like her son. She seems about as thrilled to see me as Mason usually is, which is to say, not at all. "Hi. I'm Cam Morelli. Is Mason around? I need to return something to him."

She seems reluctant to divulge Mason's whereabouts. Eventually, she says, "Try Annie's Brews," then closes the door before I can utter a thanks.

The quaint coffee shop is lively on this sunny Sunday, overflowing with high schoolers or commuter college students. My eyes rove the vicinity, seeking a beanie or curled-up figure shaky from caffeine overdose. There's not a single Mason Gray in sight.

He must be at the gallery. Well, I'm here, so I grab him a cinnamon-twist latte with extra whipped cream. Knowing him, he's probably had five cups this morning. Knowing him, he's probably craving one more.

So then I'm on my merry way to the local gallery. When I pull up to the parking lot, there's a single car. Probably a guest, since Mason doesn't have a vehicle. Did he walk here this morning? Good for him, getting in his steps, but the roads are twisty and winding—it would be safer if I drove him so he doesn't get hit by some high schooler taking a corner too fast.

I clamber out of the car, sparks twirling in my stomach. It shouldn't make me this nervous, the whole "dropping something off that he forgot at my house" mission, but my body is reacting like I'm on my way to assassinate my first hit to prove my worth to my father. Or something.

I stride to the gallery door, pushing inside.

Mason's standing behind the cashier counter in fitted jeans and a turtleneck decorated with fall leaf patterns. He catches my eye, and I almost grin like a giddy fool.

Then I notice he's not alone.

My stride scrapes to a stop. There's a tall man behind the counter with Mason. His clean stubble lends maturity to his features, but I think he's in his early twenties. His skin is smooth, his face strong and squared, his arms thick enough that I can tell he either works out or plays a college sport. He looks like the kind of standard attractive person who'd appear on the front page of a men's clothing catalog.

The man shifts to see me. His eyes are cool and calm, a frosty blue, but he's wearing a giant, beaming smile that warms the air. Yet there's something disconcerting in his stance, lax as it is, and a prickly sensation squeezes my chest.

I think I've interrupted something.

"Mason," I call out, breaking through the ice gluing me to the carpet and pressing forward. It's a clear path to the cashier's desk, but my journey there is difficult. Every step makes me feel like my shins and calves are battling quicksand.

"Cameron," Mason says. His eyes are two cold, empty caverns, devoid of recognition or awareness or . . . anything. His fingers are curled with such visceral tightness that his knuckles are bone white. Normally I pride myself on reading people's moods, but the atmosphere around Mason is painfully dull and uncolored—it's like reading a corpse.

"I brought some things," I say, glancing awkwardly at the man beside him.

"This is Cameron? The football kid who's *working out* with you?" The man's grin widens, still bright and welcoming. So why is it suddenly so cold? The sparks in my stomach have been extinguished, and the air is so chilly I can almost see my breath furling out. I nearly extend a hand to him—he seems familiar with Mason—but keep my arms down. An invisible dome encircles them, and my gut says I shouldn't pass through.

"Hi," I say uneasily.

The man's eyes plunge through mine with unnerving intensity, like he's trying to tear into my skull. "I've distracted you enough, Mason. Please consider thinking over everything I've said."

He walks around the counter, boots clicking fancily against the tiles. The moment Mason is outside of his reach, I hear myself exhale.

Then there's a hand on my shoulder, so powerful that it nearly buckles my knees. His touch saps the color from my skin as he bends down a couple of inches to look directly into my eyes, his own flickering with measured resentment, that smile still arching into his face.

"Pleasure to meet you, Cameron," he says, softly enough that only I can hear him. His breath is as cold and minty as his eyes.

He straightens up, fingertips needling into my skin beneath my jacket, before wandering off. He pauses when he's a foot from the exit.

"Mason? One more thing."

Mason's staring at the countertop like he fell asleep.

"There's a banquet coming up to celebrate my graduation and promotion," the man says, straightening his jacket's lapels. "Your mother RSVP'd for the three of you. If not before, I look forward to seeing you then."

He walks out of the gallery, the bell chiming.

I want to vomit. Who *was* that? I feel like tendrils of invisible ice have snaked along the building walls, plunging this place into an arctic void. My palm trembles around the cup from Annie's Brews—I'm clenching it so hard the lid popped off. A trail of coffee has poured over my fingers, but I can hardly feel the burn under the lingering sear of frost.

"Why are you here?" Mason asks.

It takes me a moment to remember why I drove all over town this morning. I hobble closer despite the weakness in my legs and place the coffee near his hand. "Your mom said you were at Annie's," I say awkwardly. "I couldn't find you so I decided to try here. I grabbed you a cinnamon-twist latte."

Mason blinks slow and careful, staring at the cup. "Why?" he whispers.

"I was already there, so I figured—"

"Why are you here?" Mason's eyes shift to mine, swallowing any brightness around them.

I pluck the aquamarine out of my pocket. "You left your necklace at my place."

He gazes at the gemstone without comment.

I skirt around the edge of the counter and hold out the clasp. "Turn around and I'll put it on," I say. "I'm an expert necklace hooker. My mom sucks at finding the loop, so . . ."

My sentence sputters off. Mason has turned and bared the back of his neck silently. Sighing, I drape it around his front, and as I start hooking the necklace, Mason's shoulders shift down, almost imperceptibly.

"Mason," I say.

No response.

"Water boy."

His head quirks.

"You don't have to wear this," I tell him.

"I do," he mumbles.

"Why?"

"It was an expensive gift and I need to be grateful."

The sentiment makes me scoff, and I pull the necklace away, dumping it in a pile on the cashier counter. "The point of a gift is that you don't owe someone for it, right?" I twirl him at the shoulders so he's facing me.

"He got me my birthstone because he knew I'd be happy," Mason says quietly. "I can't be unappreciative, or . . ."

His voice trails off, like he doesn't have the strength to finish his sentence.

I'm not getting through to him, so it's a good time to put my words into practice. "I brought you something else," I say, reaching into my jacket flap and pulling out a crinkled sheet of paper.

"What's that?"

"A gift. A shitty one. But I figured you'd want to see." I smooth out the crease so he can see the painting. It's a dinky thing I spent time on this morning—we have old art supplies in the basement closet, so I whipped something up, doing my best to depict a looming mountain and bulky gray clouds. The forefront features a crudely painted stick figure couple sitting in grass.

Mason takes the picture with bemusement. "Um . . . what is this for?"

"You said you suck at painting." My attention wanders to the countertop, where I spot another painting far more meticulous than mine. "See!" I cry out, gesturing to it. Mason must've been in the middle of making it, because it's of a similar style to the half-finished canvas in his room. "Your art is good. I created this garbage to show you. I didn't even purposefully fuck it up—I'm just that untalented."

Mason's dark hair is hanging in his eyes. His fingers curl in tighter around the paper's wrinkled edges.

"It's none of my business what you do with it, because it's a gift," I say, feeling sufficiently awkward amid his silence. "I figured you could look at it whenever you're feeling down about your art. Because it's just so fucking terrible. Like, I worked on it for two hours. *Diligently.* I'd understand if you throw it out the moment I turn around, since it's so ass-ugly—"

I choke on my words. Mason has set the painting aside and stumbled into my chest, hugging me. His palms tremble as they flatten against my spine and rise slowly toward my shoulder blades, like he's trying to find where best to hang on to me.

"Water boy?" I squawk.

"Quarterback," he mumbles into my jacket.

My heart swoops into my stomach before skyrocketing into my throat, clearly uncertain of how to handle this. His head is an inch below my chin and smells like crisp apples. Does he have fall-themed shower products? Probably. Definitely.

Do I hug him back? The thought of holding him against me makes my body temperature scorch hot, even after everything that happened last night.

By the time I decide, Mason is drawing backward, his lanky arms sliding away. The corners of his eyes are swelling and scarlet. "I don't get it," he whispers. "You go out of your way to bring me my necklace . . . buy me my favorite coffee . . . paint me a picture you hate just so I'll feel better . . ."

It sounds sappy when he says it like that. "It doesn't mean anything," I claim, because I'm not some soft, squishy little boy. "I was bored. Then I grabbed you coffee because I was already in the wrong place, so I figured I might as well, since you're a caffeine enthusiast. And you had a breakdown when your necklace was damaged, so I drove it here."

Mason smiles faintly at my pathetic ramble. "Cameron Morelli," he says, so frail and broken that I want to reach inside of him and put his shattered pieces together with my bare hands, regardless of how many times they might nick my fingers. "If you keep doing things like this, I might start to regret rejecting you."

My brain latches onto the word "regret." Is he serious? "Then I'll ask you out again," I say, donning an impish smile.

Mason's eyes glow with faded amusement. "Oh? And when will that be?"

"Whenever you least expect it."

"Planning on jump scaring me into saying yes?"

I shrug. "If that's the only way I can date you."

A flush works through Mason's cheeks, and he gives a small indignant scoff. "You don't have to pretend you're interested," he mutters, shifting away from me, his fingertips grazing the edges of my painting. "You'll get bored of my face eventually."

His hand wanders toward the aquamarine necklace pooled on the countertop. I snag his fingers before he can poison himself on its surface. "Sit on the counter," I snap. "Shorty."

"Huh?"

"Just do it."

Mason pinches his brows with puzzlement but does as commanded, hopping onto the edge of the cashier counter so he's raised a few inches higher. I can look him in the eye now without bending over. I step toward him, but his knees are in the way, so I nudge them apart and wheedle my waist between them.

"Cameron?" Mason's voice cracks over the word. The faint, lingering blush in his cheeks spreads farther as he leans back, but I snatch his head, forcing him to look at me.

"Stop with the self-deprecation," I say sharply. The hearth in his captivating brown eyes has started to rekindle, but it's not the intensity of flickering firelight that should be dancing against his irises while he's in his favorite place. "I asked you out because of how you look, yeah. But you're more than a pretty face. I don't know why you hate yourself, but I like being around you. Even though you'd rather suffer a thousand deaths than date me."

Mason's face twists with mystification, brows arching, lip flinching down. I try not to notice the way his kneecaps rise to frame my hips, like he wants to wrap his legs around me. Like he's falling into a new habit.

"Then I'll ask you again," he says, digging his index finger into the break of my chest. Like always, his touch is a cooling serum, relaxing the tension in my limbs. "What about me, exactly, has bewitched you, body and soul?"

I can faintly recall my previous answer.

Your face. I fuck with it. Please go out with me.

Not my wisest moment. "You want a laundry list of reasons I sort of like you?" I ask skeptically. "I'm not poetic, so that's the best I can do."

Mason looks like he's trying to smile, but there's a film of ice still stiffening his features. "Laundry list is fine," he says softly.

I can still feel the sharpness of his index finger against my chest. It's pumping me with low doses of electricity, increasing my awareness of this situation. Mason Gray's cute face is a foot from mine, allowing me to see each of his dark lashes, the purplish tone beneath his eyes, the feathery softness of his hair. The way his chest shifts with each breath. The snugness of his turtleneck.

You have bewitched me, body and soul. Mason said that was from a Jane Austen movie. I didn't fully grasp its meaning, but I'm starting to get it. Thinking about Mason has become indescribably magnetic, damn near impossible to resist. When I dropped him off last night, the emptiness of my car became consuming. I lay in bed, making adjustments to his workout regimen over and *over* because I wanted an excuse to keep thinking about him.

And here I am now, and he's in the most kissable position I've ever seen, the insides of his thighs bracing my waist, his other hand flat against the countertop behind him, fingertips splayed over the tip of my shitty painting. It's confusing. I've never yearned for anyone. Kissing, wandering hands, shortened breaths . . . I've never cared much for it.

But I want to overwhelm Mason Gray. I feel like he's wrapped in chain mail, impervious to anything that requires him to bare his heart, deflecting any warmth people want to share with him. Every so often, though, if he moves at the right angle, I notice a chink in his armor. If I don't slide in quickly enough, it disappears, and he returns to being fully hidden.

Within those glimpses, I catch sight of someone else. Someone warmer, happier, more expressive and openhearted. He feels like a fragile decoy of himself, and I want to see what he's like when he's not hiding. His expressions, movements, and words are the distant echoes of another person. What would it take to make him feel like himself?

I guess I'll give him the laundry list.

"You think you're boring because your personality isn't loud and annoying like mine," I say, setting my hands casually atop his thighs. "But you're ignoring everything else that makes you worth being around. You're compassionate, and kind, and witty, and intelligent. You make people feel calm, and you go out of your way for others without needing a reward. Also, I don't know what kind of deal you made with the devil, but she gave you a smile so fucking beautiful it makes me feel like I might as well die because there's nothing else worth seeing in this world."

I shrug again, embarrassment warming my face.

"But don't let it get to your head. I know you're capable of asshol- ery. Especially toward me. It's just that, I guess . . . I don't know. If *bewitching* is a real power that exists in this world, the way you smile and laugh would probably be proof of it. Or something."

Mason stares at me, unresponsive. I wait, patient, hoping my words will shred some of that spiky armor. I notice the barest twinkle come ablaze within his honey-brown irises. It flickers in and out, like it's attempting to stay lit against a frigid breeze. I want to cup my hands protectively around that little flame—to shield and nurture it until it's a wildfire.

"I'm sorry about yesterday," I say, flinching. "I should've asked before sticking my lips on you. I thought . . . it seemed like . . . anyway." I clear my throat. "It's probably bad taste to bring that up and then ask again, but I really, *really* want to kiss you on this counter. Is that okay?"

Mason looks lethargically between my eyes, like he's trying to decipher my intentions. His slender fingers are still nestled against the break of my chest. "I rejected you," he says, as if reminding me will stir some underlying hatred to make me shove him away.

"You did," I agree.

He blinks slowly, his impassive, level expression never wavering. "If you want," he says.

That's not good enough. "Do you?" I ask sternly.

"Do I what?"

"Want."

Uncertainty pulls his brows together, like he's not sure why I asked, or why his own interest matters. After a torturously long moment, in which his knees are still barely framed on my hips, and his face is inches away, he says, "One."

I shift forward. He's unbearably still, but I can feel the warmth of his exhales against my chin. Tentatively, I lean my lips against his cool ones, the rest of my body as unmoving as his own. I linger for two seconds before drawing away to observe him.

It's simple and quick and elementary. I don't think he wants anything more intense. His hand, which has been sprawled on the counter behind him, lifts so he can graze his index finger against his lower lip. It's like he saw the kiss happen but didn't feel it. That wouldn't be surprising—his mouth is probably as numb as the rest of him.

"What are you feeling?" I ask quietly.

Once again, he looks at me with faint mystification, like I surprised him. "I don't know," he admits. "Nothing."

"What can I do to make it *something*?" I hope I don't sound as desperate as I am. Why does he feel so unreachable right now? What's changed since last night? At least in my basement, he reacted to me—he was nervous, flustered, conflicted. But this?

Is he even conscious?

"You can try again," he says listlessly. "If you want."

"Tell me what *you* want," I plead.

That flame in his eyes is wavering again despite my attempt to kindle it. "I ruined something good by wanting too much from it," he breathes. "So I just. Don't anymore. It's fine."

"It's not," I snap, scooping his face up. I notch my thumbs in his temples, hoping the warmth in my palms will melt some of his ice. Hoping he'll look at me, rather than through me. "Tell me what you want. There must be something."

His right hand has been rooted on my chest, but he loses the strength to keep it up, because it collapses into his lap, joining the other. "I want someone to . . ." It almost sounds like he's choking on the words—like he's afraid that if he speaks them in full, he's going to be punished. He's blinking faster now, and I realize that despite his unwavering expression, his eyes are wet again. Suddenly, he shoves his hands over his face.

"You can say it," I assure him, my thumbs moving to stroke the backs of his fingers.

"Ridiculous," he rasps.

"It's not ridiculous."

"Pathetic."

"It's not. *You're* not."

Mason's fingers claw into his own face like he wants to rip it off. It's causing his skin to flare red, so I gather his wrists and pull so he can no longer conceal his expression. His eyes and nose are cherry red and his face is drawn with such visceral pain that it drives a stake of nausea through my stomach. "I want to disappear," he croaks. The water becomes too thick to blink away. Several shimmering droplets escape his lashes, sliding down his pearly cheeks.

Those agonized words are like shivs to my heart. I tighten my grip around his hands, working my fingers through his, digging them deep into his skin. "You're not allowed to," I mutter. "You're stuck here, and worse, you're stuck with *me*. So tell me what you really want, or I'll keep holding you hostage. Like in the corn maze."

The reference jogs him, and his glazed stare sharpens.

"You said you want someone to . . . what?" I prompt.

He looks at his own hands wrapped in mine for several seconds. One more blink causes a torrent of tears to scour his cheeks. "I want someone to be gentle with me," he cries.

I stand there quietly.

"I'm tired," he chokes out, bending his head forward and resting it defeatedly against my collar. "I make everything worse, no matter what I do, no matter how many times I try to change, no matter how often I say I'm sorry or that I'll be better or that I'll make it up to them. I can't smile right. I can't walk right. I can't wear the right clothes or say the right things or bruise the right way. I want . . . I w-want someone to not be so angry with me . . . I want someone to be gentle . . . when they look at me and touch me . . . and kiss me . . ."

He takes two fistfuls of my jacket and pulls, like he wants to bury himself in it. I oblige, leaning into him, gathering him against my chest because I'm not sure what else to do.

"It's scary, wanting to kiss you," he whispers.

"Why?" I mumble into the top of his head.

"Because *you're* gentle." His voice is frail and nearly incoherent against my jacket. "But you're also fake. Is this an act, or do you mean the things you say? Are you kind because you want something, or because you're genuinely kind? If . . . if it's all a lie . . ."

"It's not." I tug him away by the sides of his head so I can peer into his eyes, my own stinging with water as well. He feels so lonely, so tired, so beaten. Seeing him like this is agonizing to me, because I get it. Maybe not to his extent, but this helplessness, this desire for such a simple thing—for someone, *anyone*, to just be kind . . .

I understand.

"It's not a lie," I tell him, cradling his damp face in my palms. "I promise. Let me show you."

He deliberates for half a second before losing interest, the emotion fleeing his face as quickly as it came. His hands fall limply to the counter at his sides, and he says, "Okay."

Suddenly, I understand why the laundry list of reasons I like him didn't faze him. I understand why my words aren't helping. I vividly recall the moment he winced away in my basement yesterday.

I promise is something he's heard before. Probably several times. I'd wager that every time someone has offered that to him, they've inevitably broken it.

I move in again, fingers threading through his onyx locks. Mason's eyes slide shut and his head arches back, preparing to receive another kiss. And I want to. *Desperately.* But I don't think that's what he needs right now.

So I press my lips gently to his forehead.

Mason's body seizes up, like I've electrocuted him. For a long, arduous moment, the world is still. I stay rooted there, refusing to budge, trying to pour as much warmth and comfort into him as I can. He gives a pitifully shaky exhale as I shift my lips to the top of his head, nestling them into his hair. I think, maybe, I've startled him again.

He chokes on a quiet sob. His hands drag along the counter, and I wonder if he's going to lift them to grip my wrists. To hold my palms against his face, maybe. Or to wrap his arms around my back.

I won't ever know for sure.

Because his fingers stumble over a silver chain.

The warmth stirring between us flickers out, like the flame in his eyes. Mason's gaze fogs over and his shortened breaths lengthen as if he's passing out.

Immediately, I draw back, pulling my hands away.

"Thank you," he says, his voice light and weightless. "I should get back to work."

He scoops the aquamarine necklace off the counter and puts it on.

"Mason . . ." I clear my throat as he hops down and collects a feather duster from the shelf. "That man from earlier . . . is he—"

"Your transcript looks good," Mason interrupts. "You'll probably be able to get back on the field this week. So keep up with studying, even when I'm not with you."

. . . Okay.

I recognize that present-but-not stare. I used to see it in a mirror every morning during middle school. Mom would have to physically pull me out of bed, and on certain days when she didn't have the patience, she'd leave me there. This was a point of tension with Dad, who'd wake to find messages from the school and his son still lying in bed, flat-faced.

I've never shaken the remembrance of that feeling. That all-consuming *nothingness*. What pulled me out of it? Those dayslong funks I would sink into, aware but not comprehending a thing, feeling separate from my body and pulled onward by life . . .

Faintly, I remember the sound of my bed creaking. Mom curling up next to me, her fingers kneading through my hair. "Cammy," she would whisper. "I know it's hard to live right now, baby. I'm here for you. Dad and I will work something out."

It didn't absolve me of that aching barrenness, but her presence got me through things. Is that what Mason needs? My reassurances aren't enough, so is this the missing puzzle piece?

I know deep in my soul that putting this much care into Mason's situation is going to fully shatter the image of who Cam Morelli is supposed to be.

But I don't care.

I really, really don't fucking care anymore.

"Can you leave that spot?" Mason doesn't look at me as he haphazardly wipes the back of an easel. "If an artist comes in and sees a stranger behind the counter—"

His voice is swallowed by my jacket as I lunge forward and swathe him in a hug, arms folding him back against me. Mason's body stiffens yet again. I realize it's not cool to take someone by surprise, so I hurl backward just as quickly.

"Sorry," I stammer. "It just seems like you could use . . . I don't know. Sorry. If you need anything, text me. Or call me. I'll be there."

I leave before I can determine whether his reaction is negative or positive.

Journal #8—April 19

It's not a big deal. I'm not sure why I'm writing about
it. My gut says I should anyway?
    The other day I was mad. He drove drunk to my
house. I tried telling him how upset that made me, but

I should've let him sober up, because he was just trying to kiss me, saying he couldn't help it because he missed me. I got angrier, and I tried to shove him away. But my hand hit his jaw and snapped his head back. Should've been more careful.

This man is STRONG. Seriously. I'm glad I'll be well protected when we're married. He knocked me flat on my ass with one hit, ha ha. It was embarrassing. But I get it. I hurt him first and he was drunk. Thankfully it happened on Friday so my face has time to heal before school.

He's stayed all weekend to hold the ice packs. He keeps crying like he did something wrong. It was just self-defense though. He's in the kitchen making grilled cheese. Even after what I did, he's being nice enough to keep me company and make me lunch? I'm surprised he didn't break our engagement.

Things are good! We want an October wedding.

He knows I love autumn.

CHAPTER NINETEEN
MASON

A banquet, huh. To celebrate his graduation. His promotion. His official entrance into the world of adulthood.

The words have been circulating in my head, a looming threat. I don't want to go. Obviously. It doesn't matter, because Mom wants me to, and Dad wants to keep her pleasant, which means she'll probably kick me out if I decline to attend. And he'll let her, or she'll become a greater nightmare than I could ever be.

I wish I could stay with someone else. But there's a reason I have no friends, and I don't want to burden anyone with my full-time presence.

Though, there is Cameron Morelli.

I smile faintly at the remembrance of his painting as I gaze at my bedroom ceiling. I need to find a good place to hang it. "You're sweet," I whisper to the darkness. Bringing me coffee and the necklace, telling me he's here if I need him. Complimenting what he can see of my personality.

Kissing me gently.

I can't fall asleep and I'm parched, so I wander into the hallway, relishing in the unusual silence that midnight brings when Mom falls asleep. My father sits at the kitchen table on his laptop, his favorite place aside from the porch, with a cigarette in hand.

I snag a glass from the cupboard, feeling the weight of his eyes. "Don't want to go," I mumble.

No answer.

"Things are over," I say, sharper, filling the glass under the faucet. "I told you the things he did. The way he treated me. You promised . . ."

"It seems like he's changed," Dad says, voice level as always. "Your mother and I think you should consider accepting his apology. He's a wealthy, mature, reliable man with a good heart. You won't find someone like that at college."

"You believe that?" I ask darkly. "Or are you just saying that to avoid conflict?"

He doesn't answer. I already know.

"I won't go," I say.

"They're family friends. It would be rude if you didn't make an appearance."

"I don't care."

"Your mother does. If you want to stay in her good graces—"

"I don't."

"Then you'll be sleeping on the floor of that local coffee shop you love to escape to," Dad snaps, momentarily escaping his aura of indifference. "All you need to do is show up with us for a few hours. You never think long-term, Mason."

That startles fake laughter out of me. "I was engaged," I say, voice rising as irritation mounts within me. "For a whole *year*."

"An engagement you broke off," Dad says stiffly.

His stubbornness is causing frustrated tears to accumulate in my eyes. Why is he acting like he didn't curse my ex-fiancé profusely when I revealed what happened? Like he didn't promise that he'd never let that man near me again?

"Again, long-term." Dad draws a steadying breath, fortifying himself for his next words. I understand why a moment later. "This man can provide for you. How many people your age can say they have someone dependable waiting for them after graduation? You should consider that some benefits outweigh the consequences."

I stare at my father, stunned, nauseated. "Consequences?" I breathe.

Dad kneads his thumbs together with another hefty sigh. "Mason . . . he'll be easier to placate than someone like your mother. It won't take much to have a loving, fulfilling relationship with him. If you avoid stepping on his toes—"

"And if I accidentally do?" I demand. "Is whatever happens next my fault?"

"Of course not." He turns his eyes to his white screen against the darkness of the kitchen, tiring of this conversation. "I'm just saying that if you're mindful of your words and actions, you could lead happy lives. Comfortable lives. Stable lives." He pauses, then whispers, "Better lives."

I slam my water glass on the counter and storm to the door.

"What are you doing?" Dad asks wearily.

"Walk," I mumble, sliding into my tennis shoes despite only being equipped with my flannel pajamas.

"It's midnight. Too late for you to be out there."

But not too late for me to reinstate an engagement to someone I never wanted to see again. Or for my father, who supported my decision to break things off, to switch on a dime because my mother has to have her way.

I thought he'd be rigid in his stance. When I broke the engagement and explained why, he snarled back at Mom. He'll do that occasionally, but it's never more than five seconds before he's bowing his head so the police don't get called for the screaming. Back then, though, he stood his ground.

Look at him. Look at what your "best friend"'s son has done to our child.

There was ravenous fury in his eyes, like he wanted to hunt the man with his bare hands.

And now he's sitting among the shadows and claiming things will be fine, dandy, if I put that lavish ring back on my finger. "I don't understand," I breathe. "You said you hated him."

Dad massages his middle knuckle into his forehead. "How many people out there will accept you for who you are?" he asks softly. "You're shy and struggle to form connections. You've never made any long-lasting friends. I see too much of myself in you, Mason. When I look at your future, all I see is loneliness. This man is kinder, more loving, more personable than anything you've seen here. He's not nearly as reactionary as your mother. He has wealth we've only dreamed of having. He's put in the work to become a better man, and things can only improve without college as a stressor in his life. I'm just thinking"—he clenches his teeth together—"long-term."

My hand breaks into a tremble around the doorknob. So, he's determined that it's forgiveness or it's nobody, and being with someone who's continually battered me down is better than not being with anyone.

I shouldn't be surprised. He chose Mom.

I storm into the night. It's frigid enough that the subdivision's tented rooftops are glazed with frost. A swirl of nippy wind swathes me in greeting, causing goose bumps to erupt along my skin. But I can't be in that house.

So I start down the sidewalks, wiping the moist crooks of my eyes. I fumble for my phone, only to realize I left it charging on my nightstand.

I'll just wander, then.

I hug my flannel sleeves and don't realize I'm crying until another breeze licks my face, nearly icing my tears against my skin. "Fuck," I mutter, scrubbing them away as I take a random turn onto a main road. The trees overhead whisper and swish as I travel the shoulder, leaves cascading over the darkened pavement and dashed lines. The stars and moon are ablaze, shedding a silvery path for me to follow.

As I walk, though, and my insides accumulate frost, movement becomes more difficult. I stagger to a stop and clench my teeth, tears thickening on my cheeks.

How many people out there will accept you for who you are?

My father's voice, tinged with pity, spears my chest. I crouch on the edge of the road in a pile of dead, crunchy leaves. Is there nothing about me worthwhile? The only acquaintances I have are the guys on the football team, and I know their fondness for me is pity. The reason they give me company is because they feel awkward seeing me by myself. The reason they call me their "rock" is because they want me to feel included.

But there's another voice fighting for dominance in my head. Warming my pulse.

If bewitching is a real power that exists in this world, the way you smile and laugh would probably be proof of it.

My tears intensify, and I'm quivering violently enough to disturb the leaves I'm crouched in. How can he say something with such intensity when we've only just started to get to know each other? Was he lying because he felt bad?

No . . . Cameron Morelli may wear a fake persona, like when he pretends he's a doofus (he only sometimes is), but his heart is genuine. And if he was telling the truth, doesn't that imply my father is wrong? My fiancé? *Me?* Maybe people see me as more than an "aesthetic"— the cute, delicate, well-behaved queer boy who lacks real substance and only exists as people's fantasy.

I'm not sure where the strength comes from, but I manage to hoist myself to my wobbly feet. He's probably asleep.

I head in that direction anyway.

Journal #9—December 27

Hello journal I keep forgetting about. This is an update.
Though I don't really need this thing anymore. I'm
nearly seventeen so what am I even doing.

I'm just frustrated and not sure who to talk to, so
I'm talking to myself. It's not some fling. He's my
fiancé. He's the only person who's seen me. The real me.
He gives me structure. He saves me from my house
when my parents are being obnoxious. He makes
decisions for me when I can't make them myself. He's
a mature, wealthy, talented, attractive man who chose
my loser ass.

I love him. I'm going to marry him.

I'M GOING TO MARRY MY FIANCÉ.

Okay, future me, that sentence only looks shaky
because I'm on my fifth cup of coffee. And the page is
wet because I just washed my hands. Remember that
when you look back. Remember things are always better
more often than they're worse.

Obviously our relationship will have flaws. I just
wish he wasn't always so frustrated. I've never lied to
him, so why doesn't he believe me when I tell him what
I'm doing? I feel awful for him. I can tell he's under a
lot of pressure from his parents.

Things should get better after we graduate. Once
all of this life movement is out of the way, things will
go back to how they used to be.

I want to make things easier for him by not
complaining. But he's been so stressed that lately,

when he's with me, he's been accidentally taking it out
on me. Luckily it's winter so I can wear turtlenecks
and jeans, but there comes a point where it's like, Do
you have to grab me like that in bed? Why are you
treating me like you just caught me with another man
and you're getting revenge?

Things are going great otherwise! I might get the
ring resized. I've lost some weight.

CHAPTER TWENTY
CAM

I dial 911.

Then I peek through my blackout curtains, butter knife from my midnight toast in hand, and see Mason Gray.

Thin ice, but I do exit out of 911.

Hearing a methodical, very human tapping noise on my window-panes at one o'clock in the morning is the most likely scenario within which I would shit my pants, bedsheets, and mattress simultaneously. Which is why my first instinct is to scoop my phone up and prepare for imminent death. Yet masculine curiosity grabbed hold—I had to see the source.

Lo and behold, it's my water boy.

I unlock the window, pulling it up. "The hell are you doing?" I hiss, peering around the blackened forestry surrounding my house. In summer, the sounds of life are unbearable, particularly with insects hiding among the tall grass. Now, though, as the autumn weather takes hold, the sounds are more muted, giving way to the scraping of naked branches and whistling wind.

Mason is dressed in *pajamas*, his eyes streaked with reddish vines, shivering like he just emerged from an ice bath. "Sorry," he whispers. "Am I bothering you?"

I shake my head, utterly bamboozled. "Come in!" I snap, nestling my arm against the top of the window frame so he won't hit his head. Hesitantly he hoists himself through the window, his tousled locks skimming my arm as he pulls himself inside. The moment the house's warmth floods over him, Mason releases a sigh of relief.

"What the hell, Mason?" I demand, drawing the blinds to conceal us from forest lurkers or nosy mosquitoes that should be dead. I flick on my bedside lamp to properly see him. "Why are you wandering around in your pajamas? You *walked* here?"

"Took a private jet," Mason says dryly. His eyes flit along my front, and I realize with mortification that I'm dressed in hot-pink boxers. I scramble for my robe and fling it over my shoulders, though I guess he's seen me in worse situations, like after the inflatable pool incident.

"What happened?" I ask sharply. If he's going to occupy my bedroom on a Sunday night, I should know *why*. Even if tomorrow is a professional development day and we have school off. This is precious sleeping time for a special boy.

Not that I mind seeing him.

"Just needed air," Mason says, light and blasé as he looks around, his eyes gravitating to the gigantic poster of Beau Rainey fastened to my wall. His lip crinkles down.

"Did something happen?" I ask. "Or was the thought of my face too charming to resist?"

Mason scoffs, and I'm glad because it means he's feeling an emotion. "Cameron Morelli, could you not be an arrogant dick so late on a Sunday? Think of the children."

"What children?"

"Me."

I sigh, flopping onto my mattress. Why won't he ever give me a straight answer?

Maybe he notices the trace of frustration in my face, because his fake half smile dissolves. "Sorry," he whispers. "I know I shouldn't be here, it's just . . . I wanted to make sure of something."

"That being?"

Mason inches closer, until his knees bump mine. His flannel shirt is sagging off his shoulders, exposing his smooth collarbone. "The things you said," he mumbles. "Did you mean them, or were you just trying to make me feel better?"

I stare at him vacantly. "What things?"

"Uh . . . like what you said about my personality." He scrutinizes me intently, then flatly says, "You forgot."

The memory unfurls in little chunks through my mind. "I didn't," I choke out.

Mason gives a small shake of his head. "Makes sense that you wouldn't remember," he mumbles. "It was a completely normal, uneventful moment for you. You have no idea what it meant to me."

I didn't think that moment *was* a big deal, but the gap in my memory is more because I was so focused on the sensation of *him*. His legs against my hips, his torso leaning back but not in a defensive position. More like he was allowing himself to be vulnerable, rather than curling in. The way his turtleneck hugged him and his eyelashes glinted in the gallery lighting. The way his lips felt cool and silken against mine.

"I mean what I say," I tell him, shrugging. "Maybe I wanted to make you feel better, but that just means I used that moment to tell you what I think. Hoping it would help."

Mason smiles with just enough genuineness that his eyes crinkle. The sight is like a rush of dopamine that causes my chest to tingle and the walls of my throat to narrow. I'm sitting, he's standing, but my bed frame is high enough that I'm only an inch below him, his straight, slender nose at my eye level.

"What?" I ask when the silence of my room becomes too thick with tension. I've never wanted so badly to sling my arms around someone's waist and kiss them. Maybe it's lust? He obviously thinks I'm a giant-dicked, tiny-brained idiot. He enjoys insulting me, rolling his eyes, flicking my forehead, and scolding me while we study. I don't know where it came from, this feeling. But somewhere in our time together . . .

I've started to like this water boy.

The thought of holding his hand, sprawling my head in his lap when I give up on studying, encouraging him during workout sessions, talking casually with him on the benches of the football field sidelines, discovering vegetarian places we can eat, watching him paint . . . it's overwhelming. I want my existence to be interlaced with his, even if all we're doing is *this*—staring at each other in the dim bedroom lighting, silent aside from quickened breaths.

"Cameron Morelli," he says softly.

Everyone calls me "Cam" or "Morelli." He's the only one who lets the weight of my full name leave his tongue. It used to aggravate me, but now there's something intimate about it. "Mason Gray," I shoot back, because how else do I respond? *Yes, that's me. 'Tis I.*

"Why do you pretend you're such a prick?"

"Who's pretending?" I snip, to which he laughs, one finger rising to conceal his lips, just one, and my God, I want to devour him.

"I like you." Mason reaches out and sprawls his hand along my jaw, eyes still watery.

I . . . wasn't expecting that.

He's so nonchalant, I can barely comprehend his words. The tornado of fire that's been contained to my chest since he crawled through my bedroom window spirals out of control, lashing into the rest of my body, setting my skin ablaze.

"You like me?" I squeak. His gaze is pouring into mine, but something feels strange. There's a hint of detachment, like part of his thoughts are lying somewhere else. And since when has he ever been so forward?

Mason nods. His fingertips are nestled along the curve of my ear, and he pinches my lobe, sending my heart into a panicked, hot frenzy. Is he coming on to me? He's made some snarky, suggestive comments in the past, but he's never actually *flirted* with me before. He's fluttering his lashes, like he knows exactly what I'm drawn to.

"Aren't you the school's biggest player?" Mason's head tips, curiosity lining his features. "Why are you so flustered? It's cute."

Okay, something is *definitely* wrong. His smile seems genuine, and there's honest desire in his eyes, but it's overshadowed by something more intense.

Desperation.

"What are you running from?" I ask, catching his wrist. His heartbeat is elevated against my thumb, though it's nowhere near as wild as mine, which means all of this . . . it's calculated. "You're using me as a distraction."

Mason's eyes shoot wide. He takes a startled step back and twists his hand free with such urgency, it's like he thinks I'm going to attack him. "Sorry," he says in a weak, broken gasp.

I rise to my feet, and he stumbles farther back, pupils dilating, arms rising defensively.

"Sorry," he says again, faster. Quieter. "I didn't mean . . . I wasn't trying to . . ."

His reaction is so visceral that I freeze, not daring to flinch. I'd been planning on grabbing a sweatshirt for him, because he's still shivering.

"It's fine," I say, swallowing. Seeing him wince every time I move unexpectedly drives a dagger of pain through my heart. I hate what it means. I hate whoever did this to him. "But if you kiss me, I want it to be because you like me back."

"I do." Mason's eyes lock on my bedroom carpet. "I wasn't lying."

And maybe this should be a critical moment where everything comes together with a perfect, fiery kiss as passionate testosterone spills out of our pores. I'm supposed to sweep him off his feet and go on a tirade about all his qualities that frustrate me but also draw me to him. But I can't. Because even if Mason *is* catching feelings . . .

He's scared.

"Why did you walk here so late?" I ask, sinking into the bed-spread.

Mason's defensive stance loosens. He takes unsteady steps toward me, and suddenly, his face is falling into the crook of my neck, and he's slumping against me. "I don't know," he whispers, his warm breath tickling my shoulder.

I'm not sure what to do with my hands. Eventually, I wrap my arms around his narrow waist, hugging him against me, slotting him between my propped legs. When he feels this, he leans more heavily into my chest.

"Sorry," he mumbles. "Can I spend the night? I can sleep on your floor."

"We slept in your bed once," I point out. "Might as well do the same in mine."

Mason melts fully into my grasp, until I'm the only thing keeping him from folding onto the carpet. I shift, rolling him onto my mat-tress and then creeping beneath the blankets. I flick the light off, plunging us into darkness as we rustle around, trying to get comfort-able. Soon after, the only sound is the whirring bedroom fan.

My body starts unwinding, despite Mason's distracting presence.

My breathing lengthens as consciousness slips out of my grasp. I want to press him until he relents, but I don't want to force an answer out of him. And I'm exhausted after spending hours in Darius's backyard, running the ball and exercising my throwing arm and getting shoved to the ground so I don't return to the football field rusty and useless.

My awareness comes back into focus when I hear Mason shift. We're facing each other, about a foot of space extending between us. I feel him grip my wrist, then uncurl my fingers. Slow and careful, like he's afraid of waking me, he cradles my hand against his face, then nudges my thumb back and forth along the scoop under his eye, emulating me stroking his cheek.

Why would he wait until I was asleep? He doesn't want me to see that he needs to be comforted? He's so desperate for affection that he's using my limp hand to find some semblance of warmth and peace?

"Just ask me to hold you," I mumble.

Mason stiffens. His hand falls away, but I keep my palm snuggled against his face, continuing to move my thumb along the dried tear streaks staining his skin. I peek through one lid to find that he's stubbornly closed his eyes, like he knew I was about to look at him.

I realize something, then.

Cam Morelli is going to die tonight.

I'm not sure he's even still alive, to be honest. After everything that's happened recently, I can't say when it was that I last consciously had my mask up. Regardless, keeping up the ruse isn't possible around him. I've only ever wanted to be perceived in this school as a fun-loving, loudmouthed jock who flirts around and wins people over with his loyalty and charisma. But I care too much now. I can't pretend to be as conceited and theatrical around the other football players when Mason is nearby, because I know how painfully easy he can see through me.

Deep within the confines of my soul, I know I'm not going to get hurt by the people in this school. It's different here. But Cam Morelli has always been a fail-safe—reassurance that if I'm wrong, it won't matter, because I'll be too popular, too likable, to become a target.

Around Mason, though, I feel safe. Even if the entire school turns their back on me, or turns their fists on me, one person won't. *He* won't. Because he likes the parts of me that I've kept shielded from this town, whenever I've accidentally allowed them to peek through in his presence.

So I'll tell him who I really am. Because I know I'll be okay.

"Back in middle school, there were times I thought I'd go ahead and die if I didn't feel my mom's arms around me," I say quietly, watching as Mason peeks through one crunched eyelid to see me. "If I could get up, I'd crawl into bed next to her whenever my dad was sleeping on the couch after a fight."

Mason is quiet, absorbing this. "Your parents fight?" he whispers.

"Not anymore." I sigh from the remembrance. The overwhelming frigidity of our house—the way the stiff floorboards cried under our feet whenever someone moved. The sound of heated voices reverberating down the hallway, louder as Mom pulled more Pride paraphernalia off the walls and Dad fought to keep it up.

"I mentioned people targeted me because of my mom," I murmur. "But it wasn't just that."

Both of Mason's eyes are open now, and he's watching me with contemplation through the darkness, his expression neutral but not cold.

"I was bullied in elementary school for unrelated things," I tell him, my heart thumping harder against my chest. I've never told anyone this. "Namely, that I acted too cutesy and 'girly.' I know, it sounds ridiculous, but that's just the kind of place we lived in."

Mason reaches out, fingertips crawling over the bedspread. He nudges aside the folds of my robe, then presses his hand flat to the warm skin of my chest. The sensation of this cool calmness pushing back against my restless heartbeat causes it to slow. Unwillingly, I'm relaxing, my breaths coming longer. Less shaky.

"I was really quiet," I continue, my left hand sliding down from his hair to scrape against the back of his neck. I think he likes the feeling, because his lashes flutter. "Soft-spoken. I picked flowers during recess and collected rocks by myself. I didn't talk to anyone in class because I was so busy daydreaming and not paying attention. I cried easily and often, even as I started getting older. After people found out about my mom, they linked my 'girliness' to me just being fruity. And everything sort of escalated."

I should be sliding into a panic. The memories are seeping into the corners of my vision. But Mason is at the center, and it binds me to the present.

"They found me *everywhere*," I breathe, fingers curling in with frustration. "They stalked me and my house. I used to sell my painted rocks at the end of my driveway, and they would start pelting me with them, then throw them down the street grates. I'd go to the park so I could cloud watch, but they followed me so they could smear me in dirt. When I walked home from school, I'd stop by a florist to buy my mom flowers. They'd appear out of nowhere and rip the flower heads off, then tell me to give her the stems."

I can see Mason's eyes glittering against the scant amount of moonlight filtering into the room around my shades. They're filled with tears.

"At one point," I murmur, "I signed up for a recreational football team. I was seeing the counselor on a weekly basis, and she thought it would be good for me to join a sport or club outside of my school. To force myself to get out there. I was good. *Really* good. I knew, if I put all of my effort into the practices and games, I'd probably be the best player on the team. Even though I'd only ever practiced with my dad in the backyard and I wasn't built like everyone else. I was just a natural, I guess."

I pause, teeth latching together instinctively with frustration. I force the rest out.

"But even though I liked the distraction, it was only ever that. A distraction. It never became a passion—just a way to escape. It didn't last. When people from school found out I'd joined a rec team in a neighboring town, they claimed the only reason was so I could get my hands on a bunch of sweaty boys tackling each other. So I eventually quit."

Mason's hand on my chest begins to slide up along my collarbone. It drifts over the side of my neck, latching itself there so he can graze a slow, methodical trail along my jawline with his thumb. I resist the urge to catch it and kiss his knuckles.

"There was this party in eighth grade." My teeth clench as the memory comes reeling back. A rough bedroom carpet under my knees, half my shirt buttons undone, my heart galloping and sobs raking my chest. A crowd of people whispering to one another. "I was told about it by an acquaintance. I didn't have friends because people didn't want to get roped into my shit. It was the first time I was invited somewhere. My parents said no, so I snuck out in the middle of the night, because I thought . . . *finally*. This is my chance to turn things around."

The sound of relentless bass and explosive laughter hums in my ears. The anxious anticipation as I wandered around groups of students, high schoolers included, feeling more and more out of place as the night dragged.

"There was a girl I started talking to. Someone who'd been nice to me in the past," I say. Only then do I notice that he's not only stroking my jaw, but his other hand has moved to the back of mine. His cool thumb is massaging my knuckles, lingering in the skin between. The feeling stirs tingles in my abdomen. "I thought maybe I was going to make a friend. But she said the music was too loud to hear me, and she brought me into a bedroom."

I distinctly remember the creaky hinges of the door swinging shut. The way the music dampened and light was squashed from the room. The sudden, mischievous glint in her eyes.

"Basically," I say through multiple voice cracks, "she tried making out with me. Pushing me into the wall, trying to take my shirt off, trying to kiss me. She kept asking if I was a real man, or if I took after my mom. I didn't realize until a few minutes later that the whole thing had been set up by others at the party."

I gnaw on my quivering lip. I still feel slimy, dirty, whenever I remember the sensation of her hands plucking at my shirt buttons. The way her lips felt against my jaw or cheek because she wasn't fast enough to catch my lips as I squirmed and pushed her.

"My parents found out and we moved," I say, summarizing the complicated process that followed. "I decided I wouldn't come into this high school at the bottom of the class. If I had to emulate all the popular pricks from my previous school to make it in Elwood, I would. So I started working out religiously and building my confidence. Or learning how to fake it."

My jaw locks again, exasperation rolling through me.

"When everyone around you becomes convinced, your brain targets the final person who isn't fooled. Yourself. And what you thought was fake suddenly becomes real." I falter, sighing, then whisper, "At least, until a water boy with a smart mouth enters your life to point out all of your fakery to your face."

Mason's expression is still level despite the water sparkling in his eyes. He elbows his way closer, removing the foot of space that yawned between us, and rests his head on the same pillow. Air tinged with lingering traces of mint unfurls against my chin.

"Cameron," he says gently, nestling my knuckles against his slender lips. The sensation, the sight, quickens my pulse. "I'm so sorry the people around you treated you so horribly. You're considerate. And sincere. And you have one of the biggest hearts I've ever seen. You deserve so much better than that."

He speaks with such soft kindness that it chokes me up. But letting my nose run would be extremely unsexy, so I sniff violently and blink away the tears.

"You had me fooled," Mason says with a playful smile. "I thought you were just some himbo jock trying to date everyone in school. But all the showboating . . . you're just keeping up the ruse."

"I'm not sure it's a ruse anymore," I admit.

"Mm. Some of it, maybe." Mason nibbles my middle knuckle, which sends heat scorching through my cheeks. "Do you feel like your friends—the other varsity players—would look at you differently if you tone down some of the fake parts?"

"Probably not," I admit. I've known that for a while, but even if there's only a 1 percent chance they'd turn on me . . . the thought is still unsettling.

"Well. I'll be there for you, if you decide to give it a shot," he whispers. "Maybe it doesn't mean much, since I'm not a hypermasculine football junkie, but I think people would enjoy seeing this version of Cameron Morelli. Even the hypermasculine football junkies."

He sprawls my palm out, hugging it flat to his collarbone. The aquamarine pendant on his necklace digs into my skin.

I want to rip it off him.

"What about you?" I ask softly.

His brows shift together. "What?"

"How long have you been hiding yourself?"

Mason's eyes flit between mine, and I wonder if I've overstepped. I must've, because he releases my palm and rolls onto his back, snapping the invisible threads between us so he can look at the ceiling. "Mm," he says.

I knew unpacking my trauma wouldn't necessarily be the key to him unpacking his own. Just because I've grown comfortable enough to share my story doesn't mean he's at the same level. But I want to *help*. How can I, though, when I don't know what he's going through?

Then he rolls onto his side, putting his back to me, and I know the conversation is over. That doesn't stop me from creeping closer and looping my arm around his waist, then burrowing my face into the back of his exposed neck. The ice-cold chain of his necklace drags against my lower lip. I huddle against him, my torso nestling along the curve of his back, one leg sneaking between his curled ones beneath the blankets.

"This okay?" I mumble.

Mason hesitates. Slowly, he nods.

"I don't know what's going on, water boy. But I've got you."

Mason's body tightens before all the strain melts away, and he falls limp. He smears his face into the pillow and breaks into a poorly concealed tremble.

I pull him tighter against me and fall asleep to the sound of his fragmented breaths.

Journal #10—no idea

I can't do anything right. Why am I so useless? His parents made him take two semesters of classes in one so he can earn a more formal spot in his dad's company. He's stressed and tired and angry. I just want to help, but now he's not answering my texts.

Is he losing interest in me? Is it because I don't want to have sex as much? Or am I just not thinking hard enough about what I'm saying? I feel like even if I sit there for five hours coming up with the perfect sentence, he still gets upset.

Maybe I complain too much? A couple weeks ago I asked him to stop biting me when we kiss because it makes my lips puffy. He asked why I'm always being so controlling. I didn't realize he felt that way. Maybe I should've let him do what he wanted, since he drove all the way home to spend time with me. I owed him that much.

Maybe he's not attracted to me anymore? He keeps mentioning that my face is still too young even though my body is maturing. He rarely lets his friends come over when I drive up to see him. Does he think I'm too flirty around them? Or maybe he's afraid I'll bore them?

Maybe he's the one getting bored of me.

But he promised he wouldn't. He's different from the rest of them.

I'm trying to be more exciting and spontaneous. I planned a surprise date when he last came home. He seemed really happy when I brought him to the ice rink so he could teach me how to skate, but I think he got frustrated after a while because I'm really uncoordinated. I should've considered that.

I made him his favorite pasta dish, too, so we could have a nice candlelit dinner at home. He said it was really sweet of me to remember that. He mentioned a while ago that he wanted to do this role-play kind of thing so I even went out and got a costume. But then he got really quiet afterward and I think I maybe didn't do a good job of "getting into character" or something? Or maybe he could tell I didn't enjoy it as much as him? I wish he would tell me why he's upset instead of making me guess.

Things are great, even if we're in a tough spot. He bought me a camera because I've been interested in photography lately. It reminded me of why I love him so much.

Hopefully next time I write, it'll be with good news!

CHAPTER TWENTY-ONE
MASON

Is this cheating?

I blink slowly, watching moonlight peek through Cameron's curtains. He's asleep. I feel each lengthy breath tickle the hairs on my neck. His brawny quarterback arm is snug around my waist, and his other arm is beneath my neck, curled in against my collar, hugging me. Just like in the corn maze, I can feel the strength and rigid lines of his body pushing against my back—but now, the only fabric separating us belongs to my flannel shirt, since his robe is splayed open.

A crude part of me wants to lift it so I can feel the heat of his skin directly against mine. Cameron's body is warm. Wanting this—wanting *him*—causes guilt to plague me.

I'm not wearing the ring. It should be fine that I'm spooning someone, because nobody owns me. Even if it still feels like he does.

My eyes are dry, and I've lost so much strength I can't even turn into Cameron's arms like I want. His weight is so comforting. I want to kiss him. I want to trace the jut of his bones and sling my thighs around his hips and taste his neck beneath my lips. Is that okay? Even though I'm wearing this necklace? Even if we were engaged? And still could be, if he's really changed?

Or even if he hasn't, because Mom gets what she wants?

I peek over my shoulder to find his handsome, serene face a mere inch away. He's sleeping soundly even after everything he just revealed to me. Faintly, I can remember the nonchalant words he spoke earlier.

I mean what I say. Maybe I wanted to make you feel better, but that just means I used that moment to tell you what I think. Hoping it would help.

Then . . . he meant it. The things he said at the gallery. That I'm compassionate and intelligent and I make people feel calm. Am I really like that? When all the footballers claim they look at me to steady themselves, that they feel like I'm a staple on the team . . . they really mean it?

I feel my lower lip wobbling. My heart feels warm for the first time in years.

"Thank you for liking me, Cameron Morelli," I whisper.

My voice stirs him, just for a moment, and he curls tighter around me. I snuggle deeper into his comforting arms.

When I next blink, it's gray daylight seeping through the blinds, and the bed is cold even though blankets are tucked around my chin. Cameron's absence jars me, and I sit up, the sheets sliding away as I peer around the room. I hear the sound of thick rain pellets smashing his window.

I start toward the bedroom door when two things catch my attention. The first is that massive poster of Beau Rainey. A nice guy who played for Alpine University. I met him once through his younger sister, who went to school with my . . . well. The second thing I notice is Cameron's closet. It's cracked open, and staring at me are . . .

Googly eyes?

I shouldn't be nosy, but I inch toward the door anyway and nudge it open. Awaiting me are several rocks of varying sizes, from quarter to egg to palm. They're all painted, some with colorful patterns or little scenic images like a tree line and sunset. Some are painted to look like ladybugs or flowers. Some have silly faces or twisting vines or erratic splotches.

The one with the googly eyes has a curly, twisting mustache.

I stifle laughter with my palm, scooping it up and carrying it into the hallway, peeking around the quiet house. Cameron is in the kitchen over a griddle, fumbling his way through spooning chocolate chip pancake mix into neat lumps. Tragically, he's now wearing a T-shirt and basketball shorts, rather than the hot-pink boxers I caught him in yesterday.

"Morning," I say.

Cameron swivels toward me, and his face becomes luminous, like he was wallowing in darkness until my arrival. Part of me wonders what I've done to deserve that reaction, but I shake my head of the negative thought. He looks like that because he likes me. Right? Is that such an impossible thing to comprehend?

Cameron is happy to see me because he likes me.

"Hey," he says. "You like pancakes? I sort of assumed because you like sweet things, and they're a good vegetarian breakfast option—"

His sentence crumbles away when I roll onto my tiptoes and kiss his cheekbone. "Pancakes are great," I say softly. "Thank you."

Redness soaks into Cameron's tan, handsome face, and I think I'd hang a picture of this next to the painting he gave me, so I could look at it whenever I was feeling down. Then he sees my palms and notices the mustache rock, and he makes a noise like he's gagging on his saliva. "Where?" he squawks. "Why?"

I smile wider, presenting it to him in my open hands. "He's adorable."

Cameron kneads his forehead with exasperation. "You were snooping?"

"Your closet was wide open."

"It wasn't."

"Cracked open."

"Hmm." His suspicious look only makes me break into a bigger smile. I can't help it. Even looking at him makes me feel giddy. It's strange, considering a mere few weeks ago the sight of him made me roll my eyes.

"Can I buy him?" I ask hopefully.

Cameron's flush spreads all the way into his neck. "Just take it, creep," he chokes out, and it makes me burst into laughter. I try to scoop him into a hug, but he pushes my wrists away with flustered disgruntlement. "Go the hell away."

"What's wrong? Are you mad that I found your adorable rock collection?"

"Mom made extra coffee," he says, thoroughly ignoring me. He flips a not-nearly-ready-enough pancake, causing loose mix to splatter the griddle. "She's in the living room. Dad left to finish up a thigh tattoo, so he's not around, thank God, that absolute dick."

I have the feeling his father scolded him this morning or something, which makes me laugh again. Cameron loves his parents—I saw it in the way they interacted at dinner. Even though he's a momma's boy, the tension between him and his father is entirely fabricated. It's refreshing, being here.

I place his rock on the counter, making a mental note to bring some money for it next time I have my wallet. I pour a cup of coffee and maybe act a little selfish by adding too much sweetened creamer, then shuffle toward the living room, leaving Cameron to cuss over his pancakes. His mother is tucked on the love seat in a flowery pajama suit, her brown hair knotted into a bun, an open book propped on her kneecaps.

"Good morning, Mrs. Morelli," I say. "Thank you for making extra coffee."

She grins, as radiant as her son, the skin crinkling around her green-blue eyes. "I wasn't expecting to see you this morning," she says brightly. "Come sit."

I only popped in to greet her and was going to return to Cameron so I could torment him about his misshapen pancakes. I stride farther into the living room anyway, swallowing when she pats the couch cushion. I sit on the love seat, gripping my coffee with two hands.

"Cam says you walked here in the middle of the night," she says.

It comes with far less bounciness than her previous sentence. She's folding her book shut, angling herself toward me. Her eyes latch with mine, colored with concern.

"I . . . what?" I croak, startled by her sudden change in atmosphere.

"Why did you show up at our house after midnight, Mason?" she asks softly.

My heart sinks into the bottom of my feet. "I just needed fresh air," I say, pushing through the rasp in my throat. "I got into a fight with my dad and left."

She straightens her posture, and I can tell she's really in *Mom* mode. "Did you let them know where you are?"

"I forgot my phone at home," I admit. "Though, Dad usually texts or calls me."

Mrs. Morelli's eyes glint when I say the word "usually." I take a massive gulp of sugary coffee, hoping it'll speedrun my waking process so I can be more careful. "I see," she says gently.

I'm not sure what she's going to ask next. She'll probably try to wriggle out my reasoning for running off or demand if I feel unsafe at home. I'll say no, because my parents don't hurt me. They're not a threat.

My house itself, though, is another story.

It has several entry points that can be unlocked by a key. A key my parents gave him some years ago, all the way back when he was my babysitter. My parents fought angrily one night over whether we should have the locks changed—Dad insisted, but Mom said he's family, and we can't cut him out. Losing him means also potentially losing any benefits that come with being connected to his family.

He can come striding through the door whenever he wants. Even when I'm in bed, sound asleep, my ear is open. My window must stay locked—it's a more discreet way of getting to me, less likely to alert my parents, so it's his preferred method.

I'm falling into a dangerous lull, Mrs. Morelli's protective gaze drawing me in, making me want to be vulnerable. Why did Cameron tell her I walked here? Couldn't he have said he came to pick me up because I was bored?

But instead of interrogating me further, she softly says, "Next time, call Cam. If he doesn't answer, call me. I'll pick you up. I don't care what time it is. So add me as a contact, okay?"

I'm stunned. I've only met this woman a couple of times, and she's offering this like I mean something to her. Somewhere in my haze, I give her my number. She releases me, so I awkwardly shamble back into the kitchen to rejoin Cameron. That was nice of her.

He's drizzling the pancakes with syrup, and when he sees me, he falters. "Oh," he says. "I should've asked if you like syrup."

I laugh through my hand. "If I say no?"

"I'd start over."

"Aw." I flutter my eyes, sprawling a palm over my chest. "You'd do that for little old me?"

Cameron scowls deeply at my tone. "Nutrients are important in the morning, so yeah."

I'm not sure what nutrients he's referring to in these syrupy chocolate chip pancakes, but the fact that he went out of his way to do this warms my heart. "Thanks," I whisper.

"Huh? Oh, no problem. I'm an expert at pancake-making now—"

"Don't touch the griddle."

"I'm just going to scrape some of the batter—"

"Stop. You'll burn yourself."

". . ."

I sigh, tugging his hand to the sink and running his reddish fingers under cool water while he sniffles.

When Cameron asks if I'd prefer to stay or leave after we eat his slightly-undercooked-yet-somehow-charred pancakes, I reluctantly choose the latter. I could probably spend days in the Morelli household, but I can't avoid life forever. So he grabs an umbrella and walks me to the passenger seat of his car, before swinging around to the driver's.

The ride to my house is silent. The weight of every second presses on my chest as I realize what I've done over the last twelve hours. I walked to Cameron's house, disturbed his rest, occupied his bed, ate his food, consumed his time. I owe him an explanation, don't I? Otherwise, am I not just taking advantage of his willingness to be there for me?

He didn't have to open his window for me, or curl himself around me, or pour his heart out about what happened to him in middle school. Yet he did because . . .

He likes me.

Was he expecting I'd do the same? Because I can't. His heart is fiery red and pulsing with heat, strong and sturdy despite the scars that give it color. Mine is a dulled gray, poison rooted at its core, ready to lash into my body the moment I let myself feel too good. The flesh is cracked and dry, the arteries crusted over, the veins and nerves suspended in thin, impenetrable layers of ice.

I shouldn't unleash my burdens on him. There would be too much to untangle and shoulder. He'd allow himself to get bogged down by my issues and traumas if it meant loosening the weight on my back. I can't do that to him.

So I'll continue hiding my story in the cavities of my chest behind barbed wire and ice, where he can't find it.

"Mason? We're here."

I blink. Suddenly, we're in the slant of my driveway, and I'm staring vacantly at the garage door as Cameron's engine thrums beneath us. The rain is thick and heavy against the windshield. "Right," I say, pushing the passenger door open. "Thanks for—"

"Wait." He pops out the umbrella, then circles around the car to me, holding his hand out. I pretend I don't see as I push myself to my feet, his umbrella slanted toward me to keep rain from soaking into my flannels.

He walks me up to the front door until we're under the porch awning. The gray rain is a thunderous ringing in my ears, assaulting the house and asphalt as I stand there, watching the swinging chair sway against the biting breeze.

"If you want to get out of your house, text me," Cameron says, pulling my attention to him. There's pancake batter stained on his T-shirt, the top of which pokes out from under his windbreaker jacket. "I'll pick you up, whatever time it is."

I can't help but smile, weak as it might be. "Like mother, like son," I mumble.

Cameron winces, like I've said something to trigger him. But then his shoulders loosen, and he sighs, a soft smile coming to his face. "Yeah," he whispers. Then his back is to me, and he's striding to his car, umbrella hovering over his head. The farther away he gets, the more prominent my bodily aches become, as if his distance is draining me of warmth. Or maybe his presence gives me so much happiness that I forget about the pains until he's gone.

Is a thank-you enough?

My heart sends a particularly stabbing pang into my chest, causing me to wince. Tears are budding in my eyes—a familiar, boring feeling at this point. My soul is ugly, deformed, rotten, mutilated. I can't let him see it.

Cameron falters near his driver's door, palm extended toward the handle. "Hey," he calls out, barely audible above the rain bullets colliding with the pavement. "Coach says if I ace my next quizzes this week, my GPA should be high enough to get me on the field for Friday."

He pauses. I hug my arms, watching uncertainly.

"I'm going to win the game," he continues. "And then I'm going to ask you out."

My breath stutters in my lungs. My eyes widen.

"You can say no again." Cameron swings open the door. "But I figured I'd let you know so you can think about it."

The tears are threatening to leak down my face. Really? After refusing to open up to him, after he caught me *using* him to distract myself, he still wants to pursue me? My chest aches, but it's also ablaze, like he's pumped raging heat into my veins. Some of the ice caked around my heart trickles away. I can almost see a tinge of scarlet return to the gray, colorless arteries.

How long have you been hiding yourself?

I couldn't muster an answer. I have one now. I was fourteen.

Nearly fourteen.

I step out from beneath the overhang covering my porch, allowing the sky's weight to crash down on me, permeating my flannel, causing my shirt to sag and my pants to weigh heavier on my hips. "Cameron," I say softly, knowing full well he can't hear me.

He does. He turns, and when he sees me standing in the rain, his eyes expand with alarm. "Mason!" he says sharply. "What are you—"

"You asked me yesterday what I'm running from."

He stares at me, glued to the driveway.

"It's . . . my fiancé," I choke out. "Ex-fiancé."

My fingers curl deeply into my fists.

"His name is Liam."

CHAPTER TWENTY-TWO
CAMERON

Mason just told me something important, yet I'm too distracted by the fact that he's standing drenched in the rain to give an adequate response. "What are you doing?" I demand, rushing forward with my umbrella to shield him from the frigid water. "You're soaking wet!"

"It's fine." He looks up at me with those big glassy eyes, trembling again. Is there ever a point in time where he isn't shaking with cold?

"Let's talk inside," I say, nudging us toward his front door, but he catches my wrist.

"I don't want to go in there," he whispers.

"You're freezing!"

"It's fine," Mason says again. "I'm used to it."

His words dig like a knife between my ribs. I stare at him in dismay, rain shattering against the ground around us, wondering why that makes it okay. His skin pales as the water's iciness sinks into his bones.

He starts to step out from underneath the umbrella. Panicked, I follow him, trying to keep it level above his head. "Stop!" I order. "What are you doing?"

"Your umbrella is too small. I don't need it—use it for yourself."

"Come on. How are we supposed to have a conversation like this?"

Mason smiles—it almost looks genuine. He tilts his head back as if to greet the water cascading from the sky, and it pummels his body with a ferocity that doesn't faze him. "I've just told you my secret and all you care about is that I'm cold and wet," he says. "Anyone else would be demanding details."

"Come sit in my car where it's warm," I plead.

"Mm . . . no. This is what I deserve."

The knife twists deeper into my abdomen. "What?" I croak.

"For the way I've been using you. Especially after everything you did for me last night," he says, shrugging. "I should feel uncomfortable, and rain is good for that."

I can't even fathom how fucked up this is, how he feels he should punish himself because I met the lowest bar of decency by taking care of him. "Fine," I growl, and I snap the umbrella shut, then toss it onto the lawn. The rain hits me like a sack of bricks, so heavy and with such force it makes my knees twitch with strain. "Then we'll be uncomfortable together."

Mason's weary smile dissolves when he sees my hair matted against my sopping face. "Don't be annoying," he mutters as I fold my arms against the chill laying siege to my body.

"Tell me about Liam."

Mason glances around the street, as if scouting for eavesdroppers, then lowers his eyes to the driveway, fumbling with his aquamarine pendant. "It's a long story. But I could show you?"

I blink through the water attempting to flood my eyes. "Show me? Like pictures?"

"My journal," he whispers.

Oh. Mason wants to share his story without having to speak in depth. Maybe his journal documents whatever happened between him and this "ex-fiancé" guy, Liam. The mere word sends a shudder of revulsion down my spine. Was Mason actually engaged to someone with a real wedding ring? Or is he exaggerating—like a swap of "promise rings" or whatever? I've never seen Mason around anyone other than the varsity team. Maybe he's from a different high school?

"I have to get it from my drawer," Mason whispers. He doesn't want to go inside.

"I'll get it," I tell him. "But promise you'll come to the car."

He hesitates, then nods.

It doesn't take me long to find what he's referring to. First, I awkwardly apologize to his father, who's sitting in the living room. He stares vacantly at me when I pop through the door. I make a mental note to ask Mason what his father's job is later, and why he's able to sit at home on a Monday watching TV. "Mason?" he asks flatly.

"He's fine," I respond.

He goes back to the news. I kick off my shoes to prevent trekking too much water through the house as I jog into Mason's room. In the bedside table, there's a ratty, worn journal plastered with peeling stickers—sharks, planets, polka dots, cars. I tuck it beneath my jacket, then return to the driveway. Mason is huddled in my passenger seat, leaned against the window.

I plop into the driver's seat. When he sees me draw the journal out, his cheeks redden. "It's embarrassing," he says quietly. "I started it when I was thirteen. But it'll give you an idea of what happened without me having to explain everything. I . . ." He swallows audibly, looking away. "I don't know that I could."

I feel tremors of trepidation deep in my body, like I'm about to unearth something that'll give me nightmares. But he trusts me enough to share this, so I'm willing to accept whatever consequences come of reading this.

Mason is starting to look around fretfully again, so I bring us down the road until we're nestled into a spot that faces Lake Ever-green, the gray surface agitated by the onslaught of rain.

I flip open the cover and begin.

Journal #11—last entry, some day, I don't care anymore

Dad says I'll heal.

Not sure that's true. Feels like I'm shattered into ten thousand pieces. How do you put something like that back together without missing bits?

I'm being dramatic. No wonder he stopped loving me.

Or maybe he didn't. He said he always will even when I threw his ring in his face. Not sure I believe him. I need space. It's strange to admit because he's been beside me since the beginning.

I know I should try to get myself out there. Find a club to join. Do something. I've wasted every year of public school staying away from my classmates, and what do I have to show for it? I'm pathetic. Fucking useless. Will anyone even care to get to know me during senior year?

Apparently they're looking for a water boy for the football team. I hear the guys are nice. Though everyone says you should keep an eye out for their quarterback. I don't remember his name, but I'll stay out of his way if I get the position.

Nothing else to say anymore. Brain isn't working.

Bye forever.

CHAPTER TWENTY-THREE
MASON

It's the only way I could think to convey the bulk of the story without going into a convoluted ten-hour ramble about everything. It's hard for me to even think about it without wanting to self-detonate. Let alone explain it aloud.

I hug my knees, wishing the heat of his car would penetrate my skin. Our seats are drenched—I hope it won't ruin his interior. The beach and lake are devoid of people, the sand soaked and the rain bouncing off the waves. Cameron's chest puffs up with a deep, silent breath, and he arches his neck against the headrest, gazing at the ceiling. His face has been surprisingly neutral, considering how expressive he usually is.

"Something happened." He tilts his face sideways to observe me with calm eyes. "He crossed the line and you broke your engagement. Is that it?"

Ah. It's only natural he'd ask. I've long since stopped being emotional about it, but my stomach still plunges with nausea.

"You don't have to tell me," Cameron tacks on, but I shake my head.

"It's fine. You know the rest, so there's no point in hiding it." His right palm rests on the compartment between us, and I scoop it up to give myself something to focus on, fiddling with his fingers. He's chilly, too, after our time in the rain, though still warmer than me. "It was a little over six months ago. One night, we were at his parents' place, drinking and watching movies. And drinking. And drinking."

The hazy blur of lights from their theater room swirls before me. I don't remember which film we were on—only the sensation of his hand on my knee.

"He kept pouring me liquor," I mumble, sifting between his soft knuckles like I'm looking for something. "We'd just gotten into an argument about something. He was mad. It's all I can remember thinking about."

Cameron's hand tenses. Slowly, his fingers curl in around mine, squeezing.

"I . . . uh. Woke up in bed." I clear through the bothersome hitch in my throat. "I was wearing my clothes from the previous night. But something was off. It was like my body knew something my mind didn't."

I don't know why the words want to evade me now. Why my voice quiets, like it's new, terrifying information I haven't thought about every single day since it happened.

"Liam walked into the room from his shower. He didn't realize I was awake," I whisper. "He came to grab a shirt. I saw his body. There were . . . scratch marks. It was like . . ."

I fall silent, unable to push through the words. I can still see it. Feel it. The weakness of my limbs and tenderness of my bones, the ache in my head from blacking out. The flash of apprehension in his eyes when he noticed I was awake. The way I had to pretend not to notice anything, like I was fine and this was fine and everything was fine, because what would he do if he knew that I knew what he did?

"I didn't say anything for a few days," I say quietly. "But I kept thinking about it. I would lie in bed and get this uncomfortable feeling,

wondering if he'd come through the door. The thought of him . . .
scared me."

I pause, tracing the valleys between Cameron's fingers again because I don't know what else to focus on.

"I felt like I was good at knowing what might trigger him. He was
a threat, but an anticipated one. I knew what he'd do when he was
angry and what he *wouldn't* do. But the way that night happened . . .
how he kept making me drinks after our argument, even though he
knew I couldn't handle that much . . . I mean, I guess it's partially my
fault too for continuing to drink—"

"It's not," Cameron says sharply. It's the first time he's spoken in
the last couple of minutes, and it startles my head up. "He's the adult.
He knew what he was doing. It's not your fault, Mason."

I can't help but wince from those words, how straightforward and
brutal they feel. I'm sure they're right. Even if they don't feel right.

"Anyway," I whisper. Moving on, because I don't have the strength
to deliberate my own innocence right now. "The point is that his anger wasn't *in the moment*. It was calculated. That was when I realized
for the first time that I needed space. I broke things off because all I
could think about was . . ."

My eyes are moistening again. I can still feel the way my body
protested movement. I can still feel chunks of his skin dislodging
from under my nails as I washed my hands, blood staining my fingertips because he forgot to rinse that part of me off. The thick, pungent
tension as I lingered in his house the following morning, pretending
like I didn't want to scream as panic swallowed me whole, trying to
find a casual excuse to leave that wouldn't make him suspicious.

Because if he could do something like that, what else was he capable of?

I feel like the breath is being choked from my lungs, so I kick the door open and sputter out, "Fresh air," then stumble into the rain I've been trying to dry myself from for several minutes. My flannel clothes immediately become drenched again, my hair flattening and icy coldness plunging deeper into my veins. I stumble down the slope leading toward the soggy beach and kick up wet, muddy sand, allowing the grains to sneak into my tennis shoes and scratch my feet. It's a miserable feeling, yet I deserve it.

Because I *miss* him.

The warmth of my tears coagulates with the frigid water pummeling my head. It's pathetic. How can I miss someone who hurt me so much? As time passes, and I've learned what it means to be alone, I'm realizing how difficult it is to not have someone there. Someone who makes you their priority. Someone who chooses *you* above all else.

And Liam did. Despite his flaws, he chose me, showed up for me, listened to me, cared for me. I relied on him when things were difficult. Being *wanted* feels good, even when it straddles the fine line between love and possessiveness.

It's why I'll go back to him.

All he has to do is keep pushing. Does it matter if he hasn't changed? What's a little pain if it means being with someone who will always pick me at the end of the day? Maybe I'll be afraid, but I'll be secure. What awaits me after high school is a sprawling house, free time to indulge in hobbies, arms snug around me at night. Even if his love is unstable or poisonous or covetous sometimes, it's still love, isn't it?

Things are always better more often than they're worse.

I clung to that line from my journal. When I was on the ground, my cheekbone throbbing. When he left to go back to college, and the tension leaving my body was so overwhelming that my knees collapsed. When he would lock the doors the moment we were back in his car, and I knew I was in trouble.

When I look at your future, all I see is loneliness.

My father's words strike me painfully deep. I stare down at the sand absorbing my shoes, the aquamarine necklace jabbing into the slick skin of my collar.

I'm interrupted from my contemplation when a heavy weight slams into my side. I stagger with a surprised gasp as two bulky arms fly around me, wrenching me between them, flattening me to a broad chest cloaked by a thin windbreaker jacket.

"I'm sorry you've suffered so much," Cameron whispers, his voice sharp in my ear despite the thunderous hiss of rain.

I stand limp in his embrace, cheek nestled into his shoulder. It's fine. It is what it is. I chose this. I could've said no when Liam asked me out. I could've walked away the first time he lashed out. I could've found ways to distance us before it reached the extent that it did. But I didn't, because I still can't function without him.

"It's not your fault," he says, like he can read the thoughts sewn into my veins and lingering cancerously in my bone marrow. "He manipulated and controlled you. It's not your *fault*, Mason."

He already said that in the car. Hearing it doesn't change anything. But if it makes him feel better about everything he ingested, I'll let him hold me.

I'm about to tune out, but he suddenly snags my face and pulls me off his shoulder, lifting it so he can stare directly into my eyes, water dripping from his thick lashes. "That man at the gallery," Cameron snaps. "Was that him?"

Oh. I nearly forgot he was there. "Yeah."

"I won't let him touch you again. I promise."

He sounds so sincere that my eyes boil hotter. "Thank you," I say, smiling weakly. The sheen of rain is so heavy now I can barely see him, despite our proximity. "But you shouldn't worry about me, because no matter how hard you try, he wins. He always does. He always will. Don't make promises you can't keep, okay?"

I curl my hands around his, both of which are still sprawled around my face, and lower them to his sides. He looks like he wants to say something else but can't find the words. His jaw trembles with strain.

I step around him so I can ascend the slope and return to his car. His fingers catch my wrist, tugging me to a gentle stop.

"Then," he says, "I'll never let you be alone."

My muscles stiffen.

"I won't let you suffer by yourself," Cameron says, his voice ringing along Lake Evergreen, cutting through the howl of rain against the steely water. "Maybe he'll keep coming back, over and over, and you'll have to try to heal yourself that many more times. And maybe he won't give up on you. But neither will I."

I stare at the muddy sand caking the bottoms of my shoes, dazed.

"I won't leave you," he continues, his grip sliding down my wrist, touch skimming along my palm and unfurling my fingers so he can slip his own between them. "If I can't stop him from pushing you down, I'll be there after to pick you up. If he makes you cry every week, I'll make you smile every day. Because that's what you deserve."

His words strike a chord so deep within my soul that it reverberates through my entire body.

What I . . . *deserve?*

The shock wave is so intense that it shatters every inch of ice within me, from my achy joints to the veins in my heart, and suddenly, for the first time in days, or months, or years, I feel alive.

What I deserve.

Cameron's touch burns my hand, and despite being ravaged with tremors, heat flourishes through me, causing my pulse to quicken and my stomach to tingle.

I always assumed Liam was the only one who could care about me because he had the exact right personality type that would make me tolerable. He fell for me before my appearance became more enticing, so I believed his love was genuine.

But it's not gentle. Or kind. Maybe it was at first, but I've long forgotten the feeling of his authentic desire for me. I tolerated his treatment because I didn't deserve anything better.

But I do. Right? I deserve a gentle love. And kindness. I'm worthy of something better.

Cameron Morelli wants to give that to me. Maybe I'm allowed to take it. This kind, gentle love.

I spin toward him, sand slipping beneath my heel, and grab his jacket, hiking him closer.

I kiss Cameron like I've been waiting for him for seventeen years.

CHAPTER TWENTY-FOUR
CAMERON

I'm not sure how I went from wanting to punt the water boy off my football field to wanting to kill a man for him in a couple of measly weeks. Yet here we are, standing on a soaking-wet beach in the middle of an autumn rainstorm for no explainable reason other than that Mason was feeling the vibes of misery.

It makes sense, all of this. Why he is the way he is. My stomach is gnarled with nausea and anger, the passages of his journal coming back to me in short, violent clips. I can almost *see* it, these horrible implications. And suddenly it's not about tutoring or football or being rejected or stomach flutters.

I want to protect Mason. And I want to hurt the person who shattered him.

Mason's kiss is short but intense and pleading, like he's been waiting for a moment like this and doesn't care that his lips are wet, purple, and quivering with cold. I'm so startled that by the time I reconcile that his lips are on mine, he's pulling away, lowering himself to the flats of his feet. "Sorry," he chokes out, staggering back when he notices my bewilderment. "It's just . . . nobody's ever said something like that to me, and—"

I scoop his face up and plant my mouth against his. The taste of syrup lingers between his lips, despite the rain attempting to wash it away. Water trickles down our faces, dripping from my lashes, hair, nose, and jawline as I draw back. "You deserve happiness," I say sharply, massaging his brows to prevent more water from falling into his eyes.

Mason's eyes leak despite my attempt to keep them free from moisture. He curls his hands around my wrists and closes his eyes, as if reveling in the feeling of someone holding him in this way, or maybe fearing that I might pull away and leave him in the rain.

"Ask me," he says quietly.

"Ask you what?"

"Out."

My brows shift higher into my forehead. I say, "No."

Mason blinks with surprise.

"I told you I'd ask you out after Friday's game," I say with a smile, and I muscle out of his grasp so I can place one hand on the flare of his hip, guiding his waist against mine. "So, I'll wait until I'm the star quarterback again. What better thanks can I give you for helping me study than the honor of being asked out?"

Mason rolls his eyes, but then he's laughing, and I momentarily forget that we're shivering, sopping-wet messes standing in clumpy sand while heavy rain wrenches leaves free from the trees framing the beach. "I feel special," he says with a sardonic nod. "Not many get to experience the pleasure of Cameron Morelli asking them out *twice*."

"You are special."

A hint of color returns to his otherwise pallid face. "We should make sure you ace your quizzes. It would be embarrassing if you asked me out after bench warming the game."

He makes a fair point. "You're saying you want to spend more time with me?" I ask, fluttering my luscious lashes.

"I'm saying you ended up embarrassed the first time you asked me out, so you should do what you can to not be embarrassed the second time."

Fair point. Again. "Then we should study today," I say, shrugging. I take his wrist and pull him up the mucky, slippery slope of the beach to the parking lot, because the purplish undertones of his ice-cold skin are difficult to ignore. "It will be completely casual since we're just friends."

Mason smiles again and I want to throw myself back down the hill and into the lake. "Right," he says. "Then I guess we can't kiss again until then."

". . . Friends with kissing benefits."

"Sounds scandalous."

We approach my car, and I startle him by flipping him at the shoulder and nudging him against the passenger door. Maybe it's wrong to look at him like this when we're not together, but seeing his wet clothes clinging to him for dear life causes flaming heat to itch my stomach. I want to see the color return to his skin and redden his face.

I'm beginning to understand why he's different.

It's because I started to get to know him. *Really* know him. In a way I've never gotten to know other partners. Even on the rare chance they were interested in me beyond my reputation, I wouldn't let them close enough to develop any actual attraction to them. Mason, though, didn't even give me the choice to shove him away. For some reason, my protective walls became fully translucent to him after a few hours of hanging out.

"Scandalous is the best kind of kissing," I say softly, using my index finger to guide his chin up. With little more than the strength of my knuckle, I pull him to his toes. The power I wield with masculine charm frightens even me sometimes.

His cold, shaky breaths unfurl against my lips. "There's an unfair power dynamic," he says unconvincingly. "I'm your tutor. It would be wrong to kiss a student of mine. Like, twice."

"Yes, your authority over me is very problematic."

He smirks, but his throat bobs like I flustered him. "I didn't know you could understand sarcasm, Cameron. Let alone use it."

"Maybe you're rubbing off on me," I say, fluttering my wet lashes seductively (again). "I'm sure you've fantasized about doing that."

Scarlet roars through Mason's cheeks, and he makes a noise of dissent, putting his palm on my face and forcing me to stagger away. It's completely deserved.

But worth it.

We clamber into my car, which is sure to reek of mildew tomorrow, but I don't care. I got to have this moment with Mason. It sounds like it won't be easy to keep that Liam bastard out of his life, especially if he has the Gray parents' favor. "I'll talk to my mom to see if you can stay with us for a while," I say, driving along the curved roads to my little house in the woods.

"I can't become a permanent member of your home just because there's a chance my ex might show up at mine," Mason says softly.

He's not wrong—my parents will probably agree to let him stay when needed, but they won't let it be the solution. It would be like sealing a bullet wound with a Band-Aid. A temporary fix that doesn't address the root of the issue, which is that this man will always be a threat to Mason unless action is taken.

As to what that action should be . . . I don't know. Mason can't just pack up and move. Nor should he have to. Why can't he feel safe and secure in his own home? It's not fair.

"What do your parents know?" I ask, muscling through the chills raking my body. I need a hot, steamy shower. But Mason gets it first— I don't like the ashen tinge in his skin.

"Everything," Mason says softly.

"Like, even . . . ?"

"I didn't give details. I just mentioned that I think something bad happened that night. Mom said I shouldn't judge him so harshly since I can't remember anything. Dad was pissed for a while. Though, not anymore, apparently."

The thought is mind numbing. "They still like him?" I ask weakly.

"'Like' isn't the right word." Mason hoists his knees into his skinny chest. "He's wealthy and knows important people and my mom thinks our engagement is the only way to get in on that. There's this banquet for his graduation they're making me attend . . . anyway. Basically, they know I have a hard time making connections and think I'll be alone forever if I don't stay with him."

My fingers whiten around the steering wheel as I pull into my driveway. What kind of lives have his parents led that they're willing to accept the abuse their son has endured? I jam the car in park and twist toward him, frowning. "Can you refuse to go to the banquet?"

"I can try. But life in my house would be miserable. Mom holds a grudge and takes it out on us, especially Dad." Mason massages his temples with frustration. "I just need to show up, eat dinner, make small talk, and go."

"I'll be there," I say sharply.

Mason's eyes shimmer, and his cold fingers creep atop my hand. "Thanks, Cameron," he whispers. "Though, it might cause issues if I show up with someone who wasn't invited."

"Maybe. But with me there, maybe he'll be less interested in bothering you."

Mason looks dubious but smiles at me anyway.

We head inside to warm up. Mom left not long ago—sadly, with the hospital being short-staffed, she's been having to go in more

frequently. But that just means Mason and I get the house to our-
selves, since Dad's still at the tattoo studio.

"Are you okay being alone with me?" I ask. "We can go somewhere public."

Mason's face softens, and he presses a hand to the small of my
back, which causes tingles to rush up my spine. I didn't even realize
my heart was pounding until his touch begins to slow it, easing my
tension. "I don't mind," he mumbles. "You make me feel safe."

Those tingles pour into my stomach. I'm not sure how he can cool
me off and light me ablaze simultaneously.

I let him wash first, and though I tell him to take his time so he
can warm up, only eight minutes pass before he's wandering out,
dressed in a fluffy T-shirt and sweatpants tied tight around his waist.
He looks so good in my clothes, all I can do is cough on my saliva, rush
into the bathroom, and slam the door so he won't see me blushing.

CHAPTER TWENTY-FIVE
MASON

Cameron kisses me deliberately, and it's not a sensation I've felt in years. Liam might've once held me this way, like I was a valuable artifact. A high-quality gemstone that needed to be treated with care.

But then he began to test my fragility—a scratch was fine, so long as I remained intact. He pushed harder, though. Bits and pieces flaked away, followed by masses that disintegrated in his palms. Over a few years, he had nothing to hold but the dust of my remains. It still shimmered, though, so he didn't mind that there was little substance left to cling to.

Cameron and I should've studied longer, maybe. I have a job to do—get this boy on the field so they can make the playoffs. The scout is coming this week to observe, and I'm not even sure Cameron remembers. After everything I've learned, I can't help but wonder just how invested he is in *football*. He mentioned yesterday that he only used it as a form of escapism before he came here. So what does it mean to him now? Why did he go back to it?

We *definitely* should've studied longer. But his waist feels good notched against mine, and his arm looks so sturdy braced on the bed beside my head, and the warmth of his hand is electrifying on the curve of my waist beneath my shirt. Or *his* shirt, which has noticeably fallen away from my shoulder.

Liam kissed me with devotion in the early stages of our relationship. Over time, his lips stopped worshipping, and instead bit, gnawed, and bruised. Cameron means every movement he takes. The way his lips caress mine is achingly hot, and leaves my stomach in fluttering shambles.

Despite the glaring fractures in my soul, he makes me feel desirable. Like there's something about me worth claiming.

I wasn't sure I could be intimate with someone after Liam. I fumbled for excuses to avoid it, because I knew the weather would be warm or because I could still feel phantom pain from our previous rounds. Kissing became something I winced away from, and his touch made me fidget with discomfort.

This isn't like that. I can *feel* Cameron's intentions. As his hand presses up the length of my waist and rib cage, dragging my shirt with it, my agitated heart nearly overloads. He knows what he's doing, taking his time, fully conscientious of every shift of his body. He's not acting out of his own desire—he's also testing the waters to see what I like.

I tighten my knees around the flare of his hips. This is how it's meant to feel, isn't it? Though his left arm does the work to suspend him above me, his fingertips rest near my hair, which he threads and twirls between his knuckles with gentle reverence, like every strand is precious to him.

How did I not realize something was missing? When did Liam stop caring about the way I felt? How could I go back to him now that I know there are others who can care about me, who are willing to wait and be patient for me to open up?

I'm feeling selfish, and maybe that's okay. I crunch my fists around Cameron's T-shirt, tugging up. He makes a noise of surprise, but pauses a kiss so I can slide it over his head, leaving his midsection bare. "Too much fabric," I say, smiling guiltily.

He returns this with a boyish one of his own. "If you want to see me naked, just say so."

"I basically have," I point out. "At Ravi's party. You were drenched in your underwear. Didn't leave much room for imagination."

Cameron's grin only widens. "So you were looking."

"Don't flatter yourself," I say with a smirk, flicking his nose. "You took me by surprise when I walked in. Your junk was right there, staring me in the face."

"Maybe my junk just wanted to say hello."

"Oh, it did. Trust me."

Cameron bursts into surprised laughter, and it makes me feel warm and cozy. He laughs the way flames crackle in a firepit. "I'm going to kiss you until you can't stand it," he whispers, and he plunges back down before I can stammer through a witty retort, working my lips like he wants to devour me. His skin is soft and smells like warm vanilla bodywash. His muscles flex tantalizingly beneath my touch, bones shifting, blood pumping, heart throbbing.

My hands entice him. I can feel how he reacts to me—the tremble of his skin when I graze his hip with my fingertips, my touch feather-light. The tightening of his stomach muscles when I arch up against his chest. The sigh when I scratch a line down his spine with my index finger.

Did Liam ever react like this, like the mere sensation of my touch was intoxicating? I don't think he cared much about my hands, despite how forcefully he restrained them.

Cameron is fully aware of my touch, and it's invigorating. Even though I'm lying beneath his weight, I feel like I have control. This heightens when I give an experimental push, and he obeys the command, rolling onto his back so I'm the one hovering over him. He's wearing that same playful smile from earlier that only deepens the flush in my cheeks.

"What?" I demand. "I've never gotten to straddle someone."

"Nothing. You're cute, is all."

"I'd rather be sexy right now," I admit.

"You are."

I blink at him in surprise. When he notices, he makes an exasperated hand gesture.

"Like, you're sitting on my waist wearing my clothes, and the shirt is falling off your shoulders, and your hair is rumpled up and you smell like my bodywash. It's making things very difficult for me."

That warm rush floods my stomach. Liam used words like "cute" and "adorable" and "pretty" but rarely things like "sexy." It always made me more conscious of our age gap—I wanted to mature faster. "What's difficult about this?" I ask, bending over so the loose fabric of my shirt grazes Cameron's bare chest, and our faces hover inches apart.

His fingertips trace an enticing trail up from the outsides of my thighs, to the curves of my hips, to the sides of my waist. "The fact that we're only friends with kissing benefits until Friday," he mumbles, eyes lingering on my lips.

I nudge my nose against his, smirking. "I told you to ask me out."

He sighs, maybe regretting his decision. Then he reaches up suddenly, hands fumbling around the back of my neck. A heavy weight disappears from my shoulders as he unclasps the aquamarine necklace dangling between us and sets it aside. I didn't realize I was still wearing it. "Do you even like jewelry?" he mutters.

"Mm . . . I don't mind it."

He catches my jawline and pulls me into a fervent kiss. Maybe he just remembered he said he'd kiss me until I couldn't stand it. And I can stand it quite a bit, so he has a lot of work to do. I won't make it easy, either. Cameron is fun to torment. So I tug and nip, testing his limits to try to make him throw in the towel. And maybe I move my hips suggestively a few times to draw out groans of frustration.

How far can I push him? Even being wrapped in his charm, I feel nagging suspicion. Part of me wants to see if I should do something to genuinely irritate him, just to see his reaction. What if I accidentally elbow him or knock my teeth against his? On the field, he punched someone for making him angry. I'd be lying if I said that moment hasn't been lingering in my mind.

Yet Cameron has made me feel precious in a way Liam maybe never did.

But I saw the strength behind his fist. The way it nearly flattened that football player. Cameron is a reactionary person. He's big, too—not as looming as Liam because of the age gap, but stronger than a typical high schooler, thanks to his incessant training. And I'm still learning the ins and outs of his real personality. What if there's a dangerous part of him I haven't seen yet?

"Mason?"

I blink, and suddenly my face is framed between Cameron's hands, and he's massaging beaded tears from my cheeks with his thumbs. When did I start crying? *Why?*

"Fuck," I whisper, wrenching back so I'm sitting upright on his navel, smearing my hands over my drippy eyes. "Sorry. I don't mean to keep crying in front of you."

Cameron's shifting off his back, though, drawing himself up to sit propped against the headrest. "Did I make you uncomfortable?" he asks.

"No, of course not . . . Sorry . . ."

"Don't apologize." He taps the backs of my wrists, which are still sprawled over my face, hiding my humiliation. "Can I help?"

He sounds so sweet and supportive. Am I allowed to say it? I told

him I'm comfortable being alone with him, so won't he get angry if I
suddenly change my mind? We've been kissing for so long—isn't it
ridiculous how out of nowhere this feeling is?

Cameron plucks my trembling hands away from my face, then
draws both to his lips and kisses the divots between my knuckles. He
sprawls one of my palms over his mouth, kissing along the engraved
lines, then shifts farther down until he's at the veins of my wrist. He
moves to my other hand and treats it with the same care.

"I'm . . . I just . . ." It's all I can manage to croak.

"You can say it."

His voice is encouraging. Even so, my heart burns with terrified
anticipation, and it only causes my face to become wetter and splotchy.
Bile stings my throat.

"I'm scared of you," I breathe.

Cameron doesn't react to this. His mouth is still grazing the base
of my palm.

"Sorry. I'm sorry. I just d-don't want to get h—" I wrench my shirt
over my face so he can't see as the weight of a thousand hands curl
around my heart, wringing it. "If you get mad, what am I supposed to
do? I can't . . ."

The panic closes around my throat. Slowly, Cameron's arms curl
around my waist, and he collects me into his chest, wrapping me against
him. For several seconds, he strokes my hair, his grip never relenting.
Eventually, he says, "I know promises probably won't reassure you. The
truth is . . . I don't know what to say."

He pauses. I lie limp against him, forehead buried in the crook of
his neck.

"You've been hurt over and over by someone you love," he whispers, breath fluttering the hair around my ear. "Even if you know I
won't hurt you, that fear might never leave. It's okay. I'll never be upset
with you for feeling that way." He fans his palm up the back of my

neck, eliciting pleasant tingles. "I'll do anything I can to make you feel safe. And I'll try to remember that sometimes, it may not be enough."

My tears stain his skin and roll down the curve of his shoulder. He's speaking so softly, it makes my chest ache. "Lot of baggage," I mumble into his neck.

Cameron snickers, to my surprise. "Good thing my shoulders are so muscular."

I tug my face back to look him in the eye. I don't miss the way he goes to catch my tears with his thumbs again, like he can't help himself. "Sometimes you say the sweetest things," I murmur. "And sometimes you make me want to shove those painted rocks in your mouth. There's never a happy medium."

"Love me for who I am, water boy."

"Who said anything about love, quarterback?"

He narrows his eyes, and I smile sweetly, to which he scowls in defeat. "Can I kiss you again?" he demands. I know why he sounds irritated—it's not because I interrupted us. He's annoyed that he *wants* to keep kissing me, even after I've sassed him.

"If you must," I say with a drawling sigh. "Though my mouth kind of hurts."

"Doesn't have to be your mouth." He twists, upsetting my balance and nudging me onto my back. He props himself over me with one arm, using the other to stroke my hair away from my face. He kisses the center of my forehead. His lips graze a path to my temple. Then to my wet cheekbone. The flat of my chin, the line of my jaw. Each kiss lingers sweetly, and when he finds the arch of my neck, a sense of warm calmness washes over me.

It's nice, being kissed like every inch of me matters. Like there's not a single part of me that doesn't deserve attention. He's at the hollow of my exposed collarbone, and I feel the surprising, hot scrape of his tongue against my skin. My breath noticeably shortens, and so he torments that spot a little longer, pouring his heat into me, until I'm appropriately flushed and he moves along.

He nudges my shirt up and continues kissing, gentle and slow yet deep and deliberate. I feel like I'm being worshipped. It seems strange, letting a boy I only partially know do something like this. Would Liam have kissed me like this if I had asked? Maybe, but I don't think he would've done it with Cameron's level of care.

Cameron makes his way to my rib cage before making the jump to my thigh. He pushes the bottom of my pants up over my knee, then kisses me there, carefully moving up my skin until his lips are against my ankle. "You have cute feet," he says, setting my left leg down and scooping up my right. He sprawls my toes back and kisses my foot, which sends more pink hues climbing into my face.

"You have a foot kink, don't you?" I ask in dismay.

"Nah, yours are just cute. I want to bite them."

And he does, the absolute creep. I squawk in horror, trying to wriggle my ankle out of his grip, but he holds fast to it with a gleaming grin and sinks his teeth into the other side, enough that it tickles. "I don't exist for your fetishes!" I cry out, but he's already moved to my ankle, and then my calf, nearly shuddering with laughter.

I throw an arm over my face, my ears burning.

By the time he finds my mouth again, I've fallen asleep under the kind touch of his lips.

CHAPTER TWENTY-SIX
CAMERON

The roar of the football field is familiar and nerve-inducing. It's been a few weeks since I joined the starting lineup. With Mason's help, my grades are finally above the required level to participate in sports again.

Yay.

That scout is here.

This is supposed to be a huge, life-changing moment as I mosey out onto the turf, helmet secured. The flooded bleachers begin to roar. Maybe it's the ultramassive head Mason insists I have, but I'm damn sure they're louder than usual, confirmed when the announcer reads my name and the entire field quakes with excitement.

I peek into the stands to find my parents—it's their first time watching since before the day they traitorously abandoned me to "spend time together." They made personalized jerseys to wear with MORELLI written on the back, which they're currently sporting.

Somewhere in the stands is the Alpine University scout, who's decided to come out to Elwood once more to assess a new star player who appeared out of nowhere. He'll be watching carefully. Depending on how this game goes . . .

I could free my parents from the financial burden of having to send me to college.

My nerves are in overload, and I'm hyperaware of every sound,

every sensation around me. This is all made worse by the fact that
Mason isn't here. Maybe it was his stint in the rain that did him in, but
a couple of days ago, he fell ill, and he's been bedridden since. I wanted
to visit him after school yesterday, but he was adamant I stay away.

"You can't get sick before your first game back," he said over the
phone, his voice nasal from his stuffed nose. He was exhausted, so I
doubt he would've appreciated me telling him how cute he sounded.
"Just focus on your last quiz."

"I was going to ask you out after the game," I whined.

"Wait for the next one."

Over my corpse. I have a can of broccoli cheddar soup I'm bringing him after the game, sickness be damned.

I'm not sure what to look at now that he's not here. The entire
team is jumpier than usual—this game determines our spot in the
playoffs, there's a scout nearby, and I'm back on the field for the first
time in weeks. Without Mason's steadying presence and unbothered
atmosphere, everyone feels wobbly on their feet.

The first-string players huddle around me, punching my shoulder
in wordless congratulations. Coach Barnett paces nearby. The stadium
lights illuminate everything in white brilliance despite the evening
darkness pouring over Elwood, and the smell of leather, equipment,
and turf flutters my stomach.

I like football. I really do.

After today, it might become my entire life.

I close my eyes against the fluorescent lighting and overwhelming
stimuli. I imagine Mason in front of me, wearing that fond, skeptical
expression, the flecks of gold gleaming in his amused brown eyes.

Quarterback, he says in my head, and he reaches out, flattening his
cold palm to the center of my chest. *Just breathe.*

So I do. When I next open my eyes, I'm ready.

Focused.

The game starts, and thoughts of Mason drift away in place of instinct and game strategy. It takes me a few plays to slot fully back into place among my team. Sure enough, though, halfway through the first quarter, the familiarity of my situation returns. The feeling of being looked to, relied on. Trusted.

I somehow forget that the scout is watching several times until Coach Barnett reminds me I'm being examined both on and off the field. That the man is analyzing my techniques, but also how I interact with my teammates. How I sprint, how I position myself, how I handle tricky situations and exploit the opposite team's weaknesses. I'm doing well, I think. Yet there's a strange little voice nagging at the back of my head.

Would it be the worst thing if I did poorly?

The answer is yes, of course. Performing poorly means sacrificing a stable future. So why is the thought even crossing my mind?

We win the game, obviously. I don't remember most of it. All the guys sprint toward me, shrieking with excitement now that we've officially earned our spot in the playoffs. Somewhere in the chaos I get lifted up onto Darius's and Ravi's shoulders as if I just cinched the championship game for them.

I should probably be screaming and crying with excitement. I could've just earned my way into a Division I college with a single game. Like Beau Rainey. I've overcome so much to get to this point, and I know I should be proud that I'm following in my football idol's footsteps.

Yet all I can think about is that damned can of soup in my backpack.

The crowd is on fire and lingers after everyone leaves the field. It's satisfying to have so many guys clap my back and tell me I played well. Especially Barnett.

"Better keep those grades up," he warns, but he ruffles my damp hair affectionately.

Darius invites me to a get-together at his place, but I decline. I have to regale Mason with all the thrilling details of the game, so as soon as I'm freshly washed and in my sweatpants and T-shirt, I'm out the door. I texted my parents to say I'd be going to Mason's, so they don't wait up for me. For now, I have one priority.

When I arrive at the Gray household, his father opens the door. His dark, tired eyes soften when he sees me. "Cameron," he says in greeting. "Mason said I should turn you away so you don't get sick."

"I brought him soup," I explain, flashing the broccoli and cheddar can.

I swear the ghost of a smile passes over his face as he steps back. "Come in if you're prepared to get sick with a nasty head cold."

I'm fully prepared. I jog down the hallway and push into his bedroom. The shades are drawn, the room swathed in darkness. There's a shivering, sniffling bundle beneath the bedsheets—Mason is curled up, snuggled into the pillow.

"Cameron?" he whispers.

"Boyfriend," I reply.

His lip quirks as his lashes flutter shut. His skin is a pallid gray, the bags beneath his eyes are violet, and his nose is dried red from tissue. "Not yet."

I kick the door closed and prop myself on his bed, combing my fingers through his hair. The moment my skin comes into contact with his, I feel all of the lingering tension and adrenaline from earlier melt out of my body, and I slump completely on top of him, sprawling out on his bed.

"Cameron!" he snaps, thumping the top of my head. "You shouldn't be here."

"Wanted to see you," I mumble.

I feel his chest move with a heavy sigh beneath my head. Then he squirms one of his hands free from his blankets and rests it against my back, rubbing gently. "How'd the game go?" he whispers. "Or how much did we win by?"

"Thirty-four to twenty-one," I say, popping my head up with a cheery grin.

"Wow . . . Maybe your ego is justifiable after all."

"I've been saying that for weeks."

He snorts and pinches my cheek. "I'm proud of how quickly you improved your grades."

"I had a reliable tutor," I admit.

"Mm. Lucky you." He takes hold of my hand, then unfurls it against his cheek, nuzzling into it. Something about how willing he is to place my palm against his face, how fully he trusts it, causes butterflies to spring to life in my stomach. I trace the scoop beneath his eye with my thumb, wishing I could transplant heat into him so he wouldn't always be cold.

"Want soup?" I ask. "You probably haven't eaten, right?"

He nods guiltily. "Sorry for stealing your Friday night."

"Is it stealing if I'm giving it to you freely?"

Mason offers the softest smile. It takes strength to leave his side, but he needs sustenance, so I rush to the kitchen to heat it up. After a few minutes, I return with a steaming bowl of broccoli cheddar soup. I help him muscle upright and set the bowl in his lap, then crawl onto the mattress. His fingers tremble around the edges.

"I can feed you," I offer.

Mason's cheeks flare red. "It's a cold—I'm not dying." He manages to draw the spoon to his mouth, though the liquid wobbles precariously.

I sigh, scooping the bowl from his hands before he can utter more than a scoff. "It's okay to be weak sometimes," I say, bringing another spoonful to his mouth. He glares at me, but reluctantly closes his lips around it. "You have me to lean on. So just . . . lean. You know?"

Mason's eyes sparkle. Either my words resonate with him or this is the best soup he's ever devoured. "Liam would've called me needy," he says with a smirk.

"Helping you when you're sick is bare-minimum relationship behavior." I wrap an arm around Mason, hugging him closer before pulling his legs sideways into my lap. "I *want* to be here. I *want* to help you get better. Plus, I get to spend time with you, so I'm winning all around."

Mason squirms and covers his face like I've humiliated him.

"What?" I demand.

"Nothing. I just want to kiss you."

"So do it."

He swats a scolding hand against my chest. "You'll get sick!" he says irritably. "Bad enough I'm basically sitting in your lap. You're inhaling all my death fumes."

"If I get sick, you'll just have to return the favor and spoon-feed me," I say, shrugging as I shovel more soup in his mouth. "We'll be boyfriends by then, so it'll be expected of you."

Mason nearly laughs into his palm but catches the habit last second, lowering his hand to his lap. "You're certain I'll say yes."

"There's no reason to say no," I point out. "Now that you know I have a thoughtful personality to go with my immaculate body and sparkling eyes."

Mason bows his head in agreeance. "Yes, Your Majesty, thou art truly a flawless being graced by the gods."

". . . You're teasing me."

"Not I."

I humph, jamming the spoon back in his mouth so he can't make another snide remark. But when I draw it out, he has more to say.

"There's something I don't understand." He shakes his head with bewilderment. "You're actually a good person under . . . the nonsense. Why are people always breaking up with you?"

I didn't expect the conversation to turn like this. Mostly, people just stick to assumptions. But I'm comfortable around Mason, even if he likes to jab me with his cruel words of sarcasm. "People usually break up with me because they think I'm not into them," I admit, clearing through an incoming rasp in my throat. "They ask me out because I have this reputation for being fun and spontaneous and sex driven. But I'm not very physical with them, and if I am, I'm not into it. They end up feeling like I'm not actually interested in them, and usually they're right."

Mason's mouth opens slowly for the next spoonful. "Then you're not sexually attracted to people very often?" he wonders.

"Almost never."

"Almost?"

"Well." I rub the back of my neck, then mumble, "There's you."

Mason's cheeks color once again. I'm sort of becoming obsessed with the sight. "Like, you want to have sex with me?"

"I . . . Yeah. I'm pretty sure." I've never really fantasized about sex, but every time I'm close to him, and our breaths are heavy and short, and his eyelashes are long and his snarky voice is in my ear and his skin is slick, I want to pursue him further. "Like, I want to make you feel good."

Mason frowns through another spoonful of soup. "I'd never want you to feel obligated—"

"It's not like that," I say quickly. "I'd want to do it. Because I'm getting to know you, and I'd like to make you feel . . . safe. With me. I think it would feel, like, nice. To know you trusted me enough. To let me. Do that. To you."

I don't know. Why my sentences. Are fractured. Like that. Probably because I'm not sure how to explain myself. Whenever I've had sex conversations with my partners, it often ended in frustration or tears on their end, like I just called them hideous. Even just encroaching on the subject makes me squirm.

"So the difference between me and everyone else is what?" Mason's head tilts sideways, curious. "You feel closer to me? Like, emotionally?"

I nod, hoping it doesn't sound silly. Mason smiles again, tickling my chin with his thumb. "I can't believe I'm saying this, but thanks for being willing to fuck me, Cameron Morelli."

I choke on my inhale. "I'm being sincere!"

"I know, and it's making me want to kiss you even more." The amused twinkle in Mason's eyes flickers out. He buries his head into my shoulder, sighing. "I started hating sex after a while. I thought as I grew older, I'd understand what was so good about physical intimacy. But the issue wasn't just my age, was it? It was . . ."

"He didn't take care of you," I say softly. "Just used you to take care of himself."

Mason shrinks into my chest. I wish I'd beaten the shit out of Liam when I met him.

"You should sleep," I say, placing the empty soup bowl on the bedside table.

I hear a small puff of laughter into my shoulder. "Clueless . . ."

"What?" I ask defensively.

"Go home, quarterback. If there's a chance you're still healthy, you should get out while you can." There's a playful lilt to his voice as he squirms onto his side, faced away from me. The realization slams into me.

I'm supposed to ask him out.

I've been so distracted that I forgot my initial intention for this night. Snickering, I wriggle under the covers and scoop him against me, hugging him. "Cameron," he groans, but I catch his jaw and tilt his face, pressing a gentle kiss to his lips.

He gasps, ripping his face free. "Don't!" he snaps. "Do you *want* to get sick?"

"Yes," I say simply, trailing kisses up the length of his jaw to his earlobe. I tug it between my teeth, and it glows red alongside his face.

"Cameron Morelli, if it turns out I have a deadly virus, you'll be comatose for the next game."

I frame his hip under my hand and tug so he fits snug against me. "Go out with me," I breathe in his ear.

He makes several incoherent noises before scoffing at my audacity. "Maybe I don't want to now," he says.

"You don't like the way I kiss you?" I roll my fingers over his shoulder, drawing his flannel sleeve with it and exposing his pale, smooth skin. I bend over and give him a gentle nibble that causes goose bumps to spring up his neck.

"You're impossible," he grumbles.

"And you're avoiding the question." I catch his hand, which was moving to thunk my head again, and draw it to my lips so I can slide the tip of my tongue between his knuckles.

The color deepens in his face. "Because you're a dick," he says tightly.

"Or because you like being teased," I suggest, carefully dragging his flannel sleeve up his elbow so I can kiss his forearm. "Go out with me, water boy."

The brief tremble of his skin under my lips doesn't help him plead his case. "What will you do if I say no?" he murmurs.

"Respect your boundaries," I say solemnly, before adding, "Or just continue taunting you until you say yes."

"How toxic," he snips, burying his face deeper into his pillow.

Is that permission? I drag my fingers up from his pale waist to his torso, bunching his shirt as I move higher up his ribs, to his chest, to his collar. I shift farther down into the bed and hold his bunched shirt up, then kiss every inch of skin I can find between his shoulder blades, my fingers fumbling with the elastic of his flannel pants. When I start massaging the flare of his waist, Mason seizes my wrist like I've electrocuted him. I make a mental note that he's sensitive there.

"Go out with me," I whisper into the divot of his spine.

"You're not even asking. Just demanding." His breath has noticeably shortened and his skin is flushed enticingly, to the point where I wonder if his fever is flaring up. Maybe I shouldn't be so mean. "How is that romantic?"

I roll over him and prop myself on my elbows, smiling at his attempt to conceal himself. "Can't you pull your face out of your pillow?"

Mason shifts onto his back to glare at me. His eyes are bruised with fatigue and his pale lips are curled down with feigned disdain. His black hair is in cute disarray from having been lying in bed and his honey-brown irises are rimmed red. Even plagued with debilitating illness, he's enchanting to look at.

"Mason Gray," I say, slow and careful. "You have bewitched me, body and soul."

"You're really going to recycle—"

"I fall asleep thinking about your smile," I continue, grazing my knuckles against his soft cheekbone. "I like the way you put me in my place. I can't stop thinking about the look on your face when you're somewhere that makes you happy. I want to do everything I can to see that side of you, to make you smile and glow."

Mason stares at me with wide, glistening eyes.

"I want to make you feel safe," I whisper. "And heard. I want to be someone you can trust and rely on. I want to become your new favorite place. More than Annie's Brews, more than the gallery. When you think of escape and warmth and comfort, I want you to think of me."

I lean over so our noses are skimming, a calm smile furling my face.

"So," I breathe, pinching his chin between my thumb and index finger. "Will you go out with me, Mason Gr—"

He seizes the back of my neck and wrenches me down into a kiss.

The next morning, I wake with chills and a scratchy throat.

Fucking worth it.

CHAPTER TWENTY-SEVEN
CAMERON

Mason Gray is breaking up with me.

"I am not," he says, staring ahead of him to the twisty, curving roads as I drive us home from practice. It's sinking deep enough into fall now that the trees are fully steeped in autumnal colors, from blazing reds and oranges to warm yellows and browns. The midnight-black asphalt before us is littered in damp, flattened leaves, making it difficult to see where the dotted lines are.

"Why are you being so shady, then?" I demand. He's been questionably quiet, more so than usual. He didn't tap my head with his clipboard even once today during practice, which is grounds for concern. "What did I do wrong?"

The edges of his mouth are pulling up, so I guess I'm not in trouble. "Everything is perfectly fine, Your Highness. How can this modest peasant demonstrate his innocence to you?"

My lip gnarls into a scowl. "Every time I think you're done being a little shit—"

"Take this left."

I choke on a curse and yank the steering wheel left, nearly sending us up onto two wheels as I swerve into the parking lot of a tiny brick building tucked among the towering trees. It's paneled with giant glass windows and there's only one car present—a neon OPEN sign is blinking in the entryway. A flower shop.

"Wait here," Mason says, and he clambers out of the car.

"Why—?"

He slams the door and heads inside before I can even finish my sentence. I'm going to find a way to make him pay for his rudeness later. As I'm devising a list of torture methods—including poking his waist mercilessly—he reappears, holding a bouquet of pink, purple, and blue assorted flowers in a glass vase.

"Okay, we can go now," he says, and then he holds something out to me.

It's my fucking *debit card*.

"*Excuse me?*" I wheeze out, fumbling for my wallet in my pocket and flipping it open. How did he . . . ? When . . . ?

"Let's head back to your place," he says brightly, like he sees nothing wrong with this.

"What the *fuck*, Mason?"

"Come on. Hop to or whatever."

I stare at him in disbelief. He stares back, smiling mildly over the flower arrangement.

"I'm adjusting your regimen," I snip, swinging out of my parking spot and back onto the road

"Oh?" I can faintly see Mason's smile widening in the corner of my eye. "Do tell."

"I'm adding an abdomen exercise. You know the one."

"You're going to tickle me as punishment for my behavior?" He gives me that lighthearted, skeptical look that sets my heart aflutter. "You say you have no kinks, but I'm starting to think you're a dirty, rotten liar, Cameron Morelli."

I slide up into my driveway and park the car, then snap my seat belt back. Mason kicks open the driver's door, scoops the flowers off the passenger seat, and clambers out. I follow after him with a huff, snatching his backpack off the floor and hiking it onto my shoulder. The unexpected weight nearly staggers me.

"What the hell do you have in here that's so heavy?" I demand.

He merely gestures at me to follow him to the front door. Sighing, I do, the obedient lapdog that I am. I fumble for my keys and jam them in the lock, then push through into the ranch house and flick the lights on. I'm not expecting anything to be out of the ordinary.

Except it is.

There are a ton of paint supplies organized atop a white sheet on the kitchen table. On the floor of the living room are an assortment of board games, all meticulously prepared so no setup is required. I blink, trying to process what I'm seeing.

Mason unzips his backpack and heads to the table of paint supplies, then begins to pull out rocks of varying sizes, placing them on the table. "I texted your dad earlier, asking if he would be able to help before he went to work," he says softly, not looking back at me. "I didn't think he'd go to this extent—I was hoping he could just get the supplies and games out. But he went a step further. So. Yeah. Surprise?"

I can't find the words to respond. All I can do is stare at Mason uselessly.

"I just thought it might be fun to . . . you know." He throws me a hesitant peek over his shoulder, before quickly breaking our gazes. "Also, here. Take these." He steps toward me and nestles the bouquet of flowers into my arms. "Give them to your mom, okay? It's been a while since you brought home flowers for her, right?"

He waits for my response, twisting his fingers near his navel. I can't even think straight. It seems like such a simple thing, so why am I so baffled?

"Sorry," Mason says, and that's what wakes me from my stupor. There's a trace of panic in his face and his shoulders are stiff with tension. "I should've asked first. Maybe this was a bad idea. Sorry. I didn't mean—"

I sweep Mason into a giant hug, wrenching him off his feet into the air, holding him flat to me. My eyes are warm and stinging with tears, which melt into the fabric of his peacoat. "This is the best surprise I've ever gotten," I whisper, holding him aloft easily despite how rigid his limbs are. "Thanks, water boy. This means . . . everything."

Finally, he moves, wrapping his arms and legs around me when he realizes I have no intention of putting him down. "I just wanted you to know that I think you're lovely," he says into my shoulder. "You don't have to hide anything from me. Okay?"

I snuggled my face deep into the crook of his neck, smiling. "Okay."

So we paint some rocks. We play some board games. I give those flowers to my mom.

Suddenly, I feel like I'm breathing for the first time in years.

CHAPTER TWENTY-EIGHT
MASON

Remember, things are always better more often than they're worse.

It's the only line in my journal I remember writing. And it was true. For every time he struck me, there were ten instances of him driving home from college to pick me up from my parents' house, a box of chocolates in hand. For every time he seethed at me, there were ten instances of him carrying me to bed when I fell asleep on the couch or washing my hair gently in the shower. For every time he was jealous when I interacted with others, there were ten instances of him taking me on dates he knew I'd love, holding my hand while I rambled about my interests.

Yet eventually, maybe even before the ring was on my finger, these pleasant moments were overshadowed by the fear that at any second, a soft and loving moment might disintegrate into hostility. And so, even when things were "better," there was always an overarching concern that they could become "worse."

And if they did, it was my fault.

I don't feel that way with Cameron. When things are good, they're allowed to be good. I don't feel the fog of apprehension hanging over my head, or a nagging voice warning me to watch my words. Even when he rolls his eyes at my snark, I know he's never upset. In fact, it's a poorly concealed secret that he likes it, even if he claims otherwise.

We've been dating for a few weeks, and he's never been upset with me for feeling a certain way around him. Since I blocked Liam's number (or since Cameron blocked it for me), my anxiety has been worse, and it shows. When I'm with Cameron, making a futile attempt to work out, I know he won't lash out. But the thought still lingers, unnerving me. He won't, but he *could*. He won't, but if he *did*, there's nothing I could do. He won't, but . . .

What if he does?

I hate it. I feel safer around Cameron than anyone else, but he's the one person who could hurt me beyond repair. I've shed my layers, exposed my secrets, pains, and fears. He holds my heart in his hand, and with a bit of pressure, he could crush this barely functional, healing organ. He won't.

But he could.

Maybe one day I'll relax fully around the person I like. I'm starting to realize how messed up I am. Even in the months without Liam, I was blissfully unaware of how deeply his nails clawed into my soul.

I want to be authentic around my partner. And my current one— who will hopefully be my future one, and maybe my forever one—is helping mold the path. If a teasing insult hits the wrong way, he doesn't sulk and make me guess why I've earned his annoyance. He doesn't withhold his love until I give him a blanket apology. He just . . . tells me.

I'm becoming more comfortable expressing when I'm upset, too. With Liam, I kept my frustrations bottled because I never knew when one might irritate him. There are moments, particularly when Cameron is around a lot of people, where he transforms into that arrogant person I rejected. He convinced himself this is who he needs to be to prevent his past from catching up to him. But I'm not hesitant to tell him when he's being a dick and needs to tone it down, because he's proven he can take it without lashing out.

Cameron watches the gallery with me, during which he helps me tidy up around the place. On particularly slow mornings when it's empty and we don't have much to do, we maybe . . . um. Misbehave. The issue is that he's handsome, and his lips are soft and taste like flavored ChapStick. Which makes it difficult for me to care about anything other than assailing them.

He's good at it. Kissing. He's conscientious about how he's moving and where his hands are. Sometimes he'll massage my ear until I'm nearly sweating and have to shove him back so I don't do something I'll regret. His favorite place to stick his hands is where I'm the most sensitive—my waist, just beneath the edges of my shirt. He rarely initiates a higher intensity level, preferring slow kisses to torment me until I whine about it.

We've gone on dates, too, involving movies or trying local restaurants. Dad seems intrigued by Cameron and sometimes even sneaks me money to go out, which is nice. I haven't admitted that we're dating, because they're probably still hoping I'll reconcile with Liam, but . . . I don't know. I think Dad has some idea about us.

And maybe he doesn't hate it.

He won't defend me for not wanting to go to the banquet, though. I've tried bringing it up to Mom, but whenever I suggest ditching it, her face tightens and her lips thin until they nearly disappear. "They're family friends celebrating a massive accomplishment," she says shortly. "You're going, or you're grounded."

At least she's not threatening to kick me out, but her definition of "grounding" is extreme. Once, she removed my bedroom door, confiscated my phone, called me in sick at school, and forced me to lie atop my bed contemplating what I'd done. She ordered Dad to obey her "nobody talks to Mason for three days" rule.

If I have to go, hopefully I'll find the courage to officially end things.

With Cameron maintaining steady grades, he carries Elwood into the playoffs. After every home game, there's some kind of party—a bonfire, team dinner, evening on Lake Evergreen. Maybe I'm imagining it, but the guys seem a little warmer than usual. Toward him, specifically.

Cameron always made himself the butt of jokes due to his immature behavior and loud personality. Now that he's toned back some of the more exaggerated parts, it feels like his friendships are becoming more authentic. He can hold conversations with them that don't devolve into jokes. He's not flaunting himself around like he's the best thing since wireless earbuds. He's still kind of clueless at times and occasionally braggy about his skills, but he's more . . .

Himself.

Though Cameron and I considered keeping quiet, everyone catches on that something's going on between us. Especially since Cameron makes no effort to stop outwardly flirting with me, and I'm maybe kind of into it.

"Hey, Mason," Darius says from the sidelines when I'm watching Cameron and the offense drill down the field, tapping my clipboard against my chin. I've never been invested in football—at least until I realized how much it meant for Cameron's future, and I've been tragically devoted to watching the scoreboard ever since. Even if he hasn't quite realized yet that he's not as into it as he thinks. "Are you and Morelli going out?"

The question jolts through my body like lightning, causing my hairs to stand up. "What?" I squeak, instinctively lifting my clipboard higher over my face. "Why would you ask that?"

"Sorry—it's none of my business." He's speaking softly, but his deep voice carries through the sidelines, perking the other boys' ears. "You two just seem closer than normal. You're still studying, you show up to parties together, and Jody swore he saw you walking into the aquarium holding hands."

Images from that afternoon tear through my head—me standing before giant water tanks, rattling off my latent fish knowledge from when I was obsessed with sea life in my younger years. I held Cameron's hand, my stomach tingling whenever he asked me additional questions to test my knowledge, like he cared about what I had to say. And then after a nice dinner at my favorite vegan restaurant, retreating to Cameron's house because his mom was in the OR and his dad was out with a drinking buddy. Where I promptly pushed him onto the living room love seat and gave my first hickey.

"I don't . . . We're not . . ." I cough on my sentence. We decided not to tell anyone because we didn't want to undergo interrogation. I don't want people placing bets to see how long I can hold Cameron down before he abandons me or whispering about whether we're compatible.

"You're not?" A knowing grin furls across Darius's face, and he leans over me. I have to resist the urge to hide my entire face behind my clipboard. "Because the team's been picking up vibes. You know?"

"Vibes?" is all I can choke out.

"Yeah. Like, you're actually smiling at him. You're constantly whispering to each other on the sidelines like you're hiding a love affair. He's been different lately, less cocky and bitchy than normal, and we've been figuring that it's something to do with you. And the way you two keep looking at each other?" Darius shakes his head, eyes twinkling with exasperation. "Fucking hell, I keep feeling like I'm interrupting something."

I think my entire body turns red. "I don't know what you're talking about."

But then we win, and everyone screams because we make it another round into the playoffs, and suddenly Cameron's sprinting toward me and tearing his helmet off and swallowing me in a deep, sweaty, desperate kiss. I must get caught up in the moment, because I forget Darius is standing *right there* until he says:

"Right. Not a clue."

Oops.

Just like that, we're out to our peers, and the whispers and gossip are about what I expect because Cameron is the school's most interesting person right now. But being able to kiss me in the hallways and hold my hand to classes makes him particularly cute and eager, so I don't regret that moment.

Liam never wanted to flaunt me around. He was afraid people would think our relationship was strange—or that's what he claimed. Looking back, I guess it's probably more like he didn't want to deal with unnecessary questions or legal trouble. He was shy of eighteen when he asked me out. I never thought of it as strange because of how mature he made me feel. Regardless, when we were on dates or wandering around, he'd sometimes wrench away when he noticed people staring. This paired with Dad's unease about our relationship made for a glaring red flag. At the time, though, I didn't understand the significance of the color.

Cameron isn't ashamed of me or our relationship. The fact that he wants to show me off feels good. Which sounds objectifying, but whatever, I don't care, because the mere thought makes me tingly.

I'm supposed to be content. This is my happily ever after, right? My prince has saved me from my demons and a cursed ring, and we're together, *working*. I feel protected. Cared for. Happy. But there's one final hurdle.

I don't owe Liam anything. Cameron has spent hours poking holes into my insistence that I should unblock him to explain myself, or consider staying acquaintances so Mom can maintain her "connection" to an affluent family that keeps pulling away because of her lack of social status.

"He's a groomer and abuser," Cameron says, over and over, though the words still hit my brain in this jarring way I can't fully accept. "He was a whole-ass adult when he made you dependent on him. He *knew* what he was doing."

I usually have a rebuttal, because Liam wasn't all bad. He just *wasn't.* "He wouldn't have sex with me until I turned sixteen," I point out, or sometimes I say, "Four and a half years isn't weird. There are several couples who have ten- or twenty-year age gaps."

To which he starts showing me *articles.* I never took Cameron to be a research guy, and I'm so impressed that it takes a while for what he's showing me to really sink in. And maybe he's not wrong. In fact, when he pulls up one paper about emotional abuse, the sight of it drops my stomach. I've read it.

I sent it to my dad months ago.

Over the last couple of years, I've tried convincing my parents to go to marriage counseling. Dad doesn't want to deal with the stress, though, and Mom thinks their relationship is fine—only that Dad should work on himself so she has no reason to be upset. It's starting to feel familiar.

I wonder, sometimes, just how thought-out Liam's plan was for pulling me under his wing. He knew the only romantic relationship I was familiar with was my parents. He knew I struggled to form connections, reassured me that I didn't need people my age. That they were too young and immature to understand me. He knew how desperately I looked up to him, how my eyes sparkled whenever he came to babysit me.

But I don't want to assume he was manipulating me from the

start. Maybe there were signs that something was wrong, like when he discouraged me from pursuing things that would expand my world, like marine biology or even summer camp.

There were good times, I swear. He's not a monster.

Or he wasn't always.

I have a lot of work to do on my self-worth, grasping the extent of the damage Liam dealt me. Once this final step is taken care of, I can move forward. The banquet. I'll break things off for good so I can look forward to the championship game and fully support my boyfriend without this gloom hanging over me. I'm ready to face him.

As ready as I can be.

CHAPTER TWENTY-NINE
CAMERON

I'd be lying if I said I didn't almost fumble yesterday's playoff game because the anxiety of today was crushing. It doesn't help that I've been pondering a text from Coach Barnett, who says the scout who came to observe me will be returning to see the championship game.

But I'm not going to think about that. Tonight is Mason's night.

I stand before my mirror, staring vacantly at the sapphire suit and tie I rented. The world is cloaked in wintry late-November darkness, and I'm hot enough that the biting breeze coming through my open window causes my skin to steam. I can hear branches on naked trees scratching together, the sound grating. My parents, who are usually bantering nauseatingly on Saturday evenings, are abnormally quiet.

They have a good idea about who Liam is—not all the nitty-gritty details, but enough to know why I need to be there for Mason. They're not happy about my decision to attend his celebratory banquet, and we tried brainstorming ways to get Mason out of it. When I brought them to him, though, he changed. He looked more resolute. Determined.

"I need to tell him face-to-face that it's over or he'll keep showing up," he told me. "You don't need to come, but I won't avoid it anymore."

Honestly, that banquet is the last place I want to be. I hate the effect Liam had on me. Standing in the gallery, I was a deer in headlights. Shaken, stunned. I remember the moment his eyes iced my veins. If he's been looking at Mason like that for years, it's no wonder his soul was completely frozen over when I met him.

After today, Mason will hopefully free himself of the shackles around his wrists. He makes a good point, too—Liam seems persistent, and unless Mason draws the line in the sand, there's every chance he'll ambush Mason at home or school to plead his case.

When I enter the living room, Mom smiles widely. "My handsome baby," she says, straightening my jacket and readjusting my tie, worry lining her tired features. "Be safe, okay? Call us if you need anything. Dad and I are going out to dinner across the street from the banquet, so we'll pop over if needed."

"Thanks." I clutch her nervous hands and smile reassuringly. "It'll be okay."

She purses her lips, unconvinced. Until Dad wanders over and settles a burly palm on her shoulder. "Sometimes we have to trust our kids can handle their issues without us," he mumbles. "All we need to do is be on standby."

Mom draws a forlorn sigh, then nods. "Good luck, bun," she says softly.

So I'm off.

When Mason allows me inside, his mother instantly jumps to demand why I'm here. Mason, half-dressed in slacks and a button-down, turns on her with fierce eyes and says, "If I'm going, I'm bringing Cameron."

The woman scowls, the sequins in her spaghetti-strap dress glinting in her eyes. Her jaw clenches tight enough for the bone to jut through her skin. "I RSVP'd for three people," she says. "You can't bring guests to an invite-only party."

"Then I won't go."

Mason's confrontational aura pops my brows. I've been to his place multiple times, and Mason is usually quiet around his parents, sometimes disregarding their presence altogether—particularly his mom. I tried deciphering their relationship for weeks, and it took me a while to realize that they just . . . don't have one.

Mason's mother looks ready to unhinge her jaw and scream, so I snag his shoulders and steer him down the hallway. "Let's get you dressed," I squeak out, nudging him into his room.

"What's your problem?" Mason mutters, eyes locked to the carpet.

"I know you're nervous." I press my thumbs behind his neck, trying to massage the strain away. "But half the reason you're going is to keep your mother from becoming a miserable wretch. Let's keep her in a decent mood, okay?"

Mason turns and swings his arms around me. I press him protectively into my chest. I wonder if his tremor will go away after tonight, or if it will continue haunting him into the future.

"I'll be there the whole time," I whisper.

"I know." He snuggles deeper into my jacket. "Quarterback?"

"Water boy?"

"You look really good in a suit."

I snicker, drawing back to pose seductively. "Is there anything I could make look bad?"

Mason rolls his eyes, then heads to his bed to finish getting dressed. He fumbles with his shirt buttons, though his fingers are too shaky, so I join him and take over. His vest and tie are burgundy, which looks good against his porcelain-white skin.

Mason's eyes remain resolute. He's ready to tackle this night despite what his body is trying to convince him.

A half hour later, we're entering the banquet hall.

The stars glimmer overhead and the parking lot is alight with dim streetlamps. I thread my fingers through Mason's as we follow his parents toward the looming glass structure, within which we can hear a live orchestra. The hallway leading to the banquet rooms is carpeted and framed with golden chandeliers and exquisite paintings that slow Mason's pace so he can better examine them. At least until his mother snaps, "Keep up, boys," forcing us to abandon them.

"We can look at them on the way out," I suggest.

Mason smiles, squeezing my hand tighter. I resist the urge to scoop him off his feet and go running far, far away.

We step into the most beautiful ballroom I've ever seen. Diamond chandeliers drip from the ceiling and jut from the room's pillared perimeter. A warm golden ambience rains over the hall, causing the silver-trimmed chairs to glint as brightly as the china meticulously placed at the rounded tables. Delicate flower bouquets are centered atop each silky cloth.

The room is flooded with a hundred upper-class people wearing fancy jewelry and clothing, swirling champagne. When we clear the entryway, we're stopped by a couple decked out in the flashiest garb of everyone. The woman is dressed in a shimmering gown with a plunging neckline, tall and elegant, her makeup smoky against her striking, ice-blue eyes. The man beside her wears a velvet tuxedo and buckled shoes.

"How good to see old friends!" the woman says with a honey-sweet smile, gliding forward to encompass Mrs. Gray in a hug. She draws back before Mason's mom can even wrap her arms around the woman. "You're stunning. I'm sure it's not often you can dress up like this, mm? Oh, and Mason, my darling little thing, come here!"

She sweeps toward Mason and gathers him into a more lingering hug, forcing him to drop my hand. "Hello," he says lightly.

"I'm so happy you made it. Liam will be thrilled." She takes his wrists, smiling earnestly at him. "Whenever we speak on the phone, all he wants to discuss is how much he misses you."

Mason doesn't smile back. "I came to talk to him," he says, eyes roving the hall, clearly seeking Liam out.

"Oh good! He's more than ready to spoil you, pumpkin." She chuckles, drawing her husband to her side, who looks between everyone with slight distaste, like we're not worth his time. At least until his eyes latch on to Mason and appear to soften.

"Mason," he says warmly. "Our boy's been out of sorts for months. You should've thrown him a bone so he could better focus on his studies."

Mason's expression remains unchanged, but their casual words make me grind my teeth. Why are they talking like the only reason he exists is for his shitty ex? I want to snap at them, but that's not why I'm here. I'm his emotional support, his quiet bodyguard. He can handle himself.

"Liam is a grown man who knows where to place his priorities," Mason says, snatching my fingers. I can almost feel his nerves shooting through me. "I'm sorry to say he'll need to learn how to live without me. Though, it's lovely to see you both."

Mrs. Gray's face contorts with horrified anger. Apparently she didn't realize Mason's goal tonight was to officially end things. Likewise, Liam's parents shoot each other a startled glance, and his mother's gaze falls to me. "And who's this?" she asks, her voice suddenly as frigid as her eyes.

"A friend," Mason says.

"You've brought a stranger to Liam's banquet?" Her knife-sharp jaw shifts. "He was so excited to see you, Mason. Yet you're only here to break his heart, all while flaunting around a new boyfriend. Isn't that rather inappropriate?"

"I couldn't agree more, Ella," Mrs. Gray says, her face straining. "But he refused to come without this boy."

They're talking about me like I'm not standing with them. Just as I'm wondering if I should speak up, Mason says, "I've moved on, and it's time Liam does the same. Though, I'll always be grateful for your support."

I wonder how much they're privy to. Do they know their son is an abuser? Did Liam and Mason hide their relationship until the age gap was more "appropriate"? I'm not sure. But being around these adults—these *parents*, neither set of which did anything to help Mason—makes my blood boil. I bite my lips to keep impulsivity from taking over.

"Well"—Liam's father steps away, drawing his wife with him—"we're sorry to hear that, Mason. I'm sure Liam will be there the moment you realize what you're missing. You're young—I suppose you still have growing to do before you can understand the weight of your mistakes. Enjoy the party."

They float away to greet other guests. I'm nearly bursting at the seams with anger. I want to unbutton my jacket and swathe Mason inside so nobody can look at him.

"Thanks, Cameron," he whispers.

I blink down at him. He lifts my hand and kisses my wrist, fully aware of his mother's glare, and the boldness flares my cheeks hot. "I haven't done anything," I croak.

"You're here. That's something."

Ugh. I can't wait for this night to be over so I can kiss him to my heart's content.

We move as a group of four, wandering the banquet hall. I stand in the back, holding fast to Mason while fancy people greet his family, eyes raking the room in search of the demon hosting this banquet. I swear people are staring at us.

The longer we venture through the hall, the more Mason unfurls. His trembling becomes more pronounced, and when Liam's father speaks through a microphone to the room, he nearly shoots out of my grip.

"Thank you for attending this special event for my beloved son," the man says with a cool, aloof smile that reads *I'm above you all.* "The spread of appetizers is now available. We'll inform you when to be seated for the main course."

"You're fine," I whisper, massaging the side of Mason's wrist.

"I don't see him," he mumbles.

"Me neither."

We make our way to the buffet-style table, which is stocked full of warm treats and handhelds. Unfortunately, the smell of food causes Mason's cheeks to tint green. He staggers away and says, "I need a second. Um."

His eyes flit to the bathroom.

"I'll go with you." I start stepping out of line, but Mason shakes his head, fanning a palm over his stomach.

"No." He steps farther away, the pale tone worsening in his skin. "Would you get me some bruschetta? I just need a moment. Alone."

He beelines for the restroom. I have the urge to follow him—who knows when Liam might try to ambush him? But I don't want to make things harder if all he truly needs is a minute to himself. So I pile bruschetta onto a fancy plate and bring it to our designated table. His parents are seated, and I don't know that I want to be alone with them, so I return to the appetizer table to find something for myself.

That's when I see him.

Not Liam.

There's a bulky, looming man chatting in a group with warm bronze skin, jet-black eyes, and tight cornrows crawling toward the back of his neck. He's wearing a formal suit and a striped tie. The sight of him freezes my heart against my ribs and ices my breath in my throat.

"Beau Rainey?" I croak.

My football idol twists his head at the sound of his name and latches eyes with me. I think I'm about to dissolve from the sheer surrealness of seeing him standing there, directly in front of me. This man I've framed my entire future after. The man who overcame so much adversity and clawed his way to success . . .

I realize the small cluster of people around him have fallen silent, and they're watching me, waiting. My mouth is hanging open, so I quickly collect myself, clearing my throat. "Sorry," I whisper, and I whirl away, because oh my God, oh my *God*—

"You want to talk?"

His voice pours over me from directly behind. I peek back to find that he's stepped outside of his group and is looking down at me with a polite, friendly smile.

"Oh my God," I wheeze out.

He laughs, the sound deep and cavernous. "Fan?" he asks.

"Huge," I breathe. "I'm . . . I just . . . I'm a quarterback, too."

"Yeah? Whereabouts?"

"Elwood High." I can't even hear my own voice. I feel like I'm choking on my own air. "I'm going to play at Alpine. Or I might. If I'm recruited. I have one more game to impress one of their scouts, so . . ."

"No shit?" Beau Rainey—fucking *Beau Rainey*—grins at me, giving my shoulder a congratulatory pat. "That's great, kid. You excited?"

I stare at him, trying to thrust the word "yes" between my lips.

It doesn't come.

"I don't know," I say instead.

His thick, fuzzy brows pop with curiosity.

"I mean, yes," I correct myself. "I'm . . . Yeah. I think I'm excited."

Beau Rainey's head leans sideways. He's observing me fondly like I'm a small woodland animal. "You think?" he asks. "Just nervous, maybe?"

I'm not sure why I said those things. I should be utterly thrilled at the chance to be financially stable and famous in the college sports world. I want to confirm it's just nerves, but . . .

It's more than that, isn't it?

"Can I ask you something?" I mumble.

He shrugs, swirling his glass of champagne. "Shoot."

"What's it like? Being a first-string quarterback for a Division I school. Like . . . did you have a life outside of football?" I ask quietly.

Beau Rainey laughs but raises his hand apologetically when my face flushes. "Sorry—not trying to tease. I mean, sure, there are classes to attend and meals to eat, but your life is the sport. Working out, treatment, conditioning, NIL obligations, traveling to games, preparing for the next season . . . Hell, we couldn't even go home for the holidays because of games. It's intense. But manageable if you're passionate, you know?"

My jaw clenches with uncertainty. Maybe he notices my expression, because he props his hands on his hips.

"You don't love it, do you?"

"I do!" I protest, though I feel a pang of guilt for saying it, and I realize I might be lying. "I like it," I correct, my shoulders buckling. "I like playing and spending time with my teammates. I like having friends. I like being relied on."

"Ah." Beau Rainey massages his chin. "Then what's the drive to play in college?"

"Money," I admit. "My parents put a lot of work into getting me to this point. I don't want to put them in more debt by going to college."

The man's face softens, and he smiles again. "There are other ways to pay for college that don't involve sacrificing your life to a sport you only enjoy playing recreationally," he says, clapping my shoulder again. "There are hundreds of scholarship opportunities out there. You could try shooting for a Division II school—it's a little less intensive, and some of them offer partial rides. Division III schools also give you a more well-rounded experience, and you could find some that offer financial aid packages and merit-based scholarships. It's probably late in your season, but it wouldn't hurt to reach out to other coaches and send them videos of your performance. You're not cornered, you know."

I don't know what to say. My vision has been so tunneled in, focused on the peak of the mountain before me. Division I. Devoting my life to *sports* for the next four years, despite the fact that I'm only into it for the camaraderie. Juggling publicity and schooling and training and . . .

I didn't notice there were other peaks nearby. Not quite as tall and substantial as the one I've been watching, but still rewarding. Still attainable.

Football is fun. I want it to stay fun. I want it to be my hobby.

Not my life.

"I . . . Thank you," I say, and it's all I can manage to blurt out among the chaotic tangle of thoughts in my head. "That really helps. Thank you, Beau Rainey."

He nods with another friendly smile. "Good luck out there."

The man turns back to the group of people he was fraternizing with. The moment our gazes break, the world comes flooding back to me. The sounds of upper-class folks chatting over expensive booze, of a gentle orchestra pumping music through the room. I'm in a banquet hall. I'm . . .

At Liam's graduation ceremony.

I feel like I've suddenly been shot through the chest. The breath flies out of my lungs, and I hurtle toward the bathroom, my vision whitening, flinging the door open.

Mason is gone.

CHAPTER THIRTY
MASON

I bend over the sink, allowing cool water to trickle into my hands before patting it gently against my face to alleviate my heightened body heat. I gaze at the empty stalls and urinals behind me as I try centering myself.

I was ready for tonight. I had everything I wanted to say rehearsed. Why am I falling apart? The more people I talk to, the more tense I feel. I know I'm overthinking, but the sensation of eyes scrutinizing my every movement is overwhelming.

The bathroom door swings open. That's my cue to quit panicking and return to the table so I can save Cameron from awkward interactions with my parents.

I turn to the exit and my feet scrape to a halt. The panic lying in wait reels through me in full throttle. My heart plunges through my body and into my wobbly legs, pinning them to the tile.

"I'm glad you made it." Liam ambles closer in his white suit, a smile painted on his handsome face. "I wasn't sure you'd come—"

"Don't." I barely have the strength to utter the word. It's frustrating. I know what I want now, and it's not him. This is a good time to tell him. Isn't it?

"Don't what?" Liam cocks his head, dark curls fluttering against his forehead.

"Don't . . . come closer."

His eyes glint with astonishment, I guess because I've never had the gall to say that. Then he sighs and massages the bridge of his nose. "That boy has done a number on you," he says, and he steps sideways, giving me a clear path to the door. "Leaving me for a kid who can't even hold down a crab puff. Miserable idiot."

I furrow my brows. "What?"

"Your boy toy just ran outside to puke."

Oh no. Did he eat too quickly again? We've been dating a month and he's nearly made himself sick at least twice because of how he inhales his food. I stride to the door, and Liam watches with an expression I don't care to analyze, because he's not my priority.

"The necklace," he says suddenly.

I stumble to a stop. "What?"

"I want it back."

It's a simple ask, but it startles me. Even when I threw the ring in his face, Liam insisted I should keep it for whenever I changed my mind. This is the first time he's asking me to return a gift. Does this mean . . . he's prepared to let me go?

I fumble through my breast pocket and pull the aquamarine necklace free. I was fully intending on returning it, so his request gets this part out of the way. I allow it to spill into his open palm, and without another word, I'm through the bathroom door, through the banquet room, and into the hall with the paintings. I decide to try the back exit first, pushing through the glass door into the night. I've entered the dimly lit employee parking lot, which is devoid of people and sprinkled with dumpsters and dark, empty cars.

"Cameron?" I call, straining my ears for retching or groaning. It's deathly quiet—all I can hear is the whish of wintry wind through stripped branches.

He must've exited through the front after all. Though, why leave the building rather than run to the bathroom? Probably because he knew I was in there, collecting myself, and he didn't want me to fly into a sobbing mess by bursting inside and hurling his guts. I spin around to reenter the building, hands extending toward the door.

There's someone leaning against it. Calm, frigid eyes tear through the dim parking lot like pinpricks of light. I stare vacantly, trying to understand before it hits me.

Cameron isn't outside at all, is he? He's probably not even sick.

My fingers fumble along my pockets, seeking my phone. It's on the table.

"Finally, peace and quiet," Liam says, donning that familiar smile that softens his face. "I can't believe you left like that. You didn't greet me, hug me, congratulate me for making it through my hellish college career, wish me luck with my father's company . . . It's like I wasn't even there."

I stare at him.

"You knew the stress I went through during college. I thought you would've been happy to see me make it to this point. You said you'd always be there to support me. But, you also said you'd marry me. I guess promises don't mean much to you." He clicks his tongue with disappointment. "Then you're shameless enough to come to my celebration with a dipshit jock who somehow won your heart. Tell me, did you show your face here just to mock me? Is a few months all it takes for you to forget you loved someone?"

His half step forward awakens me. I mirror it, slowly, hoping he won't notice. I don't know what to do. I don't . . .

"Can we drop this?" Liam asks. The hum of the streetlamp on the curb is an incessant bug in my ears. "You brought him to make me jealous. To make me realize how much I fucked up."

"That's not true," I breathe. My eyes flick around the parking lot, seeking routes, but there's only the nearby street and banquet hall door. I can't outrun him. "Cameron's here to support me . . . It's nothing to do with jealousy . . ."

I try desperately to steady my voice. This is it. I'm confronting Liam like I said I would. But I didn't anticipate that it would be here now. Under the elongated shadows of streetlights without another soul nearby to see.

"Come here," Liam says flatly.

I stay rooted to the asphalt, ten feet away.

"Come. *Here*," he repeats.

The first order glanced off my skin, but the second one pierces, poking into my chest like a fishing hook. He's at the other end, trying to draw me forward with his frustrated stare. Somehow, I manage to keep my feet planted.

"Is your brain-dead jock rubbing off on you?" he whispers, inching toward me. Again, I mirror him, though I'm fully aware this movement is putting me farther from the door. "Why are you looking at me like you think I'm going to attack you? Quit being dramatic. I told you I've changed. But you won't give me the chance to show you how."

"I don't owe you anything," I snap. Chills claw up my arms, freezing me alongside the biting evening air.

"All I'm asking is that you give me a chance." It's an aching plea, and it stirs the remnants of guilt floating around my chest, causing my eyes to water. "I worked on myself for you. I bettered my mental health so you'd take me back. I've apologized. And finally I'm at the point where I know how to treat you and care for you. But you don't even want to look at me."

Liam's fists quiver. My body pulls me backward, though he closes the gap immediately, driving me to the curb.

"Really?" he whispers. "You have nothing to say? After everything I've been through for *you*, you're okay with tossing me to the curb? Like *trash*?"

There's a familiar tremor in his voice that churns nausea in my stomach. "I . . . I'm glad you're a better man," I whisper, heel smacking the curve of the parking lot. There's nothing behind me now, but a strip of grass and a wire fence. "I hope you can treat your next partner better than you treated me."

"There is no next partner." Liam's eyes become more desperate. "It's you, Mason. Didn't we decide that years ago? Why did you accept my proposal if you didn't believe in *us*?"

"I thought it was us," I croak, eyeing the door behind him. I'm not fast enough to dodge him and grab the handle, am I? I've been working out with Cameron, trying to gain muscle, weight, and stamina. But one month on the elliptical doesn't amount to much against someone like Liam. "I just . . . don't think we're compatible."

"But *why*?" he demands. "I thought you loved me."

"I've moved on, so you should, too . . ." I can barely utter the words—each one gets quieter as Liam stalks closer, separating the gap between us. The angry speech I prepared to hurl at him has disintegrated. Casually, I tack on, "It's cold. We should talk inside."

Liam stops in his tracks. He tightens his fists, breathing deeply, eyes flickering with ire.

Is this my chance? "I'm sorry," I say softly, trekking sideways, rounding his position toward the door. There's so much I want to say. I want to yell at him, shove my finger in his face, call him out for the pain and emotional torment he's caused me. But despite the rehearsal and my own angry, flared emotions, one fact remains, more powerful than my own intentions.

I'm still scared of him.

I stride toward the door, heart hammering. It's right there. Nine feet away. Eight. Seven. I can't quicken my pace. It's like the morning after I blacked out. I have to pretend everything's fine and I'm not ready to peel my skin off because the agony of this situation is too much.

Five. Four.

He's changed. He's better. He's letting me go.

Three. Two.

A hand seizes my wrist, hard enough to make my bones throb, and heaves me away from the door with such strength that I feel the ache in my shoulder. "Really?" Liam's voice is a low, dangerous snarl in my ear. "You think you can just *move on*, Mason?"

His grip is so tight that I squirm despite my instincts to stay still. I try shoving, but he merely seizes my other arm, yanking me face-to-face with him.

"All the work I put into undoing my personality to make you *happy*." He pins me against the rough brick wall, his fingers bone white around my wrists. His irises are frigid flames, searing into mine with such spite that tears glass my eyes. "You're going to give me another chance. Because you told me to put in the work, and I *did*. You can't decide you don't love me anymore."

". . . Okay."

"I have a house waiting for us. I took a position in my father's company to support you—so you could pursue whatever dreams or hobbies you wanted. I gave you everything, and this is how you're going to treat me?"

. . .

"Your age and maturity are only so much of an excuse. You have no idea the kind of pain you've caused me. I can't believe you had the fucking gall to show up holding hands with a boy who convinced you he's better for you than a mature, reliable, financially stable man."

. . .

"So, here's what's going to happen. First, you're going to apologize."

. . .

"I'm waiting."

"Sorry."

"For what?"

. . .

"For what, Mason?"

". . . Not giving you another chance."

"But you are. Right now. So what else are you apologizing for?"

". . . Being immature."

"Right. You're young. You'll make mistakes. But I can't let this be one of them. Down the road, you'll thank me for knocking sense into you."

. . .

"Don't look at me like that. I promised I'll be better for you, and I intend to keep that promise. Which is apparently more than what you can do."

. . .

"So this is what happens next. We go inside and tell our parents the good news. You tell your little boyfriend to walk his ass home. After the banquet, I'll properly propose again. We'll pretend the last several months didn't happen. Okay?"

. . .

"Hello? Am I talking to a fucking wall?"

"Okay."

"That's better. So let's head inside and—"

Suddenly, Liam's grip around me disappears. His eyes widen as he stumbles, having been wrenched back by a blurred force. Before I can come fully into focus, I'm being swathed in someone's arms, my head nudged into their chest.

"I'm sorry," he whispers. "I promised I wouldn't let him touch you again. I'm so sorry."

I blink into the sapphire-blue vest. These arms . . . they're not as long as Liam's, but they're gentler. Warmer. "Cameron," I whisper, my eyes sagging. "Can we go home?"

"Yes. We'll walk across the street. My parents are hanging out at a bar a couple minutes from here."

"Okay."

The person around me is yanked back again, sliding through my stubborn grasp. Suddenly, I'm watching him get thrown to the ground, hard enough and at the perfect angle for him to bash his chin into the asphalt. I feel the color drain from my cheeks as Cameron's skin splits, causing blood to surface.

"Unbelievable," Liam whispers, his outline quivering with rage. "The moment this guy comes within sight, you toss me aside again? You're already this unfaithful?"

"Mason, go," Cameron orders, his fingers scraped and bleeding as he puts his hands beneath him. "You've been through enough—"

Liam plants a foot in Cameron's side and thrusts, flattening him out on the street. The sight feels worse than a thousand daggers plunging into my chest. Hot tears lick my cheeks as I stand against the brick wall, paralyzed.

"Mason, *leave*," Cameron snaps again, eyes locking with mine. His own are resolute, but there's a ring of anxiety around his irises. "I can handle this prick. Go get your parents."

Cameron is shaken. It's not just because of Liam's threatening presence. This sight, this feeling, is familiar to him. Being on the ground with people looking down on him . . . It's a nightmare he can't rid himself of.

Yet he's willing to put himself through it. For me.

"Kids your age are so damn annoying," Liam says, looming over Cameron. "Mason, I thought you were different. But you're just like everyone else. Immature, bratty . . . needing a good *lesson*."

He reels his foot forward, and Cameron grimaces, preparing for the kick. It doesn't come. Liam falters, foot hanging mid-swing.

"Get away." The words are so pathetic, so weak, yet I can still force them out. I'm shaking violently, but I can still hold my stance, shielding Cameron. The tears are thick and relentless, but I can still glare at him.

"Move," Liam says sternly.

My body's instinct is to obey. I remain still, knees quaking.

Liam stares at me with incredulous eyes, and suddenly, he's throwing his head back and laughing angrily. "Are you kidding?" he cries out. "You bitch and moan about how much I hurt you, and now you're standing here with the boy you're cheating on me with, basically begging me to smack the shit out of you. What am I supposed to do, genuinely?"

"Mason, *stop*." Cameron's finally on his feet, though he's grasping at his side. He snags my shoulder and tries pulling me behind him, but my feet stay flat.

"No," I say. His touch reinvigorates me, easing the tremble in my limbs. Somehow, I manage to meet Liam's icy eyes. "I'm not your property."

"Mason," Cameron pleads, but I continue over him.

"You *have* hurt me." My fingers curl into frustrated fists. All the while, Liam stares with a mixture of emotions—heated disbelief being the most prominent. "You tried to isolate me. You'd say I was special, then make me feel worthless. You accused me of horrible things so you could own parts of me. My smile. My social life. My passion."

The words are spilling out, despite knowing this isn't the time or place for this. But I can't help it. With Cameron's comforting presence at my back, I can finally say it. For the first time, Liam is the one frozen solid, unable to move.

"You never had feelings for me when I was thirteen, did you?" I choke out, blinking through the thickness of tears. "You saw my homelife, my social struggles and quiet personality, and it was *perfect*. You knew all it would take was a little attention to win me over."

Liam's exhales are coming more forcefully. Though the streetlamps framing the parking lot are dim, I can see redness pouring into his face.

"You thought you had me in your pocket after proposing," I breathe, my fingers fumbling for Cameron's free palm. His hand slides into mine, coarse and still damp with drying blood from his fall. "You pushed and pushed because you thought you could get away with it. You liked that I was becoming scared of you."

"That's not true," Liam spits, to which my nose flares with annoyance.

I shout, "*Yes it is!* If you loved me, *truly* loved me, why hurt me so much? Stopping me from going to homecomings, parties, bonfires . . . punishing me whenever I raised my voice, pointing out my flaws over and over . . ." I can't figure out if I want to scream or dissolve into a sobbing breakdown or shove him or do all simultaneously. "I was never a person to you. Just a trophy. A box to check."

I step forward.

Liam steps back.

"I'm not your toy anymore!" I yell, tears dripping into my burgundy suit. "You don't get to push me around. I don't owe you anything just because you bought me gifts or did me favors. I'm allowed to have friends, feelings for other people. I . . ."

My breath hitches. Cameron's thumb presses into the back of my palm. Encouragement.

"I deserve to be happy," I say. "Especially without you."

Liam's jaw is set in a tight, firm line. I can almost see the force he's applying to his teeth—it causes his face to tremble.

Then, suddenly, tears are grating down his cheeks.

"Really?" he whispers, clutching his head. He chokes on a forced, manic laugh that causes Cameron to shift closer to my back, as if preparing to yank me away. "You think that lowly of me? You, my best friend, my fiancé . . ."

His knees fold, and he strikes the ground, staring unblinkingly at the asphalt.

"All I've ever wanted is to love you," he breathes.

My inhale hitches. His words poke into the cracked seals around my heart, allowing guilt to leak into my chest. I almost step forward to wrap my arms around him.

But he doesn't deserve it.

"Come on," Cameron mumbles, drawing me toward the banquet hall. I guess this is our chance to escape before Liam gets his second wind.

And yet . . . why does he look so miserable? Why is he crying? Is it another manipulation tactic? The way he spoke about "bettering himself" like it was a *chore* says everything about how little he wanted to treat me well.

So why?

"You don't see it, do you?" I ask quietly. "You thought the only thing you needed to fix was how angry you got. That the only way you hurt me was physically, and if you could fix that and tack on enough apologies, it would solve us."

Liam holds his head like his world is crumbling around him. Maybe it is. Maybe somewhere deep inside, part of him *did* care. He's not some unnuanced cartoon villain laughing from the shadows as his plans unfold.

But when did this "love" spiral into obsession? Is it fair for me to assume he wanted to manipulate me from the start? Or did part of him genuinely find comfort in me, one of the only people who looked up to him and didn't care about his wealth or popularity, while his parents expected him to shoulder every expectation without complaint? They've always pulled his strings behind the curtain, crafting him into a respectable individual worthy of inheriting their wealth. So many times, he told me he felt he had no control over his life, no direction aside from the path his parents pointed him toward.

Then was I the result of that?

In his hectic life throughout which a step out of line was met with reprimanding from his parents, isn't it natural he wanted to latch on to something he could control? Maybe he felt butterflies when I smiled, and this, combined with his desperation to have something to call his own, drove him to acquire me.

Maybe he didn't even realize it.

I shouldn't give him the benefit of the doubt, especially when there were so many intentional moments of manipulation. The night he got me blackout drunk. The way he cried after he hit me, and then his tears would vanish after I apologized for overreacting. The jealous accusations when I told him I was going to a school event, which were relentless until I canceled and stayed home, away from my peers.

Yet there were many soft, loving moments, too. When he'd bring me somewhere I was desperate to explore or fall asleep draped around me while we watched movies or call me every night to let me rant about my parents or to make sure I'd eaten.

It doesn't matter. Nothing excuses what he did. He opened wounds in my heart with his hands and shattered pieces of my soul with his words. Whether each instance was accidental or intentional makes no difference. The fact is that I shouldn't be required to heal, over and over, or cover my chest to prevent the possibilities of further injuries.

I'm not sure I'll ever stop shielding myself. I've allowed Cameron peeks, but I can't say I'll ever allow him to fully hold my heart like I allowed Liam. Time will tell if I can manage to find all the shards that crumbled away each time Liam struck my self-worth. My fervency for life. My face.

"It's over, Liam," I say, shoulders slumping under the weight of my own words. "Don't come to my house, or text me, or go to my parents, or show up at my school. I won't talk to you."

Liam sits there on the ground like he's been frozen in time. The tears rush down his face, but his expression is stoic, his hands still latched to his head. Even after everything, this is the best he can offer me.

The chance to leave.

So I do. I draw Cameron toward the banquet door and pull the handle in.

"I love you," Liam whispers.

My stride pauses in the doorway. "Your love isn't love," I murmur. "Hopefully you'll realize that before you charm someone else looking for an escape."

I tug Cameron into the building and let the door close, cutting Liam away. Permanently.

Before promptly collapsing against the carpeted hallway, gasping for air.

Cameron doesn't speak. Just kneels and scoops me into a hug, tucking my head beneath his chin. I'm not crying. I'm too exhausted and I've shed too many tears over Liam. My legs are so weak I can barely get them under me, but I manage to, with Cameron's support.

"Let's go home, okay?" he says.

I look at him through the blur of fatigue, then gently stroke some of the dried blood from his chin. I don't care that my phone isn't on me or that I haven't spoken to my parents as he draws me to the front doors.

"That painting," he says. "What do you think?"

He's pointing at one of the gold-framed pictures he noticed me slowing down for when we first entered the building. "It's pretty," I mumble, examining the flecks of gold atop splotches of black. "Not a big fan of abstract, but the colors work together nicely."

"Eh." Cameron shrugs, ushering me past it. "Your stuff is better."

My eyes sear hotter. "Thank you," I whisper.

"It's the truth."

"Not just for that."

Cameron's brows shift up, as does the edge of his mouth. He taps the back of my hand with his index finger, then guides me away from this mess.

Just like that, it's over.

CHAPTER THIRTY-ONE
CAMERON

It's called a Domestic Relationship Personal Protection Order, apparently. Or an ex parte PPO. It's like an emergency restraining order that prohibits someone from approaching you without the consequence of being arrested. To everyone's astonishment, Mr. Gray steps up on Mason's behalf to file it, since Mason's still a minor. My parents help us fill the petition out for the judge and organize for Liam to be served the order. Liam hasn't filed a motion to terminate it.

Maybe he'll let it be.

Though, there's still no physical barrier preventing Liam from going where he wants. But after seeing my scraped chin and bloodied hands, Mr. Gray changes the locks on the doors and makes new keys, so Liam's is null if he decides to storm Mason's house. I can still feel tension in Mason's hand when we're out at parties or on dates, and his eyes constantly rove whatever building we're in or backyard we're occupying.

Still, this gives him peace of mind. The road to leaving Liam fully behind will be long and difficult, but what am I there for if not to wipe away his tears and remind him how much hotter I am than that dick?

It seems Liam's retreated with his tail curled, but his cooperation might not last. He pursued Mason for months after their first breakup, assuming they'd get together if he said the right words. If he tries causing issues, I'll be there. To, like, call the police. Because this guy can kick my ass, evidenced by how easily he tossed me aside that night. I've always prided myself on my fitness and strength, but it doesn't amount to much against athletic guys who have four years of height and build on me. Among all of the games of football I've played in my life, not one sack compared to the way Liam hurled me onto the ground that day. In that moment, it suddenly made sense to me why the scout told Coach Barnett last year that I still wasn't an adequate weight to be considered seriously as a recruit yet. If Liam had thrown junior-sized Cameron onto the ground like that . . . my bones wouldn't have made it out intact.

Mrs. Gray hasn't brought up Liam since the banquet. Maybe she's ashamed they let things get to such a perilous point. Maybe she's seeing another side to Mason she forgot existed. Someone happier, who laughs and paints when he's bored and brings a fancy camera everywhere so he can take pictures of lovely things. (The roll is filled with images of me, I bet.)

There's a shift in the way Mason's father looks at me and how he speaks to his son. His voice is firmer, his eyes sharper. Mason claims that recently, he caught the man browsing articles that Mason sent him. Couples therapy, domestic abuse, mental health counseling, and the like. He doesn't know if it means anything, but . . .

Hopefully it means *something*.

Mason's shitty home life is half the reason he wound up so deep under Liam's thumb. His mom doesn't seem to care. I've never seen a mother and son have less presence around each other, and it breaks my heart. It's partly why I invite Mason over for dinner so frequently—my parents dote on him, flatter him, and ask why he's dating low-life scum like me when he's clearly superior. Mason laughs through every dinner, and the sight makes it worth it. Especially afterward when he consoles me for sniffling and whimpering about it.

I also invite him for dinner frequently because it means I get to see him. I have a pretty big crush on the guy, after all.

Also, Dad makes nutritious meals perfect for pre-workout sustenance. Mason isn't pushing the workout thing as hard as he used to, though he'll still walk on the treadmill or practice curling while I'm exhausting the elliptical. Then we wash up, and afterward he forces me to study. Kissing him as a distraction only works sometimes.

Then there's the whole reason this studying setup happened in the first place. So I could play football.

And I'm playing damn good football.

It's the championship game. The stands are flooded and it's loud enough to sound like a crowd at a professional football game. We're tied in the fourth quarter with twenty seconds on the clock, because of fucking course. The last game of the season, of my high school career, can't be a simple win that we carry away without struggle.

I can hardly hear Coach Barnett shouting in my ear as we huddle around, helmets bumping and foreheads slick. If there's a scout here watching me, I don't care. I don't want this game to be about my college career. I don't want the anxiety of my future hanging over my head during the last game I ever get to play with these guys.

With my friends.

Everyone from school is present, wailing and stomping the bleachers. My parents are in the front row, waving pom-poms. A couple of TV crews linger around, and the fluorescent lighting sears hot over the field despite December's icy coldness.

"Let's do this," Barnett growls, and I stuff my mouth guard in, then start jogging onto the field, bursting with determination. I can't run the ball—it has to be a long pass, or we'll never make it out of our own territory before the clock ends.

Someone snags my wrist, and I swivel, frowning. Who's trying to distract me?

Oh. My face lights with a smile instead.

"Helmet off," Mason instructs. He's dressed in his water boy jersey with a baseball cap secured over his forehead, beneath which tufts of black hair poke out and his warm eyes peer at me expectantly. I do as requested. He grabs my shoulder pad and yanks me sideways, kissing my cheek. "For luck," he says, righting me.

My cheeks flush warmer. I spit the mouth guard out. "I'm going to win the game and kiss you in front of everyone again," I snap, before stuffing it back in and resecuring my helmet. I leave before he can respond, but when I glance back, his eyes are wide and his face peachy pink.

Good.

The crowd roars as I return to position and my men fan out. I try keeping my breath level as my gaze darts around, seeking routes across the field before the ball has even been snapped. I bend behind Nate and brace for impact.

He snaps the ball.

I nearly fumble it (wouldn't that be fucking spectacular after what I just promised Mason?) but manage to secure it. My head whips around to observe the field. Eleven seconds. Ten. Nine. Ravi can't shake the guy marking him. Seven. Six. The line of defenders breaks apart— one of their linebackers is bulleting toward me. Four. Three. Anup is trying to find an opening.

No, he's *going* to find it.

I hurl a Hail Mary pass toward the end zone with a grunt and a leap of faith.

The linebacker collides with my knees and sends me toppling onto the frosty grass. I think he yells something in triumph at me, but I don't hear it. Not this time. I simply watch the ball spiral through the air, breath stuck in my lungs.

Anup's arms extend as he lunges for it. He seizes the ball and trips over his momentum, stumbling, falling. Right into the end zone.

The clock runs out and a resounding buzzer echoes through the field.

I gasp in relief, tears in my eyes as I force my wobbly feet under me. My teammates swarm me, pushing me around, slapping my helmet, screeching through my face mask. I rush over to where Anup is sprinting toward us, then yank him into the group so we can share the credit. The crowd's roar is thunderous, shaking the foundation beneath us. Mom is crying tears of pride. Dad nods like he knew I had it in me all along.

Then Mason. I faintly see his face over the haze of testosterone choking me on the field. He's smiling—that eye-crinkling, glittering, heart-melting smile—his clipboard set aside so he can clap for me.

Ah, fuck. I'm falling in love.

I sprint across the field, wrenching my helmet off, arms and legs pumping to carry me toward the sidelines. I scoop Mason off his feet, then plant a fat one on his lips before the world. Or at least two high schools and a local news crew. I'm sweaty and gross, but if Mason minds, he doesn't say so. He merely snickers against my mouth and whispers, "Go celebrate, quarterback."

I place him on his feet but can't help myself and take his jaw, lifting him to his tiptoes so I can kiss him again. "I'll be back, water boy," I say.

The color deepens in his flushed cheeks. "I know," he murmurs.

So I race back onto the field to rejoin the celebration. But I keep to my promise. Moments later, I return with the team, and when Mason sees the giant boys barreling toward him, he hugs his clipboard in terror. He cusses with surprise when everyone lifts him up on their shoulders.

"To our water boy for always keeping us hydrated!" Nate cries out.

"And for cleaning our shit up every game," Darius adds.

"And for getting Cameron's bitch ass back on the field!" Jody tacks on.

"I'm not a bitch, actually." I scowl, though the smile returns when I look up at Mason. His face is a comical, cherry red.

"Um," he squeaks out, bemused, "can you guys put me down?"

"No way. You're a lot easier to carry than Cam."

Mason sighs in dismay and looks at me pleadingly. But he doesn't hate this, even if he's pretending to, so I leave him up there a while longer, letting people thank and congratulate him for an amazing season.

Eventually, he's returned to his feet, and it's so Darius and Ravi can empty our ice cooler over Coach Barnett's head, causing him to shriek curses that send everyone within earshot into a laughing frenzy. Even Mason nearly sinks to his knees, clutching his stomach, tears sparkling in his lashes. His unrestrained, unapologetic mirth makes my chest ache with happiness.

"You're beautiful, Mason Gray," I whisper.

He doesn't hear me.

But I'll make sure he gets the message later.

"Can I talk to you guys about something?"

Dad pauses, his forkful of garlicky chicken Alfredo hovering an inch from his lips. "Depends," he says. "Will it make me want to kill you and then myself?"

I look at Mom in utter dismay. She betrays me by shrugging.

"I'm serious!" I choke out.

"So am I."

"Nico," Mom says, finally shooting the man a stern glare that makes him sigh and lower his fork to his plate. She gestures at me to proceed, and she's got this glint in her eye that makes me wonder if she expects I'm going to tell her bad news.

And it is. Sort of. I'm not sure how they're going to take this. If it's even fair for me to say any of this, after all they've done for me. I've been avoiding the subject for a while and probably would've continued to do so if Mason hadn't promised me he'd paint me a custom picture of anything I want after I talk to them. I know exactly what I want and exactly where I'm going to hang it on my wall.

To be honest, I'm surprised my parents haven't brought it up them-selves. I guess they probably assume I'm fully set on doing what I've been planning, and haven't thought to interrogate me about it, aside from offering me encouraging quips about how well I played this sea-son and how I make a great leader, even if I wasn't the team captain.

"So, the football thing." I stab awkwardly at the slab of chicken on my plate, glad I have something to look at while they pour their gazes into my face. "You know that scout from Alpine University has been out to examine me. And I think if he wants to recruit me . . ."

My fingers tighten around my fork.

"I might turn it down."

My parents are quiet. Waiting.

"I know it would be really beneficial financially, but I . . ." I pause again, the words clogging up my throat. I have to cough several times just to spit the rest out. "I don't think that's what I want. Football is fun, but that's just it. I want it to stay fun. I want it to be something I can escape to. I don't want it to completely eat away my life. I don't want to make a career out of it."

They don't respond. Part of me wants to sink under the table so I can't feel their eyes, but I keep steady, knowing I still haven't explained myself enough.

"I'm sorry," I mumble, a familiar stinging surfacing in my eyes. "I

know things have been tough since we moved. I know taking a position like that is a once-in-a-lifetime opportunity that hardly anyone
will ever get to experience. I know it could keep us from sinking into
more debt. I know that turning it down is selfish. So. I'm sorry. I
promise I'll find another way to—"

"Cameron."

Mom's voice is gentle. It draws my gaze up to hers, and I'm startled
to see that she's smiling weakly, her own eyes glazed with tears.

"Sweetheart," she whispers, "you have never *owed us* for anything."

My mom always has this way of luring the latent tears down the
rest of my face. "But it's my fault we had to move," I croak, snatching
my napkin so I can dab the water away. "If I hadn't been . . . If I had
stood up for myself, I . . ."

"Cameron Morelli," Dad says, more stern than normal, and it
worsens the flow I've been trying to stem. "Our decision to move was
based on several factors. We had been considering it for *years*, but it
took a while to gather the funds for a down payment on a new place
here in Elwood. You and your mother faced the worst of what that
miserable little town had to offer."

He folds his thick, hairy fingers together atop the table, pinning
me with his stare. His level face is lessening the painful ringing of
panic in my ears.

"Yes, we may have quickened our decision because of what we saw
happening to you," he continues. "We may have moved before we
were fully ready. That was our decision. Not just for you, but for all of
us. It was the best choice we've ever made because suddenly, we were
happy again. The three of us. Things are *good*, Cameron."

He reaches across the table with his ridiculous wingspan and
clutches my left fist, which has been lying there, clenched and white.

"You don't owe us for that decision," he murmurs. "It's our job to provide a safe, loving, accepting environment for you. Seeing you smiling and making friends . . . that's payment enough."

. My breath is haggard and my face is sopping wet. Mom also reaches out, settling her hand atop his and mine.

"We're sorry if you ever felt pressured to do something you didn't want to because of this," she says softly. "If you don't want to play football in college, or if you only want to play on a rec team, or if you want to drop it altogether, we'll support you. All we have ever wanted is your happiness, Cammy. Don't factor money into what you want to do, okay?"

Cam Morelli would've walked away from this conversation eons ago with a shudder of revulsion at his own weakness.

But I'm not him. I'm myself again. So I lunge onto my feet, skirt around the corner of the table, and fling myself into my parents' arms, bursting into sobs that wave across my entire body. I don't know where I'll be next fall, if I'll be playing football, if I'll choose to focus on other, new interests and hobbies. But it'll be okay.

Because I don't feel alone anymore.

CHAPTER THIRTY-TWO
MASON

It's cozy and calm, this little party. Despite the chaos the footballers are sowing in the backyard. The trees are frosted, the awnings slick with icicles, the chimney puffing smoke. The Morellis' radiator works overtime on the back porch, giving my shivering legs reprieve whenever it oscillates. The mug of steaming hot cocoa and marshmallows in my hand soothes my New Year's Eve chills.

Cameron, Anup, and Jody are trying valiantly to build a snowman, though the snow is so loose and fluffy, it's difficult to pack. Ravi and Darius are tossing a football around, typical jocks even outside of the season. Faintly, I hear the Morelli parents talking in the kitchen as they clean up appetizer plates from earlier. It's kind, the way they all speak to each other. I wish my dad could hear what it's supposed to sound like, but he isolates and doesn't like meeting people, so I'm not sure I could convince him to come around.

Though, I should still try. I was lucky enough to find someone who didn't give up on me. Maybe I shouldn't give up on him, either.

It's been a few weeks since Liam's banquet. His number is still blocked, so if he's texting me, I'm not getting them. Cameron's constant, lingering presence around me, anticipating trouble, helps me rest easier. I've been spending several nights at his house, and while it's not permanent, it gives me peace of mind while the dust settles. I don't have to fear Liam tapping on my window at night to confront me about the emergency restraining order. If he's pissed, he hasn't taken it out on me, and that's what matters.

Cameron heaves a giant snowball atop their "base," then turns toward me with a toothy grin. "It's looking great, babe," I say with a thumbs-up.

"Damn right. Anup, give me the buttons. Time to suit him up."

Anup snickers, fumbling within his massive parka jacket. "Shouldn't he get a head?"

"This *is* his head."

"So he's just an ass and a face? No body?"

"He has a face and a body," Cameron complains. "Just no ass."

"Then how is he going to have gay sex?"

". . . Okay, he has an ass and a head. No body."

"Morelli lowers the IQ of everyone within a mile radius," Jody drawls with a sigh, to which Cameron hurls a snowball at him, cracking him right in the face.

"Hey," I call out, wagging my finger at Jody while he curses and smears the snow off his face. "That's my boyfriend you're talking about."

Jody grimaces at me. "I know, and I wake up confused about it every day."

I laugh, then catch my own wrist to keep it from covering my smile. Sometimes I forget about the habit—it's so ingrained within me that it'll take a while to dig the instinct out. Though, I've been getting better about it. "He may be a big himbo jock, but he's *my* big himbo jock," I say, watching fondly as a full snow war ensues, in which Cameron begins to pelt every available teenage boy with snowballs aside from me.

I love seeing them like this. Cameron would attend game dinners or see his teammates at parties, but rarely did he ever just hang out with them. He kept everyone at an arm's length and made his personality just obnoxious enough that most of the guys didn't bother trying to pursue deeper friendships with him, even if they liked his company.

He organized this event himself with some of the first-string players. Watching them all fool around and simply be together as friends . . . it's nice. I'm happy that he's happy. And I'm doing my best to be involved, and to reassure myself that my presence around them isn't a burden. That they actually maybe like me. Even if I hate myself.

I'm not sure how much of it is intrinsic versus how much was hammered into me. But I'm living in spite of that. I'm letting myself enjoy things. I even have my watercolor paintings hanging on my wall, but only because Cameron pinned them for me. I've started advancing my guitar skills from video tutorials. I'm not great at any of these things, but Cameron's constant insistence that I don't need to be (even though he thinks I am) pushes me through the self-deprecation.

I love the way Cameron loves. I feel his devotion in how he caresses my arm when guiding me somewhere, or the way he strokes my hair when I'm using him as my pillow. Even when he's terrorizing parties with "the boys," he's always ready to drop everything to kiss my head and warm me with his hugs. His zest for life is intoxicating— I want to join him in his unrestrained joy.

I'm not always successful. But I'm getting better.

I can't give Cameron all the credit, even when he teasingly claims it since he's the one who convinced me to pursue therapy. It's been difficult to open up about everything I've been through, but being in a controlled, confidential environment with someone who doesn't give me pitying looks makes me a bit more willing to talk.

I lean against the snow-scattered railing. The backyard is faintly illuminated beneath the golden light cascading over the porch. Flakes drift from the sky, lazy and unhurried, coating Cameron's winter hat.

Mr. and Mrs. Morelli join us on the porch, and all the football players jog over to take up party blowers. They've placed a TV in the kitchen window so we can hear the announcers begin the sixty-second countdown to the New Year. Cameron slings an arm around my shoulder with a beaming grin, his cheeks flushed from the snowball fight, his damp hair matted down. I always get weak in the knees when I see him like this, all out of breath and riled up.

"Fifty-nine! Fifty-eight! Fifty-seven!"

The night is oddly quiet despite everyone's cries. Cameron's house is shrouded in trees that separate it from their neighbors, so it's isolating but cozy. Safe.

"Thirty! Twenty-nine! Twenty-eight!"

Cameron pecks my temple with every number. He's whispering them in my ear, his voice low and soothing. "Seventeen," he whispers. "Sixteen. Fifteen."

He's probably going to kiss me in the most dramatic way possible. Despite his more authentic self shining through, he still likes showing off, and maybe it's more endearing than I thought. Because I know he's more than showmanship. He's everything I didn't know I needed.

He's everything I didn't know I deserved.

"Nine! Eight! Seven!"

I don't know what the future will bring. The college application process is weeks away. We have one final semester before adulthood reels into the picture. We're testing our compatibility, too—we're extremely different people.

"Three! Two! One!"

But maybe that doesn't matter. Because we can offer each other the things we want the most. Comfort. Support. Vulnerability.

"Happy New Year!"

Cameron is about to dip me at the waist, but I grab his jacket and hoist myself against him, then lock my arms around his neck and kiss him deeply while hoots of joy ricochet through the air alongside the incessant clangs of pots and pans. When I pull back, his eyes are wide and glistening with amazement. "I didn't expect that from you," he admits.

"Sometimes I can be bold and surprising, too," I say with a cheeky smile.

He leans in, bumping his nose against mine. "Maybe you can show me that side of you more often."

"Hmm . . . maybe. I'll think about it. If you're patient."

He pinches my lower lip between his teeth, giving an experimental tug that reddens my cheeks. "I'll wait an eternity," he whispers. "If it means that one day, I can see every little piece of what makes you Mason Gray."

I laugh despite the tears I'm growing accustomed to surfacing in my eyes. There's nothing I can say that would be adequate.

So I kiss him once again, the world around us an incomprehensible blur.

CREDITS

ART AND DESIGN

Jim Hoover

Kristie Radwilowicz

CONTRACTS

Jennifer Skrzypinski

COPYEDITING

Andy Hodges

EDITORIAL

Dana Leydig

MANAGING EDITORIAL

Alexandra Aleman

Gaby Corzo

Ginny Dominguez

MARKETING

Christina Colangelo

Alex Garber

Lisa Kelly

Bri Lockhart

Danielle Presley

Talisa Ramos

Astrid Rojas

Emily Romero

Shannon Spann

Felicity Vallence

PRODUCTION

Vanessa Robles

Miranda Shulman

PRODUCTION EDITOR

Marinda Valenti

PROOFREADING

Crystal Erickson

Sola Akinlana

PUBLICITY

Lathea Mondesir

PUBLISHER

Tamar Brazis

SUBSIDIARY RIGHTS

Helen Boomer

Kim Ryan

SALES

Emily Bruce

Abby Fritz

Micheal Gentile

Becky Green

Kimberly Langus

SCHOOL AND LIBRARY MARKETING

Venessa Carson

Andrea Cruise

Judith Huerta

Carmela Iaria

Trevor Ingerson

Summer Ogata

Gaby Paez

Maggie Searcy

Cody Tigue

LISTENING LIBRARY

Kelly Atkinson

Emily Parliman

Rebecca Waugh

NEW LEAF LITERARY

Suzie Townsend

Sophia Ramos

Olivia Coleman